Return of the Prophet

Book One of the
Lemniscate Legacy series

Phil Moore

The moral rights of the Author have been asserted
Cover design: Phil Moore via Midjourney
Published by Virtual Worlds
virtualworlds.com.au

PB ISBN: 978-0-6459806-2-2

VIRTUAL WORLDS

Prologue

In the year 2050, the messiah of the modern age – the Prophet Tobias – was assassinated. His rise to fame had been swift and his celebrity lasted only a few short years, but his effect on human affairs was profound. At the time of his death Tobias could claim a worldwide following to rival that of any movie star or pop diva. They were not just fans, but devotees. His critics condescendingly described him as the 'Rock-Star Messiah', and he attracted many enemies among established political and religious authorities who saw the Tobianist 'cult' as a threat. The Prophet Tobias himself rejected all organised religions, seeing them as part of the problem – a philosophy that appealed to his largely secular following.

Upon his death, Tobias's body was cryonically preserved, in the hope that one day he could be revived to continue his mission. This was despite reincarnation being one of the core tenets of Tobias's philosophy. Also, ironically, the book Tobias wrote shortly before his death – the *Shentama* – became the foundation of a new religious order. It was to be expanded upon, translated and re-interpreted many times over the next two-hundred years until becoming almost unrecognisable from the original work.

The assassination of Tobias triggered a worldwide conflict known as *The Reckoning*, which lasted for 20 years. Ostensibly about

4

religious freedoms, it was also a clash of political and economic powers fighting over dominion of nation states, or in many cases civil unrest within nations. It was a war unlike any before – a global ideological jihad – and in its wake a true world government emerged, with Tobianism officially acknowledged as one of the world's major faiths.

An uneasy peace lasted for 30 years, during which time Tobianism developed its own doctrine, priesthood and rituals borrowed and adapted from other faiths, becoming a strange amalgam of Judeo-Christian and Asian practice, with a few of its own ideas thrown in. They even had their own holy city – Lorna: the city of the Prophet. At the heart of this new city a Great Temple was constructed, built on the site of one of the original Tobianist monasteries, atop a remote mountain. Lorna and the Great Temple were now the centre of the Tobianist faith – their very own Mecca. The cryonically preserved body of Tobias was enshrined here, making it both a tourist attraction and a pilgrimage for the faithful.

The uneasy peace shattered in the year 2102 when the tomb of the Prophet was vandalised. Cardinal Hierophant Baligaya, then leader of the Tobianist Church, used this sacrilege as the pretext for what came to be known as *The Great Purge*. The body of Tobias was moved to a secure location within the Temple, never to be seen again. Another worldwide conflict erupted, this time far more brutal and oppressive than *The Reckoning* had ever been. A ruthless, systematic cleansing of rival faiths or anyone marked as a heretic to the Tobianist cause. When the dust finally settled at the turn of the new century Tobianism had effectively become both the spiritual and political authority of the world. The Tobianist Regime had begun.

All other faiths were forced underground, their practice outlawed. Scientific research and development, already hindered by the thirty-year darkness of *The Great Purge,* was now regulated by the Church, as were cultural and artistic pursuits. Censorship was strict, and anything the Church deemed inappropriate or heretical was quashed or driven underground.

Despite the oppressive nature of the regime, a true lasting peace had indeed been achieved. And despite the Church's tight controls on technology and culture, some great advances were nonetheless realised.

A new commemoration – the *Festival of Renewal* – was instituted, a worldwide celebration and the spiritual highlight of the year. As part of the festivities the face of the Prophet is streamcast across the world from his crypt deep within the Temple of Lorna. For one week of the year at least, he is remembered, though even this macabre tribute has become a travesty.

Two hundred and forty years after the death of the Prophet, Tobianist rule is all anyone has ever known, while the body of the Prophet remains cryonically frozen in a crypt deep within the bowels of the Great Temple of Lorna – neglected and forsaken by the Church that bears his name.

Part 1

Death is not an end ; it is a renewal of life.

Shentama
– The First Tenet

1

I am not the way
I am a light unto myself only
Let no man seek to make ritual of what I say
Nor legend of what I do

Shentama
– Stanza 1

S tumbling blindly through the ancient catacombs, Althea Roget's thoughts kept returning to the fragility of life and the inevitability of death. Not her own death, but the untimely demise and future resurrection of the most important man in her life – the Prophet Tobias. She had never met him of course. He died over 200 years before she was born; but his legacy was profound. Her life was devoted to him. It wasn't religious fervour; it was more personal than that. Tobias was the father she never knew, the lover she'd never had, the God to whom she prayed at night. Her faith in the Prophet was unshakeable. And yet, what they were about to do was the ultimate sacrilege – to steal the body of the Prophet Tobias from his cryonic tomb.

Travelling with her in the gloomy catacomb passages were

Patric and Isaac, two young interns who volunteered for this mission and were probably now regretting it. It all sounds so very exciting until you find yourself lost in a labyrinth dragging an empty coffin. Isaac stumbled on the uneven floor. He would have dropped his end of the casket were it not for the grav-lift fulcrum that kept it floating a few centimeters above the ground. The casket was really a portable cryonic chamber; it just looked like a coffin.

Grav-lift (or GL) technology relied on quantum locking of super-conductive plates along the base of the unit. This created a levitation effect that could bear many times its weight. One of the few major scientific advances made in the Tobianist era, it was used in everything from storage and transportation to amusement park rides and levitating cameras. It was also remarkably quiet, except when 'rolled' over a non-conductive surface for too long, triggering a loud, crackling discharge of static electricity. This occurred now as they pushed the casket over a particularly rich vein of limestone, causing Isaac to jump.

'What's the matter?' Patric teased. 'Nervous?'

Isaac shook his head unconvincingly. He knew they were alone (who else would be foolish enough to venture down here?), but the slightest noise triggered his amygdala. His nerves were primed for a fight or flight response. The eerie gloom didn't help. It felt as if they were descending into the very bowels of the earth – a direct pathway to hell. As a loyal Tobianist, he wasn't supposed to believe in hell – but myth and imagination were hard to suppress when faced with such evocative reality.

The lower catacombs were centuries old, created by ancient lava flows. It was a maze of random channels, with tendrils snaking deep into the earth. These eventually joined with the man-made tunnels beneath the Great Temple. They moved into a passage with evidence of this human excavation – they were getting close. Here the rock was crudely pounded to make the passages more navigable. The Great Temple and the city of Lorna were built upon this vast, sprawling network of man-made tunnels and natural caves. No one truly knew the extent of it. If detailed surveys had once existed, they were now lost in time.

Althea carried a battery-lantern and a crude, hand-drawn map scrawled on Temple parchment. The orange glow of the lantern made Althea's pale complexion appear sickly, and her thick red hair shimmer as if on fire.

'Where did this map come from anyway?' Patric asked quietly, breaking the silence.

'I don't know,' Althea admitted. 'It was supposedly drawn by a priest who got lost down here once. Wandered these tunnels for weeks before he found his way out.'

'How'd he survive that long?' Isaac stammered.

'Rats. Moss. Mushrooms. He died two days later of food poisoning.'

Althea's matter-of-fact tone only compounded Isaac's fears. 'How do we know the map's any good?'

'We don't,' she answered plainly. 'But it's all we have.'

The conversation stalled and they continued in silence. This mission really was an act of faith.

The map had been acquired by Althea's colleagues in the Dissention Society (DS for short). She thought it was a stupid name, making them sound like a debate club rather than an enclave of rebel activists, but what else could you expect from a bunch of left-wing intellectuals. While the origin of the map was dubious, it had so far proven accurate in guiding them through the labyrinth to the tunnels beneath the Temple. From here, it traced routes to the surface within the Temple, and to the crypt of the Prophet, but was otherwise incomplete. Branches and side-tunnels were indicated but not filled out. Althea had already noticed a number of disconcerting errors, but none had thwarted their journey so far.

The map came to them through an anonymous benefactor, just as they were planning this bold experiment. It was an incredible coincidence, but as the second tenet of the Prophet states: *Choice, not chance, determines your destiny.* In To0bianism, there was no such thing as coincidence. Everything was connected.

The DS was further assured that Temple Guards did not patrol this deep into the catacombs, and there was no surveillance; no doubt because only a damn fool would attempt approaching the Temple from underground. So after years of preparation, everything just started to fall into place and the time had come. Nothing was without purpose. Choose your path and the universe provides. Althea could feel the thrust of destiny in their actions.

They entered what the map indicated was a long straight passage. The walls here were narrow and crudely carved. The ceiling low and claustrophobic. The air rank and stagnant. It had been a long time since anyone had walked these halls. They hiked for half-an-hour through the narrow passage, far longer than the map suggested. Had they missed a turn?

They came to a junction that wasn't on the map.

Althea traced her finger along the route trying to see where they had taken a wrong turn. She couldn't see it. The map was just wrong. She sent a pip from her comkey. A high frequency note rang out from her polymer bracelet, echoing through the tunnels. A hologram of the area surrounding them appeared projected in space above the bracelet. It was next to useless. The image revealed several paths they could go – all leading into further darkness. She tried to conceal her panic from the others, but they knew they were lost. Rats, moss and mushrooms sprang to everyone's mind.

'It's not on here,' Althea confessed.

'Well… which way do you think?' Patric asked.

Althea looked up, her apprehension waning as she noted Patric's calm expression. You could always pick a true Tobianist by how they handled themselves under pressure. Those who live the Word, live in Peace.

Althea felt guilty. Every moment was a test of one's faith, and Isaac and Patric seemed to be handing the challenge a lot better than her. She smiled weakly in apology.

'Don't worry,' reassured Patric. 'I'm just as scared as you are. I just don't want to show it in front of Isaac.'

'I'm not scared,' Isaac countered. '... I'm petrified. But I'm not about to turn back now.'

Living the Word is not so hard, Althea thought, it's the 'Peace' bit that's tough. She studied the two passages forked ahead of them. For no particular reason except that it felt right, she said 'Left', and they continued on.

The map got them into the catacombs, it had served its purpose at least that much. But it was useless now. To help them remember their way back, Althea tore away pieces of the parchment and left them on the ground at each junction. Breadcrumbs to mark the way. She just prayed they could remember the route for the first part of their journey, as soon there would be no map left to guide them.

At each junction they encountered Althea tried not to dwell on the choice, trusting her instincts to guide her. She just kept moving, not even a pausing to drop the shred of map parchment. Something was guiding her. Whether it was a vague sensory trail – a smell or distant sound – or something more metaphysical she couldn't say. But within twenty minutes they glimpsed a dim light at the end of the passage, and there was a collective sigh of relief. Just in time, as there was no more parchment left to mark their way.

They stopped at a T-junction. The passage here was wider. The stone floor smooth and polished, and the walls better hewn. Small lights were embedded in the limestone walls, spaced evenly along the passage, creating a surreal chain of bright and dark patches. They were directly under the Temple. She remembered this bit from the parchment map that was now in scattered pieces. Assuming it had been correct, the passage sloping upward to the right led to somewhere in the Temple. The tomb of the Prophet was in the opposite direction.

'This way,' Althea pointed, and turning left they continued their descent. Stairs were carved into the stone in places. Most runs were two or three steps, so were not a major problem. Then they came upon a staircase that was dangerously steep and long, and curved.

'That's gonna be a problem,' Patric mused.

'Do you want me to take the front?' Isaac offered.

'… No. I'm stronger than you. I'll do it.' It was not intended as a slight, merely a statement of fact.

Carrying the casket down such a steep incline was hard enough, but with no friction against the floor due to the grav-lift, it wanted to slide freely down the rutted stairs. The boys had been swapping ends periodically to share the load on gentle inclines, while the unit's magnetic brakes prevented it from slipping away. But the brakes would not work at this angle, so once they began their descent they couldn't afford to let up for a second. Patric bore the full weight of the casket. There was little Isaac could do at his end but hold it steady. Progress was slow and precarious, with Patric pressing against the slippery walls for support. They couldn't afford a single slip, lest they lose control of the casket and it slid to the bottom of the stairs to be destroyed. Aside from the receptacle itself there was some fragile engineering in the casket that would not survive such an impact, and their mission would fail.

…But they reached the bottom of the staircase safely. The moment the casket was on level-ish ground again, Patric engaged the brake and collapsed on the cold, stone floor. 'Give me a minute,' he gasped.

They waited…

Looking back, the staircase loomed over them discouragingly. No-one said it out loud, but they were all thinking it: How the hell are we going to get the casket back up those stairs fully laden?

'Okay…' Patric muttered eventually, struggling to his feet. Isaac now took the lead as they continued down the passage.

Their goal was in sight. The passage terminated at a large metal door – old, unadorned, and securely locked. There was a key-code panel on the side with an eight-digit LCD display. The display was broken, and the keys were dirty and wet, but it was sturdily built and still operational even after two hundred years. This was from a time before comkey bio-recognition. When fingerprints and retina scans were regarded as cutting edge, and a simple keypad was still the most secure way to lock a door.

Althea took a deep breath and punched in the passcode. The code that three of their colleagues had died to retrieve. The code on which the future of the world depended. The code that came from the same anonymous person who'd provided the map.

– P.R.O.P.H.E.T

It was such a ridiculously obvious password that it was either true, or a complete fraud.

She hit ENTER ... nothing ... then came a mute clunk, a grinding and whirring of gears, and another much bigger and very satisfying CLUNK!

Althea grabbed the handle and pulled the heavy door open. The years had not been kind and the metal hinges creaked loudly, straining under the weight. The shrill metallic sound reverberated up the passage, further amplified as the waves bounced and shuddered off the polished stone walls, rising and weaving through the catacombs. Anyone within a kilometer would have heard it. After the relative silence of their long trek the sound was deafening.

Looking past the door, Althea noticed a few small lights glowing in the oppressive darkness. The crypt was otherwise invisibly dark. Cold, stale air escaped into the passage. It smelled like ... ammonia.

Raising the lantern, Althea stepped inside. The room was small, much smaller than she expected. About four meters square. They never showed the whole crypt during the Festival streamcasts, but still, she imagined something larger – more befitting the resting place of the Prophet.

To the left was a large mechanism and control surface, the source of the glowing lights. This was the cryonic life-support that had been operating 24/7 for nearly two hundred years. Despite several maintenance upgrades over the years, it still looked like a relic from a much simpler time. To the right were cabinets with cleaning supplies, spare parts, and some old electronic gear – all gathering dust. It resembled a broom closet more than a tomb. Somewhere to dump all the things you no longer had use for but couldn't throw away. A place where they could be abandoned and forgotten.

Althea barely noticed all this, however. Her gaze was drawn to the cryonic chamber at the back of the room. In the dim, orange light of the lantern she discerned the outline of a large, foggy tube, rising from a concrete plinth like a column of frosted glass. It glistened in the feeble light.

Patric stuck a black patch over the lens of the AV camera mounted above the door, ensuring it would remain blind to what they were about to do. Then, reaching for the control panel on the wall, he flipped the switches and the lights in the crypt sparked on. There were dozens of small pin lights strategically placed about the room, illuminating the cryo-chamber for the benefit of the camera. The chamber itself was frosted by a fine coat of ice crystals, but Althea could still make out the shadowy figure floating behind the translucent glass. She stepped forward reverently, her legs becoming heavier with each step, struggling to bear her passion of this moment.

This was him. Really him. The body of the Prophet. Frozen in time. Cryonically preserved. Unchanged since the day he was killed.

Althea wiped a hand across the cold surface, clearing away the ice crystals, revealing the face of Tobias.

His eyes were closed and he looked ... peaceful. Floating in liquid nitrogen. Sleeping through the ages: Through The Reckoning – the World War that was fought in his name, through the establishment of the first Tobianist council, the building of the Great Temple of Lorna, the Great Purge of 2070, and the ultimate rise of the Tobianist Church – his Church – to become the spiritual doctrine of the entire world. Would he be proud ... ashamed ... angry?

She hoped to find out.

'Althea?' Isaac interrupted her reverie. He was right. They must work quickly. Though the camera was obscured, it was still possible the Temple Guard were alert to their presence. They could be discovered at any moment.

They had rehearsed the transfer dozens of times, and despite the age of the equipment, there were thankfully no major problems and the body of the Prophet was safely invested in their portable cryo-chamber within forty-five minutes. A quick check of the readouts told Althea the temperature was a stable 77.15 kelvin and the chamber seals secure. The only thing she hadn't anticipated was how cold it was going to be. Their fingers were frozen through, despite the gloves they wore. The original cryo-chamber now looked oddly relieved. It had sustained the body of the Prophet for nearly two hundred years and was overdue for retirement.

They pushed the portable chamber out of the crypt and into the passage. If they were discovered someone would surely have arrived by now. It looked like they were in the clear. Again, their anonymous benefactor's information had proven correct. Althea dismissed the fleeting thought that this was proving all too easy. After all, destiny was on their side.

They pushed the laden casket up the passage with a newfound fervour. Surely nothing could stop them now.

Then they reached the stairs.

We are not so free that we can see
All there is to know
We are not so free that we can know
All there is to see

Shentama
– Stanza 192

'**A**re you all right, Rene?' Joanna could always tell when something disturbed him. No matter how much he tried to hide it.

'Yeah,' Rene reassured. 'Just cold.'

'Cold?' Dan interjected. 'How can you be cold? This place is a sweatbox!' It was a bad joke, as were most of Dan's attempts at humor. Rene rolled his eyes but otherwise made no attempt to engage his friend in yet another fruitless joke-off.

The place in question was their favorite club, *The Sweatbox.* So named for the dance floor and the glistening bodies of beautiful young things that populated it every Friday and Saturday night. It was one of the few places in Lorna that still offered live music – under strict protocols of course.

Unfortunately, Rene didn't like the music of his generation.

He found it tedious and tuneless, though that may be the fault of the protocols. He was an old-school kind of guy who would rather listen to jazz or classical than anything produced in the last hundred years. For a twenty-two-year-old this was considered weird.

Dan was weird also, but a different kind of weird. Where Rene had always been the serious young man, even as a child, Dan was the court jester. Always trying to raise a smile. While Johanna was so *not* weird … it was weird. None of them quite fitted with the world around them, so they clung to each other instead.

The three of them came here often. Not for the music and dance (though they occasionally indulged in that, despite Rene's distaste of rhythmic monotony), but because there was an upstairs restaurant – *The Loft* – that offered good food, cheap alcohol, and a somber atmosphere in stark contrast to the noisy night-club beneath their feet. It was a place the bohemians of Lorna liked to hang out. Relaxed, gloomy, and slightly decadent. Rene didn't consider himself a bohemian, but it was oddly comforting to be around them. Fellow weirdoes.

He also liked the games. After their meal he and Dan would often play *Go* over drinks. They played the old-fashioned way – on a wooden board with little white and black stones. AV displays were frowned upon in The Loft, as were most other outward signs of tech. It was a refreshing respite from the rest of the city where AV murals adorned every wall; and comkey terminals and bright GL train or hopper stations were on every second corner.

Rene placed a white stone on the board.

'How come you never laugh at my jokes?' Dan asked his friend.

'I'm laughing on the inside.'

'What do you get when you cross a temple guard with a heretic?' Dan asked.

Rene sighed. 'I'm not sure I want to hear the answer to this.'

'A conflict of interest.'

Rene blinked. 'How is that funny?'

'I think it's funny,' Joanna replied.

'Thank you,' Dan nodded in appreciation. 'At least Jo has taste.'

'Well, of course. She is with me after all.'

Dan was taken aback. 'Oh! Was that an attempt at humor? Is that a smile I see creeping across your face?'

'It's your move, asshole,' Rene quipped.

Dan carelessly placed a black stone on the board. 'I've decided it's my mission in life to make you laugh, Rene. You're so earnest all the time, like you're carrying the weight of the world. You need to recede. Recline your mind. Abate your fate.'

'Oh God, now he's rhyming.'

Johanna laughed. 'He does have a point. You take things far too seriously.'

'I thought you were on my side,' Rene grumbled.

'I am. Always,' Joanna reassured. Then simpered: '… But he does have a point.'

Rene placed a white stone. 'You're move.'

Dan took the opening. 'Okay. You want to get serious? There's something I need to talk to you about.'

'This better not be what I think it is.'

'What do you think it is?'

'You know what I think it is.'

'… All right, well, kind of,' Dan admitted. 'But this is different.'

'Dan,' Rene countered, suddenly getting serious again. 'You can do whatever you like. It's your life. But I don't want to get involved with any pseudo-intellectual anarchist group – '

'– That's not what this is!'

'– I don't agree with their politics and I think it's dangerous.

Nothing personal. It's just not for me.'

'So you support the Church, then?' Dan challenged a little too aggressively as he placed his stone on the board. Beneath every court jester dwells the heart of a political agitator.

It was an argument they'd had many times. Rene neither supported nor opposed the Church. He just wasn't interested. Politics and religion were things outside of his own life. Why couldn't Dan leave it at that? Rene placed a white stone adjacent to a cluster of black ones. 'I don't want to get into this, Dan.'

'Of course not. You're like everyone else. Just pretend nothing's going on. It's all peachy keen and the world isn't falling apart around your ears.' Dan placed a black stone.

'Now who's taking things too seriously?'

'I don't joke about religion or politics,' Dan protested. Considering he had just told a joke that was both religious and political, this conflicting declaration was perfectly in character.

'And yet you talk of little else?' Joanna was the pragmatist of the group. If it weren't for her refereeing these debates they might have come to blows on several occasions. It was odd how their cheerful banter could quickly turn to heated argument in a matter of seconds. Yet they remained the best of friends. In the three years Rene and Joanna had been together they had made several attempts to hook Dan up with someone, but it never worked out. Somehow a fourth wheel upset the dynamics of their little trio.

A waitress approached and began to clear the table.

'Can we change the subject?' Rene pleaded.

'What else is there? You want to talk about sex? I'm not getting any, how about you two?'

Dan said this just as the waitress was leaning over him to get his empty glass. She rose abruptly and stared at him, her ample breasts pointing indignantly in his direction. Dan grinned back impishly. 'Are you getting any?' he asked her.

Not sure whether to be offended, flattered or merely amused, the waitress stammered wordlessly, until Rene broke the tension. 'Another round please,' he uttered calmly, placing a white stone. The waitress nodded compliantly in response and strode away.

Johanna noted this. There were times Rene had the most peculiar effect on people without even realising it. As if his voice alone influenced one's emotions.

Dan continued as if nothing had happened. 'Or would you rather discuss the weather? Lovely weather we're having. Not a cloud in the sky. Just like yesterday and the day before and the day before that.'

He was being facetious. The weather had been fine for years. Geocentric Weather Control was implemented fifty years ago and ever since, the weather had always been fine. Devastating storms were a thing of the past. Tidal waves and hurricanes were found only in archival AV records. The only time it rained was at night after curfew, precisely timed and directed to irrigate the trees, gardens and parks of Lorna, while not interfering with human activity. It was a finely tuned global system that averted the destruction of crops and homes, and made arid areas of the planet habitable for a population of twenty-five billion. The technology had both revolutionised and homogenised modern life. Rene hadn't seen rain since there had been a glitch in the system back when he was a child. He remembered it as both fascinating and terrifying. Nature unleashed. He was grateful for the stability Weather Control brought.

But Dan was right. The fact was if you wanted to have a serious discussion about anything these days, it always came down to politics and religion – which were one and the same. Rene acknowledged this, but it didn't matter if you supported the Church-State or some heretic faction opposing it, the end result was the same – people with agendas squabbling over power and influence. As much fun as it was to vent one's frustrations, Rene just found the whole debate tedious and futile.

'I don't support the Church,' Rene said for the record. 'I don't support anyone. Your turn.'

'And that's your problem, right there,' accused Dan confidently. 'You gotta pick a side.'

'No I don't.'

'Then why are you writing propaganda for them?' Dan said this a little too loudly – perhaps on purpose – and heads were turning.

Normally it wouldn't have mattered, but given the political bent of *The Loft* patrons, Rene was the odd one out here. A weirdo among the weirdoes. 'It's news, Dan. Not propaganda.' It was a lie and Dan knew it. Rene had never been very good at that. 'It's your turn.'

'Aren't they the same thing these days?' Dan placed a stone.

Rene had to concede that one. He always wanted to be a writer, so falling into a journalist position at the most respected news outlet in the city – *The Guardian* – for his first job was something of a coup. What he didn't realise was how much influence there would be from above. Not just editorial or corporate, but from the Temple itself. Of course, the Church had a financial interest in everything these days, but he hoped there would be more independence of thought at such a prestigious journal. He was wrong.

Rene placed a white piece, surrounding several black ones and capturing that territory.

'How did you do that?'

'How long have we played this game, Dan? And you still don't know the rules.'

'I know the rules. I just play it differently to you.'

'So losing is a strategy? That's interesting.'

'I'm trying to lull you into a false sense of security before I strike.'

'Can't wait to see that.'

Joanna enjoyed watching the boys spar. The drunker they were the funnier it got.

'Anyway,' Dan blurted. 'That's what I wanted to talk to you about.'

'What? My false sense of security?'

Dan paused. He would have loved to respond to that one, but it was tangent to his real purpose. He stayed on track. 'No. I mean your job.'

Rene eyeballed his friend suspiciously. 'Which game are we playing now?'

Dan smiled. 'Have you ever come across the name Jason Asar?'

'No.'

'Or Doctor Asar? He's a doctor.'

'No. Why?'

Dan became circumspect, which was most uncharacteristic. '... No reason. But let me know if he comes up.' He placed a black stone on the board. 'Your turn.'

'What are you up to, Dan?' Joanna asked.

'Me? Nothing.'

'Okay,' said Rene. 'Now I know something's up, if you won't even talk about it.'

'I was just asked to see if you'd heard anything. You know, given what you do for a living.'

'Writing propaganda,' Rene mimicked.

'Who asked you?' insisted Joanna, returning to Dan's earlier admission.

Dan didn't answer, but the smile was now gone from his face. This was not lost on Rene, stirring some familiar and all too painful anxieties.

'Dan. What's going on?'

'… Open your eyes, Rene. William could see it. Why can't you?'

Rene's mood turned black. 'And look where it got him,' he replied coldly. Dan knew better than to bring up Rene's older brother. It was a mistake to mention him.

Joanna saw where this was going and quickly stepped in. 'Daniel.' She used his full name – like a disappointed mother might.

Dan knew he had crossed a line – again. '… Sorry.' The apology was heartfelt.

Rene's expression softened. 'I'm not so blind as you might think. But I don't want you ending up like Will.'

'This is dangerous stuff, Dan.' Joanna reminded him. 'In here we're relatively safe,' she indicated *The Loft,* 'and I venture we're not the only ones discussing… well… let's face it – revolution. But this isn't a game. Will stuck his neck out, and however noble the cause, he's gone now. And for what? An idea? A crusade? There's been too many wars in the name of God. Tobianism's no different. All religion breeds is hate and intolerance. I know the *Shentama* as well as anyone. And as inspiring as it is, it's just words. Yet people get themselves killed over it. People like you. And nothing changes. You just leave the rest of us behind to clean up the mess. And I'm sick of it!'

Joanna stopped herself. The boys looked at her in astonishment. She didn't usually say much, but when she did…!

Joanna had helped Rene through what was the worst time of his life when Will died. But it wasn't until now he realized how Will's death had affected her. Rene reached out and gently touched Joanna's hand. She was shaking. Not one for emotional outbursts, Rene could tell she was angry with herself for slipping.

'Read your palm? Tell your fortune?' An old woman had crept up on them and was hawking her skills as a psychic. There were a lot of them around lately, offering easy answers to the weak of spirit in troubled times. The fact that what they peddled was illegal under Church law just pushed the old spooks underground. This one struck Rene as particularly old and raggedy. Her clothes were ancient, though clean. She wore a bizarre cloth hat that flopped over her face, and her standard issue comkey medallion hung from her neck on a fake silver chain as a fashion accessory. She can't have been very good if this was all she could afford to wear.

'Want to know the future, dearie?' she asked Rene with an intent gaze.

'Don't bother, granny,' said Dan. 'He doesn't believe in any of that stuff.'

'You don't have to believe it for it to be true. And I'm not your grandmother, dearie.' This last aimed at Dan had a venom to it that put him even more firmly in his place. Dan was besieged by angry women tonight.

She returned her attention to Rene, waiting for his answer.

'How much?' Rene asked, feeling charitable.

'As much or as little as you feel it deserves.' If that's how she set her price Rene could see why she wasn't very successful. The woman extended her hand invitingly. Rene offered his palm.

Joanna was suspicious but Rene just smiled reassuringly. 'It's about time I knew what my future was, don't you think?' He was trying to lighten the mood.

The old woman ignored the quip and focused on his palm. After a moment, a curious expression came over her face. 'You have two lifelines. One of them bound to your line of fate.'

'Is that ... normal?'

'It is most uncommon.' She kept looking, now more intently. 'How old are you?'

'Twenty-two'.

'Do you wear any jewelry? A pendant or ring?'

'Just this,' Rene held up his hand to show his comkey ring. Comkeys could be embedded in anything, usually a wearable object or 'ampule' of some kind. For some it was a fashion statement, for others like Rene, they used whatever was most convenient; as long as it contained the comkey chip and was carried or worn at all times. This was so the DNA bio-lock to one's body was maintained. Rene and Joanna had their chips embedded in their pledge rings. It was both practical and symbolic.

'That'll do.' The old woman waved her fingers, demanding he hand the ring over.

Rene turned to Joanna, then back to the hag. 'I'm not taking the ring off.'

'Fine,' she said sarcastically, then grabbed Rene's hand and placed his palm on her forehead so the ring was touching her skin. They looked ridiculous.

Dan smirked audibly but she either didn't notice or chose to ignore him this time. Rene didn't know whether to pull his hand away or submit to her 'reading'. He felt ridiculous, but didn't want to offend the woman, so he tolerated the embarrassment for now. People in the room were glancing at their table – in turn offended or amused. The woman held the ring to her head for the longest time, not saying a word. Even Joanna, normally very tolerant of 'spooks', was becoming annoyed.

'Excuse me,' Rene finally ventured. 'Can I have my hand back?'

The old woman raised her other hand, commanding him to wait.

Then finally she drew a slow, deep breath, and handed Rene's hand back to him.

Rene was afraid to ask now, but he had gone this far. 'So what's my future?'

The old woman stared back at him intently. 'Ask me again next time we meet. You are not ready yet.'

'Is that it?' asked Dan, disappointed. 'Could you be any more cryptic?'

She turned on Dan angrily, but her expression quickly softened to one almost of pity. '*You* must learn to keep your mouth shut, and your loyalties to yourself. For the moment at least.'

Then she turned to Joanna. 'Yours is the hardest road, my dear. But you must stay the course, else all is lost.' The two women remained locked in a portentous gaze, until Joanna finally looked away. The woman had an intensity that belied her scruffy appearance.

'Here.' Rene waved his ring near her comkey medallion and a green 200 appeared on the holo-display with the comforting bell-sound of credits exchanged.

'Thank you.' Again, the old woman held her gaze on Rene a little too long, as if she wanted to say more, but restrained herself. Then abruptly she turned on her heel and shuffled away.

'Well, that was bizarre?' Dan declared. 'You really thought that was worth two hundred?'

'She looked like she could use it. Whose turn is it?'

'I don't want to play anymore,' Dan said.

Rene was grateful. 'Neither do I.'

Life is defined by possibility
Not by limitation
See past the horizon of what is
To the greater vision of what could be
The extent of your limitations is a measure
Of the space between ignorance and understanding

Shentama
– Stanza 19

F ather Alban had always thought heavy robes were a bad idea. They were hot, they dragged on the ground getting dirty, and in these God-forsaken catacombs they also got wet. The deeper he journeyed the damper it got, and the heavier his robes became.

All clerics had to wear them; it was the uniform of the faith. But aside from their inconvenient fashion he was proud to bear the insignia of the Prophet on his chest – a small embroidered red lemniscate over the heart. The medallion that hung from his neck and which doubled as his personal comkey also bore the shape of the lemniscate insignia. Most clergy wore their comkeys this way. It was both convenient and symbolic of their devotion to the Prophet Tobias and his Church.

The day Alban became a priest and was accepted into the Temple Order was the proudest of his life. Since then, he had worked in many capacities at the Temple; mainly administrative duties due to his facility with numbers and ledgers. He also maintained a priory in the city – a small chapel in the Western Borough called *The Light of the Prophet*. It was a humble residence but kept him in touch with the faithful. He attended whenever his Temple duties permitted, performing the occasional pledge ceremony, induction rite or funeral service.

But his most important responsibility for the past seventeen years had been to prepare the Prophet for the annual Festival of Renewal, where his face would be streamcast around the world from his crypt deep beneath the Temple. This was a great honor, and one Alban took most seriously. He was not one to question the wisdom of the Cardinal Hierophant Cairn or the Church Council, and it was true that having the crypt so deep in the catacombs beneath the Temple was a very secure place to house the body of the Prophet. Still, lately, he had wondered if it might not serve the faith better if the Prophet were more ... accessible.

Back in the early days, after *The Reckoning*, people used to visit the tomb of Tobias. They would make pilgrimages. Leave offerings. Pray for miracles. It became the focal point of the faith, and the Great Temple of Lorna grew up around it.

Now there was no tomb. Not really. With the threat of vandalism and fears his cryonic life-support might be compromised, Tobias had been moved over a century ago to the crypt deep beneath the Temple. A giant fountain now stood in place of the old tomb in the middle of Festival Square beyond the Temple gates. Father Alban saw the logic in it. Still, it was a terrible shame.

The job was easy, really. He just had to do some dusting. Wipe down the surface of the cryo-chamber which frosted over with ice crystals from the moisture in the air. It was all for the camera. As far as Father Alban knew no-one else ever came down here. The cryonic machinery pretty much looked after itself, and not even the clergy were permitted this deep into the catacombs. Even the location of the crypt was a mystery to all but a select few. So unless a member of the Executive Council of Cardinals or the Cardinal Hierophant himself was inclined to visit the body of the Prophet, Father Alban was the only person who ever came down here.

Every time he did it gave him a profound sense of loneliness. It was hard to explain, and of course he was bound not to discuss it with anyone. But every year when he looked into the face of the Prophet, an overwhelming loneliness gripped him. The tragedy of what had happened to Tobias – cut down in his prime – haunted Alban. He had changed the world by the age of thirty-five, but think how much more he might have achieved. When Alban looked at that face, so nearly alive ... it just got to him. That's what made him want to join the priesthood in the first place. Seeing that face on the AV every year.

Alban shook his head clear. It was best not to dwell on such things. Nothing would come of it, and it just upset him.

The passage seemed especially damp this evening. Small globes suspended on the right-hand wall lit the way. A few were broken but enough were still in good order for him to see his way, and he always carried a battery-lantern just in case. He didn't use a map; he knew the way well enough by now. It would be easy to get lost down here though, with so many passages going off in different directions.

Once he wandered into the wrong passage and ended up in the old cave cells of the monastery. Before the Great Temple was built on this rock there had been a Tobianist monastery, the first ever, and the faithful used the underground caves as their sleeping quarters. Alban couldn't imagine how they could bear to live in such a place. But that was a long time ago, back when Tobianism was nothing more than a cult.

The monastery was built on the ruins of an old city, which itself was built on a dormant volcanic mountaintop which came to be known as Temple Mount. It was not especially high or treacherous; but had a large, flat mesa-like area at its peak where the top had been blown off centuries before by an eruption, giving it a strategic advantage. It was also reputed to be where the Prophet Tobias had spent some of his so-called 'wilderness' years before his fame. The old priests would hide in the caves under the monastery when besieged by pagan forces during *The Reckoning*. They expanded the tunnels using little more than hammers and pickaxes, connecting them with natural limestone formations further underground – caves and courses created by ancient lava flows and subterranean waterways. They devoted years of hard labor to create a safe refuge for themselves. Little did they know their faith and determination would change the course of human history. And that from their bones the Great Temple and the city of Lorna would rise up.

Alban had only explored a small part of the labyrinth beneath Temple Mount, and despite the historical import of it all, the place creeped him out. He made a point of never getting lost there again, conscientiously sticking to his designated route, ignoring the many tunnels that fingered off into stifling darkness. From the moment he entered the catacombs, via an innocuous door in the Temple library, the walk to the metal door of the crypt took about twenty-five minutes. It wasn't far if you stuck to the path.

He came to the curve of steep hewn stairs. As he began his descent, he noticed something and paused to take a closer look. Holding up the lantern he saw there were scratches on the lip of the top step. Fresh scratches it seemed. Two sets of them, one on each side of the step about a meter apart. In fact they were more like grooves than mere scratches – deep wounds on the otherwise smooth rock ground.

What could possibly have done that?

He continued down the staircase. Nothing else seemed out of order, and as he reached the metal door of the crypt all appeared as it should. He punched the code into the keypad beside the door.

– P.R.O.P.H.E.T

There was a *clunk* and then ... nothing. That was odd. Usually, the mechanism made a lot more noise.

He cautiously pulled on the handle and the door gave. It was open. A chill ran up his spine. Had he left it open when leaving the crypt a full year ago? Or had someone else been down here? Perhaps the Cardinal Hierophant did sometimes visit the crypt after all. He pulled the door fully open. It made the familiar metal groans, reminding him yet again that he had forgotten to bring lubricant for the hinges. He stepped inside, turned on the lights ... and seconds later collapsed in a faint on the cold ground. The body of the Prophet was gone.

The body of the Prophet lay on an operating table, naked but for a sheet covering his hips and genitals. The thaw had been a long process, gradual and meticulous. Any cell damage, especially in the brain, heart or other vital organs meant the procedure would fail.

They only got one shot at this. The reversal of cryonic preservation was a poorly understood science and had never been done before with a complete human body. If they got it wrong, they will have damaged the body irreparably and future resuscitation would be impossible.

Doctor Jason Asar was the closest thing to an expert in the field. His research of the past forty-five years, and his driving passion to fulfill the original Tobianist dream, had kept him going. The dream that the Prophet might one day be resurrected to continue his ministry. This was possible thanks to the foresight of Mr. Benjamin Thorald – a twenty-first century entrepreneur who made his fortune investing in technology start-ups. He was one of the few billionaires who didn't see Tobias and his teachings as an existential threat, becoming instead one the Prophet's most devoted supporters. Thorald ensured the body of Tobias was not interred in a tomb or grave, or cremated so his ashes could be scattered to the wind, but that he be cryonically preserved in the hope of a scientific resurrection one day. Asar had made it his life's work to bring that day about.

The process had been trialled with dozens of primate test subjects, until eventually an effective procedure was established. Timing was everything. The proof was Elly, the bonobo that had undergone the procedure and survived to this day. After some recalculations to account for the difference in body mass, the process would be the same for the resuscitation of Tobias.

During the thaw they removed the cryoprotectant (the organic anti-freeze of cryogenics) that had been pumped into his blood vessels causing vitrification of the cells and replaced it with water. The water carried a serum Asar had developed to counteract the toxicity of the cryoprotectant, which had a habit of denaturing cell proteins during the thaw process. This had been one of the tougher challenges in the early tests, with subjects' muscle tissue and organs turning to jelly. As soon as the lungs were viable a primitive cardiopulmonary bypass machine was hooked up. With blood artificially flowing, a specially formulated 'super' oxygen was then pumped into the body. This served two purposes. First it would replace the hydrogen sulphide that paramedics had injected into his body at the moment of death, placing him in a form of clinical suspended animation. This was common practice at the time for critically injured patients, postponing death to allow for a possible revival. This was not to be for Tobias, but it made the prospect of cryonic preservation viable. At the same time, it would revive and repair organs that had suffered from Ischemic Injury. This injury was caused by the prolonged lack of oxygen due to the cessation of blood-flow during the time between death and implementation of the cryonic procedure. The brilliance of this process was that it also contained modified induced pluripotent stem cells. Stem cells drawn from Tobias's own tissue, but 'supercharged' chemically to accelerate the healing process. These were carried with the oxygen around all parts of the body and repaired any tissue damage that might have occurred in the freezing process. They even repaired Tobias's bullet wound, leaving only a faint scar over his left breast.

The Prophet had been killed by a single bullet from a sniper's rifle. A well-aimed shot that had pierced his heart, killing him instantly. The bullet had been removed before his interment and the wound surgically repaired, but this was merely cosmetic. He was already dead. The stem cells now flowing through his veins would repair the damaged organ, just as they repaired other parts damaged by the cryonic process.

When the team saw this work on their test subjects – who had been deliberately killed in the same way – it was miraculous. A kind of accelerated healing, rebuilding a mortally damaged organ like the heart in less than two days. This breakthrough of medical science made everything else possible.

The whole procedure took all of fifty-two hours. By the time it was complete the formerly vitrified body looked less like a corpse and more like a man in a deep sleep. He still lacked any body fat so the face was gaunt, the limbs shriveled, and the torso somewhat emaciated; but once revived, an intravenous protein drip and, in time, a few good meals would fix that.

The entire team stayed awake for the two days of the thaw and regeneration, so they were all thoroughly exhausted. Yet no one dared sleep at this vital juncture. There were six of them. Doctors Jason Asar and Althea Roget who led the team, Patric and Isaac (who were just students – though brilliant ones), and Doctors Berger and Trevelle, associates from the Lorna Institute and two of the most trustworthy allies one could hope to find. But it was Asar who was the driving force behind the operation. His medical skills had got them this far and Althea trusted his judgment implicitly. There was no one better suited to the task. He was after all, personal physician to the Cardinal Hierophant himself. As a psychologist Althea's role in all this would come after the resuscitation. To monitor Tobais's recovery and help him adapt to this new world.

Small wireless sensor patches had been attached to Tobias's skin near all the major organs. Most were on his skull ready to monitor any brain activity. The monitors were operational, but for now displayed nothing – no signs of life. The CPB pumped air into the lungs and circulated clean blood through the arteries. It was eerie watching the chest of a man who had been dead two-hundred and thirty years, rise and fall with a smooth rhythm that had all the hallmarks of life.

Although the body had been carefully washed and dried, the hair remained matted and clung to his skull in clumps. It had also lost its trademark auburn color, now almost jet black, and was so brittle they feared it might break if they tried to wash it any further, so they let it be. It was just hair. Aside from the hair the rest of the body looked eerily healthy. The skin was pale, but then Tobias was known to have had a pale complexion, and the famous freckles were clearly visible around the nose. Something obscured on the AV streamcasts by the liquid nitrogen haze of his cryo-tube.

The operating theatre was part of an old hospital called *Saint*

Olivier's in the so-called 'abandoned' quarter of Lorna – the AQ. This was all that remained of the old city upon which Lorna was built, south-west side of the Temple mount. It had been significantly damaged during the bombing raids of *The Great Purge* and was destined for demolition and reconstruction. But that never happened. Over the years it became a slum, and was eventually abandoned as the city of Lorna grew up around it, its residents moved into the cheaper areas of modern Lorna – mostly in the west. The AQ became a ghost town as nature slowly reclaimed the site. Its crumbling skyscrapers vandalized and overgrown with vines. The once immaculate, paved roads cracked and bursting with weeds. Rats and insects populating the dark corners of the derelict quarter. A modern ruin, visible from the new city, connected to it, yet shunned and ignored.

Of course, it was not completely abandoned. People still lived among the ruins, but they kept very much to themselves. Asar had no idea who they were or how they lived. He only knew them by their nickname – *the lost*. Like the rats of the AQ they kept to the shadows, avoiding contact with any intruders. Asar and his colleagues were here because *Saint Olivier's* had a working operating theatre and other useful facilities. They had spent several months making the place habitable. The building was falling apart around them, but it was discrete. It also had the advantage of being close to the entrance they would use to access the catacombs.

With the physical restoration of the body complete, all that was left now was to attempt resuscitation. The moment of truth.

Asar nodded to Althea Roget. She pulled over the old defibrillator unit, removed the two patches, and peeled off the plastic backing; then stuck the patches to Tobias's chest – one high on the right, the other low on the left. Insulated wires trailed from the patches to the small machine. That they had to use such primitive tools was insane; but they had no choice. Roget turned the unit on. After a moment there was a gentle beep indicating it was ready.

She turned to Asar. He nodded. Roget in turn nodded to Patric, who turned off the cardiopulmonary machine. Tobias stopped breathing. The mask was removed from his face. They now had four minutes before irreparable brain damage set in, assuming of course the brain was intact before his cryonic interment and the super-IPS cells had done their work.

Roget pressed the large green button on the defib unit. Tobias didn't move. Then a calm female voice spoke from the unit: 'Shock delivered. Begin CPR now.' Asar began heart compressions – hard and fast. After a few seconds he stopped and Althea pressed her mouth to Tobias's and gave him two deep breaths. Asar continued the compressions.

'Stop CPR,' said the defib unit. 'Don't touch patient... Analyzing...'

Everyone watched the body, hoping to see some sign of life ... but it didn't move. And the machines didn't blink.

'Shock advised' said the defib. 'Don't touch patient... Press flashing shock button.'

Althea pressed the green button again.

'Shock delivered.'

Tobias's tongue spasmed forward and back a couple of times. Everyone caught their breath. Was he alive?

'That's just a reflex,' said Asar. 'We're not there yet.'

'Continue CPR,' the defib intoned calmly.

Asar continued his heart compressions... Althea her mouth-to-mouth.

'Stop CPR.'

Asar stopped. He had always been the strong leader. Supremely confident. Now for the first time Althea noticed a dark shadow traverse his face. He was terrified they had failed.

'Don't touch the patient … Analyzing …'

Althea had not given up hope. Everything had gone so well so far. Fate was with them.

'Shock advised … Don't touch patient … '

Althea returned to the defib machine – ready.

'Press flashing shock button.'

She pressed it hard, as if the extra pressure would drive some of her own life-force into the body.

'Continue CPR.'

Asar began again the heart compressions. An anxious sweat was now dripping from his forehead. The minutes were ticking by.

The others were helpless to do anything but watch and pray.

Asar pumped firmly on Tobais's chest. He was a man possessed. Each thrust carried with it the years of work, of heartbreaking setbacks and small victories that culminated in this moment. These four minutes. Soon his life's work would be at an end – one way or another.

Asar paused, Althea breathed air plus all the will she could muster into Tobias's lungs. Then Asar began again.

The monitoring equipment remained mute. So far their efforts had done nothing to revive the body, and Althea began to worry. Her hope was fading. This was taking too long. For the first time since they had begun this mad endeavor she feared they would fail.

'Stop CPR.'

Asar stepped back and stumbled, about to faint. Berger caught him.

'Don't touch the patient… Analyzing…'

Berger helped Asar to a nearby chair.

'It's not working,' Asar muttered, despair overwhelming him.

'… It's not working …'

'Shock advised,' said the defib calmly. 'Don't touch patient …'

Althea looked to Asar, but he was lost in a reverie of grief. Had he given up already? He just kept on muttering 'It's not working,' softly to himself.

'Press flashing shock button.'

Althea pressed the button one more time.

Again, Tobias' tongue spasmed … Then he swallowed and seemed to take a shallow breath… Then nothing. Another reflex.

'Continue CPR.'

Asar didn't move. Berger looked at her anxiously. Althea stepped up and continued the heart compressions. 'Come on…' she whispered so only Tobias could hear her. 'Come on…'

She became oblivious to the others in the room, bound completely in the moment. All she knew was to press life back into this body. Nothing else mattered. Nothing else existed.

'Stop CPR.'

Althea didn't hear it. She kept on.

'Stop CPR.'

Two firm hands – Berger's – gently grabbed Althea's arms from behind and she stopped.

'Analyzing…'

She turned to Asar, who seemed to have recovered his senses and was watching the body of the Prophet. Slowly Asar raised his arm… and pointed.

She looked down. Tobias was breathing. Short, sharp breaths. But with each one his breathing became slower and deeper.

'Check pulse,' advised the defib unit.

Althea placed her hand against Tobias's throat. There was a pulse. A definite pulse. It pounded in her ears – or was that her own heart?

Her head cleared and she could now hear the room once more. The heart monitor beeped a steady rhythm.

She looked at Asar. He was smiling and crying all at once.

— ∞ —

Rene collapsed.

He had suddenly felt dizzy, but before he could reach the couch his legs gave out under him and he crumbled to the floor.

A pair of strong hands grabbed him and lifted him up. He couldn't remember whose they might be. He couldn't remember where he was or what had just happened. In fact he couldn't even remember who he was. It was strange feeling so disoriented, and yet oddly comforting. If he were in any danger he wouldn't have known it. Is that what had happened? Was he in danger? Was he hurt? He couldn't tell. He wasn't afraid. Quite the opposite. He had never felt so calm. Like waking from the deepest, most restful sleep he could imagine. Only he didn't want to wake up.

He heard someone whispering to him. 'Come on...'

Who was that? The voice sounded familiar.

'Hey, come on. Wake up.'

He felt a hand touch his face – at least he thought it was a hand and thought it was his face. It kept touching him…

… Or was it slapping?

'Rene? You still there? Hello...?'

The voice was becoming clearer. A man's voice. A friend's...

'Stop hitting me,' he heard someone say. It was him.

'So you're alive. What happened?'

Rene opened his eyes. He was looking up at the ceiling. Lowering his gaze he saw Dan smiling at him.

'What happened?' Rene asked.

'That's what I said.' Dan raised his hand. 'How many fingers?'

'Huh?'

'How many fingers am I holding up?'

Rene had to focus – both his brain and his eyes. 'Two.'

'Good. No brain damage then. You fainted.'

'Did I?'

'Take my word for it.'

'Why?'

'You tell me? You were in the middle of a sentence and just collapsed.'

Rene couldn't remember. 'What was I saying?'

Dan laughed. 'You said, and I quote: "Revolution never solved anything, it just – ", and then you fainted.'

'It just causes more bloodshed, and ...' Rene struggled to think but his mind was still too foggy. '...I forget the rest.'

'It doesn't matter.'

Rene sat up slowly. He looked around. He was sitting on a couch. This was ... his apartment. It was afternoon. Sunday afternoon. They had just returned from lunch. Just the two of them.

'Don't tell Jo,' Rene told his friend. 'She'll only worry.'

'How do you feel now?'

'I don't know. Fine, I guess. Just ... thirsty.'

'Good idea.' Dan responded. 'I'll get us a beer.'

'No. Water... Just water.'

Dan went into the kitchen and got himself a beer, and a large glass of water for Rene. Rene downed it in one breath.

'Well that hit the spot,' said Dan, taking a swig of his beer.

'Why was I talking about revolution?' Rene asked.

'You weren't. I was. You were trying *not* to talk about it, as usual.' Dan studied Rene's reaction, which remained implacably calm. 'You sure you're okay? Perhaps we should have the MediScan give you a once over.'

Every household had a MediScan. It could test and medicate for anything from common viruses and broken bones to tumors and heart disease. It was both an emergency first-aid station and preventative checkup machine. Doctors were not entirely redundant, but most minor to middling conditions could be handled by the MediScan machine.

'No, no. I'm fine,' Rene eventually answered. 'It's strange. I felt like ... I was someone else for a moment. I mean, still me but ... someone else.'

Dan didn't really follow. '... Right. And who are you now?'

Rene just smiled at his friend. To tell the truth ... he wasn't entirely sure.

Thoughts are boomerangs
They will return
Manifest in your reality

Shentama
– Stanza 147

The Cardinal Hierophant Cairn was not a happy man. He disliked receiving bad news, and this was very bad news.

Father Alban lay prostrate on the tiled marble floor of the Hypogeum Basilica. It was one of several within the Temple grounds. While enormous, it was not the largest. It was, however, the most sacred being built directly above the tomb of the Prophet.

The Cardinal Hierophant liked to hold court here when necessary. He preferred it over his offices as the grandeur of the space lent a certain imperative to any discussion. It also meant he could sit on the throne, looking down on those who came before him.

Alban had insisted on speaking with the Cardinal Hierophant personally. Of course, being a mere cleric, he was denied. But he made such a fuss, refusing to talk to anyone else. Eventually word got to Cardinal Kasper, Temple treasurer and right-hand man to Cairn. He met with Alban, but even his powers of persuasion could not make the priest reveal what he was all worked up about. All he would say was: 'I must speak with the Cardinal Hierophant. Only he can hear what I have to tell.'

Kasper checked Alban's record. The priest had been a loyal cleric for nearly thirty years, with the highest security clearance for someone of his station. But it wasn't until he saw that Alban had responsibility for the crypt that he took the man seriously. Kasper immediately arranged an audience with Cairn, and twenty minutes later the three of them were in the basilica where Alban finally revealed what he had seen.

Cairn immediately checked the Temple's security system from a console on the throne armrest. The crypt camera was part of an extensive network of bio and AV sensors that were strategically placed throughout the grounds, and even spread beyond the walls of the Great Temple into Lorna itself. They monitored every movement, every comkey signature, of every person who had ever entered the Temple gates. The AV camera in the crypt was old tech, but it was on the network and easy to find if you had the right clearance, so it should have appeared on Cairn's console. It's feed however showed only a black screen.

Cairn turned to his treasurer. 'Why is there no picture?'

'I don't know, your Eminence,' Kasper replied cooly. 'Perhaps the sensor is broken.'

Kasper was a hard one to read sometimes. A short, skinny man, he nonetheless had an intensity that belied his physical stature. A schemer with a fearsome intelligence, he could be a dangerous enemy or a valuable ally. Cairn wasn't entirely sure which he was, so he kept him close. In Temple politics there was no such thing as friends, just degrees of enmity and expedient fellowship. He didn't trust Kasper, but he knew him. He understood how his mind worked. And he respected him – despite the fact Kasper wanted his job. Which was more than he could say about anyone else in the Church Council. Oh, to be an innocent again like the good father now kneeling before him.

Cairn turned to the priest. 'What was your name again?'

'Alban, your Eminence.'

Cairn scratched his beard thoughtfully. An imposingly tall man, he made an impressive figure when seated in the throne of the Cardinal Hierophant as he was now. He wore the same black robes of the faith as Father Alban. Historically this signified that he, the Cardinal Hierophant, supreme leader of the Tobianist Church, was himself a mere priest of the faith like the good father supplicating before him. Yet his robes were made of a much finer cloth, there was red trimming around the collar and hem, and the lemniscate insignia of the Prophet on the left breast was in gold and of much finer embroidery. He also wore a matching mitre headdress that was reserved for the rank of Cardinal. These small differences distinguished Cairn from the common rabble. They were the same... but different.

Being a member of the Executive Council, Kasper's robes were likewise more distinguished than a common cleric's, except his insignia was silver, and his mitre slightly smaller. The democratic principles of the early Church didn't really apply any more. In Cairn's view, egalitarianism had no place in running a global theocracy.

Cairn remained silent for the longest time. Kasper, familiar with Cairn's long contemplations, waited patiently. Alban on the other hand became agitated: *was Cairn waiting for him to say more?* He looked to Kasper for guidance, who shook his head gently.

Eventually Cairn spoke. Without looking Alban in the eye he said: 'You did the right thing, Father Alban. However, you should have been informed. Tobias was moved so the cryonic equipment could be upgraded. Don't worry, the body of the Prophet is quite safe, and will be returned before the Festival of Renewal begins.'

He looked now directly at Alban, a penetrating gaze. 'On behalf of my staff I apologise for worrying you so, and I appreciate you making the effort to tell me this in person. But please, have no fear. Everything is in order.'

Alban felt uneasy with this explanation, but it made sense. The equipment definitely was in need of an upgrade; and he had no reason to doubt the Cardinal Hierophant. In his panic of the moment, he had overlooked this possibility. 'Yes, your Eminence,' said Alban, bowing his head to the floor in shame.

'Was there anything else?' Cairn asked calmly.

'No, your Eminence,' Alban could barely get the words out. He felt a fool. His career in the Temple was surely over.

'May the word of the Prophet guide and protect you.' Cairn used the blessing to end the conversation, clasping his hands right over left in front of him, as was the custom.

Alban got to his feet and returned the gesture, bowing one last time, then quickly turned and shuffled away. He walked the full length of the basilica, his steps resounding off the distant walls as he approached the massive wooden doors at the other end. It took him a full minute to complete this humiliating walk and for the doors to close behind him.

When at last they were alone, Cairn turned to Kasper. 'Get me Captain Marius. NOW!'

—— ∞ ——

Tobias slept for the longest time.

After the initial euphoria at his revival, the team became concerned he was in a coma. They could not wake him. But his nerves responded to stimuli – a few pinpricks on the pallid skin – and his brainwaves showed a steady Delta, indicating he was simply in a deep sleep. It was not surprising really. His body was incredibly weak and in need of nourishment. They put him on a nutrient drip, kept him warm, and moved him to a room on the ward for observation.

After several hours Althea noticed something rather odd. Tobias remained in a deep Delta sleep, yet he seemed to be in a constant state of REM (Rapid Eye Movement). The two normally did not go together. REM sleep was associated with dreams and the brainwaves should have been closer to Alpha and Beta, faster and more active. Yet Tobias's brain activity remained slow and deep. Nor did he seem to be going through any kind of normal sleep cycle. His brainwaves remained in Delta. Perhaps it was a kind of coma after all, Althea thought. Necessary for his body to recover. He was the first human ever to be revived from cryonic suspension. Maybe this was normal.

But that had not been the case with Elly, their bonobo test subject. She woke almost immediately and had demonstrated a normal sleeping pattern ever since. Althea just couldn't understand it.

Everyone else on the team was asleep. It had been a very long day … two days. Asar insisted Althea also get some rest. The monitors would alert them if there was any change in Tobias's condition. But she was determined to stay with him till he recovered consciousness. She sat by his bed, keeping vigil for a man she didn't know and yet had loved all her life. She still couldn't believe they had done it. It was surreal to be sitting here holding the hand of the Prophet Tobias. She was dizzy with elation – or was that just sleep deprivation?

Eventually she nodded off, her hand still wrapped around his. So she wasn't watching when the EEG monitor's wavelength gradually increased in frequency and amplitude. She didn't hear the heart monitor's gentle beep become faster and stronger. And she didn't see his eyes open for the first time. In fact, it wasn't until Tobias leapt out of the bed, wrenching his fingers from her hand, that she woke and found him standing naked on the far side of the room in a defensive crouch, scanning his surrounding anxiously.

'It's all right,' she reassured him. 'You're quite safe. No one's going to hurt you.'

Tobias stared at Althea, confused and frightened.

Althea slowly rose from her chair. 'It's all right. You're in a hospital. You were shot. Do you remember?'

As she crept closer Tobias stepped back. The drip was still embedded in his arm and it tugged as he moved away from the bed. Tobias flinched, then ripped the needle out in a panic. He then noticed the other sensors attached to his head and body and scratched them off in a frenzy. A terrified, guttural noise cracked from his throat, more animal than human.

Althea tried to stay calm – something was very wrong. 'Please! No-one's going to hurt you. Do you understand me?'

Tobias wasn't listening.

The door burst open. Asar took in the scene, astonished to see a naked Tobias standing opposite, his arm bleeding from where the drip had been violently yanked.

Startled, Tobias grabbed the drip stand and leapt onto the bed. He raised the stand above his head and swung it ferociously. Althea stumbled back against the wall, the metal legs narrowly missing her head.

Tobias flung the stand at Asar. The ageing doctor retreated but the metal projectile clipped him in the back as he turned – knocking him to the ground. Tobias leapt off the bed and out the open door. He moved with such speed and agility that Althea couldn't help but be impressed.

Seconds later the others arrived at the door, roused from their sleep by the commotion.

'Where'd he go?' Asar demanded through grit teeth as he struggled to his feet in agony with a broken rib.

'Who?' asked Isaac dumbly.

'Tobias, of course!'

Isaac looked in the room to see the bed empty. Althea stepped past him into the hall.

'He went that way.' She turned to Patric who was just arriving. 'Get a sedative ready. If we can't talk him down we'll have to knock him out.'

'What happened?'

'He woke up,' Althea answered, then bolted down the hall after Tobias.

The old hospital was big. They had only powered one section of the building; the rest remained as they had found it – derelict and dark. Althea scoured the halls, watching and listening, as she tried to make sense of what had just happened. Tobias didn't seem to understand her. Was there brain damage? Physically he was well recovered. Motor and sensory functions had returned – with a vengeance. Cerebellum and cerebrum were clearly operating well. But higher functions like language, reasoning and possibly memory, were either absent or suppressed. Given his physical condition brain damage seemed unlikely. Cognitive function was inextricably bound with sensory.

Where then was Tobias? All his responses were primal; where had the higher functions gone? Or was he simply terrified? It was uncharacteristic behavior for the Prophet of history – a man of peace, composure and devastating intelligence. But he was only human after all. Even as Althea thought this, she didn't believe it.

Something was very wrong.

Tobias was scared. He didn't know where he was or how he got here. If he had thought about it, he didn't know *who* he was either. But he didn't think about it. Why would he? He simply was. He was also cold, bleeding, and in pain; but for now, at least, he was safe. Having found a dark place to hide he licked at his wounded arm. It tasted wrong. He didn't know how it should taste. Just not like this.

His mouth was dry. He felt hunger ... and the need to urinate. That was soon remedied. It was difficult at first, as if his body had forgotten how. Once the flow began it stung for a moment, but then the pressure quickly cleared whatever was blocking it and the pain subsided. He felt much better with an empty bladder.

There was too much light out there. Nowhere to hide. It was a strange light that came from nowhere. No warmth. What darkness there was felt even colder. Shadows were not supposed to feel like that. In this place the shadows were real. And there was a comforting smell, now made stronger by the odour of his urine.

He listened. He could hear them in the distance, running about, but they were a long way off. The one with red hair didn't scare him. But when the others arrived, shouting and moving aggressively, he panicked. He could tell they were scared of him, but he wasn't going to wait around for them to find their courage.

Moving deeper into the shadows of the room the comforting smell grew stronger – pungent, earthy. He heard a noise and stopped. A grunt, breathing ... something was in here with him. He saw movement in the shadows. The source of the smell. It was like him, but smaller. It spotted him and scuttled to the back of its space. It seemed to be trapped. He moved closer.

Elly retreated to the back of her cage as Tobias approached. She could tell he was more curious than threatening, but remained wary.

Tobias came up to the bars of the cage and reached in, palm facing up in a gesture of friendship. Elly reached out in kind.

Their fingers touched.

Elly moved closer, until they looked at each other through the bars of her cage by the spilled light of the open door. Tobias sniffed at the bonobo. A female. Lost like himself. Yet she seemed content. He tapped at the bars – *trapped*?

Elly raised her hand and stroked the bar – *yes, but it's okay*.

He tapped the bars again, more intently – *but you're trapped*?

Elly extended her arm through the bars, pointing across the room.

Tobias walked to the desk. He turned back to Elly, confused. She indicated – *up*. Hanging on the wall just above the desk was a key. Tobias took the key from the wall and brought it to Elly. She moved to the side of the cage where the door was. Reaching through the bars Elly inserted the key into the lock and turned it. The cage door opened.

Elly stepped out of the cage and looked up at Tobias. She reached out her hand.

Tobias hesitated but felt he could trust her. She was like him. He took her hand.

She led him back across the room to the open door. As she stepped into the light of the hall Tobias balked. Elly looked at him gently – *it's all right*.

Tobias followed her into the light, and they walked hand in hand up the hall. Elly seemed to know where she was going as they turned the corner into another long corridor. After a minute's walking, Althea Roget appeared at the other end of the corridor. She stopped short when she saw the naked Tobias being led hand-in-hand by the bonobo up the middle of the brightly lit hospital corridor.

Tobias stopped.

Elly, seeing he was anxious, let go Tobais's hand and continued up the corridor alone, picking up speed as she got close, then leaping into Althea's arms. Althea caught the bonobo, as she had done dozens of times before, and carried her on her hip as one might a two-year old child. Elly turned back to Tobias as if to say – *See? It's okay.*

She stroked Althea's face affectionately – *you can trust this one.*

Tobias remained on his spot, crooking his head to one side as he considered the two females standing before him. Althea didn't move. She realised if she did anything to break the tenuous trust Elly had established, she could blow it. Tobias had to come to her.

Althea stood her ground and waited.

Elly called out to Tobias quietly. You didn't have to understand what she was saying to get the meaning. Tobias began to move towards them when Patric emerged from a corridor behind Tobias, carrying a tranquilizer gun. Before Althea could do anything Patric shot Tobias in the shoulder.

Tobias screamed like a wounded gorilla – suddenly hurt and full of rage. He whirled around to confront his attacker. His roar echoed down the corridor and he charged at Patric with frightening speed. Terrified, Patric turned and ran for his life, dropping the gun. But the tranq' quickly kicked in and Tobias crumbled to the floor mid-stride, unconscious before he hit the tiles.

The essence of dogma is not what it teaches
But how it teaches it
It has no power save that which you give it
Allowing others to rule over you
It is to walk in the steps of another

Shentama
– **Stanzas 211-212**

C aptain Marius was an excellent driver. At least, *he* thought so. The fact that he managed to narrowly miss so many pedestrians as he careened through the streets of Lorna was due less to his driving skills than to the agility of the people he was *'buzzing'*. It was a game he didn't get to play nearly enough in his opinion.

Meanwhile, the unfortunate Cadet Fairchild assigned to share the vehicle with Marius was throwing-up over the side. At least one innocent bystander did not escape unscathed when hit by the debris the young guard was involuntarily jettisoning.

They were flying through the streets in an open-top four-man GL cruiser – though some still referred to them inaccurately as *flying cars*. They didn't so much fly as float thanks to their superconductor resistors. The Temple had an extensive fleet of GL vehicles, from small runabouts like this one to massive transport vehicles. While private ownership of such vehicles was restricted, public and commercial transportation relied heavily on GL technology. Indeed, the rail-less GL train network of Lorna was a model for the rest of the world. For personal use, small electric vehicles called *hoppers* were freely available to all citizens from stations scattered across the city. These autonomous people carriers had a maximum speed of only 100km p/ hour, but they served the greater community so well that to own one was largely unnecessary. The only people permitted to own GL light vehicles were wealthy and influential corporate executives, political and church leaders, and of course, the military, police and other emergency services. The main reason for these restrictions was security, and to avoid congestion. Without thousands of small vehicles clogging up the thoroughfares of Lorna, the city was a utopian model of urban planning and social engineering. Transport and communications were integrated into the design of the metropolis from the very beginning. The system worked remarkably well – at least on the surface. But like all Utopian dreams, people have a way of screwing it up.

The Temple Guards were a case in point. They were soldiers of the faith, instigated by the First Council to protect the clergy as a contingent of bodyguards – nothing more. An elite but small force; and given how the Prophet had died it was an understandable precaution. With the construction of the Great Temple this small elite force became a full military unit operating outside civil law. They answered only to the Shentamic law of the Church – more specifically the Great Temple. As such they were regarded as the most devout of Tobianists, even more so than the clergy. Under Shentamic law the clergy were seen as the left hand – the hand of introspection and prayer, while the Guard were the right hand – the hand of service and action. Faith in action was seen as the greater good. As the Prophet wrote:

... There is only action and stillness
Through action is change effected
Through stillness is change prepared

The Shentama
– Stanza 48

Captain Marius was a man of action. As a soldier of the Church, his every action was an act of faith. He had fulfilled many important assignments for the Church Council over the years. They relied on him and the Temple Guard to weed out heresy and rebellion; to maintain order in the city of the Prophet; and to suppress any dissidence that threatened the Tobianist Church-State. Marius had risen through the ranks to Captain because he got results. How he got them was irrelevant. You could justify a lot with God on your side.

Needless to say, he loved his job.

This assignment was no different, despite coming direct from the Cardinal Hierophant Cairn himself, who'd stressed urgency and secrecy. When Cairn told him what had happened Marius was furious. To think someone had actually sought to sabotage the upcoming Festival of Renewal by desecrating the very tomb of the Prophet. Thank God they had been stopped in time by an alert cleric; though if one of his Temple Guards had interrupted the vandals they would not have escaped. Such a shame the brave cleric who had fought off the vandals died soon after from his wounds. Marius would have liked to question the man. As a result, there was little to go on. The one clue they had was that the vandals were probably part of a group of intellectual radicals calling themselves *The DS* – whatever the fuck that stood for. Dumb Shits? Dickhead … Shits? Marius didn't care. They were intellectual fuckheads and he knew where to find intellectual fuckheads. The Lorna Institute.

Without slowing down in the slightest, Marius steered the GL cruiser off the road and onto the cobbled walkways that led to the Lorna Institute; then directly onto the grassy commons that fronted the main entrance. Students relaxing and picnicking on the lawn scattered in a panic as Marius led his convoy of fifteen GL's travelling at speed, towards the science faculty building.

Marius laughed out loud at the sight of all the junior fuckheads bouncing off their asses and dashing for cover. This was even more fun than buzzing people in the street, and was probably the first real exercise any of them had had since their mothers chased them from their homes.

'Look at 'em scurry!' he exclaimed to his passenger, the very green cadet Fairchild who was now clutching the sides of the GL for dear life. 'Like a herd of wild rabbits hearin' a gunshot. Fuckin' freeloaders!' he shouted at a pair of fleeing students, clipping one of them in the head as he flew past. Captain Marius paid no mind as Fairchild turned to see the young man go down hard – and not get up.

Marius drove full throttle towards the steps of the science block, pushing on up the marble staircase. It was only once he reached the top landing that he turned the GL hard into what would have been a skid had there been wheels, the sound of screeching rubber replaced by a violent discharge of static electricity, as the vehicle came to a clean stop right next to the front doors. The rest of the entourage chose to park at the bottom of the staircase, and double-timed it up the steps to join their captain.

'Come on, pup,' Marius said to the cadet as he leapt out of the vehicle. 'You're with me.'

Marius called to Lieutenant Makoto running up the stairs. 'Bring two men with you, Mak. The rest can wait out here.' Without waiting Marius marched toward the science block.

Lieutenant Makoto quickly chose two men to accompany him and caught up with Marius's GL, which the sickly young cadet was still climbing out of.

'Come on, lad,' Makoto said to him as he walked past. 'Can't keep the Captain waiting.'

Marius stormed through the front doors and marched down the main corridor. Heads turned and people retreated when they saw a contingent of Temple Guards approaching. Such a sight was rarely good news, and generally meant someone was about to be arrested – or worse. Lieutenant Makoto and the others followed behind as closely as the Captain's quick pace allowed without breaking into a run.

Marius knew exactly where he was going. Chief intellectual fuckhead and suspected dissident – Professor Berger. Dean of the Lorna Institute's science faculty and a man Marius had dealt with before. He was a smarmy bastard who managed to evade Marius's previous attempt to catch him out. But not this time.

Marius burst through doors to the rear offices. He could see Berger at the other end of the long room through the glass walls of his corner office, sitting behind his desk apparently on a call with someone. Marius walked past the diverse chorus of underlings at their desks, past the Dean's receptionist and her feeble attempt to bail him up, and stormed into Berger's office – at least as much as the safety hinges of the glass doors would allow one to storm.

Berger finished his call. 'Thank-you. He's here now.' He looked up calmly. 'Captain Marius. Good to see you again. How can I help you?'

Makoto and the other guards caught up. 'You lot wait outside,' Marius told them. 'No-one comes in.'

'A private chat,' said Berger with a slight smile. 'We haven't had one of those for a long time.'

Marius glared but kept his cool, sitting in the chair opposite.

'Of course, do sit down,' invited Berger after the fact. 'Would you like something to drink?'

Marius didn't answer.

'No?'

Berger waited for the captain to say something, but he didn't. They sat looking at each other for several seconds until Berger felt compelled to break the silence.

'So ... to what do I owe the pleasure?'

Marius watched Berger intently. He really had no idea what to ask or how to proceed. This was just a hunch, after all. But he figured Berger knew something that could kick-start this investigation. He had hoped to catch Berger by surprise to gain the upper hand but clearly someone tipped him off. He knew from past experience that the man was not easily intimidated – but he loved to talk. Berger's intellect was his greatest asset, and weakness. So Marius chose to wait and see what cracks might emerge.

'Looking forward to the festival?' Marius asked.

'Yes ... certainly.'

'What's your favourite part?'

Berger was confused. He could tell Marius was fishing for something, so he played along. 'I think ... the public mass... ... in Festival Square. Not so much for the speeches and sermons, which are, of course, very inspiring, but just the sheer humanity of it. So many people in one place. So many true believers all gathered together with a single purpose: To honour and remember the Prophet Tobias. I find it … very comforting. What's *your* favourite part, Captain?'

'Why do you find it comforting?' Marius responded.

'That the words of the Prophet are not dead. That through his Church, thanks to things like the festival, we are reminded how his teachings are still very much a part of our lives.'

'And you really believe that?'

'Of course,' Berger lied. 'Don't you?'

'What about the heretics?'

'What about them?'

'They believe in nothing.'

'I wouldn't say that.'

'They reject the teachings of the Prophet. They reject the Church.'

Marius could see Berger biting his tongue. 'Indeed. But …'

'Yes?'

'You didn't come here to discuss the festival.' Berger was changing the subject by getting back on topic, even though he didn't yet know what the topic was.

'No. I didn't.'

Marius had an idea how he might unbalance Berger. Physical intimidation didn't work well on him, despite him being a spineless wimp. His intellect and sense of superiority gave him courage. If Marius could catch him out intellectually first, then the physical threat he intended would be much more effective. Plus, bringing this arrogant prick down a peg or two before things got rough would be fun.

'I wanted to ask you: Are all scientists heretics? Or just the dumb ones?'

'The Prophet was not opposed to science,' Berger replied calmly. 'Nor is the Church.'

'That's not what I asked.'

'Why do you assume a 'dumb' scientist must be a heretic?'

'Because a smart one would know better.'

'Well … you have a point. But if it were not for science the body of the Prophet would not have been preserved for all these years. The Church is built upon the cornerstone of science.'

'Why do you say *the* Church? Not *your* church or *our* church, but *the* church?'

'Now your just arguing semantics, dear Captain. Of course it is *our* church, it is everybody's church – '

'Except for the heretics.'

'– Except for the heretics,' Berger conceded.

'And the dumb scientists.'

'Why do you persist in characterising 'heretics' as somehow dumb? And I daresay there are no dumb scientists. The very term is erroneous.'

'So I was right. All scientists are heretics, even the smart ones.'

'I am not a heretic.'

'Are you sure? By your own logic you must be.'

Berger was clearly getting irritated now by this stupid debate. 'How do you arrive at that conclusion? Faith and science are two sides of the same coin – '

'Ah. So they are different sides?'

'You're missing the point. Heresy is whatever the Church decides. It has nothing to do with faith. One can still believe in the teachings of the Prophet and not agree with the Church.'

'But that's heresy.'

'That's what I'm saying.'

'So you do believe in the Prophet?'

'Of course!'

'But not the Church.'

Berger caught himself, '… No … no, that's not what I'm saying.'

'That's what it sounded like.'

'I'm a loyal Tobianist. I believe in the Prophet, and his church.'

'But you just said heresy had nothing to do with faith. Surely it has everything to do with faith.'

'Of course, you are right. Forgive me, Captain.'

'Then how can the cornerstone of the Church be science? Science does not rely on faith but facts. Yes?'

'This is true,' Berger agreed warily.

'Then it follows that all scientists are heretics.'

'No –'

'That you are a heretic.'

'No, not at all –'

Marius abruptly rose from his seat, withdrew a handgun, and moved in one smooth motion around the desk. 'And as such you are a threat to the Church, to the body of the Prophet, and to all true Tobianists.' He drilled the barrel of the weapon into Berger's temple. Berger collapsed out of the chair and onto the floor. Marius knelt over him pinning his head to the floor with the gun.

Outside the room, through the glass, everyone in the office watched as Marius asserted himself.

'I should just kill you right here. Then there'd be one less heretic fuckhead in the world to dishonour the memory of the Prophet and spoil a perfectly good festival.'

Berger pleaded: 'I'm not a heretic. I'm not a heretic!'

'What are you then, fuckhead?'

'I believe in the word of the Prophet – '

' – But not the Church. So you're a heretic. Bye-bye.'

'NO! Please! I believe in the Church.'

'But you're an intellectual fuckhead. You guys don't believe in nothing.'

'I'm not a … fuckhead!'

'Are you sure? You look like a fuckhead. You've got this big office an' all.'

'I'm not that smart. Really!'

'Prove it.'

'…How?'

'Tell me something that shows you're not an intellectual fuckhead heretic. Show me a little faith.'

Two minutes later Marius strode out of Berger's office with a satisfied gleam in his eye. The staff who witnessed what just happened shrank into the walls, hoping not to end up as collateral damage.

'Bring him along,' he ordered Makoto without breaking stride. 'I may need to question him some more.' Then to his young cadet: 'Come on, lad. You're with me, remember!'

Reality is a symbolic construct of the idea that created it.

Shentama
– Stanza 116

Rene enjoyed his work, but there were times it just wasn't worth it. Walking through the lobby of Stone Mote Towers (nicknamed the *corkscrew* due to its winding helical architecture) he felt uneasy. As if he was in the wrong place. As if he had better things to do than 'go to work'.

He'd had the strangest dreams last night. No … not dreams. Nightmares. He was being chased. Surrounded by enemies. Lost and terrified. He felt anxious, even now. The nightmare was still with him. It peered over his shoulder at breakfast, sat beside him on the train, and was right there beside him as he entered the corkscrew. It would not be ignored.

He glanced up at the AV walls of the lobby – searching for any kind of distraction. A Warrior Games highlights reel was playing. One player, wearing a ridiculous helmet of leather, steel plate and feathers was smashed into the ground by his opponent – a huge, bald black man wearing a tank-top and wielding a gigantic hammer. The strike drew a roar from the crowd, as blood oozed from the fallen warrior's helmet onto the baked earth of the arena. The victor raised the hammer above his head and slowly turned on the spot, accepting the crowd's tribute.

Rene didn't normally watch the Games, finding no entertainment in ritualised violence. But right now, it was a welcome diversion. Watching someone else die made you appreciate your own life just a little bit more.

He caught the elevator to the 29th floor. The elevator moved diagonally as it rose, spiralling up the superstructure until finally weaving back inside to open on the offices of *The Lorna Guardian – Official curator of The Temple City and Guardian of the Word*. The masthead suggested a good old-fashioned news-site, but of course it was nothing of the sort. It merely served as a catchall name for officially curated content; and in Lorna, all content was officially curated. Dan would argue it was not curation but censorship, but that's just how things were. News was a commodity like anything else.

Rene's by-line for the digest section focused on technology trends. It was about gadgets and games, bots and infotech. Inoffensive, uncontroversial stuff. It had nothing to do with religion or politics, and that suited Rene just fine. But more and more he was expected to write puff pieces on how well the government was doing with new tech. Lorna was once the world leader in social infrastructure, technology and design. But that was a long time ago. The city (and the Great Temple) remained the central authority of the Tobianist world, but it no longer led the way. Nevertheless, stories about the great advances made by the Lorna Institute, for example, dominated his column of late. And now he was being asked to do the same for the Church. Pieces on how they used new tech to spread the word of the Prophet, or how the festival streamcast each year was some kind of revolutionary technical achievement, when it was far from it.

If he could, Rene would be writing about how the Tobianist Church had hindered tech development for nearly two centuries. As far as he could tell human society had advanced little since the beginning of the Tobianist Era. A kind of modern Dark Age where innovation was both celebrated and shunned by the Church. Science was the cornerstone of Tobianism, as Dan was fond of reminding him, and yet was considered a threat to the Church's authority. Science and religion simply didn't mix. The same as religion and politics didn't mix. There had been some advances of course – GL technology, weather control, comkeys – but the pace of progress was nothing compared to what it had once been.

And yet for two centuries, the Tobianist Church had governed the world in relative peace. Poverty, famine, wars (at least big ones), even natural disasters had been all but eliminated. And it was largely due to the Church and its autocratic rule. Perhaps it wasn't so much a *Dark* Age as a *Dim* Age. Boring, but safe. This was at the heart of Rene's ongoing disagreement with Dan. At the end of the day, the Church was doing a pretty good job; and a little freedom sacrificed for peace and stability seemed a small price to pay.

With morning coffee poured, and pleasantries exchanged with fellow workers he didn't really know, Rene sat at his desk to begin the workday. As a writer, he could do all this from home, of course. Do it better and faster, and without even having to get dressed. But management insisted people come into the office at least a couple of days a week, for face-to-face interaction and networking opportunities that everyone relished or avoided in their own way. Still, it got him out of the house.

The AV sprang to life as he sat down, triggered by proximity to his comkey. Immediately a story caught his attention that got the day off to a suitably dismal start. According to a source within the Temple, heretic scientists had attempted to vandalise the tomb of the Prophet. They were stopped before causing any damage, but had escaped and were now being hunted by the Temple Guard. The story itself, while shocking, was not uncommon. Vandalism on Temple property happened all the time, despite tight security. That their target had been the tomb of the Prophet was alarming, but it was surely doomed to failure. With everyone under constant surveillance, you couldn't get away with much in Lorna. Rene was about to wave the item away when he noticed the name 'Doctor Asar' as a scientist connected with the crime. A cold chill ran up Rene's spine. The report said Asar was personal physician to the Cardinal Hierophant himself. No sooner had Rene read this than a second more profound chill swept through his body, as the communiqué was instantly redacted and vanished from his screen, as if it had never existed.

Dan had asked about Asar just last night, but when pressed was uncharacteristically mum about who he was. To see him now in connection with a criminal raid on the Temple suggested Dan was in a lot deeper than Rene had imagined. Perhaps deeper than Dan himself was even aware. He wondered if he should he tell Dan. Would that make him some kind of accessory? Rene had no desire to get caught up in whatever mess Dan was in, but if it meant his friend was in danger then he had to do something. He had to at least warn him. Rene feared it was his brother, Will, all over again. Noble intentions that brought only misery to those around him.

Rising from his desk Rene walked to the tall windows and looked out over the city. It was a magnificent view. From here he could see clear across to Festival Square and the Great Temple. 'You shit, Dan,' he muttered to himself. 'What have you got yourself into?'

—— ∞ ——

Tobias slept peacefully as Doctors Althea Roget and Jason Asar sat in an adjoining room, watching the unconscious Prophet on the monitors. There were three floating GL cameras in the room each getting a slightly different angle. A wide shot from high up in the room, one on the side, and one directly over the bed with a close-up of the Prophet's sleeping face. It had been ten hours since Patric's tranquilizer dart had felled Tobias. The effects of the drug should be fading soon and he could wake at any moment. As before, there were wireless sensors stuck to his pale skin. And as before, the readouts all showed a steady heartbeat and deep delta brainwave pattern; the pseduo-coma that had so baffled Roget last time.

This time they were better prepared. They'd found a bed with nano-bond restrains to securely tie down Tobias's wrists and ankles. Though the restraints were quite old their carbon nano-tube filaments were still viable. The room was locked, and with remote AV monitoring they could observe him without placing themselves in danger. Asar had sustained two broken ribs from the last incident. They were minor fractures, but the pain made it difficult for him to breath, with daggers in his chest every time he inhaled. Despite being in a hospital and having a good supply of drugs for Tobias and their primate test subjects, they lacked the simple pain relief medication that would have helped him right now. He would have to wait till Berger returned that night with some pills.

They had to keep up the appearance of normality. Asar had taken time off from his practice, and Roget was calling in sick for a few days, but it would have looked suspicious if Berger and Trevelle had also abandoned their duties at the Institute. Especially given Trevelle was professor of theology and had responsibilities with the Temple to fulfill. The students, Patric and Isaac, couldn't be got rid of even if they had wanted, such was their commitment to the cause. But no one would miss them for some time.

Althea had not been injured during Tobias' escape attempt, but she was deeply troubled by it. What was blocking his recovery? It had to be psychological. Elly had recovered completely, so was it something particular to humans, or perhaps just to Tobias? Or perhaps Elly herself had been unique. A fluke. Perhaps it had to do with how long he had been in stasis. Was it simply too late to restore full consciousness after so many years? Was the tissue damaged beyond repair? Despite these doubts, she knew the Prophet was still in there somewhere. She couldn't explain it, but she felt his presence. Remote and disconnected… but present. She guessed it was just fear blocking him from coming through. He'd made a connection with Elly, even if only on a primal, emotional level. Perhaps Elly could help bring him 'round.

'I don't think that's a good idea,' Asar had said to Althea when she told him   over dinner.

'Why not? She's the only one he's made any connection with so far.'

'After what happened he may think she betrayed him. It could make things worse.'

'How could things be any worse?' argued Althea.

'The procedure worked,' said Asar. 'He's alive. We just have to work out what went wrong.'

'Nothing went wrong. There's no brain damage, no physical injury. He's not a vegetable. There is consciousness there. It's just – ' Althea couldn't finish the sentence, but Asar knew what she meant: It just wasn't the Prophet.

'Perhaps it simply wasn't meant to be,' Asar said despondently. 'Perhaps … I was wrong, thinking this could change things.'

'It still can. We can't give up on him yet.' Althea was determined. 'I know he's in there somewhere. We just have to find a way to draw him out.'

'I'm open to suggestions. But without the Bonobo. Without endangering anyone.'

Althea had another idea. It was a long shot, but they were desperate. She didn't tell Asar about it though, lest he reject it as well, before she'd had a chance to try it.

— ∞ —

'Who's Doctor Asar?' Rene asked Dan as he entered the apartment.

Thrown by the question, Dan looked at Joanna for guidance, but she was as surprised by the question as he was. 'I can't tell you,' he answered honestly.

'All right then, I'll tell *you*. He holds three degrees in medicine, political science, and robotics. Though his specialty for many years has been micro-biology. He invented artificial blood, and patented a process for growing replacement organs. He is a lecturer at the Lorna Institute in advanced medicine, and also runs a private surgical practice mainly for wealthy and influential clients, including the Cardinal Hierophant. Politically, he's a self-proclaimed libertarian and loyal Tobianist. Though some have questioned this. Oh, and he's wanted for questioning by the Temple Guards over a recent attack on the tomb of the Prophet. There's a lot more of course, but those are the highlights. So let me ask you again, Dan. Who is Doctor Jason Asar and what is he to you?'

Dan had never seen Rene so upset. He wasn't shouting, in fact he wasn't even angry. But he was clearly upset, speaking more out of concern than enmity.

'Rene?' Johanna ventured anxiously, but Rene motioned for her to hold as he maintained his look at Dan, waiting for an answer.

Dan sat down, and without looking up said quietly: 'I've never met him. I didn't know anything about him, except that … he's part of the DS.'

'What's the DS?'

'They're just one of many insurgent groups around. More your hot-air types though – you know, all talk and no action. They keep pretty much to themselves. But they had something planned and we've been asked to keep an eye out if those names came up in any Temple communiqués. I really don't know what they were up to, or what would happen if their names did come up.' Dan finally looked up at Rene. 'Are you saying there was a report on Asar?'

'Yes. For all of ten seconds,' Rene answered. 'Then it was erased from the system.'

'What does that mean?'

'It means the Church doesn't want it known they're looking for him, or what he is supposed to have done.'

'Why would they attack the tomb of the Prophet?'

'You tell me. You're the rebel.'

Joanna, who had been quietly listening to this exchange, decided to weigh in. 'Dan, who else have you talked to about this?'

'No one.'

'No one else knows of your involvement with these groups.'

'Well, aside from others in the group.'

Joanna was firm with him. 'You're quite sure.'

'Of course. Who else would I tell? You're my only friends. You're the only ones I trust. Apart from Barty.'

'Barty?' Joanna asked.

'Bartholomew. The leader of our group.'

Rene saw what Joanna was getting at. 'None of your girlfriends, perhaps?'

Dan was about to say *no* but stopped himself, '… well, not much.'

'How much is 'not much'?' asked Joanna.

Dan couldn't answer.

— ∞ —

'How many of these rebel groups are there?' Cairn demanded. Captain Marius wore his dress armour, as one must when summoned before the Executive Council. They were in the Council chambers with all twenty-three member Cardinals present and silently watching. An emergency meeting had been called, which meant only one thing – Cairn had something he wanted to rail about.

'As far as we can tell, about thirty-five, Your Eminence.' Marius responded calmly. 'But it varies. They're not very organised. None of them are big enough to be a real threat.'

Cairn took exception to this last statement. 'You think so, Captain. And yet one of these groups infiltrated Temple security and came close to vandalising the tomb of the Prophet. We have no idea who they are, or where they are, or what their true intention was. You say there are thirty-five *dis*organised groups, and yet somehow they manage to infiltrate the most secure building on the face of the planet! Tell me, Captain, how is this possible?'

Marius was suddenly on the defensive. 'I don't know, Your Eminence.'

'Then find out!'

'Yes, Your Eminence.' Marius quickly bowed and left the room.

The Council members were used to Cairn's temper, but that didn't make him any less intimidating. The only one not intimidated by Cairn was Cardinal Kasper, who sat at Cairn's right hand. To Cairn's left sat Cardinal Woolf, a corpulent and generally likeable man, the exact opposite both physically and in personality to Kasper. Yet ethically he was perhaps as venal and opportunistic as any man on the Council. You didn't get to the rank of cardinal without a strong sense of self-preservation and a little hypocrisy.

As cardinal, you represented your country at the Great Temple, becoming part of the Tobianist world theocracy. There were still local political leaders – governors, ministers, and presidents – many of them secular in nature, but the Temple was the heart of global power and faith, which made Lorna the unofficial world capital. There were one-hundred and ninety-two representative cardinals at the Temple, a caucus that met regularly in the Great Hall, voting on all manner of things affecting the world. It was all very democratic. Then there was the Executive Council. This was an elite group of twenty-three men (for they were all men) who decided Church policy and law. These were the most powerful people on the planet, each one as devious and cunning as the next. They were *this close* to the seat of the Cardinal Hierophant, and all hoped to be next in line for the office. In many ways, the Council was just as fragmented as the rebel groups, twenty-three separate agendas, twenty-three people ready to stab you in the back at the first opportunity. Cairn understood this because he was, after all, one of them. That's how one becomes Cardinal Hierophant.

Kasper whispered into Cairn's ear: 'They must understand how serious this is. But we cannot tell them the whole truth.'

Cairn addressed the Council. 'Understand this, we are dealing with terrorists. Heretics with no honour or principles, and nothing to lose. A single man with wicked intent could be the undoing of this Church. That is how vulnerable we are right now. That is how dangerous this ... attempted desecration was. This Church represents the word of the Prophet on earth, and we must do everything in our power to defend that. We have been too lenient with these rebel groups. They must be stamped out, before they become a real threat. For the sake of the Church, for the sake of the Prophet Tobias, and for the sake of the

Temple.' Cairn wanted to scare them. Kasper was right. He couldn't reveal the whole truth, but they had to understand how serious this threat was. The best way to do that was to make it personal. 'If the authority of the Great Temple falters, gentlemen, or even appears to falter … we are all ruined.'

— ∞ —

'Do you think we're in any danger?' Joanna asked.

One thing Rene liked about his pledge-mate was she called it as she saw it. 'I don't know,' he admitted. 'It depends who else Dan has talked to, and how much he said.'

Rene got into bed; Joanna was already under the covers beside him. 'I don't think he would have said much,' Joanna reasoned. ' He just likes to boast. I doubt any of his transient girlfriends would take it that seriously. I just wish he was a bit more … '

'Discreet? Responsible? Mature?' Rene was only half-joking.

'Self-assured,' Joanna countered. 'He's just looking for approval. For someone to say they're proud of him.'

It occurred to Rene that Dan sought that approval from him. They had grown up together and he was his best – indeed only – friend. Though he didn't choose the role, Rene was big brother and mentor to Dan; just as Will, his own big brother, had once been for him. Dan may be reckless, but Joanna always rose to his defence. She was big sister to them both.

'I don't think we're in any danger.' Rene reassured her. 'Despite his boasting I seriously doubt Dan is a key player in any of these groups. Can you imagine him as a rebel leader?'

'You underestimate him.'

'If that's true, then we're in serious trouble. Because if he's being watched, then we're being watched.'

Joanna thought on the implications of this for a moment. 'How would we know?'

Rene couldn't answer that one. It kept him awake for some time trying to work it out before he finally fell into a fitful sleep.

7

The gift of prophecy is the ability to read time
To see the Now in all its manifestations
To know that anything is possible
And everything is fixed
Fate and free will are two sides of the same coin

Shentama
– Stanza 55

Tobias woke up.

He opened his eyes slowly. It was dark, though a soft, ambient light illuminated the gloom. He listened. A low hum murmured from the thing beside him, but that was all. He looked around the room. It was the same as the one before, but not the same. He tried to sit up, but something held him down. His wrists and ankles were tied down. He pulled against the restraints hard. No luck. He was trapped. He felt no fear, though. Not this time. This time he was just angry.

A light flickered to life above his head. A large, rectangular light floating in the air above him. Strange symbols appeared and then … movement. Images. It wasn't a light. It was a window – a window to another world. Or lots of worlds. It kept changing. And there was sound. Strange noises. Voices and … something he couldn't define. It seemed unnatural, and yet not. A jumble of sounds that somehow belonged together. The image kept changing. The window kept moving. But it didn't move. He didn't move. The sound shifted and flowed, like water dashing around rocks in a stream. It was peculiar. He didn't understand how this was possible. It was unsettling. He watched the images and listened to the noise. He had no choice. A man appeared in the window. He spoke:

'Death is not an end, it is a renewal of life. We are all immortal, and we all share in the great adventure. And I love a good adventure, don't you?'

Althea Roget studied Tobias closely as archival footage of the Prophet beamed from the old AV display suspended above his head. She watched from an adjoining observation room, where tempered glass windows overlooked the operating theatre. Her hope was to trigger some glimmer of recognition of the man he once was.

The image cut to an interview on a late night talk show:

'You've said you had no intention of becoming a Prophet,' the host asked, 'yet that's how many people see you.'

'I prefer to call myself a teacher. At least, that's what I put on my visa application. Can you imagine the questions I'd get at customs if I put down 'prophet'?'

This prompted a round of laughter from the studio audience.

'It's said you can predict the future, is that right?'

'No. But when I meet people, I see … possibilities.'

'What does that mean?'

'I glimpse the choices before them and the paths those choices would lead them down.'

'So you see their future.'

Tobias shrugged. 'In a way.'

'What do you see in my future?' the host asked, only half joking.

Tobias paused. He looked at the man intently, suddenly serious. 'Are you sure you want to know?'

The host became anxious. 'Maybe not.'

Tobias smiled warmly. 'Don't worry, it's not all bad.'

'What about, like – world affairs? Can you predict who'll win the next election?'

I don't make predictions or prophesies. That would be irresponsible … and pointless.'

'So, what do you say then to your followers and the press, because they're calling you a prophet?'

'I take it to mean simply: teacher. I'm very flattered, of course they think I am more than that. After all, I could be called a lot worse things. But I am just a teacher. Or writer.'

'Yes, you've written a book. *The Shentama.*' The host produced a hardbound copy of the book and placed it face-forward on the desk so the camera could get a good shot of it.

'I was wondering when we'd get around to it,' Tobias joked.

Another peal of chuckles from the studio audience. The book was presented with a simple white jacket, with a figure-8 lemniscate (or infinity symbol) in the centre and the title embossed discretely underneath this. Althea noted how much thinner the book was than the modern *Shentama* she was used to reading.

'What does the title mean? *Shentama*? I know it's not Jewish. Is it Japanese or Chinese as some people have said?'

'For some reason this has been a major topic of discussion. I don't know why. It's just a name. It means whatever you want it to mean. But for those that care about such things, you could examine the etymology of the word and find meaning.'

The host waited for Tobias to explain further, but he didn't. 'You're not going to tell me, are you?'

Tobias smiled knowingly. 'Now I wouldn't be much of a teacher if I just gave you all the answers. You've got to do a bit of work yourself.'

Althea watched the face of Tobias bound to the bed in the operating theatre. All she saw was confusion. The film then presented a montage of the Prophet meeting politicians, famous people of the time, and religious leaders; speaking at rallys and festivals; and being portrayed as either a saint or a demon in the press. A voice-over accompanied the images:

'In five short years Tobias had become a phenomenon. A spiritual rock star with a worldwide following thanks to his canny use of the media. Some declared him to be the second coming of Christ. Others, the anti-Christ. Others saw him as an altogether new kind of spiritual leader, or the same old thing just with a modern spin. However you saw him, there was no denying the Prophet Tobias had become a spiritual and political force to be reckoned with. A twenty-first century messiah.'

Tobias began to struggle violently against his restraints. Althea took this as a sign the therapy was working. He was fighting it, but it was getting a reaction.

The narration continued: 'His book, *Shentama*, was in two out of every three households. The biggest selling book in history with over four billion copies sold. And despite Tobias's opposition to becoming a formalised religion, his followers established their own order, complete with clergy and a canon of laws based on the philosophies outlined in the *Shentama*. Within months, Tobianism had millions of registered faithful and was on its way to becoming the new world religion. But for a man with such unprecedented influence and power, the Prophet lived a simple life. He owned no property, gave virtually all his earnings to charity or research projects. And spent his life travelling and teaching.'

Tobias was now screaming at the top of his lungs and thrashing wildly, but the nano-binds held. The screen above him continued to flicker and babble, oblivious to his cries. It showed the Prophet of history speaking at a massive outdoor rally as the voice-over continued:

'The assassination of Tobias shocked the world – ' The image of the Prophet being shot down mid-sentence appeared on the screen – a sniper's bullet to the heart, causing him to stagger and collapse on the stage. Althea flinched. It was a horrifying image she never got used to seeing. '– But this only served to make a martyr of him, triggering the greatest conflict since World War 2. The war now known as *The Reckoning …*'

Tobias ripped his right arm free as the nano-bond restraints tore apart under the adrenaline-fuelled pressure. He pulled at the remaining bonds and was soon standing on the bed punching the screen. It bounced away, undamaged, so Tobias grabbed the humming box next to the bed and hurled it at the screen. It shattered, and tiny fragments of glass rained over him.

Asar burst into the observation room in time to see Tobias standing in the middle of the theatre, howling up at them through the one-way glass. It was a terrifying image of an uncontrollable beast.

Althea was distraught. This man was not the Prophet. He wasn't even human.

— ∞ —

Captain Marius entered the Hypogeum Basilica to meet with

the Cardinal Hierophant. It was an experience he always dreaded. No matter how assured he was upon entering, he felt less of a man once he left. He could feel his penis shrivel into his abdomen even as he walked down the long aisle toward the throne. The architecture of the place just sucked the self-esteem out of you. Which was a shame, because Marius was feeling pretty damn pleased with himself about now. Not only had he fucked young cadet Fairchild that morning and was still in a post-coital glow, he had also just received vital information from their captive, Professor Berger. Every man had his breaking point. It was just a matter of finding the right tools for the job. Berger held out longer than Marius had expected, his estimation of the man rising slightly. He may have been an intellectual fuckhead and a revolutionary, but at least he had conviction. Pity about the heart attack, he might have been able to tell them more. For some reason the condition didn't appear on his medical records.

As he strode down the aisle the doors to the basilica closed with a resonant *boom* behind him. Cairn sat in the throne, watching his approach. Cardinal Kasper sat in a smaller and less ornate throne by his side. If Marius didn't know better, he would have thought there was something going on between the two of them. They were always together. But he couldn't imagine anyone would want to fuck Kasper, the man looked like death warmed up.

'Hurry up, man!' Cairn bellowed across the hall.

Marius started to jog. His dress armour rattled when just walking, now it positively jangled his approach. As he reached the base of the dais, he fell to one knee and bowed. 'Your Eminence.'

'Yes, yes. All right. Get up,' said Cairn impatiently. 'What have you found out?'

'He gave us a name.'

'… Yes?'

Marius was hesitant to say it out loud. He knew the reaction it would get. '… Asar.'

'Doctor Jason Asar?' Cairn articulated slowly. He wanted to be sure there was no mistake.

'Yes. According to Berger, Asar is the leader of the rebel group known as the DS – '

'DS?'

' – Dissident Society, Your Eminence.'

'What a stupid name,' interjected Kasper.

' – It was him that planned the raid on the tomb,' Marius finished.

Cairn considered his next question carefully. The answer, and how he chose to respond, could determine the very future of the Church.

'Did he say why?'

'Why were they trying to raid the tomb?' asked Marius.

'Yes …' Cairn responded through grit teeth.

'Not exactly.'

'What *did* he say … exactly?' Marius was trying his patience. He was a good soldier, but he had the intellect of a kumquat.

'Not much else really, Your Eminence. He died soon after.'

'Died?' asked Kasper incredulously. 'Pray tell, Captain. How did he die?'

'A heart attack.' Marius admitted. 'Had we known he had a condition we might have gone a bit easier on him. But, as it is – '

'– As it is, Captain,' Cairn interrupted. 'You've managed to kill the only witness who could have told us what Asar was up to and where he is now.'

'Oh, we know where he is,' Marius said confidently. 'They're hiding out in some old hospital in the AQ. Not sure exactly where but we're tracking it down now. Won't take long to find them.'

'A hospital.'

'Yeah, Saint … something-or-other.'

'How many men do you have, Captain?'

Marius sensed Cairn was anxious too many people knew about this operation. He wanted to reassure him. 'I've got special ops on this, Your Eminence. Thirty-two men and women. They're the best, and completely trustworthy.'

'How many all together?'

Marius was thrown by the question. There were several classes of Temple Guard: the Elite Guard, who were bodyguards to the Church Council; the Regular Guard who maintained order and security throughout the Temple grounds; and the Regional Guard, who were the faith's forces in all cities and regions outside of the Temple grounds.

'You mean within the Great Temple?' asked Marius.

'I mean in Lorna.'

Kasper was just as confused by Cairn's line of questioning as Marius.

'There's about five hundred Regular Guard garrisoned in the Temple barracks. One-thousand or so of Lorna's own Regional Guard, plus a further five-thousand are billeted throughout the city who've come as additional security for the festival next week. So that's…' Marius tried to do the math.

'Six and half thousand,' Kasper finished.

'Good,' Cairn said. 'I want every single one of them on this. I want to crackdown on all the rebel groups you know of. Every meeting place. Every home. Every agitator, sympathiser, benefactor and sponsor. Anyone who has had anything to do with any of these groups. I want every heretic and heathen in the city rounded up and imprisoned.'

Marius was lost for words. This was a massive operation, and frankly overkill for what he thought was just another failed rebel misdemeanor.

'Do you understand me, Captain?'

'Yes, Your Eminence.'

'Are you up to it?'

'Yes, Your Eminence. It's just …'

'Yes?'

'… Can I have that in writing?'

Cairn chuckled. 'Of course. Kasper will prepare an authorisation for you immediately. Complete with official seal.'

Marius bowed, 'Yes, Your Eminence.' He turned and ran at full sprint down the aisle of the basilica, a broad smile creeping across his face. He didn't care what the reason was, or even the legality of the action. This came from the highest authority on the planet. They were going to fight back. *The Reckoning* and *The Great Purge* were well before his time. For two hundred years there had been effectively no war; no major conflict. Just localised hostilities and skirmishes. Marius wasn't a policeman. He was a soldier. A Temple Guard. A defender of the faith. Finally, he had a chance to prove it in battle.

This was going to be a historic day indeed.

Once Marius had left the hall, Kasper calmly turned to the Cardinal Hierophant. 'Are you sure that's wise? The Council won't like it.'

'The council will do as I tell them,' Cairn snapped.

'This could become known as a second Great Purge,' Kasper warned. 'The first was not our finest moment. Are you sure you want this to be your legacy?'

'That is exactly what I'm hoping to avoid. If we act now, we can nip this in the bud, before these groups get organised. I know Asar, and there is more to the theft of the body of the Prophet than simply disrupting the festival. If he succeeds, we will have a revolution on our hands. And the Church – our very civilisation – is in jeopardy.'

Kasper began to wonder if Cairn was losing his mind, this was too melodramatic. 'Succeeds in what? What are you afraid he'll do?'

Cairn turned to Kasper with a cold, hard stare. 'Something noble.'

What you see of the world
reflects your view of the world
As your view of the world reflects your self
For who you are is defined by your world
And your world is defined by you

Shentama
– Stanza 157

Dan's group met in an abandoned house in what was once a nice suburban street in the south of Lorna but had, through neglect and the ravages of time, become one of the less desirable parts of the city to live. It was not as bad as parts of the Western Borough or the AQ, though. Locals did their best to keep the streets clean and safe. Indifference was not a natural consequence of poverty, so despite the age of the houses, some were well-maintained and quite homely. Which made those that had not been as well looked-after all the more conspicuous.

The house they adopted as their meeting place was not so run down as to be an obvious haven for rebels and heretics. From the outside it looked positively habitable. Inside it was practically empty. A few chairs in the room where they met; an office with a desk and lightly stocked drinks cabinet; and a single bed, just in case. The kitchen was stocked mainly with beverages and snack foods, and there was a basement no-one ever went into. The desk, bed and a few other bits and pieces had been left behind by previous tenants. Everything else they had brought in over the course the past year, carried in the dead of night to avoid detection by the neighbours. Though Dan seriously doubted the neighbours were ignorant of their presence or their purpose. They just didn't care.

When Dan began attending these meetings, he was excited by the intrigue and danger, but also believed he was doing something tangible to bring about change. He was with people who believed as he did. But the more he got to know them the more disillusioned he became. He couldn't help feel they were just playing at revolution. All they ever did was graffiti slogans on churches, deface public property, or just complain and grumble about the Church. Lately, the topic of discussion was the Festival of Renewal and how big a farce it had become, or complaints about how many Temple Guards had arrived in the city to maintain order. Security for the festival was insane and got worse every year.

Dan stopped going to the festival years ago, or at least, the opening ceremony at the Great Temple. It was hard to avoid since it took over the entire city for a week. There were cultural and sporting events planned around it. Street fairs, music, food and theatre, a special Warrior Games death-match event, and a massive firework and laser-light show to cap things off. For a whole week everyone became infuriatingly pious. Dan was all for a good party, but he couldn't stand the holier-than-thou's and their narrow-minded, petty, hateful sermonising. He'd got enough of that from his parents. He wasn't anti-Tobias. He was just anti-Church. The dogma, the politics, the tacit martial law it imposed, the stifling of free speech and progress. It was all very subtle of course, religious oppression evolved over years of well-intentioned autocracy. A benign dictatorship that crept up so slowly no one even noticed it anymore. Despite all the good things the Church had done – and Dan was prepared to admit there was *some* good – the church of the Prophet was nothing more than a front for power-mongers and corporate oligarchs. It was a dangerous time to be an atheist.

Of course, others in the group shared these sentiments, and Dan had spoken them aloud many times to a willing audience, usually with vigorous nods of agreement and equally vociferous responses. After a while it all became tediously repetitive. There were just two reasons he kept coming back.

The first was Gabrielle (they didn't use surnames in the group). There were a couple of women who regularly attended – the other being a shy young thing named Maya who rarely spoke up. Gabrielle was forthright and candid, a quality Dan found attractive. She also seemed to be the most connected among them, often referring to other groups she knew of and their secret activities – exploits that went beyond mere graffiti and vandalism. Dan didn't always agree with Gabrielle, but she made for a healthy debate. He found her enthusiasm for the cause stimulating, and her brash impudence a turn-on. They'd had sex twice – once on the single bed upstairs, the other time against an AV wall displaying religious artwork while on their way home, as a kind of protest. He kept coming to meetings hopeful that side of their relationship would continue.

The other reason he kept coming was Bartholomew, the leader of the group. After Rene and Joanna, Barty was perhaps his best friend. Indeed, his only other friend. They just hit it off, despite Barty being better educated and having very different tastes. Most of the others in the group were as bad as the hard-core Tobianists they complained about – petty, narrow-minded, and with a dose of bitter thrown in. In a way these gatherings served as nothing more than a support group for the disenfranchised. No real change was ever going to come from such a bunch of misfits.

Dan recognised this all too well because a year ago that had been him. Barty encouraged him to think of the big picture; beyond the trivial, shambolic effort of his peers. True change was not going to come through slogans painted on walls but through a passionate and cohesive call to action. '*To create a new world, we must first destroy the old*'. That's what Barty said. While Dan didn't necessarily agree with all of his theories, they'd had some vibrant conversations about what this new world might be and how to achieve it.

'Greetings comrade!' Bartholomew called as Dan entered the lounge room of the house. He looked around, Maya sat across the way and smiled at him, and there were five others whom Dan recognised from earlier meetings. Gabrielle was standing with Bartholomew.

'Hi everyone,' Dan greeted as he made for the pair. 'Barty, Gabrielle.' Dan nodded.

'Hey Dan,' Gabrielle smiled.

'Daniel!' Barty was always pleased to see him. 'Anything to report?' This was both a personal *how-are-you?* And an official request for information. Barty tended to be bellicose in all his interactions.

'Nothing untoward,' Dan replied with a smile. It was a running gag between them. 'Although, I have heard a little something about that *thing*.'

Barty tilted his head, understanding. 'Ah. We should discuss this in private. Let's repair to my office, shall we?'

'Be right there.' Dan waited for Barty to leave before speaking with Gabrielle. 'How've you been? I've missed you the last couple of meetings.'

'I've been busy.'

'Nothing too dangerous, I hope.'

'I'm here, ain't I?' There was a twinkle in her eye as she said this. Dan had missed their verbal spars.

'Well, I hope you didn't come back just for me. After all, you mean nothing to me,' Dan teased.

'And you mean even less to me,' Gabrielle responded in kind. 'If you have time later, I can show you how little I care.'

Dan tried not to grin. It looked like he was gonna get laid tonight. 'I look forward to it.' Dan moved to touch her face, but she gently knocked his hand aside. *Not here.*

As he turned to leave, she called after him, 'Dan, can you keep a secret?'

'Yes.'

'Good.'

They had kept their relationship furtive so far. She wanted to keep it that way.

The office was really a converted bedroom, so small the desk and drinks cabinet took up most of the available space. The cabinet contained mostly spirits; Barty had a fondness for bourbon, and knew Dan liked the occasional scotch.

'Libation?' Barty offered and began pouring, not waiting for an answer.

There was also a small bookcase that had no books, just a couple of cheap ornaments and a childhood trophy. It was the only real decoration in the entire house. In a built-in closet hung several spare suits – always black, always clean. Barty was never seen not wearing a suit – like an undertaker on call. A couple of chairs, and a portable AV on the desk. This was where Barty stored his contacts and 'secret files' as he called them.

AV's could take many forms, from solid entertainment walls like those found in homes or on the streets, to small polyurethane sheets or cloth. Some were mini-holographic projectors or wearable lenses, while others, like this one, came as a scroll that could be unrolled as required, its cylindrical metal case turning into a simple desktop stand. Practically anything could be an AV screen, and frequently was, keeping people constantly connected, for better or worse. All modern AV systems, regardless of size or form, scanned one's comkey and its synced genome signature, which must always be carried with you by law. This meant you could sit in front of any AV anywhere and your personal profile would appear immediately. It also meant authorities could track who was using any system at any time, and monitor everything one did. People had come to accept this as normal, since the pros of being always connected far outweighed the cons.

Of course, dissident groups didn't want the authorities knowing anything about their activities and what they were doing on their AV systems, so the scanner was illegally disabled, the operating system replaced with something less 'secure', and a crude local biokey added to safeguard access. Very old-school. All data was stored locally, and the device was disconnected from the global network. Effectively quarantined. It was a completely self-contained, isolated system. These were called Black AV's.

You couldn't get away with doing this to a registered domestic or office system. They had to be completely off the grid to go unnoticed. Just having one in the same room or house as a registered system was dangerous as their proximity could be detected through radiation measurements. In fact, just wearing your comkey near one was a risky proposition. Being cut off from the network their usefulness was limited, but it meant you could store information confident it was not being monitored or tracked. Dan didn't know how Bartholomew had come by this one, and only he, as leader of their group, had access. He didn't trust anyone else to come near it. Not even Dan.

Barty handed Dan a large scotch.

'Thanks.'

'What have you got, Daniel?' He always called Dan by his full name, said it sounded more dignified. This was despite preferring the diminutive *Barty* for himself.

'You wanted me to find out if my friend Rene had heard anything about Doctor Asar?'

'Yes?'

'There was a bulletin that the Temple Guard are searching for Asar because – ' Dan found it still hard to accept ' – he staged an attack on the Tomb of the Prophet inside the Temple.'

Barty looked up from his bourbon. 'If that's true then the DS is more militant than I thought.'

'Thing is,' Dan continued, 'as soon as the bulletin appeared, it disappeared. Like it had been recalled or something.'

'Why was that, do you think?'

'Rene figured the Church didn't want anyone to know about the attack, or that Asar was behind it.'

'I daresay he's right,' Barty agreed. 'If that were to become public knowledge it could seriously damage the Church. Assuming of course it's true.'

'Or even if it isn't,' Dan suggested.

'Indeed. I wonder how the news got leaked in the first place?'

'Why would they attack the tomb though? What would our cause gain by doing that? If anything, it makes us look like fanatics.'

'Don't you see?' Barty explained. 'It strikes at the very heart of the Church, literally and figuratively. It's a most audacious act. I wish

I had thought of it myself. Even if it fails, and it sounds like it did, it would still put the fear of God into them. The Temple would know we were serious.'

Barty sat in front of the Black AV. It recognised his face instantly and unlocked. He dashed off a few lines, making some quick notes.

'My friends aren't going to get into any trouble over this, are they?' Dan asked. 'I haven't put them at risk just by mentioning this guy's name?'

'I don't see how,' Barty reassured, as he rose from the chair and picked up his bourbon. 'So, you and Gabrielle, huh?'

Dan snorted self-consciously. 'How did you know?'

'It's pretty obvious.'

'She wants to keep it a secret, so don't tell anyone.'

'Hey, I'm all about secrets. Do you like Stravinsky?'

Dan was used to Barty's non-sequiturs. He thought he did it sometimes just to tease him. 'I don't know. Is that a kind of pasta?'

Barty exploded into laughter. 'No! Oh, Daniel you are priceless! He's a composer. Twentieth century. My favourite piece of his is *The Firebird.* I must play it for you sometime. It speaks to my soul. It is chaotic and sublime all at once.' He slapped Dan on the shoulder, launching once again into oration. Dan found it highly amusing. 'One day soon I hope to do something as audacious as Doctor Asar and become the firebird of the revolution. We will rise from the ashes of tyranny and write a new history for ourselves and our children… and our children's children…and our children's children's child – '

'– How many of those have you had?' Dan asked, referring to the bourbon.

'Not nearly enough, dear boy. Come, let us re-join the others and see what daring conspiracies we can devise. The challenge has been set. The gauntlet laid at our feet. We must rise to meet it!'

Once back with the rest of the group Barty took Gabrielle aside briefly and said a few words in her ear. Dan observed this from a distance.

'What do you think he's saying to her?' Maya had appeared next to him.

'I don't know,' Dan answered honestly, watching Gabrielle's inscrutable reaction. He wasn't about to reveal to Maya what he suspected.

'You know what I think?' Maya offered. 'I think he's trying to get into her pants.'

Before Dan could even think of a response Maya walked away. It was the most words she had ever said to him.

The meeting began well thanks to Barty's enthusiasm and high spirits. He dared them to be bold and think big, but as usual it had little effect. Maya sat quietly in the corner, while the others could only think of what they already knew to do – painting slogans on walls or other public mischiefs. Admittedly, Dan couldn't come up with anything better that didn't sound stupid or dangerous. Gabrielle usually had good ideas, even if they were impractical most of the time. Tonight, however, she remained silent, and the group again descended into arguments about their real intentions, and yet another bitch session on the Church in general.

Throughout the meeting Dan was eyeing Gabrielle, but she deliberately avoided his gaze. Dan seriously doubted their relationship was a secret to the group; if Barty had worked it out then others must have as well. They were probably all gossiping behind their backs.

For some reason Maya's insinuation nagged at him. He had no reason to suspect she was right – that Barty had designs on Gabrielle – and frankly, even if he did, their relationship was hardly exclusive. Dan had no hold over her. It was just a bit of fun. Still, it troubled him, and he cursed Maya for planting the seed in his head.

By the end of the meeting, he had managed to dispel the thought from his mind, but a glum funk had now come over him. As things were breaking up Dan searched the room for Gabrielle but couldn't find her. 'Have you seen Gabrielle?' he asked Barty at the door.

'She left already.'

'Oh. I thought …'

'You thought what?'

'… Doesn't matter,' Dan responded.

'Go in peace, comrade. Stay safe.' It was the kind of farewell Barty always gave. This time somehow it felt hollow.

Dan smiled weakly and nodded. He left the meeting, disappointed; and a little worried. Gabrielle could be impulsive, but she wasn't capricious. He re-ran their brief conversation through his mind, trying to work out what he had missed. Had something happened to change her mind? What did Barty say to her?

As usual after a meeting, he avoided public transport to prevent his comkey being tracked, instead walking the empty streets of Lorna alone. It was dark but not yet curfew. Few people tended to go outdoors at night, not when there were air-conditioned arcades and skywalks, and GL rail-tubes connecting most buildings. Dan liked walking the streets. Though cold and a bit gloomy, it was ironically safer than if he took the train. It also gave him time to think.

The thought of Bartholomew and Gabrielle together kept bouncing around his head, which only frustrated him. To get his mind off that he considered Doctor Asar, Rene and Joanna, and his own place in the world. It was hard to know what the right thing to do was. Dan felt vandalising the tomb of the Prophet was wrong, and was baffled why a group of scientific eggheads would do such a thing. He also agreed with Barty that their so-called revolution would never get off the ground unless they were more audacious.

But it was the opinion of his most trusted friend, Rene, which nagged him the most. Rene was the smart one, and despite their quarrelling Dan almost always took his lead. He respected Rene. That's why he so wanted him to join the cause. They could use someone like him. But if Rene was not comfortable with something, Dan would heed this. He trusted his friend's instincts. Something about this whole Doctor Asar business smelled funny. It didn't add up.

Dan chose to walk an unfamiliar route. Partly because he liked to explore, and partly because he thought it might confuse anyone trying to track his movements. As a so-called 'rebel' he was conscious of the data his comkey was always transmitting about where he went and what he did. Despite these misgivings he used the Magnetic Proximity (MaP) Locator in his comkey to direct him to Rene's apartment. After all, he didn't want to get lost.

One side-effect of the Church's uneasy relationship with technology had been the collapse of the GPS system people once used to get around. It was replaced with something more earthbound and arguably more accurate, MaP location, which used the earth's magnetic fields to geo-position a person to within a few meters. Another aspect of Church rules was the stricture of a public curfew. Every city had one, though the times may differ from region to region. In Lorna, curfew was from 10pm to 6am. It had been in force so long now that people just accepted it, along with all the other little prohibitions the Church imposed on their lives. Dan thought it a great pity. Thanks to weather control it was a glorious starlit evening, not a cloud in the sky, and he was perhaps the only person out to see it.

What Dan didn't realize was that he was not alone; and hadn't been since he left the meeting.

There is nothing that cannot be altered
If one desires it enough
Be certain of your desires
Mark closely your thoughts
For they create your path
Your fate is manifest
According to your deeds

Shentama
– Stanza 133

Althea was at her wits end. She had no idea what to do next. It was Patric who'd suggested electroconvulsive therapy, and Asar went along with it. Althea opposed the idea as barbaric, but after the failure of her own brand of shock therapy she couldn't really argue against it. Electroconvulsive therapy (ECT) was widely used in the early 20th century, but had been largely discredited since then. It remained in use for extreme cases of mental disorders – primarily depression – but was completely abandoned by the mid-21st century in favour of drug and laser surgical therapies. This was largely due to the Prophet Tobias's own crusade on behalf of those with mental disorders. The irony was not lost on Althea.

Patric's reasoning was that since a form of ECT had brought the Prophet back to life, perhaps another dose now his body was stronger would complete the revival. If the block was purely mental, this might somehow 'jumpstart' the brain. It was a fair assumption based on no evidence whatsoever; but Althea couldn't find a good reason not to do it, so the delta-sleeping unconscious Tobias was transported back to the operating theatre where a jury-rigged ECT machine was setup.

Patric had taken the defibrillator they had used to revive Tobias and adapted it for application directly to the head. Althea feared it could end up frying his brain, but at this point that might just be a godsend. Being something of an electrical wiz, Patric had been instrumental in getting power to the hospital, sourcing the defib' machine and the GL casket, and getting all the old equipment they had scavenged back into working order. Isaac had been his assistant. They tracked down some old literature about ECT machines and together they adapted the defib' to suit. Though it was hardly the same as a proper ECT machine and there was no way to really measure the amount of charge being applied, Patric assured the Doctors the result would be the same. They just had to carefully watch his reactions to each charge to judge how they were doing.

The electrodes were placed either side of Tobias's head, near the temples. Having ruined the only proper restraints they had, his wrists and ankles were now tied down with sheet cloth. Nothing stronger could be found. If they didn't hold, Patric had his tranq' gun handy.

Asar hobbled about the room anxiously. His broken ribs still troubled him, and Berger had not returned with any painkillers for him. In fact, they had not heard from Berger or Trevelle for a couple of days and Asar was getting worried something might have happened to them. That was the problem with sedition, effective communication was near impossible.

Althea sat at the back of the room and observed. She did not help in any way, but nor did she hinder their efforts. She was ambivalent about the whole thing, and frankly too depressed to hold out any hope of success.

After some final adjustments Patric was ready and turned to Asar for the go-ahead. Doctor Asar nodded apprehensively, he knew this was make or break. Patric set the charge to a low level and pressed the button to send a burst of electricity through the prostrate body of the Prophet. Tobias tensed, held for a few seconds with toes curled, a strange rhythmic shudder rippling through the muscles, then relaxed as the charge released automatically. The effect was almost imperceptible.

Everyone watched and waited for something more to happen.

Nothing.

Patric turned the dial a few degrees, increasing the charge, then pressed the button again. This time Tobias convulsed more as the back arched, the toes and feet curled, and the face contorted into a frightening grimace. The charge released and the body relaxed.

…Nothing,

They checked the EKG. The brainwaves still showed as a flat delta. No change.

'Turn it right up,' Asar ordered.

'Are you sure?' Patric questioned. 'Wouldn't it be safer to – '

'Turn it up!'

Patric turned it up to maximum. He had no idea how much charge this was about to send through Tobias, except it was a lot. He pressed the button. Tobias jerked, his whole body shaking violently with rhythmic convulsions. His arms and legs strained at the makeshift bindings. A strange gargly growl tore from his lungs, growing louder and louder until it became an unbroken howl of pain.

Althea couldn't stand it anymore and ran from the room covering her ears, as the tormented cries of Tobias echoed down the polished hallways of the hospital.

— ∞ —

As Dan approached Rene and Joanna's apartment, he could hear a terrifying scream come from within. It was Rene. Dan ran to the door, which opened for him instantly as his comkey came within range. Upon entering he saw Rene writhing on the floor in some kind of epileptic fit. Joanna stood over him horrified, screaming his name in a blind panic. Dan dashed across the room to Rene and held him down, trying to contain his convulsions lest he break something or hurt himself. He ended up hugging his friend from behind, his arms pinned to his chest, their legs intertwined, with Dan convulsing in sympathy.

Then it stopped.

Dan kept his grip tight for a few seconds, then slowly released Rene.

Rene rolled over, exhausted, and looked up at Joanna. In a faint voice that seemed to come from a remote part of his mind he asked: 'What happened?'

Joanna couldn't answer, she had no idea what just happened.

Dan leaned over Rene. It took a moment for him to recognise his friend. "Dan… When did you get here?'

'Can you sit up?' Dan asked.

Rene tried to sit up, but a strange vertigo hit him and he lay back down. 'No.'

Joanna, still confused and distraught, lay down on the carpet beside Rene, while Dan found his way to the couch. She stroked

Rene's face gently and looked deep into his eyes. 'You were having some kind of fit,' she told him, as one would to a child after waking from a nightmare. 'You just suddenly collapsed and started shaking. How do you feel now?'

Rene tried to remember, but his head was mush. He had the strangest feeling of being tied down. He felt his wrist but there was nothing there.

'I'm okay … just dizzy and kind of … kind of drunk, actually.'

— ∞ —

As the current was turned off, the convulsions stopped, and Tobias relaxed. He opened his eyes and stopped screaming all at once. He turned and looked directly at Patric who was standing beside him. Patric stumbled away in a panic. Tobias was still tied to the table but the look in his eyes was enough to terrify anyone. Patric fumbled for the tranq' gun on the table beside him but ended up knocking it to the floor. Tobias sat upright in one quick move, noticed the cloth straps on his wrists and ripped them away easily. Then he pulled away the bindings on his ankles and before they knew it he was on his feet and running out the room.

'After him!' Asar screamed.

Patric and Isaac hesitated for just a moment. Patric snatched up the tranq' gun and together they ran after Tobias.

— ∞ —

Rene fell into the couch, thanks to Dan's help. His whole body was weak and heavy, as if his muscles were exhausted after a long run. It wasn't a bad feeling, there was no pain. He just felt drained. And a little disoriented – like he had been smoking some of Dan's imported hash.

'Has this happened before?' Joanna asked.

'Once,' Rene answered without thinking.

'It wasn't like this though,' Dan was quick to explain. 'That time you just fainted.'

'You knew about this?' Joanna gave Dan the dirtiest look.

'He asked me not to tell you.'

'I didn't want to worry you,' Rene said.

'All I ever do is worry about you, Rene. That's my job! When was this?' Joanna demanded.

'A couple of days ago,' Dan answered.

'I've run a complete physical since then,' Rene reassured. 'Didn't find anything.'

As good as the MediScan units were, they were not infallible. 'Then clearly the machine missed something. You need to see a doctor.'

'Okay. First thing,' Rene answered. 'But right now, I'm really tired. I need to go to bed.'

Then they heard the doorbell.

On Captain Marius's order the advance guard bashed down the barricaded doors and stormed into the hospital. It was easy to find where the rebel doctors were holed up. They just tracked their comkeys. Idiots. Even in the AQ where reception was patchy, all you needed was a mobile receiver.

The Temple Guard were issued with power gloves as part of their uniform. These light multi-function gloves were not only effective protection for their hands, but served as their primary weapon. By just pointing at your target you could trigger an intense electrical arc called a *haze* that would project from the index finger of the glove for a distance of up to ten meters. The technology was an advance on the old Taser guns from back in the day, designed to persist in the victim's central nervous system, paralysing them for several seconds after contact. Larger forms of the weapon could travel much further and were potentially fatal, but the gloves could be quite destructive on their own. They were also rather noisy. These power weapons had the advantage of not killing your target, just immobilising them. Marius however preferred a good old-fashioned handgun. One that used actual bullets. The ammunition was expensive, made primarily for shooting clubs that were into antique stuff like this, but he found firearms more elegant and precise. Power weapons also had a habit of misdirecting to any large, earthed metal source, making them unreliable in his view.

As Marius and his men stormed through the hospital corridors, they encountered two white-smocked young men running towards them. The men stopped in their tracks, then turned to flee. Marius did the right thing and ordered them to halt. But as soon as one of them produced what appeared to be a weapon, he had no hesitation in shooting the fucker. The white-smocked man fell hard. Marius had aimed for the knee but hit him in the hip. The end result was the same. One down.

The other whitesmock stopped running and raised his arms in surrender. Marius marched up to him and spun the scared young man 'round to face him. 'Where's Asar?!'

— ∞ —

Joanna, Rene and Dan all looked at the two-way AV mounted on the front door to see who was outside. It was a middle-aged man with scraggly dark hair, waving amiably at them through the lens.

Joanna turned to Dan. 'Do you know him?'

'It's Barty. He's from the group. But I don't know what he's doing here.'

Dan moved forward to open the door, but Joanna stopped him. 'Wait. Did you tell him where we lived?'

'No, of course not,' Dan protested. 'He must have followed me here.'

'What does he want?'

'Let's ask him?' Dan moved again to open the door, but again Joanna pulled him up. 'You can trust him. He's a friend,' Dan reassured, but Joanna was unconvinced.

'Tell him this is your place,' Joanna insisted. 'You live alone.'

'I *do* live alone.'

Joanna glared at him. This was no joking matter. 'Just do it, will you. But wait till we're hidden.' She moved to Rene sitting on the couch and helped him to his feet.

'What are you afraid is going to happen?' Dan asked.

Joanna looked at Rene as she answered. 'I just have a bad feeling about this.'

The doorbell rang again.

'Why are we hiding?' Rene asked, his mind still struggling to catch up.

Joanna didn't answer but called to Dan as they left the room: 'Just give us a minute. Then answer the door.' They disappeared into the bedroom.

Dan waited. Looking at the two-way he could see Bartholomew was anxious about something. He kept looking around him. He rang the doorbell again.

Dan pressed the *talk* button on the two-way, and his image appeared on the opposite side of the door for Barty to see. 'Hey, Barty. What are you doing here?'

'Dan. Hey … Need to talk with you. Something's come up.'

'Can't it wait?'

'… It's about Gabrielle.'

That got Dan worried. 'Is she okay?'

'Can I come in?' Barty asked. 'I don't want to discuss it through the door.'

Dan opened the door.

'Hey,' Barty reached out and shook Dan's hand. 'Sorry, dude.'

'What for?'

If Barty answered Dan didn't hear it, because two heartbeats later he lay unconscious on the floor.

— ∞ —

Althea was brooding in the cage with Elly cuddling up beside her for comfort when she heard the commotion – the distinctive clatter of Temple Guard armour. They were discovered. She scrambled out of the cage, turning back as Elly leapt into her arms – she knew something was up, even if she didn't understand what. With the bonobo clinging to her shirt, Althea ran into the shadowy corridors of the hospital, away from the noise. Once out of range she slowed her pace till her eyes adjusted to the darkness. The windows were smashed, and a cool breeze drifted in from outside, along with a pale moonlight to guide the way. The smell of decay and mould was carried in on the breeze, the aroma of the old city. The corridors and rooms in this part of the hospital had been untouched for over a hundred years. There were signs of vandalism and theft, but that was ages ago. Since then, the place had been left to rot, and a thick layer of dust covered everything.

Despite the dark she knew her way around. They had done an extensive recce when they first set up here, leaving these areas untouched to avoid attracting attention. She made her way downstairs to the casualty ward; once the busiest part of the hospital, now crumbling and deserted. They had used this exit to access the catacombs. That was just a few days ago when she was full of hope, filled with the anticipation of what might be and of great plans fulfilled. She couldn't believe how naïve she'd been. The Prophet belonged to history. They should have left him there.

Althea heard a loud banging up ahead. *Guards?*

Cautiously turning a corner, she spotted Tobias bashing at the locked exit doors with an old fire extinguisher. The doors once had glass in them, but this had been smashed long ago and replaced with heavy wooden boards.

Elly jumped from Althea's arms and called out to him, running down the corridor to Tobias. He stopped pounding the door and turned to see the ape trundling towards him. Elly paused a few meters away, not sure if Tobias trusted her anymore. He studied the bonobo intently … then looked up at Althea lurking in the shadows. She made no attempt to approach. Tobias put down the extinguisher.

Elly stepped forward and examined the doors for a moment. There was a crossbar one pushed to open them, but they were locked in the centre with a large padlock. She turned to Althea and extended her hand – asking for the key.

Althea didn't know what to do. If she refused, Tobias might attack and even kill her, but could ultimately be captured by the Temple Guards, and that might not be a bad thing under the circumstances. If she handed over the key Tobias would be released on an unsuspecting Lorna. What responsibility did she have to this creature now? She had helped return him to life, but it was not the life she had expected or wanted. His death would surely be a mercy. And yet …

She felt herself reach into her pocket and produce the key. It was an emotional, not a rational, act. Perhaps she felt guilty for the pain they had already caused him. It was not his fault after all – he was what he was.

Althea feared she would regret it for the rest of her life, but she tossed the key to Elly. The Bonobo caught it and looked back with an expression of incredible empathy, as if she understood Althea's dilemma, and was grateful for this gesture. She then unlocked the doors, pushing them open to reveal the side entrance of the hospital and beyond that the streets of the abandoned quarter in the old city.

Tobias turned to Althea offering the first glimmer of humanity she had seen from him. He nodded his head slightly – thank you – then fled into the night.

—— ∞ ——

Joanna and Rene were hiding in the laundry. Moments after Dan had opened the door they could hear several people entering the apartment, and the clatter of Temple Guard uniforms.

'Where are the others?' they heard someone say, as the intruders dispersed and started searching the apartment.

Joanna had chosen the laundry for a reason. She opened the fire escape access panel on the wall. It led to a form-fitting chute made of clear synthetic fabric, which spiralled down an internal cavity in the building's wall and emerged some thirty stories below at ground level. Every apartment had one, though they had never had cause to use it before.

'You can't be serious,' Rene said.

'Do we have a choice?'

'What about Dan?' But Rene already knew the answer. They could hear the guards approaching by the trail of destruction they were wreaking outside. They would be discovered any moment.

'Come on.' Joanna urged.

'You first.'

Joanna hesitated.

'Don't argue with me,' Rene insisted. 'Just go.'

Joanna grabbed the bar at the top of the access hole and lifted herself into the chute feet first. 'You'll be right behind me, won't you?' she asked, afraid Rene would try to go back and save his friend.

'Of course. Now go.' He gave her a quick kiss and practically pushed her down the chute. Joanna flew down the narrow tube. It squeezed gently against her form, controlling the speed of the descent while still allowing a swift escape velocity. She didn't cry out, but Rene could hear the rustling of the fabric as Joanna plunged toward the ground. He turned to the door, wondering if there was anything he could do for Dan – assuming he was still alive.

Just then the door burst open and a guard spotted Rene. 'He's in here!'

Rene grabbed the bar and lifted himself into the chute, but the guard grabbed him before he could slide down. Rene threw a feeble punch at the young guard. For his trouble he was dragged bodily from the chute and thrown to the floor. Then the guard raised his arm and Rene could see he was wearing a power glove. This was gonna hurt. A tendril of electricity hazed from the guard's index finger hitting Rene in the solar plexus. An intense shock burned through his whole body. His muscles tensed and his bladder emptied. It only lasted a few seconds, but it was enough to completely immobilise him. Then the guard gave him a gratuitous kick in the stomach just to make sure he didn't get up.

A concealed circular exit opened on the side of the apartment building and Joanna spilled out onto the street. It was dark and empty.

Well past curfew, so not a soul was in sight.

She got to her feet and watched anxiously for Rene to emerge from the hole. Moving closer she listened for the sound of him sliding down the tube, but there was only silence. Panic set in. She looked up the tube but there was only darkness. 'Rene!' She called.

… No answer.

The tube exit closed automatically.

'Goddamit, Rene. I knew this would happen. Fucking Dan and his crusades.' She was at once angry and terrified. Joanna was a strong woman, but it was only because of Rene. He was her rock. His calm, thoughtful approach to things balanced her impulsive nature. Without him she only half existed.'… What am I supposed to do now?' She pleaded to no one, tears streaming down her cheeks.

She moved across the street and stood vigil over the fire escape exit for a good two hours before deciding to leave. By then, she had no more tears left to cry.

—— ∞ ——

Cairn wanted to handle this himself. He didn't trust Marius or the Temple Guard with something so delicate. So when he arrived at *Saint Olivier's* hospital and strode into the operating theatre it took everyone by surprise – everyone except Jason Asar, who merely glanced up at Cairn before lowering his eyes back to the floor.

The guards snapped to attention as Captain Marius led Cairn into the room. This was both an honour and an ill omen. What was it about this particular raid that called the Cardinal Hierophant himself away from the Temple and into, of all places, the AQ?

'Leave us,' Cairn demanded, addressing Marius and his men.

'Yes, Your Eminence,' Marius responded. 'I'll just leave two men as a precau – '

' – You will not. I'll be quite safe, Captain. Take the other prisoners. I want to speak with Doctor Asar alone.'

'Yes, your Eminence.'

Marius rallied his men and they led the two young whitesmocks – Isaac and the stretcher-bound Patric – out of the operating theatre, leaving Asar and Cairn alone.

Cairn waited. Then stepped forward to where Asar was seated.

As protocol demanded, Doctor Asar rose from his chair, wincing at the pain of his still fractured ribs, and bowed in the presence of the Cardinal Hierophant.

'So, Jason. Here we are.'

'Yes, Your Eminence.'

'Are you hurt?'

'It's nothing, Your Eminence.' Asar gently held his chest with one hand, trying not to grimace with the pain.

'Did one of my guards do that?'

'No. It's from an earlier accident.'

'You should get a doctor to take a look at it. You might have broken something.' Cairn was genuinely concerned.

'I'll be all right. Thank you, Your Eminence.'

'Sit down if it's hurting you. I don't mind.'

Asar sat back down, the tightening of his muscles sent a stab of pain through his chest. He tried not to grunt too loudly.

'So tell me, Jason. Where is he?'

'Where's who?' Asar responded dumbly.

'You know who.' Cairn looked around the theatre at all the equipment, and at the table in the middle of the room, with its torn strips of sheet hanging limply from the sides. He dreaded what might have happened here, but he had to ask. 'Did you succeed?'

'I don't know what you're talking about.'

'Oh, come now, Jason. I know what you were planning. I know why you stole the body of the Prophet. Do I have to say it out loud.'

Asar knew there was no point trying to deceive Cairn. If there was anyone within the Church who could discern the true nature of Asar's intentions, it was him. He understood this was more than just an act of vandalism.

'No,' Asar answered softly. 'We did not succeed.'

Cairn studied Asar's face, watching for his tell. Asar had a habit of over-blinking when he lied. It was something Cairn had noticed quite early in their relationship, and was one of the reasons he had agreed to Asar becoming his personal physician. The man was a terrible liar. This time, it seemed he was speaking the truth, and yet, something was not right. He looked at the operating table. Clearly someone had been strapped down there recently. 'Then where is he?'

'I don't know.'

Cairn was surprised. *How could he not know?* 'Did something go wrong?'

It occurred to Asar then, that even though their original plan had failed, and the Prophet of history was not restored, he may yet be able to turn the situation to his advantage. The Temple Guards clearly had not yet discovered Tobias. He might have even escaped the hospital altogether. As long as Tobias was alive and free – regardless of his condition – he was a threat to the Church. For the first time ever, he saw that Cairn was actually afraid. He played on that fear.

Asar looked at the Cardinal Hierophant intently, and said, in a clear voice: 'Nothing went wrong. The Prophecy is fulfilled. Tobias walks among us once more, and your days are numbered. The Age of Renewal has begun.'

Asar had never been one for evangelical pronouncements. It was oddly out of character, and yet it sent a chill up Cairn's spine. Asar blinked only once as he spoke these words. At the beginning. He was not telling him the whole truth, but even a half-truth of this magnitude was frightening. It was a contradiction. *How was this possible?*

'So you *did* succeed. And yet… something went wrong.' He watched Asar's reaction. Try as he might he could not hide a flicker of apprehension. 'What was it, Jason? Not the result you were hoping for? Not the man you were expecting? You seem disappointed.'

'I've done what was right. I have no regrets.'

Asar had decided to play the noble martyr all of a sudden. To Cairn though, Asar's treachery went beyond mere heresy. It was a personal betrayal of the deepest kind. The damage he had done the Church was incalculable, but he had also been the only person Cairn had every truly liked. The only one he felt he could confide in. Kasper he neither liked nor trusted. And there was not a single person on the Council he could call confidante, let alone friend.

'How could you do this to me, Jason? I thought we were friends.'

'We were never friends,' Asar replied with such venom it startled Cairn.

Cairn did not respond. Instead, he straitened his back, slowly turned, and strode out of the room.

As Cairn entered the corridor, the Guards who had been waiting just outside the room snapped to attention. Marius, caught off guard, hurried to catch up with Cairn and escort him back to his GL vehicle.

'Your Eminence. With your permission, I'll take the prisoners back for further interrogation. Perhaps we can find out more about their network and other rebel groups. They must have had help, possibly from someone inside the Temple. I'll make sure we find out who else was involved…'

Cairn was barely listening. He was mulling over the best course to contain disaster without drawing public attention to the truth. The *truth*… that the Prophet Tobias was alive and walking among them in the Temple City of Lorna. It beggared belief. But for all his foolish heresies, Asar was a brilliant man and not one prone to exaggeration.

As they exited the hospital and approached the vehicle Cairn recalled Marius had said something about further interrogation. Not a good idea.

'Your Eminence?'

'Hmm?'

'The prisoners, Your Eminence.'

'Oh, yes. Kill them.'

'Your Eminence?'

'You heard me. Kill them all.'

With that Cairn closed the door to his armoured GL and with a nod to his driver, they sped away.

Part 2

Choice, not chance, determines your destiny.

Shentama
– The Second Tenet

10

Your creation is never lost
Even unto the past
Though the moment passes
Though the mind forgets
Your creation is now and always
A part of the All–In–All
Which is your Self

Shentama
- Stanza 47

Tobias ran for over an hour before he finally slowed to a relaxed walk. Not because he had to, he wasn't being chased. It was just good to be free. To feel the wind on his face, the earth beneath his feet. He had no idea where he was, but it didn't matter. Not another soul was about. He was alone in the world, with just the stars and moon to keep him company.

He had already forgotten about the hospital, about Elly, the red-headed woman and the others. All he remembered was a vague sense of having escaped something unpleasant. The details faded into the abyss of dream and were lost. All he understood was the here and now. And right now he was cold, tired, and very hungry. But also happy.

He left behind the overgrown, derelict buildings of the abandoned quarter and found himself walking paved streets with even taller structures around him. It was like a desert canyon – imposing, yet devoid of life. At first, only the comforting glow of moonlight and deep shadows surrounded him, but as he journeyed deeper into the canyons, cold light spilled from a web of overhead skywalks that connected all the structures, lending a peculiar aura to the streets below. The smell of decay faded, replaced by a strange metallic odour. Clean, lifeless and unsettling. He was about to turn around and return to the more familiar smells of rotting leaves, pungent flowers, dead insects and dirt when something caught his attention. A gigantic mural on the wall of one of the buildings. The picture was littered with bodies and desperate faces. They were on a makeshift raft in the middle of the ocean, scrambling for rescue as they hailed a distant vessel on the horizon. Or at least most of them were. Some had turned away as if they cared little for their own lives anymore. The waves loomed over them as their jury-rigged sail strained against the ocean wind. It was an image of desperation, death and vain hope.

Tobias didn't understand it and was incapable of putting a name to what it portrayed. All he saw was people suffering, but it captured his imagination. One face in particular drew his attention. It was near the very middle of the painting. It was the face of a man alerting others to the ship on the horizon. He was the only one who appeared to be thinking of someone other than himself. The only one who still had a grain of humanity left. The only true survivor. Tobias looked at the face of this man, as a drop of water fell from the sky and formed a tear on the man's cheek. More drops hit the mural until it was awash with tears.

Tobias looked up and let the rain spatter his face. He opened his mouth and drank it in. What had started as a light shower quickly became a downpour. The torrent washed away the day's debris from the streets, slapping the paved surface with a field of watery flowers. Little waterfalls spilled from the high rooftops, dashing onto the pavement below and flowing into hidden drains.

The AV-wall was made to withstand such elements, unlike the subjects it portrayed, and unlike Tobias, who at first revelled in the deluge, but once he had drunk his fill was desperate to find some shelter from the rain. He ran up the empty street, leaving behind the mural of *The Raft of Medusa,* and within minutes had entirely forgotten that he had ever seen it.

An hour ago, all Rene had hoped for was to get some sleep. His most pressing concern had been the welfare of his irresponsible friend, Dan, and whether he should go to work early the next day to try learn more about the mysterious Doctors Asar and Roget.

But that was an hour ago.

Right now, he was locked in a prisoner transport, hands bound, mouth gagged, surrounded by several other similarly constrained captives. Dan was next to him, though he was still unconscious from whatever drug had been used on him to gain entrance to their apartment. Rene didn't know any of the other prisoners, but he suspected they were all involved with dissident groups like Dan. Or perhaps, like him, they were just guilty by association. No-one could speak due to the gags, but the expressions of shock and confusion as each new round of prisoners was loaded into the transport said it all. Everyone was frightened, and in an odd way, ashamed. Some of them clearly knew one another, but after a glimmer of recognition they avoided eye contact, as if to acknowledge each other was somehow an admission of guilt. They were probably right. There were cameras and biosensors inside the transport studying their every move. They didn't know where they were going, but everyone could guess their ultimate destination would be the prison city of Gerda.

Gerda was reserved for the worst criminals from around the world, and heresy was one of the worst crimes possible. It ranked higher than murder or rape in the eyes of the Church and was the one crime for which there was no appeal. And usually no trial. If found guilty of heresy you were a heretic for life. No amount of penance could change that. It was also the only crime that still imposed a death penalty in extreme cases. According to the Church, the life of a heretic was a life was not worth living, so the sooner a new life could be brought about, the better for the unfortunate heretic's soul. All other crimes were forgivable by comparison. It was a barbaric law, but one Rene was ashamed to admit had never really bothered him before, since it didn't affect him. Until now.

Dan stirred and raised his head. He looked around, and in a panic tried to stand up, but soon found that his bound wrists were secured to the bench between his legs and only succeeded in slamming his hands into his crotch. Falling with a thud, he banged his head on the metal siding behind him. Groaning, he then realised he was wearing a gag. Dan shook his head violently, as if he could just throw the thing off. It was only then he noticed Rene sitting beside him, watching this dismal attempt at escape.

He grunted '*Hi.*'

Rene grunted '*Hi*' back.

Dan grunted something else, and from the look in his eyes and the tone of the grunt, Rene could tell he was trying to say, '*Sorry.*'

Rene nodded.

Dan looked around the transport to see if there was anyone he recognised. He stopped on one face down the other end, a young man from his group who was looking at the floor. Dan called/grunted to him, '*hey*!' The young man didn't move. Dan tried again, but the young man still refused to look at him. Dan gave up and turned back to Rene. Then it occurred to him, *where was Jo?* He looked around the transport again – No. He grunted to Rene, '*Jo?*'

Rene shook his head.

Dan was shocked, thinking she was dead. Rene quickly shook his head, nodding over his shoulder to indicate she got away. Dan sighed with relief. Nevertheless, they were screwed. Neither of them knew what was going to happen next, but whatever it was, it wouldn't be good.

Something tapped gently on the metal sides of the truck. Then again … and again. They had no idea what it was at first, but as it grew more insistent they realised it was starting to rain outside. The trickle soon became a downpour, violently lashing the sides of the truck, creating a terrifying din that drowned out any further attempts at conversation.

Joanna wandered the streets for the longest time, not knowing what to do. She couldn't go to any of her friends in case they were implicated and arrested along with her. She couldn't go to *The Loft*, that place was bound to have been raided. In fact, anywhere she could think of was off limits because it was either a known rebel hangout or would endanger innocent people. She was totally alone.

And then it began to rain.

She was startled at first, until she realised what it was. She had watched the night rains from behind glass for so many years she had forgotten what it actually felt like. Weather Control didn't allow it to rain during the day when people were out and about. It always held it back until after curfew. She had occasionally taken wet showers, where one washed with actual running water – it was an extravagance still found in the more expensive resorts and spas – but this felt nothing like that. The water was cold, hard and somehow threatening. She ran for cover but was soaked through by the time she found shelter under the entrance to a small church. With no idea what else to do Joanna knocked on the church doors.

In time, a light came on. Some rustling of locks, then a timid cleric opened the doors and peered out.

'It's after curfew,' he told her. 'What are you doing outside?'

'Getting wet,' Joanna replied.

'Well… I guess… you'd better come in then,' the cleric stuttered, opening the door for Joanna to enter.

He closed the door behind her with a squeak and a clang, shutting out the rain and the night chill. Not sure what to do with her, the cleric looked her up and down. 'You better get out of those clothes. You'll catch your death.'

'Do you have something I could wear?'

The cleric fumbled nervously, tugging at his robes. 'Um… perhaps.'

'What's your name?'

'Father Alban.'

'Hello Father Alban. I'm Jo.'

—— ∞ ——

Cairn hated being contradicted, especially by someone who was probably right. But like everyone else in the Temple, Kasper had his own agenda, and Cairn was not about to let it sway him from what he

122

believed was the right course of action. Cairn had larger issues to deal with. He was thinking beyond his own personal safety or position. His concern was with the future of the Church.

'Declaring martial law is going to look bad not just for the Church, but for the office of Cardinal Hierophant,' Kasper continued to argue. 'If you don't care about your own legacy think about what this will do to The Temple and Tobianism itself.'

'That's what I am thinking of. That's *all* I'm thinking of. You don't seem to realise how dangerous this is.'

'You said yourself Asar told you something went wrong with the procedure. The Prophet is not walking among us. It's physically impossible.' Kasper was right of course. It was too incredible to take seriously.

'I knew Asar,' Cairn reminded him. 'He may have been a heretic, but he was not stupid … or crazy.'

'Okay. For the sake of argument let's say you're right. What harm can he do? No-one would believe he was really Tobias. Who would take him seriously? I think we can trust in people's inherent apathy to disregard him as just another crackpot lookalike. The more attention we give it, the worse it is for us.' Kasper tended to play devil's advocate in these discussions. Cairn wondered if he did it on purpose to manipulate him – as he did with so many others on the Council. Kasper's real intentions were always hard to gauge. But Cairn was not so easily swayed.

'We can't take that chance,' Cairn responded. 'This is the biggest threat the Church has faced since the Great Purge. You know better than anyone, Kasper, we are no longer the Church of the Prophet, despite what it says above the Temple Gate. Tobianism will not survive if the Prophet himself denounces it. We've brought peace to the planet, and order to the chaos of multi-theism that came before.

The Tobianist era has been the most successful and productive world order in human history. And you would risk it all. You would have us trust in the rabble, that they would not pull it all down around us for the sake of some archaic, idealistic dream. The world is not made by dreamers like Tobias. They cannot control their own destinies, let alone the course of human civilisation. It is up to us, the shit-kickers of this world to make it work. And we do whatever it takes to achieve that. Tobias is nothing more than a symbol now. His body a relic of history. He belongs dead.' Cairn paused in his tirade as a thought occurred to him. A solution that would be swift, invisible, and in a way, elegant. 'But you know, Kasper, you are right about one thing. We can trust in the people, as long as we spin them a good tale. Something they can believe. Something they can act on. Something that will inspire the mob. A call to arms, to defend the faith. Who needs the Temple Guard when we have the whole population of Lorna at our disposal?'

Kasper remained circumspect. 'Are you suggesting we declare anarchy?'

Cairn smiled. He thought Kasper was joking. 'Not anarchy. A hunt. We announce that a dangerous criminal has escaped from Gerda and is loose in the city. We lift the curfew, declare a public manhunt for the escapee, with full indemnity to anyone who kills him. Perhaps even a reward. The mob will do our job for us.'

Kasper was shocked. He chose his words carefully. 'I doubt anyone would put their own lives at risk to chase down some escaped prisoner.'

'You don't know the rabble like I do, my friend.' Cairn was supremely confident. 'Trust me. They won't do it for the Church, and they won't do it for the city. They'll do it for the sport.'

"

As all things must change
So too does the phoenix we call spirit
Moving ever on to new adventures

Shentama
– Stanza 120

Father Alban gave Joanna a spare set of brown novice robes, apologising it was all he had. They sat in the lounge of his small lodgings adjacent to the church, eating a stew the Father had prepared. For a cleric he was a pretty good cook, Joanna thought. An AV was on in the background, showing some romantic drama. Joanna didn't watch much AV content, and shows like this were the reason why. But the good father seemed to enjoy it, as he tried to explain the characters and plot to his guest.

'…You see, she was in love with the other fellow, Xavier. But then she found out he was cheating on her. Which was bad enough, but then the other girl was selling industrial secrets to a rival firm, and was really just using Xavier for his connections – '

' – This is very good,' Joanna interrupted, commenting on the stew. 'Did you make it yourself?'

'Yes. Although I must admit the recipe came from one of the ladies in my congregation. A widow. I performed the service for her husband two years ago. Tragic death. Fell from a skywalk while repairing it. His workmates all took the day off to attend. Lovely gesture. I wish more people took the time to – '

' – Do you live here alone?' Joanna again interrupted.

'Yes, of course. I have a young novice who helps me during services and other occasions like funerals and weddings, but – '

' – So you're not expecting anyone else tonight?'

Alban paused and looked at Jo puzzled '… I wasn't expecting *you.*'

'Can I stay here tonight?'

Again, Alban paused, troubled by her request. 'What are you suggesting?'

Joanna laughed out loud. 'No Father! I just need a place to sleep. I'll leave in the morning.'

'Where will you go, then?'

'…I don't know,' Joanna admitted.

'Are you in trouble?'

'… Yes.'

'Should I be afraid of you?'

Joanna smiled. 'No. But it's not safe for me to stay here more than one night. Not safe for you.' He was an odd little man but Joanna trusted him, despite him being a cleric for the very Church that was hunting her down. If he knew the whole story he would be obliged to report her to the Temple Guard. As it was, she didn't want him to be seen aiding and abetting a heretic.

Alban was no fool though. He knew the Guard had been cracking down on dissidents and heretics. 'You know, I never did understand what was so bad about people having an opinion different from the Church. As the Prophet said, we each have our own path. My path led me to become a priest. And I am a very good priest. Very loyal. I am honoured to serve the Church in whatever way I can. I don't … question the authority of the Church. I don't speak out of turn, or challenge what has been handed down to us over so many generations. It just … it just seems to me … a pity we can't be more … tolerant. After all … not everyone has the same path.'

For once Joanna was at a loss what to say. It was only then, in the silence that fell between them, that they heard the announcement on the AV. The drama had been interrupted with a news flash.

'… the prisoner is considered dangerous and should be approach with extreme caution. Those not wanting to participate are advised to remain indoors and not let anyone unknown to them enter. To repeat: A dangerous criminal has escaped the prison city of Gerda and is believed to be in Lorna. By order of the Cardinal Hierophant curfew is suspended, and a city-wide amnesty is declared to any and all persons able to capture or kill the fugitive. This has been confirmed with Captain Marius of the Temple Guard, who are already hunting for this man…'

Alban turned to Joanna. 'It's just as well you are here tonight. The streets are no longer safe for anyone it seems. Even loyal Tobianists.'

Tobias could hear them in the distance. Just one or two at first, roaming the streets aimlessly, making all kinds of noise. Once the rain stopped more emerged and they began to travel in packs. They shouted to one another, intimidated each other, laughing and threatening in turn as the groups crossed paths. Anyone travelling alone through the dim city streets was a target, and from the hands of the hunters came a crack of thunder and a strange lightning that burned the air. Tobias didn't understand it, but from the reactions of those who either ran or fell injured, he could tell these things the hunters wore on their hands were dangerous.

He watched them with amusement. They behaved as if they had never hunted before, flashing light all over the place from handheld lanterns, stomping around like they were trying to flush out their quarry rather than catch it by surprise. Several times he crept straight past them when they got too near his hiding spot. He didn't know who or what they were searching for, but they outnumbered him ten to one so he thought it best to keep his distance.

At first the hunters were easy to evade, but eventually their number grew so large it was almost impossible to avoid one group without being spotted by another. Caught in their light, Tobias heard that now familiar crack of thunder, and the wall ahead of him shattered as something struck it violently, leaving a large hole. A pack of the hunters set after him and there were more terrifying cracks and sizzles as they fired at him. Sometimes they came close enough that a cold blue light would flash nearby and the air around him turned bitter and sharp. But he managed to evade them, disappearing into the shadows up another canyon. He soon learned that their weapons could not reach him if he was far enough away. And he could easily outrun them.

He always knew where they were by their constant shouting. Tobias couldn't understand them, but it all seemed rather pointless. Their noise drew other packs to the chase, they converged, and soon Tobias was being constantly pursued through the streets by a noisy, angry horde. They fired their lightning at him, but their aim was poor or he was out of range. They often hit each other by accident. Tobias was faster and more agile than all of them as he dodged and weaved through the moonlit streets, but no sooner had he evaded one group when he was confronted by another, and then another. Desperate to find cover he heard the distant sound of running water. It was familiar and comforting. He followed the sound, weaving through the canyons as more and more pursuers emerged, finally stumbling into a vast open space. With no more canyons or shadows to hide in he was suddenly exposed and vulnerable. He couldn't turn back so pressed on towards the water.

Festival Square was about 300 metres square, limestone paved, with a high surrounding wall and grassy parkland set back at either side. In the middle of the square was the fountain of the Prophet: an impossibly tall, twisting sculpture with water flowing from the top, down the intertwining spiral curves of the structure, into a pair of large circular pools at the base. The fountain represented the flow of life and the eternal cycle of all things. It represented death and rebirth, the renewal of life that was at the core of the Prophet Tobias's teachings. Its shape was a variation on the mathematical symbol for infinity, a lemniscate, which in Tobianist lore represented 'eternity.' Because of this, the fountain had come to be known as the figure-8 fountain. The shape of the structure itself and of the pools at its base both looked like a figure-8. Another interpretation had the fountain representing a double-helix of DNA, since it actually spiralled many times with multiple threads of varied sizes that produced a different visual effect when viewed from a distance or close-up. It was one of the greatest public sculptures of all time, a masterpiece of balance and form that managed to represent everything the Prophet had stood for. But no-one remembered who designed it, and no-one seemed to care for its aesthetic or deeper meaning. For generations now it was simply the figure-8 fountain – a good place to meet.

On the far side of the square was the entrance to the Great Temple, its massive gates closed, lest the citizens of Lorna decide to extend their hunt into the temple grounds. Festival Square was also one of the few places that remained fully lit at night. With the fountain perpetually flowing, the sound of the water and the lights at the top of the iconic sculpture served as a beacon for pilgrims to the Great Temple. It was not just the centre of Lorna, but symbolically of the whole Tobianist world. For all these reasons Tobias had ended up in the worst possible place. With no cover, brightly lit, and dozens of hunters using the landmark as a meeting place now surrounding him on all sides.

Tobias took all this in in an instant, barely breaking stride as he charged into the melee, violently pushing startled hunters aside on his path to the fountain. A brave few tried to stand their ground, raising their hands to attack, but he quickly barrelled over them. Most however made no attempt to defend themselves, instead running from him in a panic. An otherwise overpowering gauntlet of hunters scattered in fear as Tobias simply ran straight down the middle of them, striking and lashing out at anyone who dared to come near. The sound of thunder and lightning rang out behind him, but with so many hunters around it was impossible for them to hit the right target. He would have laughed at their incompetence if he wasn't so busy running from them.

Reaching the pools at the base of the giant fountain Tobias dived resolutely into the water. It was cold but clean, and while not deep, he was able to travel beneath the surface for most of its width. That he knew how to swim was a muscle-memory from some distant life. Something he just knew. Listening from beneath the water he heard the muffled cries of the hunters and the violent splashes of them entering the water all around him. By the time he broke the surface he was near the base of the fountain. Turning, he could see them approaching from all sides, wading waist-deep through the shallow pool with their gloved hands raised above their heads.

A lightning bolt was aimed at Tobias by one of the hunters standing at the side of the pool. It fell short and landed on the surface of the water. Every hunter who had been wading toward the fountain froze in their tracks as the electrical charge surged through them. Tobias also felt it. A violent tingling gripped his muscles and caused him to lose control of his body completely. The effect ended as suddenly as it had begun, but if that was what the lighting gloves could do Tobias wanted to be sure he wasn't on the receiving end of one again.

Hunters collapsed and sank into the water, struggling to regain control of their limbs. Tobias started to scramble up the structure of the fountain. His own arms and legs refused to obey at first, but eventually they loosened up and he was able to climb clear of the pond and disappear inside the structure.

Up close, the fountain was a giant twisting maze of metal pipes and water channels. Tobias was soon deep inside the tangle of steel, climbing up through its skeleton of intertwined metal and water towards the head. Below, the hunters were either rescuing those affected by the lightning, or arguing amongst themselves. None were inclined to follow their quarry up the fountain sculpture.

Tobias reached the top, where he found a small platform that he could sit on. He was high enough that the hunters couldn't see him amongst all the twisted metal, flowing water and bright lights. Looking down on his pursuers, they were like confused insects surrounding the fountain and its twin pools. A few randomly shot their lightning at the fountain but they were too far away, and no-one dared cross the water for fear they might get zapped again. For now he was safe, though trapped.

What Tobias didn't realise was that he was being watched very closely. Not by hunters, but by two who had been observing his progress for several days, ever since his regeneration. Disembodied and ethereal, they looked down upon the scene as if viewing an abstract of reality where time and space are constrained by the senses. Where experience and mortality defined one's life. An existence they had once known, and would perhaps know again, but were now apart from. To some they were called angels. To others, spirit guides. Whatever name you gave them, they remained invisible and detached. Merely observing.

Matthew and Will were not supposed to intervene, but it was becoming clear something had to be done. The balance of things was disrupted. Or as Will would have it: 'It's all out of whack.'

'Now do you understand why I wanted you to come?' Matthew asked Will.

'No,' Will replied bluntly. 'Remember, I'm new at this. Do you do this sort of thing a lot?'

'All the time. Where we can, we offer a little encouragement, try to nudge people in the right direction. But it's more to help them see the path before them so they can make a clear choice. We don't force anything one way or another. As much as we would like to sometimes.'

'Free will, huh?'

'Precisely. Only Tobias here has no will of his own. He is driven purely by instinct.'

'So why didn't it work? The whole regeneration thing.'

'Because the spirit of Tobias has moved on. Once the connection between body and soul is severed it cannot be restored. A new body is sought. A new life begun. And the journey continues.'

'So he reincarnated,' Will was starting to get it now.

'When the body of the Prophet was compelled back to life, it stole some of the life-force of its original soul. Just enough to sustain the body, but not so much as to harm its new host. The soul is now split between two bodies.'

'Does that happen very often?'

'It has never happened. And it cannot be allowed to continue. Against all our guiding principles, we must intervene. Otherwise the fate of the new host is in jeopardy.'

'I thought you said there was free will.'

'There is, and there is destiny. The two go hand in hand.'

'I don't understand.' Will was never very good at philosophical discussions. He preferred things in black and white.

Matthew turned to his inexperienced companion. 'Understand this, Will. Your brother Rene is the Prophet Tobias reborn. That is why you are here.'

'I wondered about that.'

'The fate of the world is synonymous with his. The return of the Prophet is at hand, and it is not Tobias.'

Will took a moment to take this in. After all, it's not every day you find out you're related to a messiah.

'Are you sure? Rene never struck me as all that spiritual. In fact he's entirely unremarkable, and I mean that in the nicest way. We grew up together, I never saw anything to indicate my brother was some kind of guru.'

'All great leaders were once children – innocents unaware of their fate. Their inevitable destinies are defined by the choices they make. Free will and fate are one and the same.'

'I'm sure to you that makes sense, but I'm not getting it.'

'We must find a way to restore the balance, without upsetting the new balance that has been created.'

'How could I possibly help?'

'He is your brother. Your bond with him may prove invaluable in what we have to do.'

'What do we have to do?'

'I don't know,' Matthew admitted. 'But whatever it is, we need to do it soon.'

— ∞ —

In Rene's experience Temple Guards were always surly and violent. Maybe it was the uniform. He was sure there must be some Guards who were pleasant and helpful, but he had yet to meet one. Of course, his only previous experience with them had been back when big brother William was arrested for a childish act of vandalism – reprogramming a Temple AV-wall mural to display pornography instead of religious art. The Church branded him a heretic since they saw his civil disobedience as desecration. He was killed trying to escape custody. Now Rene was in the same boat, lumped in with Dan as a heretic sympathiser.

The prisoner transport arrived at the Temple Guard compound inside the grounds of the Great Temple. Here they were bundled, along with prisoners from several other transports, into the holding cells. Rene never knew the Temple had its own prison, but it didn't surprise him. The vast complex surrounding the Great Temple (which was just one gigantic structure among many) seemed to have everything a city within a city could want. Including some things most cities didn't have – like its own military force. He and Dan were thrown into a cell together with two other prisoners. Their gags and binds were removed, and once the Guards departed they were finally free to talk.

But they didn't. And neither did anyone else in the entire block. There was still the very real possibility they were being observed. Besides, what was there to say?

Rene shivered. For some reason he was unaccountably cold. Dan took off his jacket and handed it to Rene.

'Here.'

'No, it's all right – '

'Just take it will you.' Dan insisted, still speaking in hushed tones.

Rene took the jacket and put it on. 'Thanks.' It didn't help much, though.

In time one of their cellmates emerged from the shadows on the far side of the room to greet them: 'Hey,' he whispered. 'I'm Rohan.'

'Rene.'

'Daniel.'

Rene glanced at Dan – since when did he ever call himself *Daniel*?

'What'd they get you for?' Rohan asked.

'Trusting an idiot.' Rene replied, but Dan threw him such a forlorn look he immediately regretted saying it.

Rohan turned to Dan. 'What about you?'

'For being an idiot.'

Rohan didn't seem to get it but laughed anyway. Dan turned the question back on him before he could probe any further. 'What about you?'

'Well, there's not much I can tell you. Not here.' Rohan's eyes darted over his shoulder and he shuffled closer to them, as if this would thwart any hidden camera or microphone from picking up what he said. 'I'm on a secret mission. You know, infiltrate the Temple. Get information on the enemy. I let them arrest me. No way they would have caught me otherwise. You think I'm that stupid? It's all part of the plan.'

'If it's so secret then why are you tell us?' Dan asked.

'Shit man. We're on the same team, right? We're in this thing together. And we gotta work together – '

'I'm not on anybody's 'team',' Rene corrected.

'You freelance then?' Rohan inferred. 'That's cool. We all got our ways. But you're here now, man. Looks like your team's been picked for you.'

Rene had to admit he was right. Like it or not he was now a rebel and a heretic, and would forever be seen as a threat to the Church. Of course, he might not live much longer for that to make any difference.

All this time the fourth in their cell had been lurking in the shadows going virtually unnoticed by Dan and Rene. 'Rohan.'

Rohan turned sharply, almost cowering at the sound of the voice. 'Shut the fuck up.'

Rohan scowled, then scuttled away into a dark corner. The fourth man emerged from the shadows and sat beside Rene and Dan. He was of stocky build, unlike Rohan, and wore a thick beard of dappled brown and grey to match his luxurious hair.

'Don't mind him. He means well.'

'Was any of what he said true?' Dan asked.

The man paused, then said: 'I'm Kane.' He extended his hand to them both. 'So, how did you two upstanding citizens come to be thrown in with us moral deviants?'

'Mistaken identity,' joked Rene.

Kane smiled. 'Happens all the time. Gerda is full of innocent people.'

Rene thought he was making fun of them. 'I'm not a criminal.'

'Neither am I,' Kane responded.

'And I'm not a heretic.'

'I meant no offence.' Kane deferred. 'Whatever your faith, whatever you may or may not have done, you're here now. We all are. And we need to prepare ourselves for what is to come.'

'What do you mean?' Dan asked nervously.

Kane dropped his head and looked up slightly toward the ceiling, then back at Rene and Dan. They were being watched.

'When the time comes, stay close.'

Dan was about to speak when Kane imperceptibly raised a hand to quiet him. He moved away from them, back into the shadows.

Dan turned to Rene who likewise shook his head to quiet his friend. So they sat in silence … and waited.

We are all divine fragments of creation
And we are all artists
Painting our lives upon the universe
Enacting the drama we have ourselves set down

Shentama
– Stanza 58

Captain Marius was not easily intimidated, but somehow the Cardinal Hierophant Cairn always unnerved him. It wasn't because he was supreme leader of the Tobianist faith, and it wasn't about the size of the throne, or the colour of his robes, or even that he was such an imposingly tall man used to looking down on everyone. Something about Cairn unsettled Marius and he couldn't put his finger on it. It used to be Cardinal Kasper who was the creepy one – scary and dangerous, but predictable. With Cairn though, Marius couldn't tell if it was madness or genius that drove the man. Either way, he was finding it hard to stick to his oath of loyalty. This whole thing was getting out of control.

'Why is it, Captain, with all the guards at your disposal, and half the civilian population of Lorna searching for this prisoner you've not been able to find him? How long does it take to catch one unarmed man?'

'Your Eminence, between the crackdown on heretics, the hunt for this escapee, and trying to police the chaos in the streets the edict has created – '

' – Are you blaming me for your incompetence?' Cairn asked incredulously.

Marius was quick to respond, 'No Your Eminence, not at all. It's just … more than we expected. The public response has been overwhelming. There were some reported sightings of a man believed to be the escapee, but communication has been difficult. And there's been a lot of casualties with people accidentally shooting each other.'

'I told you the rabble would respond, didn't I, Kasper? This proves I was right.' Cairn relished times like this when he could show Kasper up. His advice was usually spot on, which made it all the more satisfying when he could prove him wrong.

Kasper revealed nothing. 'Indeed, Your Eminence.' He turned to Marius. 'Why are there so many civilian casualties, Captain? What are they using as weapons?'

'Mostly power gloves, some old firearms. Whatever they can get a hold of.'

'How is it civilians are carrying around weapons like these?' Asked Kasper, truly concerned. 'I thought only law enforcement or the Guard were allowed access to power weapons.'

'Normally yes, Your Eminence,' Marius replied humbly. 'But there is a healthy black market in older models. It's something we have been trying to stamp out for years.'

'Don't worry about civilian casualties, Captain,' Cairn interrupted. 'Just focus your efforts on finding that prisoner.'

Cairn ignored Kasper's disparaging look. He simply didn't understand what was at stake here. A few civilian deaths through misadventure were a sacrifice Cairn was prepared to make for the greater good.

'It would help, your Eminence, if we had more information on who he was,' Marius ventured. 'If I had his comkey genome I could find him in no time.' Regular citizens had to carry their comkeys with them at all times – a kind of enforced free will. To wear one was a choice, not to wear one was illegal. Prisoners of Gerda no longer had free will, so their comkey chip was implanted under the skin, usually on the bone in the centre of the ribcage. This made them easy to track.

'He doesn't have one,' Cairn replied. 'It was removed.'

'Of course.' Prisoners often tried to remove their comkeys, though the explosive countermeasures usually caused this to end badly for them. 'And the crackdown, your Eminence?' Marius asked. 'Our holding cells here at the Temple are already filling up.'

'Keep on with that. I don't want any chance of some rebel crusade spoiling the festival. Ship them off to Gerda if you're running out of room. They can be processed there.'

'Yes, Your Eminence.'

Joanna didn't sleep much. She could hear people wandering the streets just outside the little church, yelling and firing weapons indiscriminately. At any moment she feared they would burst in, but they stayed outside the walls, respecting the sanctuary of a place of worship. She was also worried about Rene and Dan. There was no telling where they had been taken or what had become of them. She was not a religious person, but as she was in a church, she found herself actually praying they were alive and well.

When she did finally sleep her dreams were filled with images of Rene trapped and in pain, or of his brother Will, who had been killed by the Temple Guard years earlier, trying to save him. She hadn't really known Will, but he had practically brought up Rene after their parents were killed when he was still a child. Will's own death had a profound effect on Rene. That he should appear in her dreams was unusual, but then a lot of weird stuff happens in dreams. Her anxieties were drawing on everything she knew about Rene and dramatising her worst fears. An imaginary theatre of hope and despair, with a cast of forgotten faces and fragmented memories. Even, for some reason, the words of the old woman that read their palms just a few nights ago – '*Yours is the hardest road, my dear. But you must stay the course else all is lost.*'

Joanna finally managed to get a few hours of fitful sleep, only to be woken by Father Alban with a breakfast of oatmeal and tea.

'It's not much, I'm sorry. But we live a simple life here.'

'It's fine, thank you.' Joanna didn't realise how famished she was until she took her first spoonful and managed to empty the bowl in less than a minute.

'Would you like some more?' Father Alban ventured.

'If it's not too much trouble.' Joanna was embarrassed, but she didn't know when she would eat again.

Alban took her bowl. 'I suggest you get dressed. We'll have to leave soon.'

'We?'

'I can take you part of the way,' Alban told her. 'But the rest you'll have to manage for yourself.'

'Part of the way where?'

Alban didn't answer. 'I'll get you some more,' he said and left with the empty bowl.

Thirty minutes later Alban led Joanna out the rear entrance of the church. She was dressed in the robes he had given her the night before so to any observer they looked like a cleric and his novice out for a walk. The chaos of last night seemed to have abated. Temple Guard roamed the streets in their GL vehicles, looking for troublemakers, and there was still the odd armed civilian wandering about; but they ignored them once they spotted the robes. Alban led her through the narrow back streets of the Western Borough. Like most of the outlying areas of Lorna it was built on a slope. The further down one ventured, away from the Great Temple which stood at the peak of the mount, the more run-down things became. She had never been here before and was surprised at how different it looked to the Temple Borough where she and Rene lived and worked. This place was older, more haphazard, and had a kind of bohemian atmosphere that she liked. She could even imagine herself living here, if it wasn't so far away from everything. But the further they travelled the more dilapidated it became. The buildings became older with broken windows and exposed construction. The AV murals were weather-worn and vandalised, with glitching images or no image at all, until eventually they disappeared all-together. The streets were mostly empty, but she could sense people watching them from within the buildings. Was it always like this, she wondered, or were people staying indoors because of last night's anarchy?

She spotted a body on the side of the road. Just lying there. It shocked her how normal it seemed – not that there was a body on the road, but that she accepted it so readily. As a society they thought themselves civilised. Above such things. Violence, war, irrational prejudices – these were things of the past. But it didn't take much for the beast in all of us to take hold. And it wasn't fear of the unknown, self-defence, or even some ideological conflict that had caused this. All it took was permission to misbehave. The true mark of one's humanity is how you respond to such a call, and how you react to its aftermath. Looking at the body of the man lying on the ground, Joanna was ashamed to admit she felt nothing but relief it wasn't her – or Rene – lying in the gutter.

Alban approached the body, bending down to examine it. He rolled the man over. He was young, wearing a power glove. Blood covered his jacket from a bullet wound in the chest. Alban searched the body and found the man's comkey – a standard issue card.

'His name was Leonard,' Alban said softly. 'He was twenty-four years old.' He seemed about to say more, but grief overtook him and his eyes welled with tears.

'Did you know him?' Joanna asked.

'No.' Alban raised his lemnis medallion, which served as his own comkey, and touched it to Leonard's, scanning his info. 'I'll let his family know.' He rose to his feet. 'Come. We're nearly there.'

Alban led Jo a few more blocks, then stopped as they turned a corner into a long dark lane overgrowing with grass and weeds. She guessed they were on the edge of the Abandoned Quarter, an almost mythological part of the Old City since most residents would never venture into it intentionally. It was the home of wild tales and bizarre speculation. Anything unbelievable or stretching credulity was said to "belong in the AQ". It had become a cliché. Now it seemed Joanna was about to find out how true the tales were.

'This is as far as I can take you,' Alban told her. He indicated a door to a dilapidated house on the other side of the lane about twenty meters away. 'That's where you want to go. I hope you find what you're looking for.'

'What's behind that door?'

Alban smiled coyly. 'I really have no idea. Goodbye, Jo. You may keep the robes.' And with that Alban walked briskly back up the street away from her.

Joanna watched him leave till he rounded the corner and was out of sight, then turned her attention to the door. It was solid metal and the windows on either side were painted black. There was a second story to the house and the windows here were likewise blacked out. The house looked abandoned and derelict, as did the houses on either side, hugging closely together with barely a space between them. Old suburban tenements that might have been quite hospitable once, but now appeared sad and neglected. But the metal door made this house stick out.

The lane was quite silent. Joanna saw no-one, but still had the sense she was being watched. She snorted derisively, 'What the hell,' and walked purposefully across the street. When she got to the door she knocked confidently. If she was walking into some kind of trap at least she was going to walk in with her eyes open.

After a moment the door unlocked with several heavy *clunks*, then opened a crack. Joanna had to look down to see who was on the other side, and at first couldn't comprehend what she was looking at. It wasn't a child; in fact it wasn't even human. It must be a primate of some kind – a chimpanzee if her guess was right. The creature looked up at her with a penetrating gaze, but its face was otherwise expressionless. Although, being a chimp, Joanna wouldn't have known what its expression meant if it had any.

After a few seconds she managed to find her voice. 'Hello.'

The creature maintained its gaze, sizing her up, then slowly opened the door to admit her. Joanna stepped inside, walking past the chimp, who closed the door behind her and reset the locks. It then calmly took her hand and led her down the hallway. She had never held the hand of another species before and it was a strange experience. At first she balked a little, but the creature simply took a firm grip of her and pulled her along. Its hand was warm and leathery, the fur on the back soft and disconcerting. It led her down the dim hall to a room at the far end of the house. Joanna tried to take in her surroundings, but her head was still reeling at the fact that an ape had answered the door and was now leading her by the hand.

It opened the door at the end of the hall and let go her hand, leaving Joanna standing on the threshold as it leapt inside the room and into the arms of a red-headed woman seated at a kitchen table eating breakfast. The woman looked up at Joanna curiously as she hugged the chimp. 'Hello. Who are you?'

— ∞ —

Rene was asleep when the Guards came to get them. He had been feeling so tired lately. Tired and cold. In fact for the past several days he had been in a kind of daze. Nothing seemed real. He also couldn't shake the feeling that he was supposed to be somewhere else. Of course, being in a Temple holding cell on suspicion of heresy was not somewhere one would normally want to be, but he still felt he was forgetting something. When Dan woke him Rene had been dreaming he was surrounded by running water. So when the Temple Guard grabbed his collar and dragged him out of the cell he was busting for a pee.

'What's happening?' he asked Dan once they were in the corridor.

It was Kane who answered. 'We're being moved. Which can only mean one thing.'

'What?' Dan asked nervously.

'Gerda.'

The very name conjured up nightmares. A prison complex so immense it had become a city in its own right. It was built originally after the Great Purge to contain the worst of the worst. It boasted the highest possible security and was located in one of the remotest parts of the world, surrounded by desert, hundreds of miles from any civilised settlement. All the world's murderers, rapists and other recidivist criminals were sent there. In time, it became the World Penitentiary, used to house practically any criminal regardless of their crime. Centralised incarceration. Local authorities no longer had to maintain their own prisons. They simply outsourced penal servitude to a third-party service provider. It was known as *The Gerda Accord*, and it was a full-service contract. All judicial processes took place at Gerda, from trial to sentencing, incarceration and, if required, punitive retribution. Everything short of capital punishment – which was proscribed under Tobianist law (except for heretics). There was no outside oversight, no impartial administration; that was the point. Once transported to Gerda, you were no longer their problem.

It was rare for anyone in Gerda to fulfill their sentence – to be released and return home. If you were sent there, more than likely you would never be heard from again. Whether this was corruption, political/religious tyranny, or just bureaucratic incompetence was unclear. It's just the way things were.

Recently, Gerda had become the Church's favoured solution for suspected heretics. Partly because it obviated the need for a public trial, but also because, ironically, Gerda was geographically not far from Lorna; and Lorna, it seemed, was full of heretics.

'Don't worry,' Kane reassured Dan and Rene as they were marched from the Temple holding cells toward the GL transports parked outside. 'It could be worse.'

'How could it be worse?' Dan protested. 'We're going to Gerda!'

'It could be raining,' Kane quipped.

Dan was about to respond to this poor attempt at humour when he received an electric jolt from the prod of a nearby Guard, a warning zap to shut-up.

Rene took the joke at face value. Kane was right. The sun was out, the sky was blue, and it was a warm summer's day. Perhaps it was the daze he'd been in lately, but Rene just took it as it came. He had no control over the situation, so saw no point in stressing about it. If only he weren't so hungry.

— ∞ —

Tobias could see the food by the side of pool. Dropped by one of the hunters it had remained there all night – a square block, similar to those he had seen others eating. Most of the hunters who had pursued him into the pools had left, many of them sent packing by the uniformed men in flying cars. Despite their protests and frantic pointing to his roost at the top of the fountain, the uniformed men ignored the hunters and moved them along. He was beginning to understand this world, though he had no idea how. Answers just came to him. The names of things, the strange customs of the people below. He recognised patterns in their behavior, irrational and predictable at the same time. The more he observed the more amusing he found them, while also understanding just how dangerous they could be. So despite his hunger, he did not climb down to retrieve the food.

The night passed slowly, and the square below gradually cleared. Come sunrise a few hunters tried again to wade across the pools to the fountain and climb up. They soon quit, unable to reach even the centre of the structure due to the perpetual torrent of water swirling down the tubes.

The last of the hunters finally left their post when another flying car of uniformed men – Guards they were called – drove by. The square was now empty, and Tobias began his climb down the Fountain of the Prophet, his eyes fixed on the parcel of food.

Accept the challenge
Face your demons
Defer the lesson no longer
New adventures await you
Beyond the dread mountain

For life is a quest
To fulfill the legend that is you
To seek and discover your self
And realise the power within

Shentama
– Stanzas 77-78

'Have you had breakfast?' the red-headed woman asked Joanna.

'Yes. Thank-you.'

'I'm Althea.'

'Joanna. Jo.'

'And this is Elly,' Althea gave the ape an affectionate pat.

'… Right …'

Althea smiled. She could see her guest was confused.

'She's a Bonobo.'

'A what?'

'Bonobo.'

'Oh,' Joanna said, still confused. 'I thought…'

'She was a chimp? Common mistake. They're closely related.' Althea looked Elly in the eye. 'But then, so are we.'

Joanna couldn't be sure, but it looked like the bonobo smiled. Did she understand what Althea was saying? How was that possible?

'Why…?'

' – Do I have a bonobo? Long story. More to the point, why are you wearing the robes of cleric? And do sit down, please.'

Joanna sat in the chair opposite. 'Oh. Thank-you. No. I'm not … actually – '

'I figured as much.'

'Father Alban. He gave them to me,' Joanna explained. 'It's kind of a disguise.'

'Don't know a Father Alban, but then, we're pretty new here ourselves.'

Althea put Elly down who trundled out of the room. Joanna watched the bonobo leave, still not sure if this was really happening. Althea continued eating her breakfast. 'What did he tell you?'

'Nothing. In fact … he seemed a bit nervous just coming here. He just pointed me to the door outside and left.'

'So you don't know where you are, really. Do you?'

Joanna didn't know how to respond.

'Where do you think you are?' Althea asked pointedly. There

was a casual tone to her question, but Joanna had to be careful how she answered. She still didn't know who this woman was.

'I really don't know.'

'Why do you think Father Alban brought you here?'

'He thought it would be safe.'

'Safe from what?'

Althea could see Joanna was suspicious. 'Look. Elly wouldn't have let you in if she didn't think you were okay. She's a better judge of character than any person I know. So whatever it is you're running from, you can relax. Your priest was right, you're safe here. I'm just trying to work out how much I should tell you.'

Joanna relaxed. Any woman with a bonobo for a pet couldn't be all bad.

'The others will be back soon,' Althea told her. 'Maybe we should wait till then.'

'Others?'

'You must be hot in those robes. Do you have something on underneath?'

'Yes.'

'Feel free to take them off. Tea?'

— ∞ —

The convoy of prisoner transports approached the Festival Gates – thirteen GLs in all, each carrying forty-eight prisoners. Escorting them was a squad of smaller GL cruisers with up to four Temple Guards in each. This was the largest number of prisoners they ever had moved at one time, so Captain Marius himself led the escort. He wanted to make sure nothing went wrong. As usual, Marius drove the GL himself, though at a much slower pace than he would have liked. Sitting beside him was cadet Fairchild, whom Marius had adopted as his personal aide. They had to maintain a so-called 'safe' speed through the city, but once they hit the open road they would be travelling at three-hundred kilometres per hour across the desert to Gerda.

The Festival Gates opened automatically for them, and they emerged from the Temple grounds into the Square. Though still early it was past curfew, and normally the Square would be busy with people on their way to work or enjoying the fountain and surrounding parklands. Today it was disturbingly empty. After last night's chaos it seemed no-one was prepared to leave the safety of indoors.

Throughout the night news reports had showed images of the hunt, calling it the worst violence Lorna had seen since the Great Purge. And this was from the official AV feeds, which normally never reported anything negative about the Church. This was just too big to ignore. In response, the Temple released a short statement blaming the violence on heretic groups, reassuring people Temple Guards had successfully crushed the revolt. They also claimed to have captured the Gerda escapee and that all danger had now passed. Marius knew this not to be true, of course, but Kasper had convinced Cairn something had to be done to mitigate the political damage caused by last night. Heretic rebels were the perfect scapegoats. As for the escapee, Marius was still charged with finding him, but it would now be without the 'assistance' of the public.

One man however seemed unconcerned by the news reports. Marius spotted him across the square standing by the figure-8 fountain. He was practically naked, wearing nothing but a pair of white shorts, and was ravenously eating something. So absorbed was he with his meal he hadn't noticed the convoy coming out of the gates. Marius wondered what he was doing out here alone and seemingly in his underwear. He looked like one of the destitutes from the Western Borough. Then it occurred to him this might be the escapee they had been looking for. He slammed the wheel forward and the GL broke away from the convoy, speeding across the square toward the fountain. Fairchild was flung to the back of the car in a heap.

'Hang on, kid!' Marius told him. He hit a button on the dashboard and two power guns emerged from the front of the vehicle. This was the perfect opportunity to use the car's built-in weaponry. Something he never got a chance to do outside of the testing range. He'd fry the fucker with both barrels.

As they came within range the man looked up from his food and saw the GL vehicle bearing down on him. Marius pressed the triggers on the steering wheel and two massive hazed arcs shot from the guns, each ten times the size and energy of a power glove, and sounding like the crack of doom itself. They spidered across the square toward their target, then diverted abruptly sideways and hit the metal structure of the fountain. Aside from everything else, the fountain was also a massive lightning rod. This completely drained the power from the GL and it dropped to the ground.

'Shit!' Marius bellowed, as the vehicle's nose ripped into the pavement, flipping several times end-over-end before skidding upside-down to an inglorious stop.

The man at the fountain ran in the opposite direction, only to be confronted by a swarm of rebel fighters wearing yellow scarves and armed with power gloves, firearms and other weapons. They ignored the man in his underwear and converged on the prison convoy. It was an ambush.

The transport stopped with a sudden jolt. Rene could hear weapons fire outside. He turned to Dan who sat on the opposite side of the container; but he was just as confused. Neither could speak as they were again gagged, their hands bound to the bench between their legs. Every prisoner was anxious – except Kane. When Rene looked at him Kane just smiled back knowingly.

Outside a battle was raging. There was the distinctive sound of power gloves and firearms. They could hear orders barked by the Guard commanders, or rowdy cheers as combatants were felled. As the fighting came closer shots and hazes ricocheted off their transport. Fortunately, it was insulated against any such attack, but it was still frightening how close they were.

The doors to their transport burst open and bright sunlight streamed in, blinding them. A large man stepped in, silhouette against the frame of the open transport doors. 'Yo Kane! You in here?' he called in a deep voice.

A team of others climbed in around him and began unlocking the prisoners' bindings and removing gags.

'Hurry it up, we haven't got all day!' Ordered the large man.

Once released the prisoners were rushed out of the vehicle into the bright sunlight. Rene still couldn't quite see what was going on when someone knelt in front of him and undid his bindings and gag. 'Stick with me, and you'll be okay.' It was Kane. He took Rene's arm and led him to the doors.

As they climbed out of the transport the large man at the entrance recognised Kane. 'There you are. I've been lookin' all over.'

'How many?' Kane asked.

'About thirty or so. The GLs are armed so watch yourself.' Rene still couldn't make out the man's face, but he was a giant physically.

'Have we got everyone out?' Kane asked the giant.

'Yep.'

'Okay. Let's get the hell out of here.'

As Kane led Rene away from the transport his eyes slowly

adjusted and he found himself on a battlefield in the middle of Festival Square. Hundreds of released prisoners fled the scene in all directions. Temple Guards shot indiscriminately after them while also fending off the rebels. Not everyone ran. Many of the prisoners joined the battle and soon the Guard found themselves overwhelmed. The convoy may have had an entire unit as its escort, but it wasn't enough.

Rene looked about for Dan. He couldn't see him anywhere.

'Come on!' Kane yelled.

'Where's Dan?'

'He'll be fine. Come on!'

'No. I've got to find Dan.'

A haze of electricity crackled past them, fired from an encroaching GL with Temple Guards at the helm. They each ducked for cover, diving in opposite directions. In one fluid move Rene rolled to his feet and kept running – all that gymnastics as a boy came back to him in the moment. As he turned back he saw the GL pursuing Kane, who was forced to run back towards the transport. Rene could now make out the man that had freed them – a large, bald, black man wearing a tank-top and with a power glove on each hand. As Kane ran towards him the giant fired with both hands – a dual arc that hit the GL, causing it to lose control and smash into the side of the transport.

Rene ducked behind another stalled transport for cover. He scoured the Square for Dan amongst the fleeing prisoners and fighting rebels, but it was the bodies lying on the ground that he paid most attention to. He hoped Dan had made it to cover in the nearby park or up one of the streets that converged on the Square.

Leaving the cover of the convoy vehicles Rene searched closer to the fountain. The battle was mostly behind him, but he was exposed and any stray shot could have easily taken him down. He looked in the faces of those lying on the ground. Most were still alive, crippled by a power glove and unable to move, their muscles still tensing in a fit of electrocution, but there were some who had been shot with good old-fashioned bullets and were either bleeding out or already dead. On any other day Rene would have been horrified by such a scene, but it felt like he was walking through a dream. None of it was real. His focus was on finding Dan.

He reached the pool at the base of the fountain. Another man was standing there, watching the battle from a distance. He was naked but for a pair of white shorts, had long matted hair, and looked strangely familiar to Rene. The man turned to Rene, and they held each other's gaze for the longest time. It was as if they knew each other. More than that. It was if they *were* each other. Rene recognised himself. He was looking into a mirror, only the reflection was of another face. Another life. A long-forgotten memory he had somehow always known. It was a face he knew, a face he had seen before many times. The face of the Prophet Tobias.

A shot rang out. The bullet zinged past Rene's ear and hit Tobias in the shoulder. He fell back into the shallow pool behind him, a howl of pain exploding from his lungs.

Rene turned to see Captain Marius climbing out of an overturned GL and start running towards them, a pistol in his raised hand. He seemed not to notice or care about Rene at all. His target was Tobias.

Tobias struggled across the pool, the water pink with blood. Rene ran towards Marius who still paid him no mind. He fired another shot at Tobias. Missed.

Rene knelt at the body of one of the fallen rebels, removed his power glove, put it on and aimed at Marius. Marius finally turned to Rene, now seeing him as a potential threat, but before he could do anything Rene pressed the button on the palm of the glove, his index finger pointing out the way he had seen it done. A haze arc ejected from the finger and hit Marius square in the chest. But Marius kept coming. Temple Guard armour was insulated against power weapons, but it wasn't a perfect shield. Marius could still move but had trouble aiming his weapon. Rene held the charge – what else could he do? As Marius staggered closer the armour's protection faded. The glove started beeping – power was low. Marius kept coming, just a few meters away, his pistol raised and ready to fire, his face contorted with the struggle to move his limbs. The glove finally gave out – its power exhausted – just as Marius fell face forward onto the pavement – paralysed.

Rene had never fired a power glove before, and hoped he would never have to again. He got to his feet, turning back to the fountain.

Tobias was gone.

'That was interesting,' Matthew reflected.

'I don't understand how that was even possible,' Will replied. 'Aren't they the same person?'

'Same soul, different people.'

'What if they'd touched or something? Would that cause some kind of weird paradox?'

'No. At least ... I don't think so.' Matthew appeared just as surprised as Will at how things were unfolding. Was this pure chance, or somehow part of Rene's destiny? Weren't they one and the same?

'Maybe we're not meant to interfere.' Will speculated. 'Maybe, it's s'pose to happen this way.'

'I think we just need to wait for the right moment. An opportunity will present itself.'

'Like what?'

'I don't know. But it's clear there is a connection between them. That may be useful.'

'How?'

'I don't know,' Mathew repeated.

'We don't know much, do we?' Will teased.

'No. But we're learning.'

The battle was over. The rebels had won. The Temple Guard were either dead, incapacitated, or retreated behind the Festival Gates. Rene found Kane as the rebels prepared to leave.

'Did you find your friend?'

'No,' Rene answered. 'He must have got away.'

'Don't worry, he'll turn up.' Kane reassured. 'Here, wear this.' Kane gave Rene a hat that would cover his face from overhead cameras. 'We gotta scarper before reinforcements turn up. Come on.' It was official. Rene was a rebel, a heretic, and an escaped prisoner to boot. But at least he was alive.

The rebels broke into small groups and scattered. Rene went with Kane, Rohan, their cellmate from the night before, and two others he didn't know. The rebels removed their yellow scarves, hid their weapons in packs, and walked casually to the nearest GL station where they caught a train to the end of the line. No one talked the entire trip. Perhaps they were afraid of someone, or something, overhearing them. Rohan and the other two could barely contain their excitement. If it hadn't been for Kane constantly glaring at them to keep silent they would have been blabbing about the skirmish the entire trip. This had clearly been a major operation for them and was the first successful assault of its kind that Rene knew of by any rebel group. It was historic.

For some reason Rene's left shoulder was aching terribly, but he'd come away otherwise unscathed. Nevertheless, he did not feel excited or even pleased to have escaped. People had died. Dan and Joanna were lost. And he didn't even know what to make of the encounter he'd had beside the fountain. He felt so completely alone, in a way he hadn't felt since Will died. Back then it was Joanna who had saved him. She had given him a reason to live. More than that – a reason not to die. There was a difference. It was the difference between choice and fate. One you could control, the other controlled you. And in the middle was a world of possibility.

—— ∞ ——

Joanna watched as Althea scanned the AV feeds for news about a rebel attack. The official feeds didn't mention it at all. After last night's coverage of the hunt the Church was suppressing anything related to civil unrest in Lorna. Underground feeds managed to get some word out, though details were scant. Then she found some footage of the ambush – live streams from the headcams of some of the rebels. It was a bloody mess. And based on these snatches it looked like they had failed.

Joanna had guessed this was a rebel safe house, and it seemed the 'others' Althea had mentioned were behind this attack. After last night's madness, and now whatever the hell this was, Lorna was becoming a city under siege. Yet all she could think about was Rene, and whether he was still alive.

Elly heard something, her attention turning to the hallway. Althea muted the AV. They listened in silence for a moment, then a muffled noise came seemingly from beneath the house. Elly spoke softly to Althea, signing a word as she did. Althea nodded. Elly scampered to the hallway and opened the door to the storage space under the stairs. Inside was a linen cupboard with several shelves stacked with sheets and towels. The noise was coming from behind the shelves. It sounded like several people approaching through what must be a hidden tunnel, Joanna speculated. Elly, Althea and Joanna stood back from the cupboard and waited. The sound was directly in front of them now. It stopped. Seconds later a dull click was heard, then the entire cupboard and its contents swung open like a door to reveal the dark hollow under the staircase, with a large hole gouged out of the concrete foundations. The top of a ladder was secured to the lip of the hole leading down into the darkness beneath the house. Standing at the top of the ladder was a tall, well-built man with a thick beard and wearing a large-brimmed hat.

'Good evening ladies,' said the man, who climbed up the ladder and out in the hallway, removing the hat.

'Did it work?' Althea asked anxiously. 'Did we get everyone?'

Others emerged from the secret tunnel behind him. The man may have answered Althea's question but Joanna was suddenly oblivious, as she saw Rene, wearing a silly cap, climb the ladder and step into the hallway. Rene spotted her and without a word they ran into each other's arms, embracing so hard it seemed they would never let each other go.

The others watched this brazen display of affection with amusement.

Althea smiled at Kane. 'Now what are the odds of that?'

14

The world you know is a reflection of your truth
It changes as you change
You create it
You control it
You are responsible for it

Shentama
– Stanza 46

It was rare to see the Cardinal Hierophant away from the eastern wing of the Great Temple, which encompassed the Hypogeum Basilica where he held audience with the general public or other lesser personages, the Council chambers, and Cairn's personal apartments. He would visit other parts of the Temple on official occasions, or to chair the assembly of Cardinals in the Great Hall; but he rarely ever went outside the Temple grounds. Aside from the annual Festival address, his last official public appearance had been nearly a decade ago, partly because it was a security nightmare, partly because AV conferencing obviated the need to be anywhere in person, but mainly because Cairn detested dealing with people face to face.

Usually one would get plenty of notice when the Cardinal

Hierophant was to visit somewhere. It was a whole production, replete with protocol and ritual, and an entourage of bodyguards, scribes, and other Cardinals with attendants. But every now and then the Cardinal Hierophant would go rogue, forgoing even bodyguards, to turn up unannounced and alone.

As Cairn marched down the corridors of the Temple hospital, word quickly spread. People stepped aside or hid in rooms to clear the way, allowing him to stride past. Cairn was the most powerful man on the planet. People admired him, respected him. But more than anything, they feared him. Which was how Cairn liked it. He understood the people better than any other leader in recent history. Despite this (or because of it) he also found them insufferable and hated having to interact with them. It wasn't a phobia, he just couldn't tolerate idiots, and practically everyone he met was an idiot.

Captain Marius was an idiot, but he was usually an efficient idiot. How he managed to get himself ambushed just outside the Temple gates was already under investigation, and something Cairn himself couldn't comprehend. He'd had a pathetically small squad of twenty-four Guard escorting the prisoners, so of course they were overwhelmed easily by just a few dozen rag-tag heretics. It had turned what was already a bad situation into a shocking farce, and made the Temple look weak. Or worse – vulnerable.

Cairn marched up to the reception counter of the hospital ward. The nurse opposite cowered instinctively, not expecting him to stop.

'Nurse.'

'Yes, Your Eminence?'

'I was told Captain Marius was on this ward. Can you direct me to him please.' Cairn was polite, but firm.

The nurse pointed the way. 'End of the corridor, room 2C.'

Cairn nodded and headed down the corridor. The moment he

left the nurse dashed away from the counter into the office where her colleagues were hiding, lest she be called upon again.

2C was a private room. As Cairn entered he found Marius sitting up in bed, an AV slate suspended in front of him on a reticulated stand, watching video of the Festival Square skirmish from several different angles. He looked up as Cairn walked in.

'Your Eminence,' Marius gasped. 'I'm honoured. Um … do sit down.'

Cairn had intended to blast the captain for his incompetence, but seeing him in a hospital bed out of uniform and suddenly humbled by the visit, threw him. The man's usual gruff exterior was absent and he looked passably human. Plus, his shock of red hair was almost comical without a helmet.

Cairn glanced at the chair offered for visitors but realised it would place him below Marius, so decided against it. 'No thank you, Captain.' Cairn stood beside the bed and looked down on Marius, his mood softened. 'How are you feeling?'

'My leg was broken when the GL crashed. It still hurts a bit but … it's okay. I should be good to leave by this afternoon.'

'Surely, you're not walking out of here.'

'No, Your Eminence. I'll be in a brace for a few weeks, but I can get around.' He tapped on the screen insistently. 'I want to start rounding up these fuckers before they try something like this again. They can't get away with it.' Marius then realised he just swore in front of the Cardinal Hierophant. 'Forgive me, Your Eminence.'

Cairn waved his hand dismissively. 'I agree, we must respond before this small victory becomes a catalyst for their cause.'

'They got lucky. Caught us off guard. I can assure you this won't happen again, Your Eminence. I'm gonna come down on these f – … people so hard they'll have to reach up to wipe their asses.'

Cairn glared at Marius, who dropped his head submissively. He admired the captain's dedication, but he was forgetting himself.

'The Church will not tolerate this kind of heresy, especially with the festival approaching. I want these radicals annihilated. Don't bother taking prisoners next time.'

This prompted Marius to remember: 'The prisoner. Your Eminence, I saw him. I had him in my sights.'

Cairn's eyed widened hopefully. 'Are you sure it was him?'

'Look,' Marius rewound the slate to the moment and zoomed in on the best angle. Cairn watched as Marius shot at Tobias from the GL car and the haze of electricity twisted away from its target to hit the fountain. 'That's gotta be him, right?'

He then watched as Marius's vehicle nose-dive into the pavement and flipped several times to land upside-down. Cairn's gaze was fixed on Tobias though, who stood by the fountain watching the crash. He had believed Asar when he said Tobias was alive, but seeing him actually standing there sent a chill up Cairn's spine. The Prophet Tobias – in the flesh. His hair was a tangled mess, his body pale and lean, but he was vibrant, alert, and most definitely alive. Cairn wanted at once to meet him, talk to him, sit at his feet and learn from him; and also destroy him, knowing the threat his mere existence posed to the Church.

As a young man Tobias had been his inspiration, his spiritual mentor, his saviour. Tobias was the reason Cairn joined the priesthood and devoted his life to the Church … to the Prophet. He had loved him. He still loved him. Everything Cairn did was for him. To protect his legacy. To preserve and reveal his doctrine as set forth in the *Shentama*. And now, as Cardinal Hierophant, to ensure Tobianism remained the world faith, and to safeguard the peace it had brought for generations. Revolutions he could deal with. He had quashed many a revolt in the past and would quash this one as well. But the Prophet Tobias reborn was a dangerous variable. Whether he supported the Church or not was irrelevant, because despite his personal feelings, Tobias simply did not belong to this Church anymore. The destiny of the Prophet had been written many years ago. This present Tobias was a man out of time.

'What I don't get,' mused Marius, interrupting Cairn's contemplation, 'is how much he looks like ... well ... the Prophet Tobias. I mean, you'd think he was related or something.'

'That's why he must be found,' Cairn insisted. 'The man is delusional. He actually believes he *is* Tobias. Imagine the damage he could do if people believed him. It's impossible of course, the man is quite insane. Just another poor wretch in need of medication. Unfortunately, in his present state of mind, he is extremely dangerous. In the interest of public safely the only solution is to kill him on sight. I pray you get another chance, Captain, before it's too late.'

'Yes, Your Eminence.'

Cairn turned to leave, but Marius called after him rashly. 'Forgive me, Your Eminence – '

Cairn turned slowly.

' – do you know what happened to my aide? Cadet Fairchild? He was in the vehicle with me when we crashed. Is he all right?'

Cairn was at first incensed by the request, but then saw the genuine concern Marius displayed for the young man in question. 'I understand he was killed.'

Marius took a deep breath, a wave of grief overtaking him. Cairn was astonished. He would never have expected such an emotional response from a hard case like Captain Marius. 'I'm sorry,' Cairn consoled.

Marius regaining his usual austere composure. 'Shit happens,' he joked half-heartedly,

Cairn left the room. As he walked back up the corridor he found, like Marius, he had to suppress his true feelings over what must be done. As much as he would love to meet the returned Prophet, speak with him, learn from him. He had to die. The great shame of it was this time no one would know the sacrifice he made for his Church; and if they did, no one would believe it. If only there was another way…

— ∞ —

Father Alban couldn't sit by and do nothing. Last night people were being killed right outside his church. It was not something a decent human being, let alone a man of the cloth, could ignore. He had no opinion one way or the other about the reasons for the violence. He didn't care what the so-called 'heretics' were supposed to have done. Nor did he judge the Church and the Temple Guard for their actions. He was not a political animal. He didn't claim to understand these things. He just knew he could not abandon people who were suffering or in fear for their lives. He had taken a risk helping Joanna, and didn't care if she was a heretic or a revolutionary or whatever the Church was calling them. She was afraid for her life and needed help. What he did was probably illegal, but to his mind, not at all unethical.

Finding the body of young Leonard lying on the street was the real epiphany though. Alban was ashamed of himself for staying cloistered within the safety of his church when outside people were dying. To argue he had been protecting the one person who came to his door asking for help was simply not good enough. He may have helped one, but he had failed so many others. He had failed Leonard. He had no idea if he could have saved him, but he didn't even try.

To make amends, Alban opened his church up with a prominent sign out the front: *"For those seeking asylum or protection from harm, whoever you may be. Welcome one and all."* Several people took him up on the offer and his church was rapidly becoming a refuge for anyone who had nowhere else to go. Alban left his novice, Oscar, in charge with instructions to prepare food and first aid for their guests, and to accept anyone who came to the door. Meanwhile, Alban scoured the streets. Whenever he found someone wounded or lost, he would direct them to the Church, then continue searching.

He heard about the fight in Festival Square. Not from the AV, which had stopped reporting anything about rebel activities in the city, but from people on the street. Approaching the city centre he encountered several groups of people fleeing the scene. They did not require his assistance. Indeed, most avoided him because he wore the robes of a priest. But he posed no threat so they just passed him by.

One such group felt 'brave' enough to taunt him as they passed, pointing their power gloves and threatening to fire upon him. They were excitable and full of bluster, like teenagers on a tear. Harmless enough, Alban thought, but as they had weapons he retreated into a narrow laneway for protection, stopping here till they were gone.

As the noise of the group abated he became aware of someone breathing heavily behind him. He could not see them in the dark, but it sounded like they were in pain.

'Hello?' he called. 'Are you alright?'

… No answer.

He ventured further into the lane, his eyes slowly adjusting to the gloom. The streets of Lorna were generally very clean, but some back streets like this, particularly in the west, tended to get forgotten about. There was a pile of rubbish at the far end – boxes, old equipment of one sort or another, discarded packaging, and what smelt like food refuse or worse. As he neared the largest pile of debris he spotted small movements and the form of a near-naked man became clear. The man was shrouded in shadow, but he appeared to be badly wounded – Alban could smell the blood.

'It's all right,' Alban said softly. 'I can help you. You can trust me.' He knelt beside the man and saw he was holding his left shoulder. A bullet wound by the look of it, high against the collar bone. The man was conscious, but only just. His breathing was shallow and laboured. With every breath he took a blood-soaked sucking noise gurgled from the hole in his chest.

Alban slowly raised his lemnis medallion to the wound, enabling the holo-display. The embedded comkey scanned the area, showing a 3D simulation of the damaged tissue underneath. The bullet had nicked the top of his lung, which explained why he was having difficulty breathing. It had otherwise passed clean through his shoulder, damaging muscle tissue, but no bone.

Alban touched the man's wrist gently. The man turned abruptly, startled, as if he hadn't realised anyone else was there until now. His eyes gaped with confusion and pain staring into Alban's face. He was in a daze, unable to comprehend what he was looking at. Or perhaps he was simply too weak to process it.

Alban recognised the man instantly. But that was impossible. Every year he had looked upon that face through the mists of the cryonic chamber. He was one of a handful of people alive who had actually seen the face of the Prophet. But it couldn't be him. The body of the Prophet was safe within the Temple and … or was it? This man was alive. Such a thing simply was not possible.

'Tobias?' Alban whispered.

The man didn't react. It wasn't him. Of course it wasn't him. What was he thinking? He sure looked like him though. Whoever he was he was badly wounded. Alban found a nearby piece of plastic wrap, tried to wipe it clean, then placed it over the hole in the man's chest. A crude but effective dressing. Instantly his breathing became easier. The soft plastic was sucked against the hole with each breath, glued in place by thickening blood, helping to seal the wound.

Alban carefully wrapped his arms around the man's neck and legs and lifted him up. He was not heavy and did not struggle. He was too weak. The man remained in a conscious daze as Alban carried him to the Church as fast as he could. This one he would not let die.

There is no such thing as miracle
That which we call miracle
Is a natural process of the All–In–All

Shentama
– Stanza 165

Rene was not one for parties, he was just glad to be reunited with Joanna. He was also still worried about Dan. Everyone else though was having a riotous good time. They had done something incredibly daring and got away with it. No one had died – a remarkable achievement given the odds; and no one was seriously injured. Over five hundred of their comrades had been rescued from custody and transportation to Gerda. It was the first blow struck against the tyranny of the Church. The revolution had begun, and they were winning.

Rene was ambivalent about the whole thing. He was of course grateful to have been rescued and reunited with Joanna, and for better or worse he was now one of them – a heretic, political dissident, and revolutionary. So while he accepted his new status as enemy of the state, he also knew he did not belong with these people. He had never been a devout Tobianist, but he still identified as one. Some of his new comrades were so zealously anti-Tobianist he was uncomfortable even listening to them.

He sat with Joanna in the corner of the room and watched as Kane held court. Rene wasn't sure he agreed with Kane politically, but he liked the man. He was a born leader – charismatic, physically imposing, and good looking. Sexy even. He had an air of authority and confidence that made you trust him. He also appeared to be something of a ladies man, with the women of the group all vying for his attention. Plus, for some reason Rene couldn't fathom, Kane had taken a shine to him.

'What do you think of our fearless leader, Kane?' he asked Joanna.

'You know him better than I do.'

'First impression?'

'He's a bit full of himself,' Joanna said plainly.

'Is that a bad thing?'

'Depends where it's coming from, selfishness or ego.'

'What's the difference?'

'It's like receiving a gift. Will he be satisfied with a thank-you, or does he expect something in return?'

It was an odd analogy, but Rene understood. 'You think he's a mercenary.'

'I don't know,' Joanna admitted. 'But when the shit hits the fan, will he be thinking about us,' she indicated everyone in the room, 'or about himself?'

'When, or if?'

Joanna looked him square in the eye. 'This won't last,' she murmured. With Rene, she hid nothing. Her brutal honesty could be a buzz-kill – but it was real.

'God, I've missed you,' he said.

Joanna smiled back. They had both been through the worst couple of days of their lives. It felt longer. To be together now in a rebel safe-house enjoying themselves was a surreal experience. Rene felt guilty. He didn't really belong here. These were Dan's people. But he was starting to get it.

He observed his new comrades. He didn't know any of them, but they seemed a good lot – despite being *heretics*. Whatever their religious or political views, he was not that different to them. We all want the same thing, he thought. It's how we go about getting it that's the problem.

When they leapt out of the Gerda transport Dan had thought Rene was right behind him. It wasn't till he was well across the Square and into the adjoining parkland that he discovered he was alone. From this distant vantage he had scanned the Square for Rene, watching as prisoners ran in all directions to escape the melee; or as others stayed to fight alongside the rebel ambushers in yellow scarves. Dan considered going back, but only for a second. It was too dangerous. With no sign of Rene he turned and kept running. It was a decision he regretted immediately … and yet he kept running.

Surrounded by other fleeing prisoners, he crossed the park and lost himself in the streets of Lorna. Everyone went their separate ways, until eventually he found himself running alone. Tears filled his eyes. The wind on his face was cold and sharp, but that's not why he was crying. He was grateful to have escaped transport to Gerda, but that's not why he was crying. And still he ran.

Rene was right: choosing a side meant nothing. Dan now understood it was not what one said, but what one did, that mattered. Your actions define who you are. And he was a fair-weather revolutionary, who talked big but bolted at the first sign of trouble. A traitor who had abandoned not just his comrades in battle, but his one true friend. And so Dan cried, because he now knew he was a coward and a fraud.

Dan didn't stop running until he was sick with exhaustion. Finally collapsing into the gutter, he wept with guilt and self-loathing. It was because of him Rene and Joanna got caught up in all this to begin with. All because he stupidly trusted Bartholomew, who had followed him to their apartment that night and betrayed them to the Temple Guard. Dan's shame turned to hatred. Barty was the real traitor. He had been working for the Temple all along. Posing as a dissident leader to gain their trust, only to betray them when the time was right. It was because of him they had been arrested. He had probably betrayed the rest of the group as well. Barty had to be dealt with before he could harm anyone else.

Dan rose to his feet with a new determination. Bartholomew had to die.

— ∞ —

Rene watched as Kane enjoyed the attention of the ladies. He then noticed across the room, Rohan, also watching Kane closely. He seemed to be studying him and was not at all interested in the party or what anyone else was doing. He just stared at Kane. It was kind of creepy.

'Jo,' Rene nodded, pointing Rohan out to her.

'Who is he?' she asked.

'His name's Rohan. He was in the cell with Dan and me back at the Temple, along with Kane.'

'He's kind of creepy,' Joanna observed.

Rene smiled in agreement. 'Said he was on a secret mission.

Though it all sounded a bit deluded. I think he might have psychological issues.'

'You mean he's nuts?'

'… He just came across as rather odd.'

'Why does Kane keep him around, do you think?'

'Don't know,' Rene admitted. 'Perhaps I should ask him?'

'I doubt you'll get him alone tonight.'

Rohan suddenly turned and looked directly at Rene, as if he had felt Rene's eyes burning into him. Rene remained impassive but held Rohan's gaze. At first intimidating, Rohan's resolve faded as Rene simply stared him down. Rohan eventually dropped his gaze, then walked away.

Joanna observed this. 'Creepy, nuts and dangerous. You keep well away from him.' She was a stern mother protecting her child from mixing with the wrong crowd.

Rene watched as Rohan left the room hurriedly, bumping into a woman carrying … a primate of some kind. The animal squealed in protest as Rohan pushed past.

'What is that?' Rene asked.

Joanna laughed. 'That's Elly. She's a bonobo.'

'A what?'

'It's like a chimp.'

The red-haired woman carrying the bonobo weaved through the crowd. Everyone moved aside for them but were otherwise indifferent, like this was normal. She spotted Joanna and headed toward them.

'They're coming over here,' Rene said apprehensively.

'Don't worry. She won't bite.'

'They bite?'

'Jo,' the woman greeted as she stopped before them.

'Althea, this is Rene.'

'Pleased to meet you.' Althea offered her hand. As Rene shook it she appeared to recognise him. A kind of déjà vu moment. Althea shook the feeling away. 'This is Elly.'

Rene turned to the bonobo, uncertain. 'Do I shake her hand, too?' Elly held his gaze disconcertingly.

'Don't worry,' Joanna reassured. 'She does that. She's just sizing you up.'

Elly extended her hand, but not to shake his. She raised it to Rene's face and placed it gently against his cheek. Rene was startled but didn't balk. Her penetrating eyes looked deep into his. Elly turned to Althea and signed something as she spoke – a few unintelligible but very articulate grunts.

'She recognises you,' Althea translated.

'I'm pretty sure I'd remember if we'd met before,' Rene said.

'I thought I recognised you, too,' Althea added. 'But you're right. I don't believe we've met. You do look familiar though. You're not an actor or something are you?'

Rene laughed. 'No. I'm nobody.'

Elly spoke again, more insistent. She pointed to her own eyes, then at Rene's.

Althea was confused. 'No Elly. That's not possible.'

She signed it again.

'What is she saying?' Rene asked.

'She thinks … you're someone else we met recently.'

'Who?'

'It's not important.' Althea covered Elly's hand with her own to lower it and stop her signing. 'Shush.' She returned her attention to Rene and Joanna. 'We're going to be a bit crowded tonight,' Althea said, changing the subject, 'but I have a room for the two of you on the third floor. Its small, but you'll have it to yourselves.

That's assuming anyone gets any sleep tonight.' She gestured at the celebrations happening around them. 'This could go on for a while.'

'I guess they're entitled,' Rene said. 'Today was quite a victory.'

Althea took exception to this remark. 'You think so?'

'You don't?'

'Violence is no solution. I'm here because I have nowhere else to go. That doesn't mean I approve of what they're doing or how they're doing it.'

'Neither do I, really,' Rene responded sympathetically. 'But I'd be a hypocrite to say I wasn't grateful. Otherwise, I'd be in a Gerda prison cell by now.'

'I'm sorry,' Althea conceded. 'As dissident acts go, it was pretty successful; and I'm glad no one was killed. This isn't the end of it, though. The Church is bound to respond, and it won't be pleasant.' Then she smiled. 'But let's not think about that tonight. Tonight, we are safe, and against all odds you two have found each other. Miracles do sometimes happen.'

'A miracle is nothing more than one's destiny coinciding with that of another,' Rene quoted. 'Impossible, yet inevitable.'

Althea looked at him in astonishment.

'It's from the *Shentama*,' he explained.

'I know. But you say it like … '

'Like what?'

'Never mind.' Althea turned to Joanna. 'You look after this one, my girl. I'm guessing there is more to him than meets the eye.'

To fear death is to fear change
To fear change is to fear life
To fear life is to learn nothing

Shentama
– Stanza 122

D an sat across the road from his group's meeting place. It was late afternoon when he had first arrived. He sat patiently through the night and into the morning, just watching for any activity in the seemingly abandoned house. In the distance he heard occasional gunfire, and once a GL car loaded with Temple Guards drove past his hiding spot, patrolling the streets. Otherwise the streets were surprisingly quiet. Curfew must have been reinstated.

As morning light chased away the darkness he spotted Barty approaching the house. A surge of loathing filled Dan. Two days ago the man had been a close friend. A confidante. Now Dan felt nothing but hatred for him.

He watched as Barty entered the house. Looking each way to check the street was clear, Dan finally left his hiding spot, and dashed across the road. As he approached, his comkey automatically opened the front door with a soft *thunk*. Cracking the door he peered inside and scanned the hallway. No sign of Barty. He slowly entered, listening intently for any movement within.

Silence…

He went into the lounge that was their usual meeting place.

Empty.

Dan made his way upstairs. Barty must be in the office, he figured – but this room was also empty, as was the rest of the upper floor. *Where had he gone?*

Moving back downstairs, Dan headed for the rear of the house and the kitchen. As he crossed the threshold a door opened behind him. Turning, he saw Barty at the top of the basement stairs, his arm raised as a haze of electricity shot from his power-gloved hand. Dan instantly fell to the ground, paralysed. Barty stepped forward, the haze still triggered and drilling into Dan's frozen body unnecessarily. Barty finally released the arc, standing feet astride Dan's head on the floor. He fell to one knee, leaning over so Dan could see him silhouette against the sunlit hallway. Dan was conscious – but completely paralysed.

'Daniel,' Bartholomew chided. 'You are just too predictable. I knew you would come back here looking for me. What else could you do?'

Bartholomew tied Dan's hands behind his back with self-bonding cord, the same stuff the Temple Guards used. 'Let me guess. Revenge, yes? You think I betrayed you. You think I'm working for the Temple. Have been all these years. And that everything I said, everything we ever talked about, is a lie. That's what you think, isn't it?'

'– Bastard!' Dan managed to gargle. He tried to move but his muscles still weren't responding. All he could do was twitch.

'Don't worry. You'll be able to move again soon.' Bartholomew then sighed heavily. 'I just wish you could understand … what it's like to lead. To be in charge. The responsibility can be quite … intoxicating.

People look up to you. Respect you. And opportunities arise that you would never have expected. There is a greater good we must consider. And sometimes, sacrifices need to be made.'

Dan thrashed violently. He was getting his feeling back now. 'You're a goddamn psychopath!'

Bartholomew grabbed Dan by the collar and pulled him to his feet, leaning him against the wall. 'I always liked you, Daniel. You have a passion I find quite endearing. An intellectual dimwit. I don't expect you to understand this, but everything I did was for your own good. If I hadn't turned you in you'd already be dead.'

'And what about my friends? They had nothing to do with this. With us.'

'Collateral damage,' Bartholomew dismissed. 'Though they must surely have been guilty of something. Everyone is.'

Bartholomew shoved Dan down the hall to the basement door. 'Come along. I have something I want to show you.'

He led Dan downstairs into the basement of the house. Dan had been here only once before, when they first made this their headquarters. It was damp, dark and quite secure, with just the one entrance. He'd never had cause to come down here again since. Meanwhile Bartholomew had turned the space into a dungeon. Battery lanterns lined the walls, filling the room with a pale orange light. There was a large metal table in the centre, and what appeared to be various instruments of torture lined up against the far wall. Before he saw all this though Dan could smell the blood. It was so intense it made him want to puke. When he saw what was on the table – he did.

'Gabrielle,' Bartholomew confirmed with a heavy sigh. 'I really thought she'd have more to say. Seems all that boasting about shadow contacts and meetings in the AQ was all hokum. Just a little girl trying to impress us with tales of mischief and intrigue. Such a waste.'

Dan composed himself and tried again to look at what remained of the beautiful young Gabrielle. Then turned to Bartholomew. 'I will kill you,' he promised.

Bartholomew was unperturbed. He pulled out a chair for Dan to sit on, placing it nearby. 'No doubt you'll try. But first, would you like something to eat? You've been on the run for twenty-four hours. I doubt you've had time to eat or drink anything.'

'I'm fine,' Dan lied. He was starving.

'Surely a drink,' Bartholomew said as he wandered across the room to a cabinet containing several forms of alcohol. Removing his power glove, he poured two glasses of whiskey and brought one over to Dan.

'Do sit down, won't you?' It was more of a command that a request. Dan sat. Bartholomew held the glass to Dan's lips and tipped it up until Dan couldn't help but drink from it.

'Better?'

Dan didn't answer, though he really needed that drink.

Bartholomew pulled out another chair and sat a discrete distance from Dan, sipping on his whiskey.

'Now isn't this civilised?' Bartholomew commented. 'Our relationship may have hit an impasse, but that doesn't mean we can't talk things out man to man. I want you to understand why I've acted the way I have. Why I lied to you all about my true purpose. I don't suppose it matters much, least of all to you. But I would like to explain myself before I kill you. You see, I do consider you a friend, Daniel. Perhaps the closest friend I've ever had. That's why I had you arrested. Otherwise, you'd have ended up like Gabrielle there. Transported to Gerda you would be out of the city and have had a much better chance to survive what is to come. I was doing you a favour. But it seems that is not to be your fate. Your fate lies here with me.'

Bartholomew flung his glass aside, letting it smash against the wall. He leapt out of his chair and began strutting about the room. 'And I tell you now Daniel, a great reckoning is upon us. Far greater than that which followed the Prophet's death two hundred years ago. More purifying than the Great Purge. We are at the cusp of the greatest spiritual revolution the world has ever known. I don't know where it will lead us, but I do know where it begins. Right here. Right now. Yesterday was the first battle of the greatest war in history. And you were a part of it, my friend. And so am I. As the Prophet said: Destiny and free will go hand in hand. We are destined, you and I, to be a part of this. We just have to will it so.'

Bartholomew moved in on Dan suddenly. Eye to eye. 'I could kill you right now if I wanted. But I don't want to. I believe we have a greater part to play in this yet, Daniel. You and I are destined for bigger things than this. What do you say?'

Bartholomew had worked himself into a frenzy, and now awaited Dan's response with eager anticipation.

'I say you're stark raving bonkers,' Dan told him. 'And I *will* kill you.'

Bartholomew turned away in a huff, greatly disappointed. 'Ohhh, Daniel. Daniel Daniel Daniel. I really thought you would understand. Oh, well.' Bartholomew picked up a large bloodied knife from the table, the same blade he had recently used on poor Gabrielle, and turned to Dan. 'Guess I'm gonna have to kill you, after all.'

Dan stood up, ready to do whatever he could to defend himself, when a noise was heard from above. It stopped Barty in his tracks. Someone was in the house.

'Now who could that be?' Bartholomew joked. He turned to Dan: 'Sit down,' he ordered, brandishing the knife.

Dan sat.

Bartholomew returned to the cabinet and pulled on his power glove, then headed for the stairs. 'Stay,' he told Dan, as if he were a recalcitrant dog. With one eye on Dan and the other on the basement door above him, Bartholomew climbed the stairs.

This was likely Dan's best chance of escaping, though with his hands bound he couldn't see how. Bartholomew stopped halfway up the stairs. They could hear someone moving around. He checked on Dan, still sitting in the chair.

Then came a woman's voice: 'Hello? Is there anyone here?'

It was Maya. She had no idea what she was walking into.

'Down here!' Bartholomew called. He backed down the stairs keeping a close eye on both the door and Dan, positioning himself at the bottom of the stairs a few paces from Dan. 'Fate and free will converge yet again,' he muttered. 'What do you think her part is to be in all this, my friend? Innocent victim or saviour?'

Dan weighed up his options. If he called out for Maya to run, Bartholomew was sure to catch her up and dispatch her before she could get out of the house. But it might give himself a chance to escape. If he did nothing, she would be walking into a trap and they would both be at Barty's mercy. Neither was an ideal scenario. Dan figured, as Maya entered, Bartholomew would have to split his attention between them, and there might be an opportunity to overpower him. It was a risk, but what else was there to do? He was not about to use Maya as a decoy to try save his own skin.

Maya appeared at the door. 'Hello?'

Bartholomew put his hands behind his back, hiding his weapons. 'Maya, my dear. We're down here.'

'Barty?'

'Yes. Come on down, it's quite safe.'

Maya cautiously descended the stairs. 'Why are you in the

basement? And what's that smell?'

'It's safer down here if they decide to raid the house. And as for the smell. Well… it is a basement, after all.'

Maya was still unsure and was making her way very slowly down the stairs. 'Who's down here with you?'

'Daniel is here. Say hello Daniel.'

'Maya – '

At that moment, as Maya turned to Dan's voice, Bartholomew raised his left hand and hazed her with the power glove. Maya was hit by the arc in the chest and fell hard, tumbling down the rest of the stairs. At the same moment Dan leapt from his seat and lunged headlong at Bartholomew. Barty was expecting this and simultaneously raised his right arm with the knife taking a giant swing at Dan. The blade came down on Dan's back, cutting through his shirt and into his skin, but there wasn't a lot of force behind it, so the cut was not so deep. Dan head-butted Barty in the chest and forced him to the ground.

As he fell Barty turned the power glove on Dan. But as the arc pulled away from Maya it caught on the metal railing of the stairs. Dan drove his heel hard into Barty's chest. Barty bucked with the pain, pulling both his arms inward. The power glove arc dislodged from the railing and found a new home against the blade of the knife held in his other hand. The electrical haze arced from the glove into the knife, up Barty's arm and through his body till it flowed through the blood-wet stone floor and into the earth. Barty's paralysed fingers were locked in place and the glove remained triggered, the current running through him for a full minute till the warning beep sounded and the power drained completely. The weapon was not intended for such prolonged use as it could be fatal. Nerve cells became irreparably damaged, the heart would stop, lungs unable to breath, and the brain turned to scrambled eggs.

Dan knew this, so rather than help Barty he moved across to Maya now lying at the base of the stairs.

'Maya! Are you all right?'

Maya sat up groggy and bruised, but otherwise, it seemed, unharmed.

'What the fuck?' she exclaimed, then looked across at Barty, his clothes covered in Gabrielle's blood, his body still twitching with electrical current in its final death throes. 'What the FUCK!?'

— ∞ —

The party was over. Most of the revellers had skulked off to their beds or slept where they lay. Rene was returning from the bathroom, about to join Joanna in the small bedroom they had been assigned, when he spotted Kane sitting alone in the upstairs office. His head bowed deep in thought.

'Can't sleep?' Rene asked through the door.

Kane looked up, then cocked his head for Rene to join him. 'Come in.'

Rene entered and sat in the chair opposite.

Kane was a little drunk, which put him in a contemplative mood. 'I'm astonished today went as well as it did,' he admitted softly. 'We got lucky.'

'Choice, not chance, determines your destiny,' Rene said, quoting the second tenet. 'You chose well.' Rene had never been one to quote the *Shentama*, but lately it came naturally to him.

'I thought you weren't religious.'

'I'm not,' Rene told him.

'Did you choose to be arrested?' Kane mused. 'Did we choose to be put in the same cell together? Was it choice that brought both you and Joanna to this very house?'

'You brought me here,' Rene responded. 'You were looking out for me. Why?'

Kane paused, as if this hadn't occurred to him before. 'I don't know, exactly. It just seemed important.'

'What? That I escape?'

'That you survive,' Kane stated plainly. 'Of all the people I've met in this life, Rene, no-one has impressed me as much as you.'

Rene was taken aback. 'You barely know me.'

Kane nodded agreement. 'Hmm. And yet…'

'I don't know what you expect of me. I'm just a writer. And not a very good one.'

Kane smiled. 'I was once a teacher. Ancient history…'

Rene wasn't sure if he meant that was his subject, or it was such a long time ago. Kane slipped into reminiscence. Rene let the silence sit. It was a welcome calm after the storm of the party. He was about to ask about Rohan, when something occurred to Kane, and he opened a drawer in his desk.

'Here, I want you to have this.' He handed Rene a pen. Not just any pen. It was a weighty, gold-plated, finely crafted writing tool, with a textured grip, pressure-sensitive nib, and embedded scribe software. The kind of pen given as a retirement gift to one truly beloved and respected.

'Oh no. I couldn't possibly – '

'– You're a writer, aren't you? You'll get better use out of it than me. Take it,' Kane insisted.

'Thanks.'

'Promise me one thing. You can write as many lies as you like. But with this pen, you write only the truth.' Kane was very drunk Rene decided. 'Promise.'

'I promise.'

'Good. Now go to your woman. She's prob'ly waiting up for you.'

Rene made for the door.

'And don't worry about Rohan,' Kane said after him. 'Let me deal with him.'

Joanna was fast asleep when Rene entered the room, so he curled up beside her and closed his eyes. Just lying next to her was enough for tonight, and despite the unfamiliar environment, he slept peacefully.

To be free of emotion
To travel the path yielding and supple
Without judgment or enmity
Is to abide in the All—In—All

Shentama
– Stanza 88

A noise woke Rene. Whether it was real or in a dream he couldn't be sure, but he found himself wide awake, feeling something wasn't right. He listened for a moment … nothing.

He checked on Joanna. She was sound asleep. Rene climbed out of bed, careful not to wake her, pulling on his pants and moving to the door. He opened it slowly, scanning the hallway. Nothing unusual. Outside the house dawn was breaking, and an early morning haze of blue light filtered through the blackened windows.

Rene headed downstairs. He found others still asleep on the couches and chairs or sprawled out on the floor. The whole house it seemed was fast asleep. Creeping past his snoring comrades, Rene made for the front of the property and looked out the side window. Since this old house didn't have a two-way on the door, a small clear circle had been scratched out of the camouflage to allow one to peer

185

outside. This was the extent of their surveillance. Cameras would have been too conspicuous. Even micro-wireless cameras, which are effectively invisible to the naked eye, leave a traceable electronic signature. Most forms of wireless technology were banned. To avoid comkey detection a Faraday field had been setup around the house, making it an electronic black spot, aside from a few credible diversion signatures which made the place look like a conventional family home on the network. No more, no less. As a heretic, one had to be wary of being constantly watched and monitored. It was a lifestyle Rene was still getting used to.

He looked at the street outside through the peephole. It was a bit gloomy, thanks to the pre-dawn light and the state of repair of the old houses in this part of Lorna, but it was otherwise quiet and empty. Perhaps his imagination was just getting the better of him.

As Rene turned he found the bonobo Elly standing right behind him, and he let out a startled cry. 'Ah! Shit. Elly. What are you doing here?'

Elly didn't answer. She couldn't of course, but she didn't even seem to acknowledge the question. Instead, she looked Rene square in the eyes. It was that same disquieting look of recognition she had given him last night. To anyone else her behavior might have been intimidating, but Rene saw a cool intelligence behind her eyes. He knelt down to her level.

'What is it?'

Elly took his hand and led him down the hall into the kitchen. She led him to a chair, then left the room momentarily. When she came back, she was carrying a copy of the *Shentama*. It was an old hardback copy, with a smooth white cover, worn edges and a creased spine, but good care had been taken of it otherwise. Elly handed it to him.

Rene felt the weight of it. One rarely saw bound books like this anymore. They were antiques, relics. This one would have been quite valuable, and probably illegal. The *Shentama* was of course free to anyone, but only the official Temple-sanctioned AV edition, which was regularly updated. Old printed books like this were found only in the Temple library, or some privately approved collections. Rene had seen one only once before, at university. His Faith & Religion tutor, being an old-school kind of guy, had an approved pressing of the modern *Shentama* that he used for his classes. He would have to update it every year and destroy the old one, but that volume wasn't nearly as impressive as the one Rene now held. Also, this old book was thinner and smaller than modern pressing; less than a hundred pages. He was holding a piece of history. He carefully opened the book. It creaked a little as he lifted the cover, a gentle pressing of cardboard and paper. Inside the front cover was a handwritten inscription:

> *For Althea*
> *The truth lies buried in the past.*
> *Let this book be your guide to finding it.*
> *With the greatest of love*
> *Jason*

Below this was the publisher's inscription and date of publication – 2062. The book was over a hundred years old, from before the Great Purge. This was beyond rare. How on earth did Althea, or this Jason, come by such a treasure?

Rene turned the page gently to reveal a photo of the author – the Prophet Tobias. Rene had not seen this picture before. It didn't show the regal, contemplative man of God that was the usual representation of the Prophet, but was instead a smiling, casual, almost humorous likeness of the man. He wore the white and ochre robes he was traditionally seen wearing, but they were more colourful and vibrant than other pictures revealed. It was an altogether different side of the Prophet. A more human side. One Rene had never seen in modern editions of the *Shentama*, or indeed in any AV records of the Prophet that had survived over the years.

Elly pointed to the picture, touching the smiling face of Tobias, then raised her finger and touched Rene on the face. As if to say: *'This .... is you.'*

'No, Elly. This isn't me. I am not Tobias.'

Elly repeated the action: *'This ... is .... you.'*

She was so adamant about it Rene had to take her seriously. He tried to think what exactly she meant. He was reminded of the encounter at Festival Square, looking into the eyes of a man who looked like the Prophet and yet was himself. He couldn't explain it, and it had troubled him ever since.

Before Rene could think of another response a sound from beneath the house diverted his attention. Someone was coming up the secret entrance behind the linen closet. A gentle click and the false door unlocked. Both Rene and Elly watched as a hand pushed the shelving aside and Rohan emerged from the shadows. He saw the two of them watching him and froze. They all looked at each other for moment, then Elly grabbed the book off the table, and fled into the next room.

Rene was left looking across at Rohan.

At first Rohan was startled to find anyone awake, then confused by Elly's wary retreat, then finally angry that Rene was just sitting there watching him.

'What?' he blurted.

'Good morning, Rohan,' Rene said calmly.

'You spying on me?'

'No. Should I be?'

Rohan didn't quite know how to respond to this. Finally, he said: 'I'll cut you some slack 'cause you're new here, but don't get any ideas. We got shit going on around here you have no inklin'. You know, deep cover shit. So you just keep to yourself, all right, and don't ask questions. S'not your place. Not your fuckin' place. You got it?'

Rene was not the least bit intimidated. Rohan was clearly hiding something. 'Of course,' he answered calmly. 'We must all know our place, after all.'

Rohan thought about this a second and found it a satisfactory answer. Subtext was clearly not his strong suit. 'Good. Didn't mean to tear you a new one just now. But you know, can't be too careful.' Rohan closed the false door to the secret passage and stepped forward into the kitchen.

'I quite agree,' Rene said.

'What you doin' up anyways?'

Rene wasn't about to get into a conversation with Rohan about his intuitions. 'Came down for a glass of water.'

'Right.' Rohan looked at the table. 'Where is it then?'

'What?'

'You're glass of water.'

'I haven't made it yet.'

'Why not?'

Rene indicated the room Elly had retreated into. 'I was waylaid.'

'Huh?' Rohan seemed not to understand the word, but he worked it out. 'Oh. Yeah.' From the contempt in his voice he was clearly not a fan of Elly's. 'Don't know why we have to have that bloody monkey around. Weirdest fuckin' pet I ever seen.'

'She's a bonobo.'

'… Whatever.'

Rohan made a move to leave the room. Rene remained in his seat. 'You comin' up?' he asked Rene.

'I still have to get my water.'

'I'll wait for you.'

'That's very nice of you, but there's no need.'

'Hurry up.' Rohan stood by the door unmoving. It seemed he wasn't about to leave Rene alone in the kitchen.

Rene rose to his feet and went to the cupboard. He took his time searching for a glass, got some water from the fridge, and poured himself a drink. Rohan remained by the door watching. Rene wasn't concerned, he found it all rather amusing actually.

He took a slow sip of his drink… then finally turned to Rohan and smiled. 'That's better.'

Rene walked across the room, past Rohan and into the hallway. As he reached the stairs he turned and saw Rohan still standing by the kitchen door – watching him intently. Rene knew now what had woken him. He'd sensed Rohan's clandestine return. Somehow he *saw* the threads of impending possibility – a premonition of imminent deed. Normally he would discount such feelings, but given everything he'd experienced the past few days he intended to give these strange sensations more credence in future. Who knows, the bonobo might be on to something.

'Good night,' Rene said cheerfully as he headed upstairs.

Rohan glared after him.

— ∞ —

The Executive Council was not being very cooperative. The Church had endured crises in the past, and Cairn had always managed to steer them safe. What doesn't kill you makes you stronger, right? If they knew the real danger now facing the Church, rather than questioning him, they would be grovelling at his feet begging for him to save them all. Greater good be damned, all they really cared about was their own skin. They lived in constant fear of losing power. Not that they actually had any of course, but the perception of power through ritual was a compelling façade. That's what ritual was for. They were sheep, they just didn't realise it.

Even Kasper, who knew the truth, didn't fully comprehend the implications. Cairn could see the future. He was no mystic, to him it was just obvious. There were two very clear paths – one where the Church survived and grew stronger, and one where it didn't. For the sake of the world the Church had to prevail. The alternative was anarchy.

'Your Eminence,' it was Cardinal Ignatius, a deceptively handsome man with thick black hair, who rarely said what he meant or meant what he said. 'I'm sure I speak for all of us when I say how grateful we are that you took such decisive action. I for one would not have been so bold as to incite a public manhunt in pursuit of a single escaped prisoner, or mandate the violent suppression of rebels that were posing no threat to the Church whatsoever.' The man's barely veiled contempt for Cairn was obvious. 'These actions, while initiated no doubt with the best of intentions, have resulted in Lorna becoming a city under siege. We have violence in the streets. Temple Guard in the infirmary. A dozen or more citizens killed. And for what? The rebels are now stronger than ever, emboldened by their ambush right outside the Temple gates. And this escapee, if he even exists, is still at large.' Ignatius fancied himself an orator and liked using big words and fancy phrasing. Cairn found it pretentious. 'Your Eminence, how can you possibly justify continuing this course of action? No good has come of it, and every hour you persist damages the reputation of the Church and the Temple City.'

'Have you quite finished?' Cairn asked Ignatius flatly. 'Have you all quite finished?' Cairn had listened patiently as most of the Cardinals got up and had their say. It wasn't often they felt compelled to speak out against Cairn, so whenever they felt the urge he let them speak their mind. It made no difference. Their opinions were irrelevant. But at least they felt as if they'd accomplished something. They felt heard.

'We will continue the hunt for the escapee. He is more dangerous than any of you realise. You cannot understand this because you are not privy to all the facts. But I assure you, his capture is crucial to the security of the Church.' Cairn wasn't about to tell them who the escapee was, but he had to throw them a crumb to explain his actions. 'However, in light of the over-zealous behavior by some members of the public last night, the mandate has been repealed. The Temple Guard will continue the search, without the assistance of the public. As for the rebels, I think the attack on our prisoner transports demonstrates just how organised and dangerous they've become. We are no longer dealing with a bunch of misfit heretics boasting to each other in coffee shops about what they will do when the revolution comes. The revolution is here gentlemen. It's on our doorstep and is growing in force. They caught us by surprise yesterday, but this will not happen again. We must respond swiftly and decisively. We must crush this heresy before it infects all of Lorna. Make no mistake, gentlemen, we are at war. The very survival of Tobianism is at stake. Any man, regardless of rank, who does not support this holy cause is himself a heretic and will be dealt with as such. Do you all understand?'

The council to a man nodded agreement, even Ignatius.

Kasper turned to the Cardinal Hierophant with an almost defiant glare. He was clearly not comfortable with this, even though he understood better than any of them the reasoning for it.

Cairn returned the gaze. 'You have something to add, Kasper?'

As one the Council turned to Kasper, perhaps hoping he would speak up on their behalf; or perhaps they were waiting for him to cut his own throat so they could watch Cairn carry out his threat. Kasper's seat was the right hand of the Cardinal Hierophant. They couldn't wait for him to make a wrong move and be removed from office. The daggers were out.

Cairn held Kasper's gaze, unperturbed. He knew Kasper was just waiting for the right moment to challenge him, to assume control of the Council and the Church. It's how he himself came to office, after all. An internal coup that made the subsequent election by the caucus of Temple Cardinals a fait accompli. Cairn was prepared for whatever Kasper might try. But it seemed the time was not yet right. Kasper lowered his eyes submissively. It was not capitulation, more a tactical retreat. 'No, Your Eminence,' he said steadily.

The Council members turned away. Kasper would not be their champion today.

Dan and Maya retreated into the house and locked the basement, shutting out the horrific scene of a mutilated Gabrielle and the electrocuted body of Bartholomew, their former leader, lying on the blood-soaked floor. They weren't sure what to do next. Neither wanted to go back down there and 'clean up'. Neither dared leave the house. So they sat in the kitchen drinking coffee, trying to behave as if everything was normal, even though both their lives were changed forever by what had just happened in that basement.

'I don't know if you knew this,' Maya said, breaking the silence. 'But Gabrielle liked you.'

'I know.'

'I mean …. Really liked you.'

'I liked her,' Dan said.

'I think Barty was jealous of you.'

'I'm glad he's dead,' Dan said plainly. 'I'm just sorry I was too late.'

'You couldn't help it.' Maya wasn't trying to make him feel better. She was just stating the facts. 'Thank you, by the way.'

Both of them were still in a weird state of shock. Grief might come later, but for now, they were just thankful to be alive.

'Gabrielle was the main reason I came to these meetings,' Dan admitted. 'Aside from, you know, the whole changing the future thing.'

'No-one else?'

Dan regarded Maya. He knew she liked him, and while she was very cute, she was also shy. Not really his type. 'Guess it's just you and me now, kid.'

Maya smiled weakly. If the circumstances were different she would have taken that as a definite maybe. For now she was happy just to have someone to talk to.

'Why did you join this group anyway?' Dan asked her. 'You never struck me as very rebellious.'

'It was a way to meet people,' she admitted coyly, then more ardently: 'And I can be rebellious when I want. I'm just not good with crowds.'

'We never had more than ten people here.'

Maya dropped her head, her cheeks flushing.

'Well, at least you're talking to me now.'

'What are we gonna do, Dan?'

Dan took a long time before he answered. He felt a paternal protection towards Maya, as if he had saved her life and was now responsible for it. 'I don't know. But we'll do it together.'

—— ∞ ——

Father Alban carried the near-naked man several kilometres through the streets of Lorna until finally reaching the front steps of *The Light of the Prophet*. The staircase was not particularly steep, but after such a long walk he struggled to make it to the top. Upon entering the atrium that adjoined the main chamber of the church he found himself surrounded by refugees. People sat against the walls or lay on the floor, some with belongings grabbed in haste, some with young children. Singles, couples and whole families had sought refuge in his little church. All from different backgrounds, but with one thing in common. He had no idea what they were doing in the atrium. Perhaps Oscar, the young novice he had left in charge, was refusing them entry into the chapel. He would have to have a word with him.

Alban entered the main part of the church still carrying the unconscious body of the man he had found and was overcome by what he saw. This part of the church was traditionally called the sanctuary, where services and ceremonies were conducted. Today it more than lived up to its name. Crowded with asylum seekers on all sides, three hundred or so people crammed into the relatively small space, filling it to capacity, spilling over into the atrium and no doubt other parts of the building. The pews were pushed aside in several places allowing small circles of people to gather on the floor. Others were using the pews as beds, or as protective covers so they could sleep on the floor beneath them. It was like a chaotic indoor camping site, and the usual orderliness with which Alban liked to keep his church had been completely overturned. As he looked around the space Alban couldn't help feeling both proud and anxious that so many had sought refuge in his little church. And all it took was a sign on the door.

He picked his way through the crowd, still carrying the limp body of the man with the striking resemblance to the Prophet Tobias. As he passed by, he looked into the faces of the people. Some had been injured and wore fresh dressings on their wounds. These were mostly men, but some women too. Like those he met in the atrium many had brought some meagre possessions with them. They must have fled their homes in a hurry and grabbed whatever they could. Some had bags of clothes, jewellery or other heirlooms, while the children clung to their most beloved toys – stuffed animals for the young ones, AV slates for the older. Even among the adults many carried nothing more than their pocket slate to maintain connectedness. Not the most practical thing to bring to a safe haven; but Alban was more concerned about their comkeys being tracked and attracting the Temple Guard.

Many he recognised as members of his parish and regular churchgoers. They nodded as he passed, and in the eyes of some he observed a heartfelt *thank-you*. He nodded back, smiling acknowledgment. It felt odd to be exchanging pleasantries under the circumstances. They were devout Tobianists; why did they need sanctuary? He drew a few curious glances as he crossed the room, but no-one it seemed was particularly surprised to see a cleric carrying a near-naked unconscious man through the church. This kind of thing was already normal.

Alban entered the anteroom where he found Oscar in a state of panic. 'Where have you been?' the young man demanded. 'Ever since you put that bloody sign up I've had people coming in here all day long. I've got nowhere else to put them, unless you're happy to have strangers sleeping in your lounge!'

'That would be fine,' Alban heard himself say. 'Now would you please help me get this man to the bed. I've been carrying him for over an hour.'

Oscar's temper abruptly switched from irritated to mortified as he stepped forward and relieved Alban of the dead weight. The man wasn't particularly heavy, but after carrying him for so long Alban's muscles had locked up, so when the load was lifted from him a stabbing pain seared through his whole upper body. He couldn't move his arms without them shaking uncontrollably, and he couldn't straighten them for a full ten minutes.

Oscar carried the man into Alban's quarters and laid him out on the bed. He looked at the man's face, not recognising him at all. Not that he should, Alban realised. He was a stranger to them after all.

'He's been shot,' Oscar declared.

Alban fell into a chair next to the bed. 'I know. Is there anyone out there who could help him?'

'There is a nurse. She's been helping me with the wounded. I'll go find her.' Oscar moved to leave then turned back. 'Do *you* need anything?'

'A cup of tea would nice.'

Oscar nodded and left the room, leaving Alban and the injured man alone. Alban turned to his unconscious guest, studying the face. The resemblance was uncanny.

'If only you *were* the Prophet,' Alban said softly. 'We could really use you right about now.'

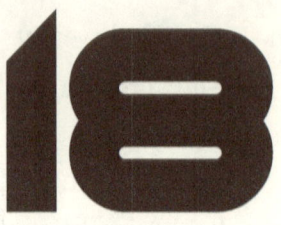

Fact is fiction given substance
Truth is imagination given form
Everything that is real is also unreal
Everything that is unreal is also real

Shentama
– Stanza 138

The house began to wake around 10am, and aside from a few hangovers, there were no major casualties from the previous night's revels. Rene didn't sleep much. After his encounter with Elly and then Rohan his mind was buzzing. He was inclined to disregard Elly's insistence that he was somehow the Prophet Tobias. Despite her seeming intelligence she was just a bonobo, after all. Yet her conviction unsettled him. She was either mistaken, insane, or right. For now, Rene chose to believe she was simply mistaken. It was not something he knew how to deal with anyway.

Something he *could* deal with was Rohan. Rene considered several possibilities for why he was out last night when everyone else was asleep, and why he became so defensive when Rene caught him sneaking back. The most obvious conclusion was that he was an informant for the Temple Guard. A mole. While Rene didn't discount this alarming possibility, he also explored more benign reasons for Rohan being out last night. A secret rendezvous with a lover perhaps? This seemed unlikely. Rene was hard pressed to imagine any woman or man putting up with Rohan for very long. Perhaps a visit to a prostitute? The Western Borough was well known for its seedier side. Another possibility was that Rohan was an addict and he was out buying drugs. His hyper-active personality sometimes made him appear like a man under the influence. Rene considered several other unlikely possibilities, but he always came back to what seemed the most logical – Rohan was a mole.

He chose not to tell anyone of the encounter aside from Kane. He would let him deal with it. Rene didn't want to start gossip that may not be true. His evidence was purely circumstantial, and his suspicions possibly tainted by his own opinion of the man. Telling no-one but Kane was the fairest and most responsible thing to do, he told himself. And Kane seemed to know Rohan better than anyone. From what Rene had observed they had an odd relationship. There must be some reason Kane kept him around. Perhaps he knew Rohan was a mole and was using him to feed the Temple bad information?

This constant speculation kept Rene up until Joanna stirred. She rolled over and saw him already awake beside her.

'Sleep well?' she asked.

'Fine.'

'I dreamt we were back at home, and we had a child.' Joanna said softly. 'A girl. At least, I think it was a girl. Can't be sure. You were wearing robes, like a priest. I asked you why and you said … *'cause it's comfortable*.' Joanna chortled a little. 'Then I was wearing them too. And it seemed like … you were someone important. And our child, wasn't a child, but was your brother, William. I forget what he said now. Something to do with … death. He told me not to worry.'

She looked up at Rene. 'I don't usually remember my dreams. Now I know why. They're fucked up. What do you think it means?'

'Probably nothing. Maybe you're just homesick. You know – family, security...'

' – Death.'

'He did tell you not to worry,' Rene reassured. 'Don't make too much of it. It was just a dream.' Even so, it made Rene uneasy. Perhaps it was the mention of Will. Any discussion of his dead brother made him get defensive.

Fifteen minutes later, after a quick shower and shave, they headed downstairs to greet the morning properly. They found Althea in the kitchen preparing breakfast with another woman. Elly sat in the corner and watched Rene enigmatically, as if they shared a secret no-one else knew, which they kind of did.

'Good, you're up,' Althea greeted. 'This is Margaret, legal attorney by trade, and provisional short order cook. Breakfast will be ready in a few minutes.'

'Can I help?' Joanna offered.

'We got it. Have a seat.'

As Joanna sat and the girls chatted, Rene opened the back door off the kitchen.

'Don't go too far,' Margaret warned. 'Kane doesn't like people outside in case a surveillance camera spots them.'

'Just having a look,' Rene told her.

The door opened onto a small patio leading to a patch of overgrown grass. A stone path snaked through the grass to a locked gate at the back. The opaque yellow plexi-fence around the yard (if you could call it that) was three meters tall, preventing anyone seeing in.

Rene closed the door. 'Do you use the rear entrance much?'

'Sometimes,' Margaret responded. 'But you're just as likely to be spotted back there as you are at the front. Most of the time we use the tunnel. It's safer.'

Rene remembered. 'That's how we came in last night. I've never walked through a sewer before.'

Althea read his expression. 'I agree, it's not very pleasant down there. At least it doesn't smell. It's also a bit of a maze, one could easily get lost. But it's the best way to get around Lorna without being seen.'

Rohan might have gone anywhere last night – no cameras, no comkey tracking. A perfect alibi. Provided you don't get caught coming back.

As the smell of the food wafted through the house others began to emerge, bleary and starved. Pretty soon the kitchen and the adjoining lounge room were filled with rebel fighters eating scrambled eggs, toast, coffee, and baked pastries, from a plate on their laps. It was amazing how much food came out of one tiny domestic kitchen. There was enough to feed a small army, which is what they were.

Kane and Rohan came down together. Rohan shot Rene a hostile look, then he noticed Elly in the corner. 'That thing shouldn't be in here. It's unhygienic.'

'She's cleaner than you are.' Althea retorted. Kane gestured for Althea to take her out anyway, to avoid a scene. It seemed he was always making concessions for Rohan, and Rene couldn't understand why.

'Come on, Elly,' Althea chimed as she led the bonobo out of the room.

Kane sat at the head of the kitchen table, his natural position, with Rohan sitting to his right. Rohan reached into his pockets and started sharpening something against a whetstone in his palm. Rene found himself seated at Kane's left hand, with Joanna beside him. Margaret approached with a plate of food for each of them.

Rohan began eating immediately, but Kane waited. Rene and Joanna looked at each another and decided to follow Kane's lead and also wait. Rene wanted a moment alone with Kane, but for now his news would have to wait.

A strange silence fell over the table, aside from the unsettling sound of Rohan devouring his breakfast. In time, Margaret returned with a particularly large serving and placed this before the empty chair at the other end of the table. The timing was perfect as an intimidatingly large black man entered the kitchen just as the food hit the table and planted himself in front of it. The chair groaned under the weight – all muscle and bone, no fat.

'Thanks Maggie!' he beamed. His head was bald and tattooed. A thick silver chain hung around his neck with a large pendant dangling from it – like the medal one might win at a sports event. He wore dirty khaki pants and a tank-top singlet that barely covered his massive frame. The guy must have spent ten hours a day most of his life just lifting weights and working out. Even at rest, his muscles were practically bursting through his chestnut skin, which aside from his pate was completely unblemished – as if to gild this lily would have been sacrilege.

Rene recognised him immediately as the man who had led the rescue the day before. Seeing his face properly now for the first time, Rene felt he knew him from somewhere else, but couldn't place where.

'You waitin' for me?' the giant asked the table.

'Of course,' Kane answered.

'Sorry,' said the tattooed giant. 'Dig in then,' he invited, and began immediately devouring the plate in front of him. The others followed suit.

'This is Tank,' Kane introduced. 'Rene, Joanna. New recruits.' He spoke as he ate, with only an occasional crumb falling from his mouth.

Tank reached across the table to shake their hands, 'How ya doin'?' He greeted with a broad smile, flashing a spectacular row of large white teeth.

'I remember you from yesterday,' Rene said. 'Thanks.'

'My pleasure.'

'I've seen you somewhere before though, and I know we haven't met.'

Joanna punched Rene in the shoulder. 'Idiot. It's Tank. From the games.'

'Of course.' Now Rene remembered. 'You're in the Warrior Games.'

Tank smiled. It was a well-rehearsed smile, but no less genuine for that. 'Used to. Retired now. It's a young man's sport.'

Tank didn't seem much older than thirty, but he was already too old for the Games. In a past era he might have been a football player or pro wrestler. These days the most popular AV sport worldwide was the Warrior Games, and Tank had been one of its biggest stars. A bona-fide legend of the sport.

'What are you doing here?' Rene asked stupidly.

'Same as you, man. Tryin' to change the world.'

Tank famously had a personality as big as his physique. Kane and Rohan were used to people being a bit dumbstruck first time they met Tank, whether for his fame or sheer size. They themselves were indifferent by now.

'Tank got back late last night,' Kane explained. 'Missed the party.'

'Looks like it was a real hootenanny judging by the debris.'

'I was worried there for a while,' Kane confessed quietly.

'You know me, Kane, I'm indestructible,' Tank said as he shovelled more food into his mouth. 'Says so on my CV.'

'Any luck?'

Tanks grinned and raised two fingers.

'Good.'

'Are we gonna start this meeting or what?' Rohan interjected impatiently.

'Just making small talk, little man,' Tank came back. 'Keep your shirt on.'

'All right, all right,' Kane conceded.

'What about them?' Rohan indicated Rene and Joanna. Clearly, he felt they should not be here for this.

'I want Rene to sit in,' Kane answered, then turning to Rene: 'If you don't mind. I'd like your input.'

'I guess,' Rene replied.

'He's been here one day,' Rohan complained. 'Not even that. Why does he all of a sudden get to be on the council?'

'Let's call him an advisor, shall we?' Kane suggested.

'We don't even know who he is! Where he's from!'

'Then it's time we found out,' Kane interrupted. 'Now shut the fuck up, Rohan.'

Tank flashed an impish smile at Rohan, turned to Rene. 'Welcome aboard, my friend. You have no idea what you're getting yourself into.'

'Then what about her?' Rohan carped. 'She can't be here for this.'

Kane sighed in exasperation. 'Would you excuse us please, Joanna.'

'Of course,' Joanna said graciously. 'Wouldn't want to interfere with men's business.' This mock was directed at Rohan, though she managed to patronise the table and the entire male sex at the same time. Joanna playfully ruffled Rene's hair as she rose. 'You play nice now. No rough stuff. I'll be in the other room with the womenfolk.'

Joanna made for the adjoining room where Althea and Elly had retreated. As she left Rene patted down his hair, a wry smile on his face.

'I like a girl with spirit,' Tank declared, beaming again that famous smile.

Rohan on the other hand was not impressed. 'Can we get on with it?'

'Okay,' Kane agreed. 'I call this meeting of the Libertarian Army, Western Chapter 25, to order – '

Rene was surprised and a little amused by the name. Perhaps they were better organised than he had given them credit for.

' – We need to decide what our next move will be. The ambush yesterday went better than even I expected, thanks to Tank and the rest of the team, and all the prisoners who joined the fight. But frankly, we got lucky. We caught them off guard. The Temple's gonna be ready for us next time, so we gotta get strategic.'

'Hang on,' Tank interjected. 'Yesterday was a rescue mission. A one-off. It's not like we've declared war on the Church.'

'No, but the Church will see it that way,' Kane responded. 'To them we're terrorists and heretics; and declared or not we made the first strike. They're gonna come after us. We need to consider how to best defend ourselves for what's next.'

'We can do more than that,' Rohan added. 'Let's get preemptive on their asses. Hit 'em first. Hit 'em where it hurts.'

'I agree,' Kane said. 'Yesterday was the beginning of something we've only talked about till now. It feels good to finally act on all the rhetoric. We need to keep at it. If we waste this opportunity our moment in history may be lost forever. The festival is soon. I think we should plan something to coincide with this.'

'You want to attack the festival?' Rene was shocked.

'I didn't say attack. But … something.'

'Why not attack?' Rohan countered. 'If we're starting a revolution then let's get serious. We fought against Temple Guards and won. We can do it again. But don't wait till the festival. Like you said Kane, we need to keep it going. Do something now.'

'Like what?' asked Tank.

'I'd make you a tea,' Althea said to Joanna, 'but it's best not to go in the kitchen when they're talking.'

'How did you end up here?' Joanna asked pointedly. 'You're not like the others. And, I have to ask, how come you have a Bonobo for a pet?'

'Like I said, long story.'

'We got time,' Joanna persisted.

'Well, for a start. Elly's not a pet.'

'What is she then?'

'… A miracle.'

'Now you're just toying with me.'

'Sorry,' Althea said. 'I don't mean to be ambiguous. It's been a secret for so long I still don't know how much I can really say. I'm a psychologist. Until recently I worked at the Lorna Institute. A group of us from the Institute tried to … well … it was a daring plan, impossible really. If it had worked, it would have changed everything. But it didn't work. At least, not the way we'd hoped. Elly was our test subject. One of many, in fact. She was the only one to survive the procedure. She proved it could be done. But something went wrong. I don't know what. And I fear we have damaged our cause far more than if we had done nothing at all. We tried to manufacture a miracle. What we ended up doing was beyond heresy. It was profane. It was impertinent… it was foolish. Elly is a constant reminder to me. She gives me hope and makes me ashamed of myself at the same time. That's why I keep her with me. She's become my conscience,' Althea looked at Elly fondly, 'and my friend. As far as I know we are the only two survivors of that bold experiment. The Temple Guard found us and killed everyone. The Church of the Prophet no longer acts in his name. Even your priest, Father Alban, dumped you on our doorstep to avoid giving refuge to a heretic. Lorna is a city that has lost its soul. Only a miracle can save it now. And I'm all out of miracles.'

'We should raid a church.' Rohan suggested. 'Raid all the churches. We can't hit the Temple yet, but we can burn down their local branches. That'll send a message. And it'll get publicity. The Temple can't cover up burning churches on the streets.'

'Don't be so sure of that,' Rene mumbled.

'You got a better idea, mister advisor?' Rohan challenged.

Rene turned to Kane, who simply looked back, waiting for a response. He turned to Tank, who silently gestured – *the floor is yours*.

'I really don't know why you asked me to stay for this. I'm not a revolutionary. I don't condone violence. And to be perfectly honest, I don't really have a problem with the Church. Or I didn't until two days ago. I'm not a Tobianist, but nor am I a radical reformationist or libertarian. This is the same kind of argument I used to have with my friend Dan, and if he were here he'd probably be all for burning down the churches, and storming the festival or whatever it is you want to do. But I can't in all conscience support anything that might see people killed. And burning down Church's just sounds like vandalism to me. There's nothing noble in that.'

'Great choice, Kane. You've brought us an apologist for the Temple,' Rohan intoned. 'What were you arrested for anyway? And how is it you just happened to end up in a cell with Kane and me? Maybe he's a spy. Maybe he's gonna lead the Temple Guard right to us. I wasn't gonna say nothing, but I found him coming in early this morning through the tunnel. Where were you, Rene? Some secret meeting? Did you tell 'em where we are? Are we about to be raided?'

'Is this true, Rene?' Kane asked.

Rene should have been surprised by this deceit, but he wasn't. And he didn't see the point explaining what really happened. Rohan got in first and anything Rene now said would just look like a lie.

'And what about his girlfriend there, Joanna? How did she come to us again? Oh yeah, a Tobianist priest brought her right to the door. And that stupid bitch Althea just let her in. Her and her fucking monkey!'

'ENOUGH!' Kane slammed his fist on the table, causing the breakfast plates and cutlery to jump and rattle, spilling leftovers on the table.

'Rene,' Kane said in a much calmer voice. 'Did you go out last night?'

'No.'

'He's lying,' said Rohan.

Kane pondered the situation for a moment. Rohan eyeballed Rene across the table with a manic confidence. Whatever it was between him and Kane, Rohan felt he had this in the bag and Rene would soon be history. Rene however, remained calm. He was not threatened by Rohan and his lies. Whoever Kane believed he would accept the consequences. Rene could again feel the threads of time converging in this moment. It was one of those moments that one's fate turned on, and as always, it came down to a simple choice.

'Someone once said,' Kane began, 'the best leaders are those who don't want the job. Who have it thrust upon them. It's only through a quirk of fate that I'm here rather than someone else, making decisions that affect so many people. Being responsible for the lives of others. Planning a revolution. I didn't choose to be here, but here I am. And all I have to go on … is what feels right. I don't know which one of you is telling the truth. But it doesn't matter. Rene?' Kane sounded almost despairing as he looked Rene in the eye. 'I don't know you. I don't know what kind of man you are or what kind of man you're likely to become. I don't know if you will betray us or be our greatest ally… All I know is I trust you. The same way I trust Tank here, and everyone else in this house. If we can't trust one another at a time like this, then we are surely doomed.'

'So you believe him over me, your own brother?' Rohan protested.

Now it made sense. They were brothers. That's why Kane put up with him. And that's why Rohan felt inadequate, doing all he could to live up to big brother's example, and most likely their father's expectations. What little resentment Rene had towards Rohan suddenly evaporated. He understood exactly where he was coming from and felt only pity for him now.

'You're not listening, Rohan. I trust him. And I cannot have you making accusations like this about people I have put my trust in.'

'Don't you trust me?' Rohan asked his brother.

Kane didn't answer…

Unable to bear it any longer, Rohan stood up defiantly and left the room.

'Well,' Tank broke the silence. 'That went better than expected.'

Every facet of creation
From word to rock
From song to bended knee
From a star to a blade of grass
From a city to a drop of rain
All of it is complete within and as part
Of the All-In-All

Shentama
– Stanza 43

When Captain Marius was discharged from hospital he was told by the doctor to 'take it easy'. His broken leg was not yet fully healed and walking on it could cause permanent damage. Marius then immediately refused to sit in a GL-chair, as it made him look weak, and walked under his own power out of the hospital. Dressed in the uniform he'd arrived in, still battle worn and damaged, he hobbled out the main entrance to a waiting GL cruiser. Lieutenant Makoto was at the wheel, watching Marius limp across the hospital forecourt. It was an odd sight – a wounded soldier in battered armour walking purposefully away from the ostentatious edifice of the Temple hospital. Something primal and broken absconding from somewhere clean and civilized.

Normally Marius would leap into a GL, but his braced leg made that impossible. As it was he struggled to get in without looking ridiculous, his frustration clear as he grumbled and grunted at his pathetic body for not doing what he wanted. Finally, he was sitting comfortably.

'Get me the fuck out of here,' Marius commanded. Makoto pushed the wheel forward and they sped away from the hospital. 'What have I missed?' he asked his lieutenant.

'Nothing much,' Makoto replied. 'The rebels have all gone to ground. We know where most of them are hiding, and we can strike any time. Been holding off though on orders from the Council. The entire guard has been deployed to find the Gerda escapee. It would help if we knew who he was and what he looked like.'

Marius remembered the conversation he'd had with Cairn in his hospital room. 'You mean you haven't been told?'

'Told what?'

'He looks like the Prophet. Thinks he *is* the Prophet. That's why the Council's so keen to take him down. In case people believe him. He's a nutter, but I guess they'll believe anything these days.'

'Okay, that make a bit more sense, then,' Makoto said, as they turned a corner and approached the barracks. 'Why weren't we told that to start with?'

'Guess they don't want it advertised.'

'Not even to the Temple Guard? That's fucking ridiculous.' Makoto was offended the Council wouldn't trust their own Guard with this crucial information.

'I know.'

'How did you find out?'

'Cairn told me. But I don't think he would have if I hadn't seen the prisoner with my own eyes.' Makoto turned to Marius, intrigued. 'He was in the Square during the ambush. Next to the fountain. Would've got the fucker too if some prick hadn't got in the way. I've been going through the surveillance footage to see where he got to, but he disappeared into the Western Borough. Not enough bloody cameras in that area so I lost him.'

'Well that at least narrows things down. We'll focus on the Western Borough, then.'

'Fuck that. I want to hit the rebel safe houses before it's too late. Get me all the intel you have on the where they're hiding. Recall everyone. I want to regroup, then we go in hard and fast.'

'What about the Council?'

'It's entirely possible the prisoner is hiding out with one of the rebel groups. This way we kill two birds with one stone.'

Tobias was still weak, but the gunshot wound he had received was healing fast. A nurse had been enlisted from among the asylum seekers to tend his wound. She was one of several medical practitioners hiding out at Father Alban's church, *The Light of the Prophet*, dealing mostly with minor injuries, but there were a few more serious gunshot or hazing wounds. The chapel's old MediScan was able to treat most of them, but more serious injuries like Tobias's were beyond a MediScan remedy. She knew what *should* be done, but not having the necessary equipment to hand, she was forced to improvise.

Tobias's left lung had filled with blood, the reason for his laboured breathing. It should have collapsed completely before now, but fortune was on his side. She sealed and dressed the wound lightly with a polymer bandage, allowing him to breathe easier, but left a gap for the blood in his lungs to drain out through a tube via the open wound. Every breath he took helped to pump a little bit more out. Sitting him upright, to avoid her patient drowning in fluids, she told Alban she'd done all she could, but he was unlikely to survive the night.

The following morning Tobias was still alive. In fact, as the nurse changed the dressing, she was astonished how much he had already healed. What should have taken weeks or months was happening in a matter of days. It was miraculous. What she didn't know was this was due to the IPS cells Doctor Asar had injected into Tobias during the revitalisation process. They were still in his bloodstream, still doing their work at repairing any damaged tissue. In a way, they made Tobias stronger and more impervious to injury than he had ever been in his former life. But to her, it looked for all the world like a miracle.

With his wound redressed, Tobias now sat up in bed comfortably, colour returning to his face. Father Alban stayed with him. He had again made his famous soup and was encouraging Tobias to eat. Alban's young novice, Oscar, watched silently from the doorway.

'Come on. I doubt you've eaten anything for days. This will help.' Alban raised the bowl to his own mouth and took a sip – to show it was safe. He offered the bowl to his guest. Silently the patient took the bowl and sipped cautiously. It was warm, not hot. And hearty. Pretty soon he was gulping it down.

'That's the way. No-one will harm you here. You're safe.' Alban didn't know if he understood, but hoped the tone of his voice was at least reassuring.

Alban thought he heard a noise and turned to Oscar in the doorway. 'Did you hear something?' Oscar shook his head. Alban turned his attention back to the man in his bed. Again, he was struck by the uncanny resemblance. If this was not the Prophet himself, he was the spitting image of the man. No-one else saw it, but Alban had a unique relationship with Tobias, he knew that face intimately from so many visits to the crypt, year after year.

'I realize you are not him,' Alban told his patient. 'I doubt the prophecy of his return was meant to be taken so literally, but I think I will call you Tobias nevertheless – just to have a name to call you by.' Alban looked for any glimmer of a reaction. Nothing. 'So, Tobias it is. Are you … I mean, is there someone I can contact for you? Do you have a home? Family? Anyone? You're welcome to stay here of course, at least for a while. I just wonder what will become of you when this is all over.'

Tobias gazed at Alban curiously. He was listening, but not comprehending. He handed back the empty soup bowl.

'Would you like some more?' No reaction. Alban raised the bowl to show what he meant. 'More?'

Tobias nodded. He understood that at least. He was like a child – Intelligent and curious, but one who had not yet acquired the power of speech.

'All right. I'll get you some more.' Alban carried the bowl out of the room, ushering Oscar outside, and closed the door behind him. The church was still crowded with people, but he had given up his own bed for Tobias and wanted to keep him isolated. Aside from the preposterous nagging feeling that this was the real Tobias, Alban had the sense there was something profoundly important about his new patient, and he must be protected at all costs. He was a fugitive, possibly a criminal, possibly even dangerous. But it was no mere chance Alban found him when he did. Tobianism teaches: *there is no such thing as coincidence.* The choices we make define our destiny, and the opportunities life presents are there for a reason.

As he was pouring a fresh ladle of soup into the bowl Alban heard a disturbance in the chapel. People were crying out, doors were flung against the walls, and a panic erupted in the room. Setting aside the bowl Alban dashed out of the kitchen. He opened the doors from the rear apartments to see Temple Guards storming the sanctuary. People ran past him in a panic, fleeing into the back rooms for safety. Alban strode purposefully up the aisle to the officer leading the raid.

'What is the meaning of this?' Alban demanded. 'This is a church for God's sake! These people have been granted sanctuary!'

'Are you saying the Temple Guard are not welcome here, father?' The lieutenant countered. 'We're on the same side, you know.' As he spoke Guards stationed themselves at all the exits from the room, and those who had already escaped were herded back inside. Alban prayed they did not enter his bedroom and discover Tobias.

'What do you want?' Alban demanded.

'Just a look 'round. Don't worry, father, we're not here to arrest anyone. Unless we find who we're looking for, of course.'

'You have no right!'

'I HAVE EVERY RIGHT!' The lieutenant blasted back. 'We are the Guardians of the faith and this church belongs to us! Now just shut the fuck up and cooperate, and no-one will get hurt.'

'Who are you looking for?'

'What part of "shut the fuck up" don't you understand?'

'Who are you looking for?' Alban repeated defiantly.

The lieutenant glared at Alban. He raised his power-gloved hand and aimed a finger at the Father's head. 'Sit down,' he said intently. Alban stood his ground. '… Please,' the lieutenant added.

Alban realised continuing his protest would be fruitless, so he sat on the floor with everyone else. The lieutenant addressed the crowd. 'We are not here to arrest you. So relax. We are searching for the escaped prisoner you will have heard about. This is for your own safety. None of you will be harmed as long as you cooperate.' The lieutenant then signalled his men, and they began to slowly walk through the crowd, looking at every single person as they passed by.

Alban watched as they studied the men in particular. Despite the lieutenant's assurance, people were anxious and frightened. Everyone here had something to hide. The Temple's announcement that the prisoner was in custody had been premature it seemed – they were still hunting him. Yet the Guards didn't seem to know who they were looking for. They hoped to intimidate their prey to a reaction, thus exposing himself. Could 'Tobias' be the prisoner they were seeking? They were bound to search the back rooms before long.

Alban began to sing:

True freedom must be twofold
The freedom to act or be still
The freedom to go or to stay
The freedom to speak or be silent
The freedom to live as you choose

It seemed an appropriate prayer for the occasion. The words were said to come from the *Shentama*, though could not be found in modern editions. It was handed down through the generations as an anthem of Tobianist values. Under the circumstances, the words had a revolutionary ring to them.

Others joined in, and soon the entire congregation was singing the *Hymn of True Freedom* as Temple Guards roamed among them.

True freedom must be twofold
The freedom to refuse or accept

The freedom to believe or deny
The freedom to love or despise
The freedom to live in the shadow of another

True freedom must be twofold
It cannot be given but must be allowed
It cannot be taken but must not be denied
It cannot be forced but must be chosen
It cannot be known but must be lived

True freedom must be twofold

The song changed the mood of the room from one of fear to brazen composure. Once the Guards completed their circuit of the room, they were now the ones feeling anxious. The lieutenant stepped up to Alban, waiting for them to finish the song before he spoke. 'Is there anyone else here, Father?' he asked.

Alban shook his head.

The lieutenant motioned to his sergeant. 'Check the back rooms.'

The sergeant took a couple of men and headed for the apartment doors. Alban was about to jump to his feet and protest, when a *beep* signalled a message on the lieutenant's field AV. Pulling it into view, he read the message.

'Belay that, Sergeant. We're ordered back to barracks.' Then to all the Temple Guards: 'Move out!'

Employing the same precision and speed with which they had arrived the Temple Guards mustered out of the Church, and in less than a minute they were gone.

Alban looked about the room, observing relief and confusion

on the faces around him. Attempting to lighten the mood and mask his own disquiet at what had just happened, he joked: 'Well … that was fun.'

No-one laughed.

— ∞ —

'Goddamit! Who gave that order?' Cairn was furious.

'Captain Marius, Your Eminence,' Kasper answered calmly, though deep down he was relishing the moment. 'He seems to be of the opinion that an assault on the rebel safe houses would be more productive. Especially with the festival just a few days away.'

They were in Cairn's private chambers – just Cairn, Kasper and the tailor who was currently kneeling at Cairn's feet, pinning the hem of what was to be the Cardinal Hierophant's new robes for the festival address, which opened the week-long festival and was streamcast across the world. It was the most watched AV event of the year – every year. So he had to look his best. Tradition demanded the Cardinal Hierophant wear something spectacular for the occasion. This was the only time a bit of opulence was not only allowed but expected. Oh, to have had the ritual and pomp of the old religions. It may have been extravagant and indulgent, but they knew how to put on a show. Tobianism was positively austere by comparison. These new robes would be worn only once. Every year a new set was specially created. It was a great honour to design the festival robes for the Cardinal Hierophant, and every year the competition among designers was cutthroat. But this was not a conversation a mere tailor should be privy to. Cairn kicked at the little man through the unfinished garment hanging from his shoulders. 'Get out!'

The tailor anxiously began to gather up his tools and cloth samples.

'Leave all that. Just get out!'

He did as he was told and made a hasty retreat, leaving Cairn and Kasper alone.

'I thought Marius was still in hospital,' Cairn said.

'He discharged himself this afternoon.'

'How the hell did he ever become Captain of the Guard? The man's a certifiable idiot.'

'You appointed him.' Kasper maintained his cool, but he did love goading Cairn.

'And you recommended him. Don't test me, Kasper. You're on shaky ground as it is.' Cairn often let Kasper get away with his little jibes, but this was not the time.

'The captain believes the rebels may be sheltering the escapee. That's why we haven't found him. A raid on their houses could help expose him, as well as deal with the heretics that caused the Festival Square massacre.'

'Are we calling it a massacre now?'

'It helps get the public on side if they see the rebels as nothing more than terrorists and murderers.'

'Marius may be right,' Cairn admitted. 'Perhaps the good Captain isn't such an idiot after all. Why didn't you think of that, Kasper?'

'Your Eminence?'

'Or *did* you think of it, and simply chose not to say anything?' Cairn was testing him right back.

'Your Eminence gives me too much credit.'

'I doubt that very much,' Cairn replied emphatically.

Kasper didn't respond. Anything he said in response to this would seem either facile or downright treacherous.

'Tell Captain Marius he may proceed,' Cairn commanded. 'Now

get that queer fellow back in here. These robes need to be finished before next week!'

— ∞ —

Kasper marched along the corridors of the Temple with a pressing resolve. While Cairn was preoccupied with 'prison escapees', rebel insurgents, and flamboyant robes, Kasper had far more important business to deal with. Rather than react to events as Cairn was prone to do, Kasper created his own opportunities. He was a patient man. It had taken eight years to reach this point. Eight long years of secret meetings and subterfuge; of quiet subservience and furtive duplicity. But the end was in sight. Soon he, Kasper, would be Cardinal Hierophant, and a new era of Tobianist rule would begin. There was just one last detail to sort.

Doctor Trevelle was waiting in Kasper's office. As the Cardinal entered Trevelle rose to his feet and bowed slightly. It was a respectful bow, but not so low as to appear grovelling. The man still had pride, despite his treachery.

'Please Doctor, have a seat.' Kasper tolerated Trevelle. He had been useful in the beginning, enabling Kasper to help Doctor Asar steal the body of the Prophet from the Temple, and then leading Marius and the Temple Guard to their hiding place in the AQ. Kasper would have got rid of him then, along with the other heretic scientists, if it weren't for one thing. The body of the Prophet was still missing. Kasper wanted it missing, but he also wanted to return it to the crypt at the proper time. He suspected Trevelle knew where it was but was withholding it as insurance against his own life. He was right to do so, because if it had not been for this complication Trevelle would most certainly be dead by now, like his co-conspirator Doctor Berger and his undisclosed heart condition.

'How have you been?' Kasper asked politely.

'Quite well, your Eminence … under the circumstances.'

'And what circumstances would that be?' Kasper knew perfectly well what he was alluding to.

'As you can imagine, it's not easy for me these days at the Institute. Asar and Roget had many friends there. They may not have helped us directly, but they supported what we were doing.'

'Are you saying your colleagues at the Institute don't trust you anymore?' Kasper couldn't care less.

'I don't really know. They barely talk to me.'

Poor Trevelle. Shunned by his peers and a traitor to his own principles, now trapped in a blackmail impossible to sustain. Killing him would be a mercy.

'There's an easy solution to this,' Kasper suggested. 'Tell me what you've done with the body, and your friends will never know your part in Doctor Asar's death. I could even make you out to be the hero.'

'I told you; I don't have the body. I don't know what happened to it … to him. I assume he escaped when the Temple Guard attacked the hospital.'

Was he really going to persist with this story? Kasper refused to believe the regeneration had been successful. He had heard it both from Cairn (who simply took Asar at his word) and Trevelle, who claimed to have witnessed it firsthand. That Tobias's corpse had risen from the dead, but his spirit was somehow absent. That he was indeed running around Lorna like an escaped animal. It was just too absurd.

Kasper had learned of their plan to steal the body and attempt revitalisation three years ago. It was a naïve, idealistic dream that conveniently ignored reality. Any true Tobianist knew it flew in the face of the first guiding principle of the faith – the renewal of life.

The irony was bewildering, but Kasper realised he could turn their ill-fated efforts to his advantage, so he secretly helped them. Enabling them, through Trevelle, to find the equipment they needed and the hospital where they performed their 'operation'. He further ensured a map of the tunnels beneath the Temple fell into their hands, so they could navigate their way to the crypt. They had fulfilled the first part of his plan flawlessly. The body was stolen and Cairn was in a panic; his authority questioned, his focus scattered. It didn't take much to then nudge the Cardinal Hierophant in whichever direction Kasper pleased.

The second part of his plan – encouraging the dissidents of Lorna to riot against the Church – had gone better than Kasper could have hoped for thanks to Cairn's impulsive over-reaction. Things were moving faster than Kasper wanted – like an out of control roller-coaster – but it was still on track.

The only wrinkle was the Prophet Tobias. He needed the body to ensure its safe return to the crypt. Timing was critical if he was to secure the vote of the Council for his accession to the seat of Cardinal Hierophant. They would agree to anything to restore the status quo, abandoning Cairn for Kasper in a heartbeat when they saw that only he could return order to Lorna; only he could restore the body of the Prophet to its resting place beneath the Temple.

Kasper turned on Trevelle. 'The only reason you're still alive, Trevelle, is because I don't believe you. I understand why you insist Tobias is alive. You want to create doubt among the people. You want them to question their faith and the authority of the Church. If the Prophet were to return it would be like a new start. A fresh slate. But it's a fantasy. You've deluded yourselves into believing one man can still make a difference. Especially if that man were Tobias himself. But it's far too late for that. There is no place for prophets anymore. There is only the Church. We are the one true faith left in the world. If you do not believe in us, then you are a radical and a heretic. So I ask you one last time, deliver me the body of the Prophet, or be a martyr to your cause and a known traitor to your colleagues.'

Trevelle was a man who cared far too much what others thought. For him, reputation was everything. The prospect of death was not nearly as frightening as the fact that he would be remembered as a traitor. Kasper knew this; it was how he got Trevelle to trust him in the first place – with the promise he would come off looking like a hero to their cause when he was able to secure such difficult resources.

But Trevelle was more honourable than Kasper gave him credit for. As professor of Theology at the Lorna Institute he had studied the life and works of the Prophet Tobias more than most people. More than Kasper himself. He was a loyal devotee of the Prophet, if not the Church that bore his name. He was what they called an Ethical Tobianist. Faithful, but not religious. The fact he had become Professor of Theology at the Temple City's own Institute was a matter of some controversy. As far as the Church was concerned, he was not a heretic, but nor was he suitably pious. They finally accepted his appointment on the basis of his intellectual objectivity, and ever since, Trevelle had proven to be a major pain in the ass for the Church. No-one knew the *Shentama* better than Trevelle, and no-one understood the Prophet's message more profoundly. Yet after a lifetime of rigorous and devoted scholarship, Trevelle, only now, in this very moment, realised the true meaning of the Prophet's words – *Choice, not chance, determines your destiny.* He looked Kasper square in the eye, a newfound resolve steeling him for what he knew was to come.

'I swear to you Tobias is alive. If you choose not to believe me I can do nothing to convince you otherwise. I have no idea where he is, but even if I did, I would not tell you. I accepted your help because it suited our needs. You thought you were using me … I was using you. You underestimate me, Cardinal. I am not so proud that I would betray everything I believe in to spare my reputation, or indeed my own life.'

'You cherish life so little?'

'Sometimes there are more important things to cherish,' Trevelle answered philosophically.

'Very well.' Kasper touched a button on his desk console. The bodyguard who had been standing just outside the office stepped into the room.

'Yes, Your Eminence?'

'Kill this man for me, would you?' Kasper told the bodyguard.

The guard was confused – was he expected to take Trevelle away?

'Now,' Kasper demanded.

'I'm not armed with a lethal weapon, Your Eminence,' the guard explained.

'Use your hands.'

The guard nodded and approached Trevelle, who couldn't believe what was happening. 'Kasper, you can't be serious,' he protested as the guard's hands wrapped around his throat and began to strangle him.

Kasper watched coldly as the life was squeezed out of Professor Trevelle. 'I'm always serious,' he told him. Moments later, with a few desperate last gasps for air Trevelle lost consciousness and with it, his uncherished life.

Those who seek power should not lead
Those who seek fortune should not lead
Those who seek fame and recognition should not lead
Those who seek prestige and status should not lead
Only those who have nothing to gain
and nothing to prove
Are suited to lead

Shentama
– Stanza 233

Captain Marius and Lieutenant Makoto entered the armoury. There was row upon row of charged standard-issue power gloves. They walked past these to a heavy metal door at the back of the room – the lethal weapons vault. Stopping in front of the vault door their comkeys were recognised and the mechanism clunked and whirred open. It required the presence of two officers for the lethal weapons vault to open. This was the first time in over a decade it had been done; and the first time since the Shanghai Treaty of 2100 they were to be used in battle.

One hundred and fifty years of peace had been boring, but safe. Authorities were permitted only to use weapons designed to debilitate or immobilise, occasionally maim – but never kill. Murder, no matter the circumstances, was strictly outlawed (except occasionally in the Warrior Games, where it was all in the name of sport and was labelled *death by misadventure*). That edict was over. Lethal force against the heretics had been approved at the highest level.

The vault door slid aside and they entered the musty room. Air conditioning had kept it dry and clean all these years, but it still smelled of age. And metal. Lights sprang to life as they entered, revealing dozens of racks housing hundreds of assault rifles, high voltage gloves, and fragmentation and plasma grenades, all neatly stacked and displayed. There were also several rows of handguns, shotguns, ammunition and other explosives. Good old-fashioned body rippers.

'Does this stuff still work?' Makoto asked, picking up a random power rifle.

'Let's find out,' Marius grinned, grabbing a shotgun and a box of shells. 'Come on.'

He led Makoto back outside. Their weapons were logged by the system as they left, with details of their chosen arms displayed on a nearby AV. The door automatically closed and sealed behind them. They walked to the indoor firing range next to the armoury. Marius loaded a few shells, as Makoto punched in details on the control slate of his power rifle for a couple of targets. On the range, two realistic figures appeared ten meters away. Makoto and Marius stood at the firing point, ready.

Makoto gestured: 'You first, Captain.'

Marius grinned, pumped the action, and aimed. Squeezing one off, the gun exploded and kicked his shoulder so hard he stumbled backwards. He wasn't expecting such a robust recoil and completely missed the target.

'Shit. Let me try that again.'

Pump – squeeze – *BANG*. This time he hit the target in the chest and left a satisfying hole. A red symbol appeared above the mannequin to indicate the subject was dead.

'Yep. That'll do it.' Marius was beaming. He fucking loved guns.

Makoto lined up his power rifle and fired. A blistering blue haze shot from the barrel and hit his target in the head. The mannequin started to shiver uncontrollably, simulating how a real person would react. Its clothes smoked and the face blacked. After a few seconds a red death symbol flashed above its head, and Makoto released the haze. 'Still works.'

'Okay. Let's get these weapons into service.'

'Two days ago a convoy of prisoners bound for Gerda was attacked by heretics right outside these walls. Two Temple Guards were killed – one them my own aide. Aside from being a major fucking embarrassment, it was a declaration of war against the Church of the Prophet. And against us.'

It was 6 am. Marius stood on a GL platform, addressing his troops in the quadrangle of the Temple barracks, before they set out to deliver a ruthless and thorough retribution. He had every Temple Guard in the city assembled on the quad outside their barracks – the Temple's own Regular Guard of five-hundred men and women, the city's thousand or so Regional Guard, plus over five-thousand international Regional Guards who had come as additional crowd control for the festival week. Nearly seven-thousand loyal and highly trained men and women dressed in battle armour and equipped with lethal fire weapons – not those piss-ant low-voltage power gloves they were usually forced to wear. It was the largest gathering of Temple Guards ever in one place. Truly a sight to behold. And for Marius, a thing of beauty.

'We will not be caught off-guard again,' Marius continued. 'We're going in hard this time and we're not taking prisoners. Remember these are heretics we're dealing with. Heretics and terrorists. They want to destroy what you have sworn to defend. Show these fanatics what it means to be a Temple Guard. Show them what happens when you defy the Church of the Prophet. Show them they can't fuck with us and get away with it!'

The assembled Guard collectively raised their weapons and barked –

HA!...HA!...HA!'

It was a chant the Guard used informally as group validation, usually in jest. This was the first time it had been voiced at such a momentous occasion and in such large numbers. The impact of so many voices raised as one was frighteningly loud. Marius smiled. This was his army, he controlled them. For the first time he understood what real power felt like.

'The Prophet said destiny and free will are one and the same,' Marius misquoted – but it was a common error. 'It is our destiny to win this day because we choose it! We have the power to make it so. We know who they are, how many there are, and we know where they're hiding. I guarantee you – this is going to be a very ... short ... war.'

As Captain Marius turned from the podium, the platform lowering to the ground, his lieutenants called their units to attention and marched them in formation to the armada of GL vehicles waiting either side of the quad. This time they would not be outnumbered. This time, they would not be taken by surprise. Today the Temple Guard and the Church of the Prophet would redeem itself, creating a new chapter in the history of the world.

Since the establishment of Tobianist global rule nearly two-hundred years ago, no country had its own military force. There was no need. War between nation states was a thing of the past. All countries were united under Tobianism. There was local law enforcement and emergency services; and above them, the Order of the Temple Guard – the soldiers of the faith. What Marius had assembled was in fact the first true army since *The Great Purge*. An army cultivated and trained as warriors of The Church. Marius knew they would prevail, because the spirit of the Prophet was with them. God was on their side.

Dan sat in the room that had been Bartholomew's office, staring into the translucent display of the portable Black AV. Maya kept lookout, watching for Temple Guard or comrades also seeking refuge at the house. Gabrielle and Bartholomew were still in the basement. Dan just couldn't bring himself to go back down there, though something would have to be done about them soon.

They had slept the night in an upstairs room, as far away from the basement as possible. Maya cried herself to sleep in Dan's arms, quietly traumatised by the day's events. He barely knew the girl, but they had now been thrown together by circumstance. A terrible moment that would bind them to each other forever. They didn't dare leave the house, and they couldn't face what was downstairs, so for now the front door and the door to the basement remained firmly sealed.

Dan poured himself a scotch as he stared at the lock screen of the AV. Usually, the device would unlock instantly with the proximity of a valid comkey, but this was disabled on Black AVs. They needed something more personal and untrackable. 'Face ID not recognised' was all it told him, then offered a handscan as an alternative.

Dan wondered how many other rebel cells Barty had compromised, and how he communicated with his masters at the Temple. Did they meet in dark places, or was this not a true Black AV? Perhaps there was a system link after all. If he could unlock the device, he might be able to see who Bartholomew had been communicating with. He might also find details on other rebel groups in the city. He and Maya needed a safe haven, and to warn the others they might be compromised. All contact between groups had been face to face. As leader of their group Bartholomew was the only one who knew who they were, and where they were. Dan didn't know anyone outside of their small circle. This 'need-to-know' security seemed prudent, but a single Temple mole was all it took to unravel their entire network.

Dan needed to get into this Black AV. To do so he needed either Barty's face or right hand to unlock the device.

Dan downed the scotch, then headed for the basement.

A hand would do just fine, Dan figured, as he entered the basement. He told Maya what he was planning, but understandably, she refused to go back down there. Dan flicked on the light and crept cautiously down the rickety staircase. The place stank of death – – of raw meat and metal. He covered his face to try mask out the smell. The blood had congealed into a burgundy-black paste on the floor. He avoided looking at Gabrielle on the table, focussing his attention on the body of Barty lying at the bottom of the steps.

He was lying on his back, his body frozen in the crippling tensed pose of electrocution, arms stuck to his sides with hands raised and clenched – one fist wrapped in a power glove, the other clutching a knife. Barty's face was likewise frozen with an expression of agony and shock – his mouth agape, his eyes open and bulging, looking up at the ceiling in a cold dead stare.

Dan knelt beside the body, averting his eyes from the face, and tried to uncurl the fingers wrapped around the knife. They refused to move – the muscles were locked. Changing position, he crouched over the body to get more leverage on the hand. Now Barty was staring right up at him, as if saying: *You really are a disappointment, you know that Daniel? A huge fucking disappointment!* Dan looked away, focussing on the hand. He managed to pry the fingers open enough that he could pull the knife away; as he did so he could hear the muscle tissue stretching and tearing under the skin. Ignoring the sound he pulled the finger all the way open. The palm of the hand was black, with a massive imprint of the knife handle burned into it. The fingerprints had been melted away. The hand was useless, he would have to use the face.

Two hours later Dan carried Barty's head up the stairs in a box. He was covered in blood. Maya had found him the box, but otherwise kept well away. The whole situation was too macabre.

Dan removed Barty's head from the box and positioned it in front of the AV sensor. It scanned – read – and failed.

Shit.

Dan held the face up and looked at it. 'What the fuck you piece of shit?' The face seemed to be mocking him, as it dripped into the box. Dan took the head into the bathroom and washed it. He also forced the mouth closed, gently pushed the eyes back into their sockets, and dried and brushed the hair until Barty looked more like his old self.

Returning to the office, he tried again, holding the face up to the sensor. It scanned – read – and *worked*!

'Yes!'

Dan held the face up triumphantly. 'I own you now, you bastard.' He put the head back in its box and set it aside. Looking at the floating holo-display all he saw was a small circle in the middle with a tag next to it – *WC42.*

At that moment a panicked Maya appeared at the door. 'Dan! There are Temple Guards outside. Lots of them!'

— ∞ —

Kane was alone in his bedroom, staring at the Black AV display, pondering what the hell to do next. After walking out of their meeting yesterday, Rohan had secretly gathered several supporters, and with the breaking of dawn that morning, before anyone else was up, they all left the house via the underground tunnel. There were no farewells, no clue to their intentions. They just left. Kane feared he might never see his brother alive again. He couldn't send anyone out after them. The streets were still far too dangerous. Neither could Kane contact Rohan directly. Their modified comkeys were disabled for wireless communications – too easy to track. Face to face was the only safe way for rebel heretics to meet and talk – passing handwritten notes, whispering in dark rooms. There had to be a better way.

A knock at the door. 'Who is it?' Kane called a little too aggressively, he really didn't want to be disturbed.

'Rene.'

'Come in.'

Rene found Kane at his desk, a scroll AV mounted in front of him, with some kind of contextual node-map displayed.

'Are you coming down for breakfast?' Rene asked.

'Have they all heard?'

'Everyone knows by now.'

News of Rohan's departure had spread quickly through the

house. Some were anxious at losing so many of their best fighters. Others were grateful to be rid of them.

'What's the mood?' Kane asked.

'Positive. But you should probably talk to them.'

Tensions between the brothers and the factions that formed around them had made things difficult for the group lately. Perhaps this was for the best. Kane doubted Rohan would make a good leader. He was self-centred, impulsive and ambitious. But then what did *he* know? Kane had been accused of being too cautious – always afraid someone would get hurt. They had a point.

The fact was, he envied Rohan's conviction. Kane wanted nothing more than to fight the Church head on. Take a stand, then win or lose they would at least have tried. But then he thought about the people who would inevitably die. Perhaps he *was* a bad leader, unwilling to risk a single death. Trying to avoid suffering and death was no way to fight a revolution. He just wasn't ruthless enough. Deep down, Kane still hoped for a peaceful solution.

For some reason, Rene fortified that hope. He didn't know what it was about the man, but if they were to have any chance at avoiding a total bloodbath, he felt Rene was somehow the key.

'Was something going on between you and Rohan?' Kane asked point blank.

'He just doesn't like me, I guess,' Rene answered plainly.

'He's not always like that. Sometimes he can be very insightful. Very … pro-active. But he tends to rub people the wrong way. There's two kinds of people in this world. Those who hesitate, and those who would kill the fat man.'

'Pardon?' Rene didn't understand the reference.

'It's a moral paradox,' Kane explained. 'Imagine a train is approaching, and five people are tied to the tracks about to be killed.

You're standing on an overpass with a fat man. If you push the fat man off you can stop the train and save the people. But the fat man will die. Sacrifice one to save many. Sounds logical, but most people wouldn't do it. They see it as morally wrong. But some people don't care about the morality. They just see the logic. They're called Sociopaths. That's Rohan. He'd kill the fat man in a heartbeat.'

Kane paused and considered Rene. 'What would you do?'

Rene thought about it for only a moment. 'I'd jump on the tracks myself.'

'That's cheating.'

'I don't want anyone to die.'

'One day, you may have to make just such a choice,' Kane told him. 'I hope you choose better than me.'

Rene didn't like where this conversation was going. In an effort to change the subject he turned to the translucent AV display before Kane. 'What's that?' From Rene's vantage across the room it was reversed, but he could see it clearly. Kane made no effort to hide the display. Instead, he motioned for Rene to join him.

'It's a map of all the rebel groups we know about. How big they are, how connected. A topology of rebel cells throughout Lorna.' On the display were several interconnected circles, each representing a different group in the rebel network. Each circle was a different size and colour, with abbreviated tags either inside or beside it – conveying information about each group. At a glance it gave a clear visual representation of the scope and number of rebel enclaves throughout the city. Some groups were strongly interconnected, with smaller circles branching off into ever smaller groups. Others floated completely detached from the rest, like clusters of islands that had yet to merge with the main network, or for whatever reason had lost their link and now floated isolated and alone.

'This is us here,' Kane pointed to the circle in the middle with the tag *WC25* next to it. 'We're one of the larger groups, or we were until this morning. This isn't live, by the way. Every now and then the group leaders meet and we update the information, share intelligence, exchange rumours. Last meeting was about two weeks ago. A lot's changed since then. Some of these cells may have disbanded or been shut down. It's hard to know. Rohan's crew could have gone to join one of these other groups. Or maybe they've broken out on their own.' Then after a long pause, 'I just wish we hadn't parted on such bad terms.'

'When's the next meeting?' Rene asked.

'It's supposed to be today. But I'm not going. It's not safe anymore.'

'Was there a man called Bartholomew at these meetings?'

'Maybe. We don't use names.'

'He's the reason I was arrested. Dan was in his group.'

Kane looked at the map of rebel cells projected before him. If there was a traitor leading one of the groups then all of this was known to the Temple. Their location, their numbers, their strengths and weaknesses. They could be raided at any moment.

'We're not safe here anymore,' Kane told Rene.

'I know,' Rene agreed. Then a cold realisation hit him and he turned to the blackened windows, knowing what was about to come. 'But it's too late to run now.'

Just then a terrifying squeal came from downstairs. That damned bonobo –

—— ∞ ——

Dan quickly compacted the scroll AV and put it in his pocket. He would examine it more closely later – if he got the chance. Temple

Guards were outside the house and it was time to leave. He took Maya's hand and they ran downstairs. The front door lurched violently with the force of Temple Guards battering upon it. They made for the back of the house but heard the shattering of glass and splintering of wood as the back door was similarly pounded. There was only one place to go.

As Dan unlocked the basement door Maya softly pleaded with him – 'No, no …' But there was no time to argue. He pulled the door open and dragged her into the basement. Maya retched, but held it in. The stench was overpowering. With two dismembered rotting bodies, and a floor stained with blackened blood, no sane person would choose to go down there. That's what Dan was counting on.

'There's no way out of here, Dan,' Maya whispered desperately. 'We're trapped.'

Dan held Maya by the shoulders and looked her in the eyes. 'I'll get us out of here – but it's not gonna be pleasant.'

Her expression shifted from panic to confusion to wary acquiescence. 'Okay. What do I have to do?'

A crash from upstairs and the thundering of footsteps – the Temple Guard had broken into the house.

'Lie down … over there.' Dan indicated the large pool of Gabrielle's blood on the floor. Maya knew what he was getting at but was still disgusted at the thought. 'Roll around a bit, get it all over you. Hurry.'

Maya did as she was told, keeping her eyes closed and her face puckered against the smell. Dan then scooped up a handful of clotted blood and wiped it on her face and hair. Maya gagged.

'Quiet,' Dan whispered firmly. 'Now keep still and don't make a sound.'

Dan was already covered in blood from his earlier visit, but now scooped a handful and likewise smeared it into his face and hair, then lay on the floor near Barty's headless body.

They lay still like this for several minutes, listening as the Guards explored the house upstairs and down. Heard them shouting as each room was searched and 'cleared'. Then came a horrified 'What the fuck!' from upstairs., One of them had found Barty's head.

Finally, the basement door was tried and both Dan and Maya held their breath.

'Oh, shit! What the fuck is that smell?'

Footsteps descended the basement stairs.

'Prophet be damned, what happened here?!' It sounded like there were two Guards entering the room.

One of the guards nudged Barty with his foot. 'Here's the other half. Looks like they all killed each other. Maybe it was a suicide pact or something.'

'Oh!' The first guard saw what remained of Gabrielle. 'That don't look like no suicide!' The guard stumbled in revulsion, stepping into the blood and losing his footing on the slippery floor. He fell hard, his armour clattering as he hit the ground almost landing on top of Maya. But to her credit she didn't flinch. 'Goddammit!'

The other guard laughed, then helped his partner to his feet.

'Hey, is this the one we were supposed to keep an eye out for?'

A Guard rolled Dan over, then grabbed his face to get a better look. 'Nah. I think it's the headless guy.'

'Shit. Guess they beat us to it. Someone's not gonna be happy 'bout that.'

'Let's get out of here. Fucking heretic psychos. Even dead they're a pain in the ass.'

The two Guards ascended the stairs, the fallen one still grumbling all the way to the top.

'Basement clear!' the second Guard shouted as they reached the top.

'Close the door!' Someone yelled at them. 'It stinks in there. What happened to you…?'

The door slammed shut, muffling the sound of Temple Guards speaking and moving about upstairs. Both Dan and Maya finally took a breath. Maya began to sit up –

'Don't move,' Dan told her. 'Wait till they're gone.'

So Dan and Maya lay there in the blood, surrounded by the decaying bodies of their compatriots, waiting for the Temple Guard to finish their sweep of the house and leave.

You cannot see the glories of the life beyond this

You cannot know the miracle of unshackled

expression

You may not go where you will, when you will

Without the limitation of time and space

You will not know the greater bounty

Until you pass the threshold called death

Shentama
– Stanza 118

E lly screamed! She leapt out of Althea's arms and dashed up the hall to the front of the house.

'Guards!' came a call from upstairs. Lookouts were posted on the second floor to watch the front and back entrances. 'Guards at the front!' 'Guards at the back!'

'How many?' Kane called out as he ran downstairs with Rene.

'Too many!' came the reply as one of the lookouts charged down the stairs after them. 'We gotta get out of here now!'

Panic spread through the house. People grabbed what they

could and fled downstairs. The din would surely be heard outside, alerting the guards they were discovered.

'Into the tunnel. Quickly!' Kane ordered. He triggered the secret latch and violently pulled the linen cupboard away from the wall, revealing the tunnel entrance under the stairs. Neatly stacked rows of towels and sheets spilled onto the floor to be trampled underfoot by terrified rebels. The delicate fraternity within the group was shattered as each sought to save their own skin.

Rene led Joanna through the crush toward the tunnel entrance.

'This time you go first,' Joanna insisted. Rene hesitated. 'I'm not going without you,' she told him firmly.

'Okay,' Rene answered. 'But not yet.'

They joined Kane, ushering the women and children into the tunnel. A panicked crush of people pushed at them – it was every man for himself.

Glass shattered at the front door. Moments later a crash came from the backyard as the rear gate was smashed in. Rene turned to the sound and saw several of their men in the kitchen ready to defend the house as best they could. When the alarm had first been raised Tank had the foresight to raid the armoury (a ground floor study) and was now handing out power gloves and arms to anyone ready to take a stand.

'Tank!' Kane called, raising a hand. Tank tossed Kane a power-rifle. He turned to Rene and Joanna: 'Get as many out as you can.' Kane then powered up the weapon and pushed through the crush to the front door.

With Temple Guards battering both sides of the house many of the men lost their courage and now pushed their way to the tunnel – their only escape. Rene understood their fear but could not abide their actions. Joanna was not so much shocked as outraged. 'Where the hell do you think you're going!?' she rebuked one man, physically pushing him aside.

The man was about to push back when Rene yelled at him: '*HEY!*'

He stopped dead in his tracks.

'Help Tank,' he told the man, who instantly complied. Joanna had never seen Rene so commanding before, or anyone respond to him so faithfully.

Kane reached the front door with Temple Guards battering against it in force. It was a good solid metalised composite that could withstand such a pounding, but the frame and surrounding wall was ordinary wood and drywall which would not survive long. The blackened windows were smashed in and power weapons thrust through the breaches firing blindly into the house. The haze from these guns hit people as they ran down the stairs or in the adjoining hallway, and even reaching into the next room. Their electric-blue tentacles jumped from one person to the next, ploughing through their victims like a web of lightning. Kane could smell the burning flesh of his comrades as they fell in agony around him, not paralysed, but dead – their chests, arms and faces scalded with seared lacerations. Some even bursting into flames as their clothes or hair caught fire.

Kane fired his comparatively feeble stun-rated power-rifle at the hands of the Temple Guards poking through the windows. They stopped firing and withdrew immediately, temporarily paralysed. Lethal fire weapons were not only illegal, they were practically unheard of in modern times. Not even the Temple Guard was permitted to use them. And yet here they were. Whenever a Guard tried to fire through the shattered windows Kane would give a quick burst to immobilise them. It would hold them off for a while, but he was just postponing the inevitable. The house would be overrun soon and anyone not in the tunnel would surely be killed.

At the rear of the house Tank had his men firing into the yard as Temple Guards poured through the far gate and across the overgrown lawn. Tank was firing double-gloved, hazing the Guards two at a time. It had been his trademark move when competing in the Games.

The Guards were exposed and easy targets, but their armour was power-shielded so it took quite a few hits before they would go down, then only to recover seconds later. Tank could see this was futile and they would be overrun in minutes if they couldn't come up with a better defence.

The Guards on the other hand were laying siege to a two-story house with a solid wall and relatively small windows on two levels. But accuracy was not required for a power-weapon to find its target. With each haze a tendril of electricity would hone in on its intended victims, looking for an earth. Some might divert to metal pipes nearby, but many would arc directly into the windows and fry several rebels with a single charge as it leapt from person to person.

Tank was shocked when he saw his comrades dropping dead around him. The smell of ozone and burned flesh was overwhelming and painfully familiar. Memories flooded back of his time in the Games, one of the few places where lethal fire weapons were sometimes permitted. The Games were a fight to the death. He had killed many people in those days in the name of sport, and after 'retiring' swore he would never again take a life.

'Fall back. FALL BACK!' Tank commanded, but those who remained standing were already retreating from the windows, knowing they were powerless against such an assault.

Rene forcibly took belongings from people, tossing them aside if they hindered their ability to climb down the ladder. 'You don't need it! Move!' His voice was so commanding no one argued. His words turned their minds compliant, their actions obedient.

Rene could see the men at the back of the house falling dead, with Tank firing a sustained double-haze out the window at the encroaching Guards, swapping out his gloves when they ran out of juice.

In the opposite hall he saw Kane desperately fending off the Guards at the front as they fired into the house through the windows. The wall buckled and cracked with the battering the door was getting. Soon it would give out entirely, the front entrance would collapse, and Temple Guards would be storming the house.

'Rene!' Kane called. 'Get the hell out of here!'

Most of the residents were now safely into the tunnel. Many of course had not made it that far and their bodies littered the hallway and rooms. Then Rene spotted Althea desperately searching through the corpses in the lounge. 'Wait here,' he told Joanna, and ran to Althea.

'Althea, come on,' Rene urged. 'We have to go.'

'Where's Elly?' She pleaded.

The Guards were at the back door. Tank grabbed the tap-head over the kitchen sink. Howling with exertion he forcibly ripped it off. Water gushed from the pipe, hitting the ceiling and raining all over the kitchen, flooding the tiled floor. As the door burst open and Guards stormed into the house, Tank ran across the room, leapt into the air and fired double-gloved at the wet floor. The haze swept through the water across the floor and into the torrents of water raining down into the room. Several Guards, the first through the door, were caught in the stream. Their protective armour was no use as the charge found its way into their wet clothes and directly to the skin. They froze in their tracks. Guards coming up behind didn't slow their charge and fell on top of the front line, knocking them to the floor, themselves getting caught up in the mass electrocution. The result was an almost comical stacks-on of Temple Guards, as wave after wave fell with the sound of rattling armour and grunting Guard.

Comical, until one of the Guards decided to fire back. His gun hazed a deadly arc towards Tank, but surrounded by water and the bodies of fallen rebels, it seemed to have too many choices for where to land. The arc split into a dozen tendrils that attacked the corpses on the floor, while other smaller ones found purchase in the streams falling from the ceiling. All of which was of course connected back to the pile of Temple Guards lying across the threshold.

Tank hit the floor, sliding on his back into the dry hallway. The charge in his gloves had exhausted but the Guards were now doing the work for him. He came to rest not far from Joanna's feet, near the tunnel entrance, as a chorus of Temple Guards screamed in agony from the lethal charge sweeping through the men. Joanna was impressed with Tank's athletic prowess, demonstrating why he was considered the greatest warrior the Games had ever known. But was then horrified by the death cries of so many Temple Guards. They may be their enemy at this moment, but they were still human beings.

The Guard who had fired the weapon must have died as the haze ended and the charge was released. Not all the Guards were killed, just those at the bottom of the pile.

'No power weapons!' barked a lieutenant at the back of the ranks. 'Use firearms if you've got 'em!'

A shot rang out, hitting Joanna in the leg. She screamed, more from shock than pain. Stumbling backwards into the hole, she fell several meters to land flat on her back on the concrete floor of the tunnel. Her head hit the ground hard, knocking her unconscious.

The front door held fast, but the surrounding wall finally gave way with the sound of snapping timber. Kane ran as the wall caved in behind him. He fled into the lounge and found Althea stumbling through the bodies.

'Where is she? Where is she?' she was pleading.

Kane grabbed her and pulled her towards the tunnel entrance.

'No! I must find Elly!'

'She's just a goddamned monkey. Come on!'

'No!'

Kane wasn't going to argue. He punched her hard, knocking her senseless, then dragged her to the tunnel.

Tank was already descending the ladder. Kane practically threw Althea into the hole after him. Fortunately, Tank was ready and caught her before she landed on top of the unconscious Joanna. As Kane pulled the linen cupboard behind him several water-drenched Guards with raised power weapons converged on the secret exit. They held their fire. One however had a shotgun and discharged a round just as the cupboard locked shut. The projectile hit the wooden frame of the door, ricocheting past Kane's ear, just missing him. But a large wooden splinter broke away and speared his cheek.

'Shit!'

Kane stumbled in the dark but managed to avoid falling down the hole. He descended the ladder, addressing Tank as he neared the bottom. 'We gotta move,' Kane mumbled with difficulty. 'They'll be through that door any minute.'

'Shit man. You got a fuckin' plank stuck in your face.'

Tank was right. The splinter was really more a giant piece of wooden shrapnel that had firmly embedded itself in, or rather through, Kane's left cheek. It might have looked worse, but you couldn't see much through all the blood.

'I'll deal with it later. We gotta blow the entrance. Did Rene get out?'

'Dunno. Didn't see him. What do you mean blow the entrance?'

'Always have a contingency, in case everything turns to shit.'

Kane looked down at Joanna lying unconscious on the sewer floor, and at Althea sitting nearby – still dazed from his blow. 'You take her,' he told Tank, indicating Joanna. 'I'll get Althea.'

Tank picked up Joanna as gently as he could. Her leg was bleeding badly but there was no blood on her head – a good sign, though she could have a very serious concussion.

Kane pulled Althea to her feet. 'Come on.'

'What about Rene?' she asked groggily.

'He's okay,' Kane told her. Then more to himself: 'I hope.'

Rene was still in the house, upstairs searching for Elly. He finally found her huddled under a box in the corner of one of the communal bedrooms. As he pulled the box away she squealed, terrified. Then when she saw who it was, relief swept across her face and she leapt into his arms, clinging desperately to his shirt.

'It's all right. I've got you.'

Rene ran for the door, but at that moment something happened downstairs and the entire house lurched and shook violently. Rene lost his footing and fell. He could hear muffled screams coming from the back of the house. His guess was the Temple Guards had finally broken through their defences and were in the house. If they went downstairs now, they were sure to be killed. Looking out the shattered windows of the room he could see the street below. There must have been close to a hundred Guards swarming into the house below him, and perhaps a hundred more at the back. They were certainly taking this assault seriously. The only way out now was up.

With Elly still clinging to his chest he ran into the hall and away from the staircase. Guards would surely be coming up that way any second. At the far end of the hall there was a latch on the ceiling.

A trapdoor with a retractable staircase that led into an attic. But he couldn't reach it.

'Elly. Get the latch,' he told the Bonobo pointing up. 'The Latch.'

Elly looked up and understood. She climbed onto Rene's shoulders and reached up, hooking a finger through the ring and pulled. A muffled click and the trapdoor lowered slowly, the staircase unfurling as it opened through a mechanism of pulleys and joints, creating a steep ladder-like staircase up into the darkness within the roof of the house.

Thank God for old houses, Rene thought. Modern constructions never had such ingenious use of space.

Shots were fired downstairs, the guards not only had power weapons but firearms as well. Rene heard them coming up the main staircase.

Elly dashed up the ladder-steps easily and vanished into the attic. Rene followed more awkwardly – such ladders were not made for rushing. Sitting in the darkness of the attic Rene fumbled for the mechanism that closed the trapdoor. 'How do you close the damn thing?' he said more to himself, but Elly reached past him to press a button on the wall nearby. The staircase retracted and the trapdoor closed. As it did Rene saw Temple Guard emerging at the top of the staircase at the far end of the hall. They looked directly at him through the closing crack.

One of the Guards raised his gun and fired a powerful haze at them. It hit the underside of the trapdoor just as it snapped shut, causing it to glow and burn. If he had held the shot for much longer it would no doubt have burned clean through. As it was the wooden staircase, now folded and compressed into a tight bale at Rene's feet, was scorched and blackened by the haze, its metal hinges expanding and breaking away. They were trapped. Rene led Elly into the middle of room, away from the trapdoor. A small, frosted skylight in the roof illuminated the room with overcast sunlight.

The Guards pulled open the trapdoor, causing the now broken staircase to clatter in pieces to the floor below. Rene tried punching open the skylight. No luck. He looked around for something solid he could break it with. Elly understood what he was doing and also searched.

Light spilled up into the attic from the collapsed trapdoor. Elly saw an old metal lamp-stand glistening in the shadows – she dashed across to grab it. A Guard's hand suddenly reached up through the hole in the floor and grabbed her by the ankle. Elly squealed in fright, then turned and hissed so violently at the Guard, her dark hairy face emerging from the shadows to confront him, that he let out a startled scream and released her ankle immediately, falling backward to land hard on the floor below. He probably thought he had grabbed onto some giant attic-dwelling rat or something.

Elly grabbed the lamp-stand and dragged it across the room. As she scooted past the open trapdoor a powered haze entered the attic and latched onto the metal stand. Elly released her grip a split second after she felt the charge enter her body, her hand ripping away violently. A pained squeal burst from her lungs as she dropped the stand to the floor.

The erratic orange-blue light from the haze bounced around the angled walls of the confined attic, creating a quite spectacular impression. Rene marvelled for a moment how beautiful it was. A pity it was so destructive.

The house lurched again. This time far more violently, as if the very foundations had been raised up and then pulled out from underneath. The attic fell dark as the haze stopped. The floor collapsed beneath them. Elly leapt into Rene's arms, knocking him backward – though he was falling anyway. The house was sinking into the ground, collapsing in on itself.

Everything became slow-motion as Rene watched the beams and walls around them buckle and snap. The dust of decades awakened in a burst of shimmering fog. He was suddenly falling into an abyss where the cries of Temple Guards and crumbling architecture merged into one. The house caved in around them, engulfing them in darkness. When they finally hit the ground, they were buried deep inside the wreckage of the building, along with the bodies of a hundred rebels and Temple Guard who had fought and died that day.

No one could have survived such a fall.

Rene's last thought as he gazed into the darkness, feeling the warm fur of Elly cradled against him, was of Joanna, and how cross she would be that he had gone and got himself killed – all to save someone else's bonobo.

'Hello, little brother.'

'Will? What happened?'

'You died.'

'...Damn. That wasn't meant to happen.'

'Perhaps it was,' came a voice. Rene turned to face him. 'Hello, Rene. I'm Matthew.'

'Hello. Where am I?'

'Look down.'

Rene looked down. Somehow, he was able to see through the wreckage of the collapsed safe-house to a small cavity deep in the heart of the rubble. He saw his body, surrounded by darkness and covered in debris. A thin translucent tendril of light snaked from the chest of his physical body to his present incorporeal self, floating somewhere above the scene. They were tethered by a spiritual cord. He also saw Elly still lying on top of his dead body, unmoving.

'Elly. Is she dead too?'

'No,' Will answered. 'You broke her fall.'

'Well,' Rene laughed, 'at least I didn't die in vain. Will she be able to get out of there?'

'She'll be all right,' Matthew said. 'We need to get moving.'

'Oh, already? What about Joanna, can't I say goodbye.'

'If things go well, you may not need to.'

'I don't understand. Are you saying I can go back?'

'We'll explain on the way,' Matthew answered.

'Where are we going?'

'To find your destiny, dear brother,' Will said with a cheeky grin.

'What?'

'You'll see.'

Matthew and Will led Rene away from his body, though the tendril of light kept him connected to it, stretching – if that's the proper term – as they flew across the city and descended on a nearby chapel …

Part 3

Freedom means allowing others to also be free.

Shentama
– The Third Tenet

You are not your body
You are more than moulded clay
You are a tree
A mountain
A drop of rain
A breath of air
A thunderbolt
A song

Shentama
– Stanza 67

Father Alban left 'Tobias' sleeping peacefully. His wound was almost completely healed. A miracle really. But he still slept an awful lot, as if his mind had more important things to do than lie uncommunicative in a cleric's bed. His young novice, Oscar, was helping several of their guests prepare an evening meal in their woefully under-equipped kitchen. When Alban entered, Oscar pulled him aside and spoke softly, not wanting the others to overhear:

'I think it's time we asked people to leave. The danger seems to have passed. Temple Guards have stopped patrolling the streets. We can't afford to keep them all here. It's too many.'

'I understand your concerns, my boy,' Alban consoled. 'But you will not ask anyone to leave. They are welcome to stay as long as they want. This is our job. To serve the people of this city in whatever way we can.'

'I thought our job was to serve the Church.'

Alban didn't quite know how to respond to this. Technically Oscar was right, they were servants of the Church. But lately serving the Church was giving Alban an acute crisis of conscience. He resolved it as he always did when confronted with such dilemmas, by asking himself: *What would the Prophet do?* It may be a naïve little ritual, but it meant he slept well at night.

'That too,' Alban said noncommittaly, and walked away before Oscar could advance the debate. Alban was no good at arguing theology or ethics. It was one reason he'd not advanced very high in the ranks of the Church. He couldn't play the game that others did so well. Oscar was a bright lad and would no doubt be Alban's superior one day. But that day had not yet come. This was Alban's chapel and he would run it his way. It was his own little fiefdom.

Father Alban walked through the sanctuary, nodding and smiling at his guests, and feeling rather proud of himself. In the old religions this might have been considered a sin, but to a Tobianist, expressing pride in something good was acceptable and healthy, as long as – like all things – it was not taken to excess. He had created a safe haven for anyone seeking sanctuary. He did not care why they came or what they had done. He did not care what their politics were – whether they were Tobianist or heretic. They needed help and he was in a position to provide it. This was the first time in his career as a priest he had felt truly useful. That he was making a difference.

Then the screaming started.

Beyond the closed doors leading to the atrium Alban heard the distinctive sound of power weapons being fired, and something he'd not heard before except in old movies – the sound of gunfire. Panicked, people moved to the back of the sanctuary – away from the noise. The doors burst open and several armed men and women charged in, firing indiscriminately into the crowd. These were not Temple Guards. They wore no uniform. Just a yellow scarf around their collars to set them apart. These were the same rebel fighters who had attacked the prisoner convoy two days earlier. The power gloves they wielded were the usual non-lethal kind, though if their haze was sustained long enough it could do some serious damage to their victims. The firearms however were deadly. Only a couple of the invading rebels had them, but they inflicted catastrophic harm to anyone in their line of fire – man, woman or child.

The man leading the charge had one of these firearms and he was the one Alban rushed, positioning himself between the rebel leader's gun barrel and a fleeing family. The man hesitated, smiled, then marched up to Alban and pressed the barrel of the gun against the priest's forehead. A chill ran through Alban's body, but he held his ground. 'You do realise you're killing your own people.'

'How do you know who my people are, priest?'

'Who are you, then? And why are you doing this?' Even with a gun to his head Alban was defiant. If he was about to die, he would die protecting his flock.

'Rohan's the name. And I don't have to explain myself to a priest.' Rohan was about to blow Alban's head off when –

'Then explain yourself to me!' a voice bellowed from behind Alban.

Rohan looked past the priest to see what appeared to be another priest approaching fast. He was tall, fair-haired and had intense blue eyes that somehow fixed Rohan to the spot. This second priest grabbed the barrel of the gun and wrenched the weapon away from Rohan, who seemed unable or unwilling to resist. Then he struck Rohan over the head with the butt of the gun, knocking him to the floor.

Alban turned and saw the Prophet Tobias standing next to him, wearing a spare set of his priestly robes. Tobias raised his arm and called out to the room in a voice that trembled the very walls: '*STOP!*'

The firing stopped.

Everyone turned to see the Prophet standing in the middle of the hall, with Alban by his side and the rebel leader Rohan at his feet massaging the bump on his head. As Tobias lowered his arm, rifle in hand, the rebels lowered their weapons in accord.

Tobias turned his attention to Rohan. Taking his arm, he helped him to his feet. 'I think you should leave now.' He offered back the gun. Rohan snatched it away, was about to do more but those deep blue eyes of Tobias's stayed his hand. They seemed to sap his very will to strike back. Rohan bowed his head, then signalled insistently for his followers to move out – as if it was his idea all along.

Before Rohan left Tobias placed a hand on his shoulder. 'I know your deeds are well-intentioned,' he said to him. 'But your method is misguided.' Rohan glared at him but couldn't sustain the anger. It wasn't the words so much as the bearing of the man that confused him. He didn't understand it.

The rebels left the chapel.

Alban considered the man standing next to him in awe: 'Tobias?'

Tobias smiled slightly. 'We have some injured people to tend, brother.'

Father Alban wouldn't have believed it possible had he not seen it with his own eyes – but then he had, and he still didn't believe it. Tobias moved through the crowd, seeking out the injured. With a laying on of hands he eased their pain and calmed their hearts. The attendant nurses still did what nurses do to clean and dress the wounds, and Tobias did what he could to help. He was not afraid of getting his hands or Alban's robes stained with blood. There were no big miracles, no feats of magic, and yet his presence and gentle ministrations brought a profound peace to everyone he touched or came near.

This was most evident when it came to those grieving for the ones who had been killed. He could do nothing for the dead. But for their families he spoke as if the departed were still there, speaking through him. He knew their names, knew things about them impossible for a stranger to know. He couldn't relieve their anguish; that would take time, as it always must. But his words helped them endure their tragedy, knowing their loved one was still with them in spirit.

Alban marvelled to see the Prophet Tobias at work – for he no longer doubted that he was indeed the Prophet reborn. All the philosophy and wisdom of the *Shentama*, all the lessons and principles it set forth, were brought to bear in that hour through his compassion for the people of Lorna. Others saw it too, though they could scarcely believe it. Even if they wouldn't accept this was the Prophet returned, they knew they were in the company of someone extraordinary.

When finally they retired to Alban's apartment, Tobias flopped exhausted into the sofa chair and looked up at the father. 'Some of that wonderful soup of yours would be much appreciated, brother.'

Moments later Alban sat with Tobias as he drank the soup.

'Is it really you?'

'You know, I'm not entirely sure myself,' Tobias answered.

'But you are the Prophet Tobias?' Alban needed to hear him say it.

'Yes. I am Tobias.' As he said this he combed his fingers through his long fair hair, brushing it away from his face. It was an unconscious gesture he was well known for.

'Have you returned to fulfill the prophecy?'

'Prophecy?'

Alban quoted: "In years to come, when my body is dust and the memory of this life is faded, I will return to continue my mission – '

' – As do we all,' Tobias concluded. He was confused. 'That was not a prophecy. It was … an explanation … of the inevitability of renewal. Of reincarnation. I must confess, I don't understand myself – how I came to be here, or even where here is.'

'You're in my church. Your church. I found you on the street a couple of days ago. You were wounded so I brought you here. Do you not remember? You were … not yourself. And yet, somehow, I knew it was you. You see, I look after your crypt. In the Great Temple. At least, I used to. When I went in there last week to prepare for the festival streamcast you were gone. Someone had moved you. I was told it was nothing to worry about but something wasn't right, I just knew it. Since then, things have got very bad. I'm sure it's no coincidence the Temple Guard is seeking out heretics in the city. Lorna has always had its share of troublemakers, but this is quite unprecedented, I assure you. What you saw out there was not normal. Things have become very dangerous, very quickly.'

' – Father,' Tobias interrupted. 'What do you mean, this is *my* church?'

Through finite means we grow and learn
Until the means are abandoned
In the understanding of the infinite one is alone

Shentama
– Stanzas 152-153

In the east wing of the Great Temple of Lorna, the spacious living quarters of the Cardinal Hierophant were conveniently located to allow ready access to the Hypogeum Basilica, the Council of Cardinals chambers and meeting rooms, and perhaps most importantly, the Temple Library.

There were actually two Temple libraries – one public, one private. The public library allowed just about anyone access to old printed books and photographs, and the massive database of digital AV records – all curated of course. Or one could wander through the museum of artifacts and educational presentations relating to the Prophet, the *Shentama*, and the history of the Tobianist Church. This was the approved history of Tobianism. It was quite extensive, and not completely self-aggrandizing. The dark days of *The Great Purge* for example were represented, rationalized as a violent coming of age the young religion had to endure to safeguard its place in the world (much like the civil wars of many nation states before it).

Out of conflict and hardship, one grows stronger. In the end, it was a noble war of empowerment for Tobianism, not that different from *The Reckoning* that had preceded it.

The other library, the private one, was only accessible to Church elite – the council of Cardinals and, in particular, the Cardinal Hierophant. This contained many more documents and recordings of the true history of the Tobianist era. The good and the bad. The known and the unknown. It contained those things banned or suppressed over the years. Rare early pressings of the *Shentama*, including three first editions – the only ones left in the world. It also had the only known unedited AV recording of the assassination of the Prophet – from news coverage of the time. Even things not directly related to Tobianism, but which challenged it in some way – such as archives of old movies and AV clips that promoted the values of rival religions, or political views not deemed safe for public consumption. Most of these entertainments and stories were 'lost' during *The Great Purge*.

In the public library you could also find a few artifacts and relics from other world religions and philosophies. These were for purely academic purposes, of course. Study of the old religions was not banned, just the practice of them. They were now little more than historical curiosities. Their rich histories and the centuries of knowledge and art sponsored by them confined to universities and museums.

But that was for the general public. The Great Temple's private library housed anything that challenged Tobianist belief or dogma in any way. The kind of unrestrained thinking that was dangerous to a monolithic religion like Tobianism. For example, some academic books that detailed the influence the old religions had on Tobias when forming his own philosophy, and in his writing of the *Shentama*. Or how the early Tobianist Church modelled its rites and rituals on those of the old religions. At first this was a way to get people to convert – the new way being not all that different to what they already knew. Over time people forgot the old ways, and through slow attrition Tobianism prevailed as a unique world religion. While all this may be fascinating from an historical perspective, the sanctity of the Church depended on suppressing such knowledge. Tobianism was a new faith, with its own traditions that owed little to the old religions. Anything that proved otherwise weakened the power of the Church, and its ability to govern.

Cairn understood this better than anyone. Suppressing knowledge was not to disadvantage people, but to control them. It was a noble lie. It avoided confusion, and engendered devotion to the Church and its laws. The mob needed clear, simple guidelines to live by. To conform was to be content. To be led meant one only had to follow. You were not distracted by unfathomable conundrums. The so-called Ethical Tobianists would claim otherwise, but Cairn knew better because he had once been one of them. It was intellect versus emotion, and in such a quarrel emotion always won out. There is comfort in constraint. Freedom in boundaries. The proof of it was in the fact the world had been prosperous and at peace for nearly two centuries. Tobianism was good for the world.

Before *The Great Purge* the tomb of Tobias had been readily available for people to pray to, leave flowers, post messages, or simply touch in the hope of a miracle. One could view his cryonically preserved face directly from a screen on the front of the tomb, and people had apparently experience miraculous cures just by looking upon the face of the Prophet. When the body was moved to a secret location deep within the Temple for security reasons, a way had to be found for the faithful to still connect with Tobias, while accepting the Great Temple as his new resting place. The annual streamcast made that possible, and it had since become a tradition of the festival. No longer did one have to travel to the temple city of Lorna to see the Prophet. Instead, the Prophet would come to you. And for those who still wanted to make the pilgrimage, the Great Temple offered far more than a crumbling stone edifice to express one's devotion.

As he watched rare AV recordings of the Prophet, unseen for over a hundred years except by his predecessors, Cairn was reassured he was doing the right thing. The public must never know the body of the Prophet had been stolen. During the opening ceremony of the Festival of Renewal, when the face of the cryonically preserved Tobias would be streamcast live across the world and displayed on gigantic AV-murals in the square outside the Temple, an isolated recording from last year's ceremony would be used instead. No one will know the difference. Nevertheless, Tobias still roamed the city alive, despite successful raids on dozens of rebel hideouts that morning. Until the body of the Prophet was safely installed back in his frozen tomb, the Church was still in danger.

The AV wall in Cairn's lounge was connected directly to the private library archive. He could browse for anything with a simple command. Cairn didn't really know what he was searching for. Just something that would somehow help him into Tobias's mind. Know how he was thinking. Where he might go. He knew Tobias had opposed establishing a Church in his name. A fact not mentioned in the publicly approved documentaries or archival recordings. How would Tobias feel about the Church now? He had also been a strong advocate of personal freedoms. It was the third tenet of Tobianism –

Freedom means allowing others to also be free

That's how it read in the original *Shentama*. The modern edition went more like –

You are free to live as you wish, within the laws nature
has provided as expressed through the Church; and
provided you do not infringe on the freedom of others
to live according to the same laws.

– depending which edition you were looking at.

Cairn thought the original bordered on anarchy. So simple and vague it was ripe for misinterpretation. From the moment he first read it upon becoming a Cardinal, it troubled him that the Prophet made this declaration such an important part of his philosophy. The amended version served the Church better. Complete freedom – without laws, without direction – was a bewildering and dangerous exercise. The history of the world was predicated on the fight for freedom in one form or another, resulting in perpetual conflict and bloodshed.

In his youth, this was a subject Cairn often imagined debating with the Prophet himself. He would fantasize of long conversations with Tobias about all sorts of things. The more he learned, the more he questioned. And with each question the Church provided a clear, unambiguous, answer he could believe in. As a result, his faith only grew stronger, until at the age of nineteen, and against his father's wishes, he left home to devote his life to the Prophet and his Church. That was nearly forty years ago.

In the twenty-two years since becoming a Cardinal to the Great Temple, and then Cardinal Hierophant, he had learned so much more. But the quest for understanding never stopped. Now he *was* the Church. He provided the answers for all those who, like him as a young man, had questions that needed to be answered. He was the chief interpreter of the Prophet's words. This was Cairn's responsibility to the Prophet and his legacy. But an even greater responsibility was owed the Church. It held dominion over the world and the life of every person upon it. No small charge.

Cairn returned his attention to the AV. Tobias was speaking at one of his public gatherings. He looked directly into camera – directly at Cairn.

'We are not the product of our parents or our environment. We are not formed by forces outside of ourselves. These things are merely physical. They offer challenges, obstacles, even crises that we must face. But they are not us. Chip away at the block that surrounds you. Remove the barriers that prevent you from being who you truly are. That is why you are here. That is why you were born. And it is why you will keep on being born, until all the rubble that binds you is removed. Then will you be truly free. And then you will understand, your only responsibility is to yourself. All the rest is encumbrance.'

Cairn wept unexpectedly. Even after all these years he still did not understand the paradox that was Tobias.

It is in disaster that peace abides
Carried on its shoulders like a child
Borne forward by tribulation
This is the way of all things

Shentama
– Stanza 148

Joanna woke with a massive headache. She opened her eyes but couldn't see a thing; it was too dark. Her other senses returned one by one. Wherever she was it was dank and moist. The air was stale and smelled of rotting vegetables, with the faint odour of oil and metal. She heard the distant sound of a whistling wind, as if through a cold and lonely tunnel. Was she underground? The wind became a breeze that licked at her exposed skin. She realized she was lying on her side. Whatever she was on didn't feel like a bed, but it was soft … and lumpy. She tried to sit up, but her head exploded and nausea gripped her throat, so she lay back down. What happened? How did she get here? Who was she with? Or was she alone? Why did she feel so awful? She couldn't remember any of it. Memories flitted through her mind: sitting with Rene in a strange house … conversations in a night club … a bonobo not a chimp … a red-headed woman … a priest … Temple Guards. It was all a jumble. She didn't know what order any of it was meant to be.

Then she realized her leg was in pain. It hurt like hell, but her headache was so intense she had barely noticed. Reaching down she felt a plasticky coating on her leg, and the outline of a hole in her thigh. Touching it didn't hurt, but the muscle tissue below ached something terrible. Someone was looking after her it seemed, but who? Then it occurred to her she was incredibly thirsty, and probably hungry – but one thing at a time.

'Hello?' she tried to call, but it just came out as a garbled grunt. She tried again: 'Hello!' This just made her head pound more so she stopped calling.

Someone heard though. A door opened and a sliver of light entered the room, followed by the silhouette of a woman. The noise outside became louder for a moment, the wind now more like the dull roar of distant machines. Or perhaps that was just her head bursting through her ears. The woman closed the door behind her and the room fell quiet again. She knelt beside Joanna and raised a straw to her lips.

'Drink.'

Joanna did as she was told. She ought to know who this woman was. She remembered her, but couldn't recall her name.

'How are you feeling?'

'Like shit.'

'How's the head?'

'Which one?'

'Don't worry. The pain should go away in a minute or so. Do you know where you are?'

'No.'

'Do you know *who* you are?'

Joanna had to think about that for a second. 'I'm Jo.'

'Good. Do you know who I am?'

She looked at the woman, trying to remember her name. She was the attractive red-head, though the black eye she now sported rather spoiled the image. Her name was on the tip of Joanna's tongue. She could hear it in her mind – three syllables – but it was clouded by a fog of pain and uncertainty. Then as promised, the pain receded and the headache stopped pressing so hard against her skull. The name came to her '… Althea.'

'Good,' Althea smiled warmly. 'Now the big one. Do you remember what happened?'

'… No.'

'What's the last thing you remember, Jo?'

'I don't know.'

'Do you remember the raid? Temple Guards attacking the house?'

Joanna did, but she recalled two raids, two houses. Which one came first? The memories were tangled – fleeting images, screaming, weapons fire … running … falling…. The one consistent thing was:

'Rene.'

'Yes. Rene was there. Do you remember falling?'

Joanna recalled flying down a fire-escape chute. Was that what she meant?

'You've suffered a pretty bad concussion. You've also been shot in the leg. I've taken care of that, but your head is what concerns me. You need to rest. Are you hungry?' Joanna nodded gently. 'I'll get you something.'

'Where are we?'

'You're lying on a couch, in an office, in one of the old underground train stations in the AQ.'

For some reason that didn't help. 'How did I get here?'

'Tank carried you.'

'A tank?'

'Don't worry about it. It'll come back to you.' Althea rose and made for the door. As she opened it Joanna remembered the most important question she had meant to ask:

'Where's Rene?'

Althea closed the office door behind her. A nervous anxiety clutched at her chest, as she walked across the station lobby to the old coffee shop. The station was a relic from a long forgotten era, when such public facilities were decorated with art deco tiling and colourful stained-glass lighting fixtures. Where curved arches, narrow pedestrian passageways, staircases and escalators ushered people from one tunnel to the next, and then to the surface. But the escalators no longer ran, the lights no longer glowed, and all of the surface exits had long since been covered over and forgotten. Travelling underground was not favoured in the Tobianist era. The old rail and road networks were abandoned in favour of elevated GL trains. Despite the world now being a very small place socially, people just didn't travel as much as they used to. Communication infrastructure obviated the need. One network had been replaced by another.

Althea thought there was something romantic about these old stations. Even now, falling apart as it was, and lit only by battery lanterns, the deep shadows clung to memories of a once vibrant city. Memories buried under generations of alleged progress. Despite historical records and hundreds of years of archived entertainments that showed what life was like in these times, they really knew very little about the people that once lived here. Their lifestyles and passions, politics and beliefs were likewise buried in the dust of time. So much had been lost in *The Great Purge*. Althea knew more than most, having studied the Tobianist era from its beginnings. Yet it was astonishing how little understanding came from so much information. Somewhere along the way, knowledge became content, content became data, and data just became noise. It was a world without wisdom or compassion. A world doomed to repeat the mistakes of the past.

A few deep breaths helped ease Althea's anxiety, but there was too much on her mind for it to wane completely. She'd just told Joanna Rene had escaped with a different group and they would find him again soon. Althea didn't know if this was true or not, so it wasn't exactly a lie. She couldn't bring herself to admit it was her fault he was lost. Rene had gone to find Elly. That was the last she saw of him. She couldn't imagine how he would have escaped the Temple Guards. She feared the worst for both Rene and Elly but clung to the hope that by some miracle they had survived. It was best Joanna did not know this yet. Worrying would only exacerbate her condition.

'How is she?' Kane asked, looking up from his mug of tepid brown coffee.

'I think she'll be okay. But we shouldn't move her for at least a couple of days.' Althea grabbed a packet of rations to take to her patient. The station had been considered too remote to be a safe-house, but served well as a storage facility. For years Kane had been stockpiling food and water here in the event of an emergency. Like the explosives laid beneath their house, he had prepared for just such a crisis. Despite his usual optimism, he'd had the foresight to plan for the worst.

'How's the face?' Althea asked Kane.

'Sore. I can't even drink properly.' With every sip of his barely drinkable coffee a little dribbled out the side as he tried to keep the liquid to one side of his mouth.

'You should use a straw,' Althea told him.

'You don't drink coffee with a straw,' Kane slurred.

'You shouldn't be drinking coffee at all.' Althea could see she would have to re-dress the wound once he was finished. Her own face was still bruised from the wallop he had given her back at the house, so she had no sympathy for him, though his actions undoubtedly saved her life.

Tank had removed the massive splinter from Kane's cheek, and the wound was sealed with a translucent organic polymer dressing that protected the skin while allowing it to heal. The dressing came as gel patches that could be cut to shape, and which used the same IPS stem-cell technology Doctor Asar had used on Tobias. It encouraged natural healing and reduced the chances of scar tissue forming. For a wound this bad though, without the facilities to properly graft it, a scar would be inevitable.

'So how did they find us?' Althea asked.

Tank responded, since Kane was having enough trouble talking. 'I think they've known about us for ages. They've just been waiting for the right time to strike.'

It was clear this had been a coordinated city-wide assault by the Temple Guard. Every rebel safe-house, meeting place, and home had been attacked. Hundreds killed. There may be others like them, who had survived and were hiding out, but no-one would risk exposing themselves. They were completely isolated.

Althea turned back to Kane. 'How long do you intend we stay down here?'

'I don't know.'

'What about the others? Do any of them know about this place?'

'No.'

'Then what the fuck are we gonna do?'

'I DON'T KNOW!'

Kane's voice echoed down the ceramic tiled tunnels of the station, ringing on for several seconds, amplifying the despair and doubt in his voice. Then he said again, gently, inconsolably: 'I don't know.'

Althea knelt beside Kane, her hand on his shoulder. 'It doesn't end here,' she reassured.

'How would you know?'

'… I just do.' Althea was thinking of Tobias. It was a vain hope, but still a hope. 'You know there are others still out there. We have to find them.'

Kane looked at her. She was right of course. Many had escaped and were now either wandering the city or lost in the tunnels beneath it, looking for a safe haven. If they could get them to the station safely and unobserved, they could regroup. At the very least they could prevent more people falling into the hands of the Temple Guards.

Kane turned to Tank and nodded. It was all he needed. Rising from the table he prepared to leave.

'I'm coming come with you,' Althea told him.

'No,' Kane interrupted. 'You need to look after Jo.'

'I've done all I can there. She just needs to sleep.'

There was no arguing with Althea when she was on a mission, so Kane let it slide. 'Make sure she doesn't get into any trouble,' he told Tank.

Althea smiled; he was learning. 'Let me give her this food and I'll be right with you.' She marched through the once glazed coffee shop doors across the station lobby.

'Tank,' Kane murmured when Althea was out of earshot. 'Get me a straw.'

One who seeks to divert you from your path
Is insecure in their own
And not worthy of esteem

Shentama
– Stanza 7

C aptain Marius hated going to meetings. They were either a big waste of time or resulted in actions he disagreed with. Rarely did he walk out of one feeling he had got what he wanted. And never after meeting with Cardinal Kasper. This was despite Kasper's support for Marius's idea to stage an all-out assault on known rebel houses and haunts. There had to be another reason for Kasper to champion the idea – some secret motive. There always was.

Marius's armour rattled unevenly as he strode down the spacious halls of the Great Temple. He was trying to mask the limp he had sustained at the Festival Square ambush, but it looked like he was stuck with it for life. He didn't mind the limp so much, it was kind of cool in fact, but it made walking in armour difficult. Things were rubbing together that shouldn't be. He would have to see about getting the leggings modified to suit his new gait.

The Temple halls were decorated with art from several generations. A museum of religious and philosophical themes, noble virtues, saints and martyrs, heroic deeds. Marius had studied many of these when he first joined the Guard, but had forgotten most of it now. He was not motivated by high ideals or moral imperatives. He just did what felt right. So far his instincts had served him well. They got him where he was, after all.

All too often the meetings he was forced to endure had people arguing these kind of intellectual goals, whether they be the Council of Cardinals or his own officers. The more people present, the worse it was. Marius preferred to act as he saw fit, then apologise later if it caused a stink. It was a calculated risk. More often than not he got results, so it didn't matter; otherwise he might have been discharged or demoted long ago. You could disagree with his methods, but there was no arguing his record.

He approached the inner sanctums of the east wing. This housed the Temple's central admin offices for each of the Executive Council members and their aids. Here the art adorning the walls was giant portraits of past and present council members. It represented the entire history of Tobianist leadership since *The Great Purge*. With each step he journeyed through the decades and the changing fashions of clerical garb. Then as the offices came into view, the faces of the present Council surrounded him, dressed in the simple but elegant black and red robes now standard for the Executive.

Kasper's offices adjoined the Cardinal Hierophant's. As treasurer of the Great Temple and effectively second in charge, Kasper commanded a large staff including his own contingent of bodyguards. Two guards stood constant vigil outside the doors to his offices and apartments. They worked in eight-hour shifts – six guards in all – just to guard the doors. There were twelve others who either accompanied the Cardinal everywhere he went or did whatever bidding he commanded. Every council member had the same security.

They were the Elite Guard. The best of the best. And the only guards not pulled from duty to take part in the recent raids.

The two guards at the door snapped to attention as Marius approached. Each carried a stun-rated power rifle, and despite recognizing him as their commanding officer, they brought their weapons to ready position, prepared to fire in the event he was a threat. Normal protocol. Marius would have bawled them out if they had done anything less. With his comkey ratified on approach, signalled by a gentle chime, the guards returned to at-ease, letting Marius pass.

Through the door into the Cardinal's offices, the Captain passed a few underlings sitting at their AVs doing whatever it is underlings do. He strode up to Kasper's office. Another guard at the door snapped to attention, weapon ready. This meant the Cardinal was in.

'Captain Marius is here, Your Eminence.' The guard announced into the comms.

Moments later, 'Come!' came the response from within, and Marius entered the room.

Despite rising to the highest rank a Temple Guard could, there were still masters he had to answer to. The trick was in pleasing two masters at once. Both Cairn and Kasper wanted this Gerda escapee Tobias look-a-like found and killed. Both also wanted to be the first and only person Marius told when this was done. Cairn was the more superior of course. As Cardinal Hierophant he was superior to everyone. But Kasper was just as formidable, and in some ways more powerful than Cairn. He had his fingers in everything and might one day become Cardinal Hierophant. Marius needed to stay on Kasper's good side.

'Captain,' Kasper greeted. 'Have a seat.'

Marius sat in the chair opposite Kasper's imposing desk, his armour squeaking and knocking as he lowered himself awkwardly.

Dress armour was not meant for sitting.

'I presume you've had no luck finding the prisoner,' Kasper began. 'Otherwise, you would have told me already.'

'Yes, Your Eminence. That is to say: No. We've not found him yet. Apart from that time – '

He had already told Kasper about his encounter during the Festival Square ambush. Kasper didn't believe it. He had not shown Kasper the surveillance footage Cairn saw, but Marius doubted it would change his mind.

'As I have told you, Captain. I believe our real quarry is already dead, despite what you may have been told … or seen. You know how easily AV footage can be altered. Surely it can't be that difficult to find a dead body in this city?'

There were a lot of dead bodies in the city, Marius wanted to say. But he bit his tongue. 'There are parts of Lorna not easily searched.' Even as he said it Marius realised this was a pathetic excuse, however true it may be.

'You mean the Abandoned Quarter.'

'Yes. We've had men in there before, but all we've ever found are squatters and derelicts. The so-called *Lost*. The place is a shambles. Very hard to navigate.'

'And yet you found those scientists in the hospital.'

'We knew where to look.' Now he was getting defensive. Not a good tactic with Kasper.

'You disappoint me, Captain. I would have thought you of all people could find an escaped prisoner. Dead or alive.'

Marius was not sure what Kasper was referring to – '*him of all people*'. Perhaps his confidence in Marius's leadership was being tested.

'We're still looking. I'm sure we'll find him soon. Dead or alive.'

'I hope so, Captain. I would hate for you to be sent back to Gerda, after all the years it took to get you where you are.'

Marius was confused. Why was Kasper talking about Gerda? What did he know? 'Your Eminence?'

Kasper leaned forward in his chair. 'Seven ... five ... three ... nine ... two.'

Marius suddenly couldn't breathe. His face drained of blood, turning white with shock. His head was spinning and he felt he was either about to throw up or faint. *How the fuck did he know that number? How the fuck did he find out?!* That had been his number when he was a prisoner in Gerda. In a former life. Before he became a Temple Guard. Before he became Marius.

'What do you mean?' he bluffed, his voice cracking as he spoke. *It was just a number. How much did Kasper know?*

'Normally, one convicted of murder is never released.' Kasper said slowly, making sure it sank in. 'It's a life sentence. And yet you escaped.'

'I never escaped Gerda,' Marius blurted, realizing he had just admitted to being there. But it seemed Kasper knew it already. 'I served my time.'

'To be released from Gerda is still escape of a sort, would you not say?'

Marius couldn't answer. Everything had got very surreal, and he wasn't sure any more this conversation was actually happening.

'You're wondering how I came to know about your carefully forgotten past. It is something I have known for a very long time. Have you never considered why you were accepted into the Temple Guard? Or how you were able to advance so swiftly though the ranks? And all despite your homosexuality.'

He knew about that too. Marius felt his life crumbling away beneath him.

'I've been sponsoring you from the very beginning,' Kasper continued. 'I secured your release from Gerda. Enabled you to change your identity and start a new life here in Lorna. Encouraged you to join the Guard and saw you safely through the system. I did this all so you could sit with me now … and return the favour.'

Marius tried to process what Kasper was saying. He couldn't believe it. His whole life had been directed according to the whim of another man. Yet it made sense. Thinking back on how things had turned out, it had always seemed someone was looking out for him. He credited fate, or his spirit guides, or some other ephemeral force. Or just plain good fortune and hard work. He would never have imagined it was Kasper.

'You see, Captain. You owe me far more than you can know. I gave you this life. And I gave it you for one very simple reason. You serve me.'

26

True freedom comes from within
In the full acceptance of self
Requiring no-one's consent
Needing no laws to confer it or enforce it
It is not bequeathed by society
But is an emotional knowingness
Unique to each person

Shentama
– Stanza 222

E lly woke, and immediately knew something was wrong. Pain racked her body. She was surrounded by darkness. She tried to move. Slowly. Carefully. Her muscles protested but she could move. Her body was intact.

She remembered falling. Lots of noise. She remembered being scared. The alpha-man was with her, holding her. The one they called Rene. Who was also called Tobias. Who was also called Prophet. He came for her. When the noisy men attacked. The men with death in their hands. They ran. Were trapped in the top room. Then everything fell down.

She felt Rene beneath her and climbed off him. The space was cramped. Dark. Surrounded by the fallen house. The top room had become the bottom room. She found Rene's face and touched it gently. He didn't move. He was wet. She smelled her fingers. Blood. She felt his chest. It beat with life. Faint and weak, but the life beat was there. He was hurt. Althea would know what to do. She would take away the hurt. Elly was hurt too, but Rene was hurt more.

She was thirsty. He must be thirsty. They needed water. And food. That would help. He came for her. Saved her from the noisy men. She would save him now if she could.

Elly didn't understand why humans killed each other. Why they feared each other so. A gift was all it took to turn stranger to friend. Why did they make everything so complicated?

She scrambled around in the dark, exploring the space. Broken beams held up the roof of their hole. Brick, earth and debris filled in the gaps. She found a spot more loosely packed. Pulling at it she was able to create the beginnings of a tunnel.

Dan and Maya lay on the floor of the basement for a good two hours after the Temple Guards left – just to be sure. When they finally ventured upstairs they saw the result of the guards' ransacking. Giant scorch marks were burned into the walls from indiscriminate power weapons fire. It was as if the Guards were pissed there was no one to kill and so decided to wreck the house instead. They removed their blood-soaked clothes and showered. Dan found them a pair of Bartholomew's undertaker suits from the office closet that hadn't been completely torn or burned. Too small for Dan, too big for Maya, but anything was better than what they had been wearing.

He also discovered in the closet a secret panel on the back wall. It gave slightly as he accidentally pushed against it while rummaging through the clothes, but was otherwise quite indistinguishable from the rest of the closet interior. Feeling around its edges he found a small latch under the cornice near the ceiling. The panel opened to reveal a hidden shelf on which rested a tall camouflage-patterned weatherproof vinyl bag with a carry strap. Dan took the bag out and placed it on the floor of the room. Unzipped it. There was a gun inside. A rifle of some sort. It was partially dismantled, and Dan was certainly no gun expert, but even he could tell this was something unusual. The barrel had a strange bulbous end, and the large body of the weapon was an imposing matte black. Whatever it was, it was something Bartholomew had wanted to keep secret. That was reason enough to take it.

They did one last thing before leaving. Dan lit a fire in the middle of the lounge out of paper and broken shelving, and they ceremoniously burned their comkeys. Dan's was in the pendant he wore around his neck; Maya's was a bracelet on her left wrist. These were already hacked to avoid being remotely tracked, but their other functions were still active. Best to get by without them from now on. Cut themselves off from the grid completely. The thought of it was both frightening and liberating.

All of these preparations were done in silence. Neither Dan nor Maya felt the need to speak, or even knew what to say. Nor did they discuss leaving the house. They just did. It was relatively safe now that the Guards had come and gone, but they didn't want to spend another minute in that accursed place. So they abandoned it, hoping the fire would spread.

Wandering the streets of Lorna in their ill-fitting, slightly ruined, matching black suits, they were conspicuous. But no one else walked the streets, just the occasional hopper that would whizz by from time to time, the occupants shooting them curious glances. By burning their 'keys they had effectively cut themselves off from society. Conformity was surrender, and surrender was death. There was no place for them now in Lorna, among the civilized sheep.

More than ever, Dan saw the Church as his enemy, and the Temple Guard as their puppet army. A legion of despots and parasites feeding on people's blind faith. Controlling them with dogma and ritual that no longer had anything to do with the Prophet Tobias or his teachings. The Church was a cancer on the world and must be destroyed. Dan had always thought this, but until now it had been an intellectual rebuke. All talk and no action. Now he would act. Blood begets blood.

Maya followed Dan without question. He was now her leader. He had saved her life, twice, and she trusted him implicitly. It was not in her nature to do otherwise. She also loved him, but she was not about to tell him so. She couldn't even admit it to herself. Fate had thrown them together, and she would see where it led. So when Dan headed west, she said nothing. When they passed by the huddled, modest homes of the indigent in the Western Borough, she said nothing. And as she saw the crumbling skyscrapers of the AQ in the distance, and understood what Dan's intentions were, she accepted it.

Almost without noticing their surroundings became empty and overgrown, devoid of human habitation. The buildings were taller and older, the streets broken and crowded with collapsed architecture.

They walked on … Two smartly dressed refugees in search of safe harbor. The setting sun cast an orange bloom over the old city. Long shadows consumed the canyons separating the buildings, the cross-streets bright and stark in the languishing light. Their footsteps crunched on the street and echoed through the empty halls of history. Dan thought he heard something and raised his hand for Maya to stop.

The footsteps continued. Someone else was walking these streets.

Moments later a figure emerged into the light and walked to the middle of the intersection ahead of them. He was armed with a power rifle, wore khaki pants and a plain collared shirt, a brimmed cap, and sunglasses. He was the model of a modern-day freedom fighter who had yet to see any real battle – all front, no experience. He stopped and looked at the two of them for a few seconds, the rifle carried comfortably across his torso; not threatening, but ready if necessary.

'What's with the suits?' he called to them.

'What's with the gun?' Dan countered.

The man raised the weapon to his shoulder and aimed it at Dan. *Does this answer your question?*

Dan lingered, wondering what might be a suitable response to a stranger pointing a gun at his head.

'WC-42.'

The man slowly lowered the gun. 'WC-25.'

'Our cell was attacked,' Dan told him. 'I think we're all that's left.'

He lowered the gun further. He believed him. 'Every cell was attacked.'

'How many of you are there?' Dan asked.

The man didn't answer. Instead, he gestured for them to follow him, and walked back the way he had come. He led them into the building that fronted the intersection. As they approached, Dan noticed the reflected glint of lookouts watching from the windows high above. They would have seen them coming from miles away.

They entered the lobby of an old office block, past the front desk and security station, past the derelict elevators, and up the stairwell.

Seven flights. They emerged into a conventional workspace, with private offices around the sides and open-plan workstations spread throughout the middle of the floor. Not all that different to a modern office really, though here everything was covered in dust, there was no glass in the windows, and no AV screens, desks, chairs, or any other evidence of recent occupation. It was like the place had been stripped bare and left to rot for a hundred years, which is essentially what had happened.

Their guide led them past the lookouts who scoured the streets below for other interlopers. The lookouts gave them a cursory glance, but then returned to their vigil. Moving along the main corridor they passed empty offices, storage rooms, bathrooms, and a kitchenette area. *All the comforts of home*, Dan thought. Finally, they came to the largest office on the floor. This had an actual desk, an AV screen, and sitting in the chair behind it, the leader of the survivors of WC-25.

'More castaways, I see,' the leader said as they entered. He studied Dan's face. 'Hey, don't I know you?'

Dan didn't recognize him. 'I don't think so.'

'Yeah…' He pointed a finger at Dan as the memory came to him. 'You're the idiot from the holding cells.'

Now Dan recognized him. The psychopath with the big mouth. Rohan. *This guy was their leader?* 'Oh yeah …. Hi.'

'So you made it out alive. Good to see. Got your comkeys with you?'

'We destroyed them,' Dan told him.

Rohan smiled. 'Good. Saves me the trouble. Don, wasn't it?'

'Dan. This is Maya.'

'Cute.'

'Rohan,' Dan told Maya by way of introduction.

'General Zielinski, if you don't mind. Welcome to the

Libertarian Army.' Rohan then noticed the camouflage bag strung over Dan's shoulder. 'What you got there?'

—— ∞ ——

Tank drove a Temple-issue GL cruiser through the train tunnels. Althea was in the passenger seat, involuntarily gripping the sides of her chair. She was not used to travelling at such high speed, in such a confined space, with so little light. Tank however was quite relaxed. This was a perfectly normal velocity for him, and given his Warrior Games training, going slower would have been even more dangerous.

After the Festival Square ambush Tank had managed to appropriate two GL cruisers and somehow get them down to the station unseen. Their consoles were modified (ie: broken) so they couldn't be tracked, but otherwise they were fully functional. They even had Temple Guard markings still on the side, plus the odd haze burn.

With headlights illuminating the way, they zipped through the tunnel like a ball of light in pursuit of the darkness. The walls whizzed by in a blur, broken occasionally by a branching tunnel or gloomy station platform. The GL floated just a few centimetres above the old rail lines. An occasional static release from the rusted metal cracked loudly, sending a hollow standing-wave echo down the long tunnel. Otherwise, the dull sound of thrumming supports as they buzzed past was hypnotically calming.

Althea's mind turned once more to Elly and Rene, which further fuelled her guilt. Elly was such a peaceful creature. Bonobo's, unlike humans or even chimpanzees, never fought or killed their own kind. They were an intensely social animal that lived in matriarchal communities in the wild. Their entire existence was predicated on pleasure and the family bond within their tribe. They were giving, loving, and nonviolent to the point of extinction. Chimps were more like humans emotionally and psychologically. Bonobos were what humanity aspired to become. They were more evolved in so many ways. At least, that's how Althea saw it. Others didn't share her view. Just because Elly didn't speak, they thought her stupid. A brutish animal. A bizarre pet. Probably no-one else cared that Elly might be dead. So many of their comrades had died that morning, what did the life of a pet 'monkey' matter? Rene cared though, and he was probably killed for it. Guilt infected her mind and just would not be ignored.

Tank brought the GL to a stop as they entered another station. Leaving the vehicle on the tracks, he grabbed a couple of battery lanterns and slung the power rifle across his back, just in case. Althea wore a backpack with first aid supplies and some food. They climbed onto the broken platform and up the cracked and crumbling staircase to the surface.

'What if we kept following the tracks?' she asked Tank. 'Where would we end up?'

'Don't know. Never been that far. All I know is this is the way out.'

Althea noticed an old topological map of the rail network on the wall of the upper platform as they ascended. It looked vast and complicated. Much bigger than just the AQ, with lines stretching under Lorna proper. Combine that with the sewerage network, the catacombs under the Temple, and God knows what other ancient tunnels were hidden under the city, and one could get just about anywhere without ever having to break the surface. But as she had learned, navigating these forgotten passages without a map meant one could very quickly become lost.

The uppermost level of the station was caved in, the exit destroyed and obscured by giant blocks of concrete and metal fallen from one of the desiccated towers above. The floor was flooded from rain that had flowed down through the debris – mould and grass taking hold in the tangled cracks of the tiles and walls. This station was not as ornate as the one they'd set up camp in – its construction looked newer. More pragmatic. Less robust.

They climbed over and through the rubble until finally emerging out a narrow slit into the moonlit canyon of a ramshackle AQ street. Althea had a vague recollection of this route, but she had been so groggy first time through, hanging semi-conscious off Kane's shoulder, that she hadn't really paid attention. *How on earth did Tank carry Joanna through all that?* she wondered. There had to be an easier route.

They were in a part of the AQ Althea didn't recognize, but Tank knew the way so she just followed his lead. 'Where are we going?' she asked.

'Well, if you were out here all alone, Temple Guards on your tail, nowhere safe to hide, where would *you* go?'

'Somewhere here, inside the Abandoned Quarter.'

'Possibly.' Tank scanned the crumbling office buildings surrounding them. The darkness within was frightening. Even Tank hesitated to brave these ruins during the day, let alone at night. 'It'd be rough going. Living in these ruins. Anywhere else?'

Althea considered for a moment. 'Somewhere they least expected.'

'What? Like inside the Temple?' Tank was joking, but he wasn't far off the mark.

'Not the Temple, but maybe a church?'

'No church is gonna protect heretics on the run,' Tank countered.

'One might.'

27

My truth is for me alone and will never serve another
If these words help to light your way that is good
But let them be the guide to your own path
And not the path you follow

Shentama
– Stanza 98

The chapel was running out of food. Father Alban had sent Oscar out to buy supplies, instructing him to visit several stores so as not to arouse suspicion. It would all be recorded of course, but Alban hoped the Temple didn't keep too close an eye on the activities of church novices.

Despite this, they went through most of what Oscar bought in a day. For the evening meal Alban and his helpers prepared again his now famous soup with bread. It was suitably humble as Tobias helped serve the meal to the crush of people crowding the sanctuary, vestibule and adjoining rooms. He wandered through the chapel handing out pieces of bread to each person as they received their bowl of watery soup. The bread was drawn from a bag he carried over his shoulder, and as the bag became lighter Alban feared they would not have enough to go round. Amazingly every person was fed.

In days to come this would be seen as a miracle of sorts. Like others before him, Tobias had fed the multitude with the merest of rations. Alban knew it was just good math, nevertheless he too felt something miraculous in the event. Not so much in the food itself, but in the act of giving it. Tobias connected with every single person. Each had their own little moment with the Prophet, and for each it was a defining moment in their lives. Just to be in his presence was a miracle.

As it turned out they had five portions to spare. Oscar had calculated everything exactly, but had not counted on five of their group being dead before dinner.

The bodies were removed to one of the church's antechambers, intended as a waiting room or utility storage area. The five deceased lay in state on makeshift tables. Killed not by Temple Guards, but by rebels. One of them was a ten-year old girl named Kayla. Already this revolution came at too high a cost.

Tobias stood by the body of the child with tears in his eyes. Alban was with him.

'I wish the stories were true,' Tobias said softly. 'That I could restore life. Raise the dead. Then I would surely return this child to her family. But even I cannot defy the laws of nature.'

'But you have already,' Alban ventured. 'You are here.'

'Yes,' Tobias mused. 'I don't understand it, but there must be a reason for it.'

'Perhaps you are meant to witness what has become of your teachings. Perhaps you have come to set things right.' Alban was sounding like a revolutionary. Tobias said this was not the prophesy of his return fulfilled, but to Alban there could be no other explanation.

' …Perhaps …' Tobias looked again at the pale, still face of the dead girl. He thought he had been doing so well. His mission had been to teach people to think for themselves. To respect one another, and not be fooled by those who only sought to control them. But everything he had said was twisted – turned against itself. It had become the very thing he wanted to avoid. And from the little Alban had told him of how humanity arrived at this place, it had been a violent and bloody process. This was not the future he had hoped to create.

But was it his to create? Was it arrogant to think he could change things? After all he had said, after all these years, people still clung to ritual and conformity. They gave up their freedoms for a little peace of mind and convenient truths. Who could blame them? A life without boundaries is a life uncertain. Not everyone is ready for enlightenment. Tobias realized his actions had been contrary to his own teachings. He sought to influence how others thought. The irony was not lost on him.

To teach people to teach themselves was surely not a bad thing. But now he saw the consequences of his life's work, and he had only made things worse. He didn't yet know why he had come back, but he knew it was not to set things right, as Alban put it. His mission ended the day they fired a bullet into his heart.

And yet … he knew there was something more yet to be done. He had seen it.

Kayla was killed by people fighting in his name, against a Church in his name, in a place built in his name. He wished he had never begun all this. The world would have been better off without him.

Alban interrupted Tobias's introspections. 'You once said: To mourn the dead is to mourn life. To resist change is to resist the very purpose of life, and the lessons it offers.'

'I did say that. And yet I weep. To believe it is one thing, to live it is much harder.'

Just then Oscar burst into the room in a panic. 'Father! They're back!'

Alban dashed into the chapel, ready to confront the rebel leader Rohan and his followers once more. Instead, he saw two new rebels walking calmly through the crowd. One was a striking red-headed woman dressed in dusty top and pants, hiking boots, and carrying a small backpack. The other was a large black man wearing a tank-top singlet, dark pants and boots and carrying a power rifle. The weapon hung from his arm, impassively pointed at the floor. They were not outwardly threatening anyone. Nevertheless, the crowd drew back creating a path for them as they passed, a wave of fear coursing through the assembled. The very sight of a weapon sparked a mute panic.

Althea didn't understand why everyone was retreating from them. Was Tank that scary looking – big, black and carrying a gun? A priest appeared on the other side of the chapel and made towards them.

'Tank. Put away the gun,' she told him.

Tank slowly raised the weapon, causing the people around them to cower further, and locked the rifle into the holster across his back. They continued in silence.

'Are you Father Alban?' Althea asked the priest when they were face to face.

'Yes.'

'We mean you no harm. My name is Althea Roget. This is Tank.'

Tank smiled his pearly-whites and nodded at Alban, who returned the greeting reticently. Even when friendly Tank was an imposing figure.

'You brought a woman, Joanna, to our door a few days ago,' Althea continued. 'Do you remember?'

'Of course, Jo. How is she?'

'She's fine,' Althea lied. 'We're looking for – ' Althea watched over Alban's shoulder as Tobias enter the room. At least he looked like Tobias. Was she hallucinating?

He wore the robes of a cleric, his hair smooth and shiny and practically glowing in the light that spilled from the door behind him. He was not at all the Tobias she had last seen though – an animal, driven by primal instincts. Had something happened? Could this really be him?

Tank followed Althea's gaze. He also thought he recognized the priest approaching them.

'Ah, yes,' Alban introduced. 'Althea, Tank … the Prophet Tobias.'

Tobias studied Althea with a penetrating gaze. 'How do you do?'

Althea's head was spinning. This was the most surreal moment of her life.

'You're alive,' she managed to say.

'Yes.'

'You're talking.'

Tobias smiled. 'Yes.'

'… I don't understand.'

'Neither do I,' Tobias admitted as he combed his fingers through his long hair. 'Yet here we are.'

'It worked,' Althea murmured, more to herself. 'It actually worked.'

'I beg your pardon.'

Althea was overcome. She fell to her knees and timidly touched the hem of his robes to make sure he was real.

'There's no need for that.' Tobias gently took her by the shoulders and lifted her back to her feet. She felt as light as a feather. His hands then moved to her face, cupping her affectionately, as a parent might a child. 'Please tell me, what do you mean: it worked?'

It had taken Elly several hours to dig her way to the surface. There were many detours, dead-ends, and spots that were barely wide enough to squeeze through. But she persisted, digging in the dark, cutting her hands on unseen metal and glass fragments, climbing over the bodies of friends or the noisy men trapped in the rubble.

Finally, she emerged into the night and could breathe clean air again. Then began her search through the remains of the house for food and water. She found an undamaged bottle and filled it with water from a large puddle. Rummaging through the place where the kitchen had once been, she managed to find a few scraps of something edible. After eating and drinking herself, she wrapped the rest in a makeshift bag made from the shirt of a dead friend, and headed back to Rene.

He was awake when she returned, but still lying where she left him. Elly carefully poured the water into his mouth. He drank. She pulled off pieces of food for him and he ate. She touched his head and smelt her fingers again. No smell. His blood was dry.

Rene tried to move and groaned painfully. She touched his chest gently and he groaned sharply again. Something was broken inside. All she could think to do was to kiss it.

In time Rene went back to sleep. Elly sat with him in the dark. She needed to find help but did not want to leave him. So she sat. Waiting till he was stronger.

Kane sat beside Joanna as she slept. He rarely got time to just be alone and think. Now that he had time, he was doing everything he could to avoid it. He tried sitting outside, drinking coffee he wasn't supposed to, watching the AV for news of the raids.

Nothing.

He even tried exploring the train station a bit more, but didn't want to wander too far from his patient. Finally, he returned to the office where Joanna was laid up and just sat with her. That way he could be doing something without having to do anything.

Kane was not cut out to be a leader, and he knew it. He became one by default when no one else would step up – aside from Rohan. But Rohan was too impulsive. Too belligerent. He rubbed people the wrong way. Kane became leader so that his brother couldn't. It was not the first time something had come between them as brothers. Perhaps they would have been better off with Rohan. Being popular was no surety one could lead well. Some of the greatest leaders in history were also the most reviled.

In a way it was fortunate they'd had this falling out. It had prompted Rohan and his followers to leave before the attack on the house, so there was a good chance they'd survived. Unless they knew. This hadn't occurred to Kane before. What if Rohan left because he knew they were about to be raided? Was he a mole, as Rene had suspected? An informer for the Temple? Did he give up their location to the Guard?

Kane didn't want to believe it. He knew his brother well enough to know he would never be in league with the Temple. It was just a coincidence. It had to be. He may have disagreed with Rohan's politics, but he was exactly the kind of fighter the revolution needed right now. Someone who wasn't afraid to break a few eggs. Someone who was prepared to kill the fat man. Kane was already obsolete.

That's why he was so glad to have found Rene. Rene didn't know it, but he was a born leader. Reluctant perhaps – but then the best leaders are. They emerge out of crisis, from unexpected places and the least likely of folk. That is how heroes are born. Theirs is a destiny few can imagine, least of all themselves. Kane didn't know what Rene's destiny was, but he was damn sure it wasn't to die in a Temple Guard raid on an insignificant rebel safe house. He felt in his gut Rene was still alive. Even though he knew the odds were against it.

Joanna stirred.

'How do you feel?'

'Better.' She sat up carefully. Kane offered her some medicated water, but she waved it away. 'Where's Rene?'

'I don't know,' Kane told her honestly. He spoke softly, conscious of her delicate state.

'Did he escape the house?'

Kane couldn't answer. He was sick of telling people *he didn't know*. It made him feel impotent and useless.

'I'm sure he'll be all right,' Joanna reassured, as much for Kane as for herself. 'Rene has a tendency to avoid things he doesn't like. He's become quite good at it. I'm sure he'll manage to avoid getting himself killed. He knows how cross I'd be if he did.'

Kane couldn't believe she was joking about it. They continued in hushed tones, as if they feared offending some eavesdropping spirit.

'You know him pretty well,' Kane said.

'Better than anyone.'

'I think you're right. Rene's meant for something more than this. I've only known him a few days, but I sense in him … something profound.'

'I know.' Joanna knew exactly what he was talking about. 'It's like… he's important somehow. He has a destiny. Not like the rest of us. An actual destiny. I keep telling him, but he refuses to see it.'

'He's avoiding it.'

'Exactly. How can someone avoid their own destiny?'

'You can't.'

'You can't,' Joanna repeated. 'Sooner or later, it'll catch up with you. And then we'll see.'

'What will we see?'

Joanna pondered on this a moment. 'We'll see who Rene really is. We'll see the man he was always meant to be. We'll see the future.'

'What kind of future do you think it will be?'

'Wonderful. Frightening. Momentous.'

'That's a lot for one man.'

'He won't be alone.'

Joanna looked Kane deep in the eye as she said this. He understood. In the silence that passed between them a pact was made. Together, and with whoever else they could call to their side, they would be there for Rene. They would help him fulfill whatever fate had in store for him. It was an odd thing, but Kane suddenly felt he had purpose again. His life was not misguided and futile. His destiny and Rene's were bound together. There was a reason for everything, and he was now beginning to see it.

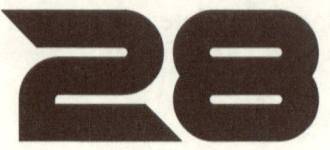

28

To lie in truth
Is to not contend with life
To eschew the judgment of others
To have nothing to prove
And therefore nothing to fear

Shentama
– Stanza 92

The Festival of Renewal was days away. Normally the weeks leading up to the festival were filled with eager anticipation and preparation. Lorna, already the centre of the Tobianist world, became the focal point for a global celebration of the Prophet and his Church. Similar festivals took place all around the world, in every city, every community. It was a week-long carnival, culminating with the renewal of the year on the 1st of January. Previous generations knew this time by another name, celebrating the life of another great spiritual teacher. It had also been a festival of a different kind for one of the oldest of the old religions. But these observances had become so commercialized and fantasized, their spiritual roots were all but forgotten.

After *The Reckoning*, Tobianism proclaimed this same period for its own festival, since the assassination of Tobias actually occurred on what was then known as Christmas day. The birth of one prophet … the death of another.

As the faith grew to dominate country after country and finally the world following *The Great Purge,* the Festival of Renewal became the dominant religious observance on the calendar, replacing all others except to those few who still clung to the old religions. As had happened with previous holidays, the Festival quickly became commercialized. Public fairs were common. Souvenirs with the lemnis symbol of the faith or the face of the Prophet adorned everything from caps and t-shirts to comkey ampules, portraits, statuettes and busts, pendants and other jewellery, plaques, plates, silverware, and a host of other nick-nacks for the faithful to waste their money on.

Despite all the merchandising, the spiritual core of the occasion was still intact. The festival began on the anniversary of the Prophet's death with a sermon from the Cardinal Hierophant, which under Cairn's reign was practically his only public appearance all year. This took place from his balcony above the grand pulpit on the forecourt of the Great Temple. Millions would gather here and in the adjoining Festival Square to hear the sermon, many of them visiting from other parts of the world. The population of Lorna trebled during the festival with tourists, pilgrims, media and added security. The sermon was streamcast across the world, viewed by 80% of the planet. Only the Warrior Games finals tended to have a larger audience. At the end of the sermon the face of the Prophet would be shown from his tomb deep within the Great Temple, and kept on display for the entire week on giant AV murals overlooking Festival Square. Screens throughout the city would also show the view from the tomb, alongside other images and video illuminating the faith. The entire (official) history of Tobianism was presented for anyone to see. Indeed, it was impossible to avoid.

During festival week the Temple was open to the public to offer charity and receive tithes. Free food was made available to any and all who visited, while a donation to the Temple coffers was seen as an act of karmic tribute. One could present petitions that the Cardinal Hierophant was obliged to consider, seek counsel from the College of Cardinals and other Temple authorities, or watch the Temple Guard stage a series of impressive martial arts and precision drill demonstrations. It was the one time of the year when the Church opened its doors to the people as if to say – *we have nothing to hide, all are welcome.*

Beyond the Temple, the city of Lorna became a massive fair with stalls, rides, and other temporary attractions filling the streets for several kilometres. It was the biggest party in the world. Curfew was lifted. Alcohol and other drugs were tolerated. And every person who visited The Great Temple was gifted a unique, and often quite valuable, souvenir of the occasion. Something different each year. This year it was to be a comkey compliant metallic GL Orb, that could be used as a personal AV recorder or holo-projector, a carry device (20kg capacity), or whatever else you could think to use a floating orb for.

That's how it usually was. This year was different.

This year, the days leading up to the festival were marred by bloodshed and violence. The Church had done its best to suppress the news or bias it against the rebels, but the world knew there was trouble in the Temple City.

After the raids on the heretic safe-houses Cairn was confident the immediate threat was crushed. They had yet to find the restored Prophet, but Cairn's priority right now was to ensure the festival went ahead as planned, and that the world saw normality restored. People were afraid to leave their homes, afraid to go to work; hiding from the Temple Guard whether they needed to or not. So Cairn did something he hated doing. He gave a public address. It wasn't that he didn't like speaking to the people. It's just that whenever one said anything publicly you were on record. Anything on record was potentially dangerous. An autonomous GL AV recorder & lighting kit was set-up in his office, and the address went out across the world. He didn't have much time to prepare what he wanted to say, so he kept it simple.

'My friends. The last few days in Lorna have been a trying time for us all. There have been cowardly attacks upon the Church by heretics seeking to challenge our divine authority. These have failed. Those responsible have been dealt with. Also, the fugitive that roamed our streets has been apprehended and is no longer a threat. Do not believe the stories you hear about Temple Guard reprisals or the destruction of property. These are simply not true. They are lies spread by anarchists, who seek to discredit the Church. I assure you – the city of Lorna is safe.

'In the spirit of conciliation, I declare an amnesty to any and all who sought to oppose the Church. You are forgiven. The Festival of Renewal begins in two days. I urge the citizens of Lorna: go back to work, start your preparations for the festival. Let us show the world that the actions of a few terrorists cannot dampen our spirits, cannot break our resolve. More than ever, this will be a festival of change and renewal. Of hope and promise. Let us rejoice in the peace and prosperity the Church of the Prophet has bestowed. May the word of the Prophet guide and protect you.' With this blessing Cairn ended the address, his hands clasped right over left, his head bowed humbly.

Perhaps now he could get on with eliminating the real threat to the Church – a resurrected Tobias.

—— ∞ ——

'Why would you do this?' Tobias asked, once Althea had explained how she and Asar had regenerated his cryonically preserved body. 'It goes against everything I taught.' Tobias was not angry, just confused. He was still getting used to centuries of lost time. 'Whose idea was it to preserve me that way in the first place?'

'Saint Benjamin,' Alban answered confidently. He knew his Tobianist history and the calendar of saints over the centuries. 'He was the first saint. A wealthy man who gave all he had to the Church. His foresight made all of this possible.' Alban had been shocked when Althea revealed how she and her colleagues violated the tomb. It was the worst possible sacrilege. But it meant a living, breathing Tobias now sat beside him in the kitchen of his humble lodgings. There was the hand of destiny in all this.

Althea however could see Tobias was not pleased. She understood their entire faith was based on a lie. Ironically, she found herself defending the Church – at least the early Church. 'You were taken from us too soon. We weren't ready. Without the Prophet we were lost.' She spoke not just for herself, but for Saint Benjamin, and every Tobianist through history with good intentions. 'We wanted you back, so you could finish what you started. And the fact that you are here surely counts for something. It was meant to be.'

In Tobianist philosophy there was no such thing as coincidence. Everything happened for a reason, even if we didn't understand why. It was the second tenet of the faith: *Choice, not chance, determines your destiny.* Nothing occurred that was not chosen by you in some way.

Still, Tobias was unsure how to respond. This was not a scenario he imagined possible.

'People are leaving,' Oscar interrupted.

'Good,' Alban said. 'Let them go.'

After Cairn's address, many decided it was safe to return home. Their numbers soon dwindled to half. Those who stayed did so not because they feared leaving the sanctuary of the church, but because they wanted to remain with Tobias. They would become his new disciples, numbering one-hundred and forty-eight men, women and children.

'...Father?'

'Yes, Oscar.'

Oscar turned from Father Alban to Tobias, tears welling in his eyes. 'Forgive me.'

Alban became concerned. 'Whatever for?'

Oscar fell to his knees, crying. 'I told them.'

'Told who?' Alban asked.

'The Guard. I told them you were here.' Oscar shook uncontrollably with guilt as he addressed Tobias, head bowed, unable to look him in the eye. 'I'm sorry! I didn't know it was you! I didn't know. I didn't know!' he prostrate himself at Tobias's feet, begging for forgiveness.

Tank grabbed the weeping novice by the collar with one hand and raised him up like a ragdoll to face him. 'When?' he demanded.

'Yesterday,' Oscar bawled, terrified by the black giant.

'Arrgh!' Tank threw the young man across the room in a rage. Oscar landed on the counter knocking bowls, knives and other cooking utensils to the floor in a clatter of kitchenware, himself falling to the ground after them like a sack of flour. He made no effort to get up. Instead, he just lay there on the floor, sobbing.

'Never trust a priest!' Tank blasted.

Alban cowered, fearing he would be next to be thrown across the room by the angry giant.

Tobias knelt beside the inconsolable Oscar, touched his hair gently. 'I forgive you. You only did what you thought was right.' He stepped across to Tank and placed a hand on his shoulder to calm the giant. Tank sat back down. 'You all have.'

'If he told them yesterday, why haven't the Guards been here already?' Tank asked.

'They have,' Alban realized. 'That was before you ... woke up.' Alban didn't quite know how to say it. Tobias's animal state still baffled him.

'They'll be back,' Tank intoned.

'We can't stay here,' Althea declared. 'Cairn knows you're alive. He's afraid of you. You're a threat to the Church.'

'How can you say that?' Alban protested. 'Tobias *is* the Church.'

'What do you think that public manhunt was all about?' Althea countered. 'There was no prisoner. They were looking for Tobias. The Church wants him dead.'

She pleaded with Tobias. 'This is why we brought you back. The Tobianist Church is a mockery of all you stand for. Of everything you tried to teach. But it's too powerful. You've seen what the Temple Guards are capable of. Revolution will only result in more deaths. The only way to confront the Church peacefully is to hold up a mirror to its hypocrisies. To have the Prophet himself declare it a disgrace. Force it to change or raze it to the ground and start from scratch. Make it the way you wanted. The way it should be.' Althea's passion was getting the better of her. Asar would have put it so much better.

Tobias didn't respond. He was not angry. In fact, his expression was more sympathetic than judgmental. He turned to Alban for his reaction.

'It is true, the Church has strayed at times,' Alban admitted. 'But I cannot condone anything that would seek to destroy it. It has done far more good than bad. There is no war, no hunger, no flood or famine. Much of this is due to the Church, its moral and political leadership.' Alban could see Althea and Tank objected to this simplistic assessment. 'My view is biased of course. And my knowledge of the world perhaps limited. But for all that is wrong with the Church, there is much it has done to make this world better than it was.' His attention returned to Tobias. 'But… you are the Prophet. The foundation of all that has been for over two hundred years. I have devoted my life to following your word. If I must choose between the Prophet and his Church, the choice for me is simple.'

Tobias nodded, acknowledging Alban's loyalty. He turned to Tank, who had calmed down, but maintained a suspicious eye on Oscar lying on the floor.

'I'm still reeling from the fact you're actually alive. This kind of stuff only happens in stories or fairy tales. If you're asking me what you should do, I have no idea. I just know, if we fight, we'll prob'ly lose. And nothing will change. Maybe it's not meant to. Maybe this is how things are supposed to be. Maybe the Father's right and we've never had it so good…' Tank hesitated to say the next bit for fear of the reaction. '…But we're not free. And we're not as civilized as you might think.' Tank directed this as much to Alban as Tobias. As a competitor in the Games, he knew how barbaric their civilized society could be. 'I'd rather fight for the life I want, and die trying, than live the life I don't. If that makes sense.'

Tobias nodded – *yes*. Kneeling again beside Oscar, he addressed the young novice. 'And what do you think I should do?'

Oscar finally looked up into the face of Tobias. 'You are the Prophet Tobias. What I think is not important.'

'Tell me anyway,' Tobias encouraged.

Oscar's confidence returned as he gazed into the eyes of the Prophet. 'This is your Church. Claim it.'

Tobias smiled: *thank you*.

He weighed their opinions as objectively as he could, knowing this was still only part of the story. There was an entire history between what he remembered, and this new world made in his image. A few days ago he was speaking before a crowd of over a million people in Central Park, New York City, on Christmas day in the year 2050. The last thing he remembered was being shot in the chest mid-sentence, regretting that he would not get to finish the talk he'd spent so long preparing. Then he woke up in Father Alban's bed, two-hundred and forty years in the future. Just getting his head around that was hard enough. Now he was being asked to lead a revolt against his own Church. His first impulse was to refuse. People had lobbied him to support their causes before. Some very worthwhile, others not so. He was very careful what he endorsed. Each one was a commitment he took seriously, and a dangerous association should things go pear-shaped. Everything happened for a reason though. He firmly believed this. He just needed a bit more information before he could decide what to do.

'I think I need to talk with this Cairn,' Tobias finally said.

The only freedom you have
The only freedom you need
Is the freedom to choose

Shentama
– Stanza 214

'I'm not a Tobianist. Not religious at all. And I don't believe in all that free will equals fate crap. People do what they do, not because they choose to, not because they're destined to, but because they're used to it. They get so used to it they don't know anything else. They're like sheep – mindless and unthinking. The only way to change the behavior of someone like that is to turn their world upside down. That'll get 'em thinkin' again. That'll wake 'em up!'

Rohan had his own philosophy on life that was about as far away from Tobianism as you could get. It was pragmatic and ruthless. Law of the jungle. Where an aesthetic saw spiritual beauty and truth in the concept of change and renewal, Rohan saw only death and decay. The only fate we can be certain of is that we all die; and whatever we do prior to this inevitability counts for very little. The universe could care less what happens on the speck of dust we call earth. We are not answerable to some unseen higher power. We are not judged against a tally of good and bad deeds. There is no karmic calculator controlling our destinies. Our life is nothing more than a string of chance encounters and pointless happenstance. So we're free to do whatever the hell we like. At the end of the day none of it really matters. This nihilistic view of the world was oddly liberating, fitting neatly with Dan's new existential take on life. Understanding the futility of existence gave one the audacity to try anything. Even take on the Tobianist Church.

Rohan had called a meeting in one of the old conference rooms. All fifteen men of the Libertarian Army were present, including Dan. The four women (which now included Maya) were not permitted to attend; instead, they kept lookout. Nineteen people were hardly an army, but it was a start.

Night blanketed the AQ with a furtive stillness. Outside the shattered windows of their derelict hideout lay a deep, oppressive darkness. Beyond the black, up the hill, the lights of Lorna could be seen, glistening against the clear sky. The illuminated spires of the Great Temple and peak of the figure-8 fountain were clearly visible even from this distance. It was actually a beautiful sight, even though it symbolized everything they were fighting against.

'The festival is the perfect opportunity,' Rohan told them. 'If we can take out Cairn during the sermon it'll send a message to the whole world. We strike at the very heart of the religion. Chop off its head and watch it panic as it tries to work out what just happened.'

Despite the mixed metaphors, it was certainly a daring plan. Others around the conference table nodded agreement, though some more vigorously than others. The table itself was large and heavy, which is probably why it hadn't been removed with all the other fixtures. No doubt it had once been quite beautiful, with deep wood stain and gleaming polish. But after decades of neglect, it was a resilient ruin in keeping with its surroundings.

'In the confusion we can then enter the Temple and take out as many robes as possible.' Rohan liked to bundle all the priests, clerics and cardinals of the Church into the collective slur – *robes*.

'What about the Temple Guard?' asked one. Dan didn't know everybody's name yet, but they had welcomed him into their war council without hesitation. Rohan trusted him and that was enough.

'They're gonna be busy with crowd control. There'll be a few of course inside the Temple, but most of the Guard will be in the square watching for troublemakers.'

'In that case how do we get close enough to take out Cairn?' asked another.

Rohan smiled knowingly. He reached behind him and placed on the table the camouflage bag Dan had brought. Unzipping it, he removed the body of the weapon, pulled out and locked the retractable shoulder brace, screwed on the barrel with its horn-like nose, connected the scope, attached the bipod to the front and placed the assembled weapon in the centre of the table. As he did this the others in the room watched in awe. They had never seen a gun like it. In its own deadly way, it was magnificent.

'It's a plasma-shot sniper rifle,' Rohan told them. 'It fires an energy field. Very fast, very powerful. Has a lethal range of two and half kilometres. This is what we'll use to kill Cairn.'

'Where did you get it?' one of them asked incredulously.

'Dan brought it.'

The entire room turned to Dan, now very impressed with their new comrade.

'Our group leader had it,' Dan explained. 'How he came by it I don't know. When our house was raided, I took it. Thought it might come in useful.'

'Useful?' Rohan exclaimed. 'This is one of the rarest weapons ever made. Most were destroyed after the Shanghai Treaty. They were thought too dangerous even for museums to have. How your group leader got a hold of it is beyond me, but it's a damn piece of luck. If I didn't know any better, I would say it was fate led you here.' The assembled chuckled, then applauded to welcome Dan to the fold. For the first time in his life, Dan felt he belonged.

'How does it work?' asked one of them.

Rohan picked up the weapon and brought it to the hole in the wall that had once been a window. Resting the bipod on the sill he turned on the gun's digital sight. A holographic display appeared showing an enhanced view of the street below. He zoomed in a couple of times to scan the distance for a suitable target. The sight had a combination infra-red and thermal night-vision so he could easily make out the buildings and streets of the unlit AQ, all neatly outlined in shades of blue, with contrasting false colours of red and yellow to indicate the weapon's range and focus. He saw movement – a rat. The heat-seeking target recognition tracked the movement, highlighting the creature with a bold yellow outline. The range meter indicated it was 2.15 kilometres away. Rohan touched the image on the hologram, locking onto the rat. The outline turned red, continuing to track its target as it scurried across the road. Without even looking Rohan gently squeezed the trigger and fired. The bell-like muzzle shot a toroid of high energy across the space like a swirling donut of latent blue fire. There was surprisingly no recoil, the gun's mechanism absorbing the force, but it sounded a tremendous deep *thrum* that made everyone balk. The distant rat exploded in a puff of vaporized guts and blood, leaving nothing but a haze of floating ash twinkling in the moonlight; the pavement glowed with intense heat for several seconds, then cooled into a tiny crater.

The men were shocked at the power of this weapon. Rohan nodded approvingly, 'Awesome.'

— ∞ —

Things weren't going quite to plan, but things rarely did. The more complex a plan became, the more agents involved, the more there was to go wrong. Kasper knew this and had prepared for every possible contingency. Whatever happened, he remained steadfast yet flexible.

Killing Trevelle was an inconvenience, nothing more. He'd been a useful agent with the rebel scientists and within the Lorna Institute, but he was not the only one. Kasper had other resources to help him track down the body of the Prophet. Besides, if other things panned out as expected, it may not matter anymore. He would still achieve his end even without the body.

Bartholomew Matheson had been a good mole among the rebel groups, spreading disinformation and reporting on dissident plans and movements. An idealist so full of himself, all it took was a bit of ego stroking and a few well-phrased promises and he would do anything Kasper wanted. He'd been Kasper's backup for the denouement of his little plan. If the coup didn't take, an assassination could be arranged. He had even gone to the trouble of securing a sniper rifle for Bartholomew to use if it came to it. When Kasper found out the idiot got himself killed during the raids, he began devising an alternate Plan B – a backup for the backup. Within hours however he'd heard from another of his agents that the rifle had fallen into the hands of one of the surviving rebel groups, and lo and behold, they planned to use it to assassinate Cairn. It couldn't have been more perfect if he had orchestrated it himself. The Prophet was right: there was no such thing as coincidence, just dumb luck and serendipity.

Kasper couldn't help smiling as he strode down the gold and marble halls of the Great Temple to the Basilica, drawing the attention of staff along the route. After all, it was a rare occurrence to see Kasper smiling.

The Hypogeum Basilica was where the public petitions and tithes would take place during the festival. Tables and AV consoles were being set up along the length of the great hall to handle the thousands of supplicants seeking an audience with the Cardinal Hierophant, one of the Church Council, or some other caucus member. The festival was no fun for the clergy, guard or staff of The Great Temple. While the city partied, the Temple became a tourist attraction, a soup kitchen, and a security nightmare. Their calm and dignified world thrown into chaos by an invasion of loud, unseemly proles.

To secure an audience with one of the council members was not easy. Most people ended up with a more junior caucus member. Even so, everyone from the Cardinal Hierophant down had to make themselves available to meet the common folk throughout the week. Kasper hated it. The entire Caucus of Cardinals – one hundred and ninety-two in all – endured a tedious week of listening to idiots tell them how to do their jobs, bitch about their pathetic little lives, or demand the Church do more for some trivial local issue. Nothing useful ever came from this archaic tradition, and it was something Kasper intended to abolish when he took over. Face to face dialogues with the faithful were a waste of time.

Usually, the doors to the Basilica were closed with a permanent sentry standing guard. No one was admitted unless Cairn was in attendance and predisposed to receiving. Today the doors were wide open as workers lay carpet runs across the expanse of polished marble in preparation for festival petitioners. Most of the interviews would be conducted in Cardinals' chambers or in conference rooms throughout the Temple. Cairn however liked to conduct them from his throne in the Basilica. Only a special few were granted such an audience, and if they had a mind to criticize or confront Cairn about anything, this resolve tended to evaporate by the time they had walked the length of the hall and knelt before His Eminence. Only the bravest or most foolish sought an audience with Cairn.

Kasper had expected to find Cairn here reprimanding Captain Marius yet again, but the place was empty. *They must be in his chambers.* He wanted to make certain Marius's position was secure. Kasper needed the support of the Temple Guard for what was to come, and Marius was key to that. Despite all of Cairn's bluster about *the people*, he had no idea how human beings actually behaved. He couldn't read the signs. Which made him easy to manipulate, but hard to control.

Kasper was about to turn around and make for the Cardinal Hierophant's chambers when a wicked idea occurred to him. Pressing on, he walked the length of the Basilica. He was so used to the imposing architecture, glorious art, and glistening gold and marble surfaces that he barely noticed it anymore; his focus was on the throne at the far end. The workers laying the carpet glanced up as he passed, but then ignored him and went back to their work. He wasn't the Cardinal Hierophant, so they were not obliged to down tools and prostrate themselves.

Kasper walked right up to the empty throne, stopping on the rostrum. He considered the oversized chair with its high back and ornate decorations for a moment. Then glanced at the smaller, though still impressive, chair to its left where he normally sat. Then turned back to the throne of the Cardinal Hierophant … and sat down.

Looking out across the vast space before him, Kasper noticed the view was subtly different from this angle. Perfectly centred, the pillars of the basilica fell into line on both sides, their perspective now keenly focused on the gaping entrance at the far end. As one approached, the throne was intimidating and formidable, but Kasper had never realized this worked in reverse. There was an overwhelming sense of symmetry that made him gasp involuntarily. Just sitting here gave one a feeling of superiority and power. It was the most powerful seat on earth and Kasper wanted it.

The workers looked up at him confused. For anyone to sit in the throne of the Cardinal Hierophant was not just a breach of protocol, it was tantamount to sacrilege. Kasper glared back at them unrepentant, and they quietly returned to their work.

Any day now.

— ∞ —

'I'm very disappointed, Captain. This impostor should have been captured by now.' With the festival imminent Cairn was beginning to panic. He was also annoyed that because of festival preparations he had to conduct this meeting in his chambers rather than the Basilica. The usual advantage his throne afforded was diminished.

'Without a comkey to track it's been more difficult than expected, Your Eminence,' Marius explained feebly. 'But he may be among those killed in the raids. We've yet to identify all the bodies.'

'Regardless, I am discharging you as commander of the Temple Guard. You are relieved from duty.'

Cairn said it so perfunctorily that Marius thought he misheard. 'Your Eminence?'

'Are you deaf, man? You're an incompetent, loudmouthed oaf. The only reason I made you Captain of the Guard was you have a talent for intimidation. And even that you managed to bungle by killing the very man who might have disclosed the Prophet's whereabouts. You were my dog, but I see now you're unfit even for that. So to make it perfectly clear, Captain, your commission is terminated. I am not demoting you. I am firing you. I want never to see your face in these halls again. And depending on how things go during the festival, a stretch in Gerda is not out of the question.'

Marius was both shocked and infuriated. Cairn ordered the death of all those scientists in the first place. Had they lived he would have had better subjects to interrogate than some old bugger who up and died at the slightest bit of torture. For days he'd been hunting an escapee with no physical description, no comkey implant, and no leads. All the violence and bad press Cairn complained about was a direct result of Marius following orders. And the man has the gall to call him a dog.

Marius was a loyal soldier of the faith. That loyalty was to the Church of the Prophet, its ministers and representatives, and most of all to the Cardinal Hierophant. In the space of a day he'd been blackmailed by one Cardinal, and now betrayed and threatened by another. Marius wanted to kill Cairn where he stood. He could feel the blood boiling in his veins. He clenched his fists to contain the rage. Striking Cairn would be an instant death sentence, so he restrained himself, took some deep breaths and tried to think logically. He had come to this meeting contemplating whether or not to tell Cairn about Kasper's blackmail. It would mean exposing his past and jeopardizing his career, but his loyalty to the Cardinal Hierophant was paramount. He was not going to do that now. Cairn didn't know it, but he had just pressed his most devoted servant into the arms of his rival. If Marius could no longer count on Cairn's support, he would have to submit to Kasper's demands, whatever they may be.

'As you wish, Your Eminence,' Marius said through grit teeth, bowing. He made for the door.

'Captain.'

Marius about-faced sharply, his armour clashing as he turned.

'Nothing personal.'

Before his temper got the better of him, Marius turned on his heel and left the room.

Storming down the corridors of the Temple, Marius saw Kasper approaching.

'Ah, Captain,' Kasper greeted. 'Any news?'

He really didn't want to deal with Kasper right now. Marius brushed past the Cardinal without answering.

'Captain!'

Marius stopped. Took a deep breath … and turned. 'No news, Your Eminence. Rest assured I will inform you as soon as I hear anything.'

'Is something the matter?'

'No, Your Eminence. Everything is fine.' It took all his effort just to maintain a civil voice.

Kasper didn't believe him but decided not to press the point. He may have guessed the reason in any case. 'Sometimes loyalty is not appreciated as much as it should be in this place. Do not count me among those who would abandon you, Captain. I value loyalty, and I reward it.'

Marius bowed. Kasper nodded slightly in return. They understood one another, and without another word went their separate ways. Marius would not have thought it possible, but Kasper was his greatest ally in this place. His patron. He wasn't sure he was entirely comfortable with this, but it was gratifying to know *someone* appreciated him.

Back in his quarters, Marius removed his leg brace and hobbled uncomfortably about the room. It still hurt. The tissue was healing well, but the bone had been broken and was not healing straight.

Climbing into bed, it occurred to him he would have to find another doxy. He didn't mind sleeping alone, preferred it in fact. But a warm young body to fuck and cuddle helped him feel human. Orgasms were good for the soul.

… A few minutes later, his soul was feeling more at ease, but he still couldn't sleep. In the space of a day he'd led the biggest operation the Temple Guard had ever undertaken, successfully raiding hundreds of rebel hideouts and safe-houses, found himself blackmailed by and beholden to the one man he most disliked in the Great Temple, and was finally dismissed as Captain of the Guard – just for doing his job. In an effort to get his mind off the injustice of it all, he pulled over the AV screen and called up the footage of the Festival Square massacre. He watched again the Tobias look-a-like they had been hunting. The resemblance was uncanny. Marius suspected there was more to this man than he had been told. This was no escaped prisoner.

His attention turned to the other man, the one that had prevented him from catching the 'escapee'. Marius found an angle that showed the man's face clearly and did a quick compare against the comkey database. Not everyone had access to this information, but he was still officially Captain of the Guard with all the security privileges that office held. Up came the details for a Rene St. Claire. Checking the comkey location info, this Rene appeared to be in one of the houses they'd raided that morning. Images of the scene showed the place was now a pile of rubble. The incident report stated it had been booby-trapped and exploded from within. Buried in the rubble were dozens of comkeys from both Guards and rebels, all inactive – their owners deceased. This Rene St. Claire however was still alive … just. His comkey feed showed him to be dehydrated, wounded, and presently unconscious. He must have got trapped in the place when it collapsed.

Marius set the AV aside and pulled the covers up. If Rene St. Claire survived the night, he'd check it out. It was a long shot, but he might know something about the 'escapee'. If he was dead, then it wasn't meant to be. Sometimes doing nothing was the best way to honour the second tenet. Don't interfere and just let fate take its course. It was surprising how often this worked. Of course, choosing to do nothing was still a choice – just a much easier one. That's what landed Marius in Gerda in the first place. He'd murdered his father, after witnessing him kill his mother. He was eighteen at the time. Had he acted sooner none of it might have occurred, and his life would have been very different. But he didn't, and it wasn't. This was the life he chose, even if he hadn't meant to.

At least that's what he had always thought. Now he wasn't so sure. For years it seems Kasper had been making the choices for him. His release from Gerda, his life in Lorna, his entire career in the Temple Guard was due to Kasper's intervention and support. Marius wasn't sure how to feel about that – grateful or infuriated. One thing he was sure of though – he wasn't going back to Gerda.

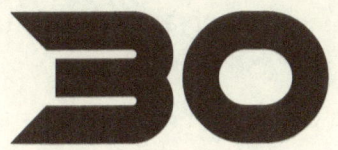

30

Love is action without movement
Love is language without words
Love is passion without desire

Love abandons self
Love forsakes ego
Love is at one with the All–In–All
Love is the All–In–All
And as you are a part of the All–In–All
You are Love

Shentama
– Stanzas 112-113

The *Light of the Prophet* was abandoned by everyone but Oscar. Alban asked his novice to stay and look after the place while he was gone. It was not that he didn't trust him anymore (though he didn't), but someone had to look after the church. Oscar begged to come with them, but with a few quiet words Tobias convinced the young novice to stay.

'What did you say to him?' Alban asked Tobias as they left the church.

'Something for him alone. But his destiny is not with us.'

Tobias said this matter-of-factly, but it was clear he saw something in Oscar's future Alban could not fathom. Despite his modest nature, moments like this reminded Alban how truly remarkable the man walking beside him was.

It was the dead of night, and the streets were now surprisingly peaceful after so many days of violence. Temple Guards were nowhere to be seen, nor were the local residents – who sensibly remained indoors just in case thing flared up again. They followed the route Tank and Althea had come by, through the narrow dark streets of the Western Borough, into the AQ, then descending into the collapsed train station and underground tunnels of the old city. It was a mute procession, with many of the new disciples never having ventured out after curfew, let alone braved the AQ. They huddled together anxiously, like children frightened of the dark. But the Prophet was with them, their fears dispelled in the faith that he would protect them. There was no safer place on earth right now than in the company of Tobias.

Tank led the party into the underground train tunnels, their uneven footsteps resonating sharply off the dank concrete walls. Four of the more severely wounded were put into the waiting GL. With grappling ropes secured to the front of the vehicle Tank pulled the GL at the head of the procession. It would be a long walk back to home base.

Tobias came alongside Althea. He spoke softly lest their conversation carry through the tunnel and be overheard. There was something he wanted to ask her.

'Are you disappointed?'

'In what?'

'In me. Am I the man you expected me to be?'

'Not exactly,' Althea admitted. 'But I'm not disappointed. Not at all.'

'Just surprised.'

'Yeah, a little.' Althea had studied Tobias her entire life. She'd read everything he wrote or that was written about him, watched archival footage, documentaries, and even fictionalised biographies of his life. But none of it had prepared her for the reality of the man. His presence and charisma. His emotional temperament. Even his sense of humour. Tobias was far more human than she'd expected. Until today Tobias had been an idealised person – perfect and unreal. Now he was flesh and blood and soul intact. A preposterous longing made manifest; fallible and astonishing all at once. So real, in fact, her feelings towards him had become a tangle of contradictions – love, disillusionment, reverence, anticipation, adoration. But mostly love. Just to be walking beside him now made her heart race.

'Is there anything you would like to ask me?' Tobias offered. 'Something you've always wondered?'

There was, but she dare not ask it. 'No. Nothing that comes to mind.'

Tobias answered anyway. 'I would sometimes be asked the most indelicate questions. I wasn't offended. To be honest I was flattered anyone cared. But it was none of their business. My personal life, such as it was, had nothing to do with my work. Of course, not speaking about it only fuelled the rumours. Made me even more notorious. So that kind of worked out.' He smiled. Fame in the 21st century was often for entirely the wrong reasons. 'It's true I never married, never had children. Was not known to be in any kind of relationship with a woman … or a man for that matter.' He laughed a little as he said this. During his former life many jumped to the conclusion Tobias was gay. His gentle nature did suggest it. 'But I tell you now, Althea Roget, I knew a great love was in store for me. I had seen it in my future, just as I had seen my death. Like so many of my visions it was unclear, vague, ambiguous. Yet when I saw you in the church, I recognized you immediately. We've shared a life before, you and I. We have done it many times. And we will no doubt do it many times more in the future. The confusion you feel is because of this. Do not be embarrassed or ashamed of your feelings. They made all this possible. The miracle you have made, you made for love. And I am grateful for it.'

Althea was speechless. She couldn't believe what she was hearing. It had to be a dream.

Tobias took her hand and gently kissed it. Then with a smile, walked on ahead to join Tank at the head of the march. Althea stopped in her tracks and watched Tobias walk away. She couldn't breathe. Her heart pounded in her chest so hard her ears thrummed; her head swamped by a haze of incredulity.

'Are you all right, Althea?' Alban had caught up with her and wondered why she was stopped.

She looked at the priest, her breathing finding its rhythm again. She reached out and pinched Alban on the arm.

'Ow!'

Althea smiled. 'I'm fine,' she finally said. 'Just fine.'

With ropes slung over each of his massive shoulders, Tank pulled the GL cruiser and its load of wounded refugees through the tunnel. Its headlights illuminated the way, casting a long, dark shadow of Tank's massive frame on the curved wall. The frictionless anti-grav made easy work of it. In fact, Tank rather wished it were harder. It had been some time since he'd had a proper workout, and he was feeling the need to punch something.

'What troubles you, my friend?' Tobias asked Tank as he came alongside.

Tank had been uncharacteristically quiet since meeting Tobias. 'Forgive me for saying this, but you do.'

Tobias smiled. 'We can't always know where our choices will lead, or what fate has in store for us. We just have to trust ourselves to the journey. It'll all make sense in the end.'

'I can't do that. I can't live with that kind of uncertainty. My entire life has been what I made it. I fought in the Games because I chose to, and I left of my own free will despite everyone begging me to stay. I'm here now because I choose to be here. We live or die by our choices.'

'We do indeed. But one does not exist alone in this world. Your choices affect everything and everyone around you. As much as we are the product of our own will, we are also bound by the deeds of others. Some we know, most we don't. I am here now because of a choice Althea and her colleagues made. I had no control over it. And yet, there is providence in my being here, don't you think? Right here, right now. So that I can tell you the sacrifice you have made, is nothing to the one to will make.' Tank looked the Prophet in the eye, more intrigued than alarmed. 'It will be your choice, but it will affect the lives of everyone. In some ways your death will have a greater impact upon the world than my own.'

Tank was shocked. Not that Tobias had just predicted his death (which he knew was inevitable), or even that it would have some significance upon the world, but that Tobias was so indifferent towards his own death. Was he talking about his assassination, or a death that was to come?

'What sacrifice?'

'I can't tell you that,' Tobias smiled. 'It would spoil the surprise.'

'Then why are you telling me this?'

'I want you to know it will not be in vain. It will be the single most important act of this revolution. You will not live to see the end, but the choice you make will change the world.'

Tank was struck dumb. Had this come from anyone else he would have dismissed it out of hand. He didn't go in for clairvoyants and spooks. But this was the Prophet Tobias. Tank tried to think what he could possibly do that would have such a huge impact. How would he know it when the time came? How could he be sure of making the right choice? Dammit! Why did Tobias tell him that!? Now he was going be worrying about it every day until it happened.

Tobias read his mind. 'Don't worry. You'll know it when the time comes. Normally I wouldn't reveal such a thing. You can never be sure how someone is going to react. But I thought it was important you know.'

The entourage reached the underground train station where Kane and Joanna were waiting. Kane had heard the rabble approaching. He stood guard on the platform, weapon raised defensively. When Tank emerged from the shadows pulling the GL behind him, Kane lowered his weapon. Anxiety rarely got the better of him, but a wave of relief coursed through him when he saw his comrades returned safe and well.

There was a tall, fair-haired priest walking beside Tank. Moments later Althea appeared with yet another, shorter and somewhat stouter, priest walking alongside her. A crowd of civilians brought up the rear – men, women and children. *Damn*, Kane thought. *They've brought me refugees when I need soldiers.*

Kane reached down to help the first priest up onto the platform. Kane looked into the face of the man, a vague recognition clouding his mind.

'You must be Kane,' the priest said, offering his hand. 'How do you do? My name is Tobias.'

'Bullshit!' Kane saw Tank nodding vigorously as he came up behind the man. 'What the fuck?'

'That was my initial reaction, too,' Tobias said cheerfully, his hand still outstretched, waiting for Kane to shake it.

Kane finally clasped the Prophet's hand. It was starting to sink in. 'Shit.'

'It's been a while since anyone cursed so much around me. It's quite refreshing.'

'Oh … fuck. Sorry.' Kane didn't know what was going on. Tobias just smiled and moved on, making room for the others coming up behind.

Tank slapped Kane on the shoulder as he passed. 'Wait'll he tells you your future. That'll really freak you out.'

Joanna heard the commotion and sat up. Her head felt fine, though she knew she had to take it gently. Her leg was mending well; fortunately, the bone had not been broken, and the bullet-hole in her thigh was already healed over. The polymer bandage Althea had applied, laced with stem cell culture and other medicinal additives was doing a good job at repairing the underlying muscle tissue. It hurt when she put her weight on it, but she could walk.

Joanna left the dark office and limped slowly through the spacious station lobby towards the hubbub. She was halfway across when Kane, Tank, Althea and two priests emerged from the lower platform, leading a throng of civilians. Her heart soared seeing them all returned safely, even Father Alban whom she recognized immediately. But her attention was drawn to the other priest. For a moment she thought it was Rene, and her heart leapt into her throat. Then she saw his face, her disappointment tempered by a strange new recognition. The tall priest picked up speed and strode ahead of the others, stopping directly in front of Joanna. A deep sadness overwhelmed him, as if he knew what she was feeling. Knew about Rene … about Dan … even what lay in her future. He was the Prophet Tobias. She knew this without question. She didn't need to know how or why. She just accepted it.

Tobias lowered his gaze and gently lay a hand on her belly. Somehow he knew before she did, but the gesture was clear. She was pregnant. He embraced her. Like a proud father. Like a loving husband. Like her dearest friend. And she wept. Uncontrollably. Unreservedly. Pain and joy fused into one cathartic moment.

Tobias offered her unconditional love; and she accepted it.

Rene felt Joanna in his arms. Felt her tears on his face. He touched her belly – a child. A girl. He lay his hands on her head and on her leg. Took away the pain. Healed her wounds. Restored her strength. He saw into their future. The child born. Surrounded by darkness and the cries of the forsaken. They stood with a great host of allies, besieged by enemies on all sides. A great battle. Thousands of spirits rising to the sky. Then Rene was alone – completely and utterly. But the choice was his to make. The destiny his to fulfill. If not now, then later. If not later, then in time. There was no escaping the inevitable. The desert would decide. The path was already walked. Every path, every person. Frozen in time. The outcome was always the same. Except for the child. The child did not belong. Her future was not decided. The child was hope. The child was freedom. The child would choose her own destiny. And the world would be forever changed.

Rene woke.

He was afraid, though couldn't remember why. Taking a deep breath he stopped short – pain shooting across his chest. A warm hand touched his brow. It was too dark to see who it was, but the touch comforted him. He felt water on his lips and drank. Reaching out he brushed the dank fur of his protector. She made a noise – startled but friendly. He spoke to her. Sounds of thanks and puzzlement. They were alone, trapped in blackness. Time was smeared. He knew something had come before this – but couldn't remember what. He knew there was a world beyond this blackness – but couldn't think what it was. None of that mattered though. All he felt was pain and hunger.

Rene sat up. It hurt to do so, but he was sick of lying on his back. It was time to get out of this place. His companion led the way.

'Should we do something?' Will asked.

'For all we know this is how things are meant to happen,' replied Matthew.

The two guides had been watching Rene closely from the moment he died. He was sustained by the spiritual link to his other body – Tobias; and Elly's attentions had also helped. He was healing faster than expected.

'What if someone finds him?'

'I suppose it would depend on who it is.'

'Do bonobo's have souls?' Will asked.

Given the circumstances, Matthew might have expected such a question; nevertheless, he was surprised. 'Why do you ask?'

'If Elly is killed, I'd like to think she has the same spiritual options that we do.'

'Yes. Elly has a soul. All creatures do. In a way, everything that exists has a kind of soul. Consciousness is relative.'

'Relative to what?'

'To one's ability to sense and interact with the world around you.'

'Does that mean I'm smarter than I used to be, now that I'm up here with you?'

'Theoretically,' replied Matthew. 'Of course, everyone's different.'

This could have been interpreted as a slight on Will's intelligence. Fortunately, the obtuse Will did not see it as one. 'Is that what made Tobias different? Was he able to see more than other people?'

It was a simplistic analysis, but quite accurate. 'Exactly. Rene will be the same in time. He will see more than others do. Not be so bound by the physical. He will have visions of the future, see inside the hearts of others, and be able to heal or influence the physical world in ways that would seem magical to others.'

'Just like Tobias.'

'Greater than Tobias. Assuming he doesn't get killed first.'

Dan was billeted in one of the empty offices of the tower Rohan's militia had established as their HQ. There were plenty of rooms to go round, so a certain level of privacy could be maintained. What they lacked however was comfortable bedding and other conveniences. Dan found himself sleeping on the rotting carpet with his backpack as a pillow. Still, it was a thousand times better than where he had last slept. Not as comfortable, but eminently more agreeable psychologically. He felt safe here.

When he woke the next morning Dan discovered Maya sleeping beside him. She had come in at some point during the night and curled up next to him. Dan propped on one elbow and gazed at her while she slept. She wasn't really his type, but she was cute. And she had guts, a kind of childish bravado. Watching her sleep, his big brother instinct kicked in. He wanted to protect her. Look after her. She was an innocent. Probably a virgin. Definitely vulnerable despite her gumption. Like it or not he was stuck with her.

Maya stirred, opened her eyes and looked up at Dan. He smiled. 'Good morning.'

She raised herself up and kissed him impulsively, held it for a while, then dropped back down to rest on the dirty carpet. She watched for his reaction. After thinking about it for a few seconds, Dan lowered himself and returned the kiss.

If she *was* a virgin, she wouldn't be for much longer.

Rohan called a meeting to plan their attack. They had the weapon, the plasma rifle Dan had brought, but they needed a safe vantage to snipe from.

'What about the corkscrew?' Dan suggested.

'What about it?' Rohan prompted.

'A friend of mine works ... worked there. Twenty-ninth floor. I've been there a couple of times. It's got a pretty good view of the Temple.'

'Can you get in?'

'Not without a sanctioned comkey.'

'Hmm.' Even if they had not destroyed their own comkeys, one still had to be sanctioned to enter private premises and offices.

'What about a ghost 'key?' Maya was standing at the door listening in.

'Men only, sweetheart,' declared one of the others, ignoring completely what she had said.

'A what?' At least Rohan, despite his usual chauvinism, was listening.

'A ghost comkey. It gives you access to public services like trains and hoppers, buildings like museums, hospitals … offices. But you don't get tracked.'

'How does that work?'

'The genome link is disabled. It creates a bogus ID that the network accepts as real, provided you don't draw too much attention to yourself.'

'How do you know about these? I've never heard of them.' Rohan was intrigued, as was everyone else.

'I make them. It's my little invention.' This might have sounded boastful, but coming from Maya there was genuine humility in the admission. As if it was no big deal, really.

A quiet fell over the room, several mouths agape is stunned silence.

'You make them,' Rohan repeated.

Maya nodded. This … girl unwittingly held the secret weapon their struggle was missing. To travel incognito, effectively invisible to the network, would free them from hiding out in the AQ. They could roam the city, let the network track them, confident their true identity remained unknown. It was safer than having no comkey at all – assuming it worked.

'How do you know it works?' Rohan asked.

'I've been using one for years. As far as the network is concerned, I don't exist. No-one's going to track one little comkey just going about its business; as long you're discreet about it.'

'If that's true, then why did you destroy it back at the house?' Dan asked.

'I was just following your lead. I can always make another.'

Rohan was convinced. 'What do you need?'

'Not much. An AV, some nano-electronics tools, which I have with me, and a working comkey to modify.'

'Do we have any working comkeys?' Dan asked the group.

Within an hour Maya was at work. Creating a ghost 'key from the disabled but still functional comkey Rohan sourced for her. It had belonged to one of their comrades who'd died a few days earlier in the Festival Square massacre. It should have been destroyed, but Rohan kept it intact just in case. He may not put much stock in the Tobianist credo of fate/free will, but it was a most fortuitous decision, nonetheless.

Dan watched Maya at work. At first, she modified the microscopic electronics, literally cutting signal paths to isolate the DNA sync of the device. This took a couple of hours. It was delicate work with circuitry so small it was measured in nanometres. She was literally moving atoms around. To do this she had a portable electron microscope and an array of precision nano-tools, geared to fit her delicate hands. Dan had no idea Maya had been carrying these around with her in that backpack. Indeed, he never suspected this meek, helpless girl was a tech geek and electronics whizz. He saw her now in a whole new light. Eventually Maya found Dan's presence too distracting and she threw him out of the room. So he continued to watch quietly from the doorway, guarding against any interruption.

Maya remained head down, intensely focused for ten hours straight. It was oddly exciting, seeing her so completely absorbed by a project. Once DNA sync was severed, she used the Black AV Dan had liberated from their safe-house to reprogram the 'key. This gave it the false identity the network would see and respond to. It was not a complete profile, but enough for low-level single-factor security systems to acknowledge, allowing generic access to public areas. If it worked, this would get them into the building and probably up to the correct level. But they still had to work out how to access *The Guardian*'s offices. A sanctioned 'key was needed for that, which they didn't have. They would have to devise some other means of entry for this final barrier.

There is no predestined fate
And there are no accidents
All is set
The future by the past
All is in motion
The future and the past

Shentama
– Stanza 137

Visions of impending life crowded Tobias's mind every time he met someone. Most of it was fragmented and vague. When he saw something clearly it was often mundane – fleeting moments of the little choices that would cascade into a major turning point in one's life, but which isolated signified nothing. Sometimes though, he saw the big turning points. They might be tragic or happy, occasioned by choice or circumstance. Often it was the manner of one's death.

Tobias was not in the habit of telling people their 'fortunes'. He was no clairvoyant. He felt passing on vague predictions of someone's future did more harm than good. Choice and free will remained integral to the fates he glimpsed. They would still occur, but the path that led one to these milestone events could yet be altered. What mattered most was how you felt about it when it happened. Foreknowledge often resulted in guilt, depression, anger, anxiety, and atypical behavior – all of which spoiled the lesson that would otherwise be learned. Only when knowledge of the future might help a person did Tobias feel it necessary to reveal what he saw.

This was the case with Tank. You cannot change the future by knowing it, but knowing it can sometimes help you change the path that will lead you there. Some people, like Tank, function better when they know what's coming. It's the little choices we make every day that are important. The little choices define the big ones that define your life.

Unfortunately, Tobias could not preclude visions of his own future. Once something was seen it could not be unseen. Every little, mundane choice he made flowed into all the others, connecting and interacting with the choices of those around him until the butterfly effect of it touched the whole world. He had trained himself not to dwell on personal visions too much. You can't live your life second-guessing fate.

Joanna was completely healed. A little psychometric 'faith-healing', along with Althea's medications, had done the trick. Of course, now she had a whole new reason to be cautious. Tobias didn't tell her anything about her future or that of her unborn child. The glimpses he had seen were both terrifying and propitious, but unlike most of his visions they were clouded with possibilities. He saw no clear path, no big predestined and unalterable milestone events. Instead, there were so many they contradicted each other, as if every choice she was to make would be profound and significant. The child's future defied destiny.

From what he had been told, and from what he had seen while

healing Joanna, Tobias gleaned that the child's father, Rene, who was presently lost to them, was himself reborn. In which case, Tobias didn't understand how his cryonic resurrection was even possible. He was somehow split between two living bodies. This might go some way to explaining why he was impaired when first revitalized. But what had happened since then that he was now fully himself, and Rene was missing? Had Rene died? But Tobias could still feel him – somehow they remained connected. And he felt that same impairment now afflicted Rene. In the end, only one of them could live.

Tobias told no-one of these concerns. He also saw no benefit in telling Joanna the hard road that lay before her. Alerting her to the unborn child was enough for her to be mindful of her actions. He didn't understand the implications of it all yet.

Perhaps his meeting with Cairn would clarify things. The festival was one day away and he had yet to decide what, if anything, he was going to do. He needed to know what the supreme leader of the Tobianist Church had to say. He also needed to see what lay in Cairn's future, and the only way to do that was to meet the man. There was more at stake here than whether or not he should support a political uprising. More even than the future of the Tobianist Church. His connection with Althea Roget defied the laws of nature and crossed centuries – just so they could be together. There had to be a reason for it.

'I really don't think you should do this,' Althea told him. 'It's far too dangerous. You'll likely get arrested or killed before you get anywhere near the Cardinal Hierophant.'

'Father Alban will be there to guide and protect me,' he reassured. Althea wondered if Tobias realized he had just paraphrased the Tobianist blessing. 'He believes getting in will be easy. Getting out will be the hard part.'

They were in the stationmaster's office where Joanna had been recuperating. It was the first time they'd been alone together, and the small room was imbued with a curious apprehension.

'I wish you would let me come with you.' Now that she had Tobias, Althea didn't want to let him out of her sight. It was an instinct both maternal and selfish.

'I'm given to understand a woman priest roaming the halls of The Great Temple would be rather conspicuous.'

'Your religion is sexist.'

'I agree. Perhaps I'll mention it to Cairn.'

Althea leaned forward and kissed Tobias on the mouth. He was startled, but did not pull away. He wasn't sure how to respond, so he just held his ground until Althea withdrew.

'Sorry, but … I've been wanting to do that for the longest time.'

'Quite all right. Forgive me if I … it's been some time since anyone kissed me like that.'

Althea grinned. 'Are you blushing?'

Tobias turned away. 'No, of course not.'

'You are human, after all.'

Tobias looked Althea in the eye. 'I'm counting on you. Both of you.'

'We'll be there.'

They had an exit plan, but the outcome was unclear. It rested ultimately on Cairn's reaction. For now, things could go either way. But Tobias did not tell Althea of this uncertainty. Instead, he gently brushed a strand of hair from her face, and returned the kiss.

'You're mad. It's the worst idea in a long list of bad ideas.' Kane figured with the Prophet Tobias on their side, the last thing he should be doing is marching into enemy territory for some powwow with Cairn. 'They'll kill him on the spot.'

'Are you going to tell him he can't do it?' Alban challenged.

'I already did.'

'What did he say?'

'He said …' Kane sighed. He knew this was an argument he could not win. ' *"My life. My choice."* What about the rest of us?'

'You just want him to endorse your revolution,' Alban argued. 'Do you really think the Prophet Tobias wants to start a war against his own religion? If there is a peaceful solution to all this, he aims to find it.'

'Of course, you would say that?'

'One doesn't have to be a priest to want peace.'

'And one doesn't have to be a heretic to want change!'

Alban hesitated; Kane hit home with that one. 'Change doesn't have to be violent,' he said at last, though it was more a plea than a statement of fact.

'If there were any other way, father…' Kane felt sympathy for the little priest. He quite liked the man, even if he did disagree with his politics.

'Tobias will find a way.' Alban was certain of this.

As if on cue Tobias emerged from the stationmaster's office. There was purpose in his stride as he crossed the lobby, combing his fingers through his hair, with Althea following close behind. All eyes were on the Prophet, so no one noticed as Althea self-consciously adjusted her shirt and hair.

'Are you ready?' Tobias asked Alban.

The little priest nodded and rose to his feet, pulling up the hood of his robe.

Tobias looked sympathetically at Kane, then Tank, Joanna, and finally scanning all the other anxious faces of their motley group. 'We won't be long,' he announced. 'Just going to have a little chat with the supreme leader of my church and ruler of the known world. Sort a few things out. Should be back by suppertime.'

Tobias smiled at the assembled, turning to find Althea standing beside him. He kissed her on the forehead affectionately. 'See you soon.' Pulling up his hood a vision flashed through Tobias's mind of a dark space ... intense pain ... struggle ... the smell of blood and death ... a comforting pelt and the face of a compassionate ape. This vision had a different feel about it. It wasn't his future he saw, it felt more like the present. Was it Rene?

Tobias stopped ... turned back to face Joanna, who sensed something was up and rose to her feet. But he couldn't be sure. He didn't want to give her false hope. After a moment's hesitation, Tobias turned on his heel and followed Alban down the stairs to the underground tunnels.

Joanna remained standing. It didn't matter that the Prophet said nothing. She knew. She saw it in his eyes. Rene was alive.

It had taken several hours, but eventually Rene emerged from the rubble of the safe-house with Elly. He was exhausted. His chest burned with pain so intense it numbed his senses. Dragging himself through Elly's tunnel had been excruciating. He'd pulled himself up on his back to avoid putting pressure on his ribs. This was a special kind of torture, agony searing though his upper body with each drag. But he fought through it, using the pain to power his climb. Anything was better than being trapped in that hole another day. To breath clean air and see the sky again made it worthwhile, even if he was vomiting from the pain.

Elly brought him some water and sat, gently stroking his matted hair. That was the last thing Rene remembered before passing out.

— ∞ —

The vision of Rene haunted Tobias as he and Alban travelled to the city centre. They were led to the surface by Tank, and from there made their way above ground until they came to a remote GL station, where they caught the train. With preparations for the Festival of Renewal in full swing throughout the city, a couple of clerics riding the train network was not at all out of place. Despite Tobias not having a comkey, Alban's was sufficient to get them onto the train, and Tobias's unaccounted presence would be discounted as a glitch in the system.

While they sat silently on the train waiting for their stop, Tobias meditated on his vision. He tried to reconnect with Rene. Nothing came at first, but he was patient. In time vague disjointed feelings and images flickered through his mind – hunger … pain … water … Joanna … sex … falling … lightning deaths … screaming … a multitude … a great battle … Dan … Will … hearing the news – heartache … agonizing chest pains … a crying baby … joy and fear … prison … revolution … the desert sun … blood and death … a soft couch … falling … pain …

Tobias realized he was watching Rene dream. A dream from a shared consciousness. A dream that was a prediction of possible future events. Like his visions of Joanna's unborn child, nothing was certain. The images were confused and jumbled, but incredibly vivid. The connection was disconcertingly lucid. He was Rene, and he was in pain. Tobias used the connection to send a healing energy to his other self. From the nature of the pain and the troubled breathing he was sensing, he could tell Rene had broken ribs. Normally a laying on of hands would help the healing process. He didn't know if this would work remotely, but their link was strong right now. He continued the healing until Alban interrupted:

'My lord …. Master….Tobias.' Alban gently touched Tobias's hand and whispered in his ear to rouse him from his meditation. Tobias opened his eyes. 'I'm sorry. But this is our stop. We need to get out.'

Tobias quickly reoriented himself. That's right – he was on a train, with Father Alban, to visit Cairn. He nodded. 'Perhaps you should call me 'brother' from now on,' Tobias said with a smile.

They changed to the Temple line. There were three stations within the Temple grounds, with one of them being directly alongside the Great Temple. These stations were mostly for tourists or other visitors. Staff and clergy who worked at any of the Temple buildings lived in apartments on the grounds, while the Temple Guard had their barracks also within the walls.

The festival was a day away, but already the Temple was open to the public as tradesmen, media, food vendors and other workers from outside prepared for tomorrow's opening ceremony. The train station, the Temple grounds and the halls of the Great Temple itself were abuzz with activity. Two humble, hooded, clerics passed completely unnoticed amid the chaos.

Which is not to say the place was insecure. Every person was being constantly tracked via their comkey, which communicated who they were, where they were, what they were supposed to be doing, what tools or equipment they carried (including concealed weapons if anyone was foolish enough to try), their medical histories, criminal record if any, even what they had for breakfast that morning. One's entire life was recorded and tracked through your comkey. So while only a few Temple Guards were in sight, guarding entranceways or patrolling the avenues, reinforcements could be called upon in an instant if a system alert went out.

Father Alban still had Temple clearance so was able to pass by unimpeded, and as far as the system was concerned, he travelled alone. The man with him had no comkey – a red flag. His DNA would be sampled from his breath as he passed a checkpoint and checked against the records of every living person. Since his DNA was not recognized the Prophet Tobias would again be ignored as a glitch and be effectively invisible.

It wasn't until they reached the offices of the Cardinal Hierophant that an actual Guard stopped their progress. Alban looked up at the Guard dressed in ceremonial dress armour, while Tobias kept his head bowed humbly, the hood discretely masking his face.

'We wish to see His Eminence,' Alban told the Guard.

'Do you, now? Is he expecting you?'

'No. But I'm sure he'll want to see us.' The little priest's brazen manner was oddly disconcerting for the Guard. People didn't usually make demands of the Temple Guard, let alone the Cardinal Hierophant's private elite.

The guard gazed at Alban suspiciously, then touched the side of his helmet, activating its built-in camera and comms. 'Two priests to see his Eminence. No appointment … what's the name?'

'Father Alban.'

'Remove your hood please, father.' Alban did so. 'You too.'

Tobias pulled back his hood. This would allow face recognition to confirm their identities. The guard's attention was drawn by the voice inside his helmet. He then looked up at the second priest. 'What was your name?'

'Tobias.'

'Father Tobias,' the guard repeated for the voice in his helmet. He looked confused and turned back to Tobias. 'Are you sure?'

'Quite sure.'

341

'One moment. There seems to be a problem finding you on the system.'

'I wouldn't be at all surprised,' Tobias said cheerfully.

Cairn was very careful when writing his festival sermon not to say something that would hold him accountable for anything in particular. Every sermon was recorded for posterity, every word scrutinized by the media and compared to what he had said in the past. The trick was in speaking specifically about nothing in particular. It had to be inspiring and positive, giving a nod to history but with an eye on the future. It had to quote the *Shentama* and offer a lesson that would fortify people's faith in the Prophet (meaning the Church). It had to acknowledge any major issues that had come up in the past year without asserting an opinion either way (to not mention recent events caused a bigger furore in the media over their omission). It had to be about twenty minutes long and hold the attention of a worldwide audience. It had to entertain.

Cairn found the best way to do this was through parables. Stories. Sometimes real, if he came across something appropriate, sometimes invented. Stories of regular folk, doing regular things, and to whom something extraordinary occurs. Something people could relate to. Something that emphasized the core tenets of the faith: renewal, free will and fate, respect for others, and self-realization.

Each year's sermon often took him months to write. He had this year's pretty much finished until a week ago. Now it all had to change. He had decided to tell the story of Tobias as a young man. Before he became the Prophet. Before anyone believed in him or followed his teachings. Before the *Shentama* was published. Back when the world denounced him as a fraud and charlatan, like so many false prophets before him. Heedless of this criticism the young Tobias remained true to his beliefs, travelling the world, healing the sick, teaching and learning. Eventually his resolve paid off, and the world accepted him as a true prophet and spiritual master.

If the Prophet Tobias could make it through those dark years, his faith fortified by the hostility he encountered, so could the people of Lorna and the world. Through adversity came strength, and through the fellowship of the Tobianist Church came security and peace. The heresies that threatened their way of life were no match for the divine authority of The Church of the Prophet. Like Tobias, their trust in the one true faith will see them through these dark days and they will be made stronger by the journey.

It was all bollocks of course. The power of the Church came not from faith, divine authority, or even political supremacy. It came from the delusion that the Church was good and just. That it offered hope. That despite its many faults, it had the best interests of the people at heart. It was the stern father you wanted to kill yet make proud at the same time; an imperfect ideology that was still better than any alternative. A benign dictatorship that had achieved what countless dictators of the past could not – true and total dominion over the world. One couldn't argue with the facts. Tobianism was good for humanity.

The Festival of Renewal was a massive pain to organize, but it served a crucial role in fortifying the authority of the Church. It reminded everyone how good they had it, and who they had to thank for it. But this was not a time for gloating or false piety. It was a time to pat the faithful on the head and tell them how well *they* were doing. An angry mob could be a powerful weapon, provided it was *your* angry mob.

Cairn was interrupted by a comm from his secretary in the outer office. 'Your Eminence, forgive the interruption. But there are two priests here who insist on seeing you.'

'Do they have an appointment?'

'No, Your Eminence.'

'Then tell them to fuck off.'

'Yes, Your Eminence.'

'... Wait. What are their names?'

'Father Alban and Father Tobias. Though I can't find Tobias on our system, and he is not wearing his comkey.'

'How did he get this far through security?'

'I don't know, Your Eminence.'

Alban. That name was familiar. And Tobias. Surely not. Many were given the name Tobias in honour of the Prophet, some might even have become priests in the Great Temple. But why was he not wearing a comkey? It was effectively against the law to be without one. And why could he not be found on the system? Then Cairn remembered where he had heard of Alban. The fat little crypt-keeper who discovered the body missing a week ago. The one who started this whole mess.

'Let them in,' Cairn ordered.

'Are you sure, Your Eminence?'

'Yes, I'm fucking sure. Let them in!'

The Guard led Alban and Tobias through the opulent outer office, towards the high double-doors of Cairn's private chambers on the far side. The office was teeming with diligent brown-robed clerics gripped in final preparation panic for the festival. A determined chaos. Alban had been here once before, seventeen years earlier when he was made caretaker to the tomb of Tobias. Officially it was considered an honoured duty, and he was indeed honoured to have received it.

Unofficially it was looked down upon as little more than janitorial. A dead-end for anyone with career ambitions within the Temple. To work in this office, so close to the Cardinal Hierophant, would be a high honour indeed, and something Alban knew long ago he would never attain. He had no regrets though. To be walking into the Cardinal Hierophant's private chambers with the Prophet Tobias himself was something he never could have imagined seventeen years ago.

The tall doors to the inner chamber opened automatically as they approached, revealing a spacious, elegantly simple office lit by muted sunlight. The Guard motioned for them to stop a few steps inside the room as the doors closed behind them. Cairn was seated at his desk – a gigantic mahogany island in the middle of the room, with nothing on it but a large, translucent AV screen and a decanter of water with some glasses. Behind him, floor to ceiling glass windows opened out to a broad balcony overlooking the Temple forecourt and Festival Square. Cairn was silhouetted by the light from these windows – a dark figure swathed by an ethereal luminance. The figure-8 fountain could be seen beyond the glass in the distance, as small aerial cameras buzzed about the space, being tested for tomorrow's opening ceremony streamcast.

Alban dropped to one knee, clasped his hands, and bowed his head deferentially. 'Your Eminence. Thank you for seeing us.'

Tobias however remained standing; his head lowered just enough that Cairn couldn't make out his face underneath the hood. Cairn glanced at the Guard who promptly stepped in front of Tobias, shielding Cairn in the event of an attack. 'Kneel before His Eminence,' he commanded.

Tobias raised his eyes slowly, observing the Guard intently. There was a glimmer of recognition, or was it alarm? Gasping, the guard took an involuntary step backwards, his armour rattling anxiously. Finally, Tobias kneeled beside Alban, mimicking his supplicate posture.

Cairn tried to get a look at his face, but the Guard blocked his view. 'You can leave us now, thank you,' Cairn ordered. The Guard was about to question the command, but knew better. He bowed, turned on his heel, and left the room.

Cairn rose from his chair, looking down on the two priests kneeling before him as he walked around the desk. 'Father Alban.'

'Your Eminence.' Alban raised his head.

'I remember you. You came to me last week to tell me the body of the Prophet was missing. You were most persistent then as well.'

'Yes, your Eminence.'

'Have you come to tell me you have found him?'

Cairn looked intently at the second priest. Feeling the Cardinal Hierophant's gaze upon him Tobias rose to his feet and lowered his hood. Cairn looked into the eyes of the Prophet.

Now was his chance. With a word the Guard would be back in the room in an instant. Cairn could order both these men be killed where they stood, and the Guard would do it without hesitation. Tobias would no longer be a threat, Cairn's position would be secure, and the festival could proceed without any further bloodshed. The crisis would be over.

But Cairn did not call out. Despite all he knew about the theft of the body and its revitalization, despite the evidence confirming what Jason Asar had told him, Cairn had still harboured doubts. Now, there was no doubt. The Prophet Tobias was returned. And regardless of his high office Cairn was still a priest of the Tobianist faith. God had just walked into the room.

Cairn dropped to his knees and bowed before the Prophet.

'There's no need for that,' Tobias said gently. 'Please, stand up.'

Cairn rose, as did Father Alban.

'I knew you were alive,' Cairn told him. 'Others would not believe me, but I knew.'

'And you have been trying to kill me ever since.'

Cairn was rattled. Alban could see it. To witness the Cardinal Hierophant vulnerable and frightened was a rare thing indeed. The man was human after all. 'I have good reason.'

'I would love to hear it. But first, could I trouble you for some water?' Tobias asked.

'Of course.' Cairn poured two glasses from the decanter on his desk. His hands were shaking. As Cairn handed the glasses to them… Tobias clasped his hand gently to steady it.

'Thank you.'

As Tobias drank, his mind wandered. Then, looking at the floor thoughtfully, he sighed: 'Hmmm.' He looked up at Cairn with sympathetic regard, as if he knew what lay in the Cardinal Hierophant's future, and it did not look good. Alban was still astonished by the Prophet's ability to know a man's future merely by touching them.

Tobias looked about the room, then walked to the windows overlooking Festival Square. 'I like what you've done with the place. A bit ostentatious, but impressive. The Great Temple of Lorna. Tobianism, the new world religion. And all from a little book I wrote two-hundred odd years ago. I gather there is also a festival in my honour tomorrow?'

'The Festival of Renewal,' Cairn responded.

'Sounds like fun. Perhaps I should go. See what all the fuss is about.'

Cairn remembered his earlier resolve. 'I would prefer that you didn't.'

'Why not?'

'It could be dangerous.'

'For me … or for you?' His voice was calm, but Tobias was not about to accept Cairn at face value.

'For both of us. For all of us. A lot has changed since you died. This is not the world you once knew. And you are no longer the Prophet you once were.'

'What am I then?'

'A myth. A fairy tale we tell our children. A hero. A god.' Cairn said this with both irony and reverence – no mean feat. 'But here you stand before me, a mere human. How could you possibly live up to the legend the Church has made of you?'

Alban had also struggled with this paradox since meeting Tobias. But the more he came to know the man, the more in awe he was of him. Not a god perhaps, but certainly something more than merely human.

'I suppose I should be flattered,' Tobias responded. 'Though it is not the legacy I would have hoped for.'

'Whether you approve of it or not, your legacy has changed the world … for the better.'

'Is it better? I don't know enough about this world yet to decide.'

'It is not for you to decide.'

Tobias turned on Cairn. He was offended that he should have no say in a world built in his image. But then he smiled indulgently. 'Please, Cairn. Speak your mind. I'm keen to know what the leader of my religion thinks of me.'

'… You don't belong here,' Cairn told Tobias plainly.

'You may be right. But is that really for *you* to decide? Your solution is to have me killed all over again before I cause any trouble.'

'I wish there were any other way.'

Tobias stood before Cairn and looked him in the eye, smiling gently. 'I believe you. Tell me why.'

'Two hundred and forty years ago, on the day you were assassinated, Tobianism was born. The religion you never wanted.' Cairn paused to gauge Tobias's reaction. The Prophet remained silent so he continued. 'Since then, wars have been fought in your name. People have died defending your teachings and the right to live by them. The Tobianist Church has committed atrocities to rival anything hitherto done in the name of God. The *Shentama* you wrote has been rewritten many times to suit the Church's needs. Technology and science, more than ever before, are in the service of the Church. It is how we maintain control. It is how we rule the world. We are a long way from what you taught, and the world in which you taught it.

'And yet, your vision of an ideal world is upon us. There is no war, no hunger, no crime. People live their lives free from the bondage of doubt. Aside from a few heretics bent on anarchy, this is a safe world. A passive world. Tobianism has brought peace. For the first time in the history of mankind we are united under one rule – The Church of the Prophet. But it is not your church. It never was. Religion is not built on a man, no matter how enlightened. It requires myth, structure, a clear doctrine of laws and commandments. And it requires a God we can understand.

'What you began has flowered into a great and powerful regime, built on ritual and faith. I know this is not what you wanted, but it is what people need. And it's how we've kept your teachings alive. If the world saw you returned, speaking against your own Church, there would be chaos. There would be war. I cannot answer for the crimes of the past. But I will not be responsible for the ruin of a Church that has finally brought peace to the world, even if it comes from the Prophet himself.

'This is the world you created. This is your legacy. You have no right to take it from us now. Forgive me, but we do not need another

Prophet. We already have one, and he belongs frozen in a cryogenic crypt, buried beneath this Temple, a relic of the past. A great man. One of the greatest ever to walk upon the earth. But who's story we, the Church, must control.'

Alban remained dutifully silent throughout this, though he was in turn fascinated and shocked to hear the Cardinal Hierophant's candid précis of the history of Tobianism.

Tobias, for his part, revealed nothing. He listened attentively, letting Cairn speak his mind without interruption, without judgment.

'Thank you for your honesty, and the history lesson,' Tobias eventually said. 'I take it then my resurrection is something of an inconvenience for you. You think I mean to tear down what you have built over two centuries, and that I have no right to do so. I quite agree. Besides, I've only been here a few days. Still getting used to the place. But I do wonder what all those people out there would think if they had heard you just now. Not something you'll be putting in your speech, I imagine.'

'Then you understand why you cannot be here.'

'I understand all too well. And that is precisely why I did not want to become a religion. For all the good the Church may do, your mission is to put blinkers on a person's soul. To bind them to you. To curb their freedoms and control their destiny. All for the greater good. But if a person is not free to choose their own path there is no greater good. An enforced peace is no peace at all. I'm sorry to say, Cairn, you've rather missed the point.'

For the leader of the Tobianist Church to be chastised by the Prophet that he has got it all wrong was a telling blow. Cairn was humiliated. But his steely composure soon returned, his temper turning toward resentment and rage. 'You are a wise man, Tobias; but you've never had to rule. Civilizations rise or fall on how well they understand the greater good. Too much freedom threatens the society that tolerates it.'

Tobias considered this for a moment. 'You think I am naïve to these things. Perhaps I am. You strike me as an honourable man, Cairn, with a fair understanding of human nature and the best of intentions. You may even be a half decent human-being underneath all those robes. But you lack one important thing, my friend. Compassion.'

'One does not rise to the office of Cardinal Hierophant without sacrificing a few sentimentalities along the way,' Cairn responded.

'If that is so, then I hope never to be Cardinal Hierophant.'

'Do you intend to challenge the Church?' Cairn was becoming confrontational, but Tobias appeared not to notice.

'I don't know yet. The dilemma for me is, as you so rightly put it, I am not of this time, and have no right to interfere. And yet, here I am. Fate has somehow plucked me from my sleep and thrown me back into the world. There must be a reason. I am beginning to understand what that reason is. It's not about me at all, really.' Tobias smiled, 'or you. Though you, Cairn, will play an important part. More important that you can know.'

'What do you mean?' Cairn didn't like being teased – even by the Prophet. 'Have you seen my future? What did you see?'

Tobias turned to Alban. 'I think it's time we left, Brother. Thank you so much for your time, Your Eminence. It's been most enlightening.'

'Guard!'

As Alban and Tobias approached the door, they were confronted by the same Elite Temple Guard who had escorted them in.

'Place these two under arrest,' commanded Cairn.

The guard mumbled something into his helmet and within seconds a contingent of Elite Guards had them surrounded.

'What do we do?' Alban whispered anxiously.

Tobias placed a reassuring hand on the little priest's shoulder as Cairn approached them. 'I should have you both killed right now.'

'Yes,' Tobias agreed, holding Cairn's gaze, '… but you won't.'

Was Tobias challenging him, or simply stating what he saw in their future? Either way, Cairn could change his mind on a whim. Their lives hung in the balance.

'Put them both in the dungeon!' Cairn finally commanded.

'Your Eminence?' queried the lead Guard.

'You heard me!'

As they were escorted back through the outer office with its industrious male clerics, Tobias called back to Cairn. 'By the way. You should think about allowing women clerics. That'll fix half your problems right there!' Whereupon the tall doors of the inner chamber closed with a gentle thud, shielding the Cardinal Hierophant once more within his private domain.

Each life has its path
Each life plays its part
You are the actor and the writer
The one among many
The many into one

They all exist in the Forever—Now
Speaking with one another
Guiding one another
Choosing one's destiny moment by moment
As if it was ever thus

Shentama
– Stanzas 131-132

The 'dungeon' was a euphemistic, though quite accurate, term for the caves underneath the Temple that were part of the vast catacombs of Lorna. They had once been cells in the traditional sense – small rooms that housed the early priesthood back in the days when to be a Tobianist was a dangerous conviction. On this site two hundred and forty years ago was built the first ever Tobianist monastery. A small fortress that protected the 'cult' from vandals and extremists.

These natural caves were carved from the limestone sediment by ancient lava flows, or by groundwater laced with carbonic acid eons ago, as was the rest of the labyrinth of tunnels upon which the monastery, and later the Great Temple, were built. Beneath the limestone, solid granite foundations influenced how large (or small) the caves were and the winding path many of the tunnels took. As a result, some of the cells were not even big enough for one to stand upright or lie fully stretched on the floor when sleeping.

The caves were converted into prison cells during *The Great Purge*, used for detaining and torturing enemies of the fledgling Tobianist Church. The ghosts of prisoners murdered in those dark days still haunted the catacombs; one reason people avoided going down there anymore. Since those days the dungeon, as it came to be known, was largely neglected, though it sometimes came in handy for detaining secret enemies of the Church. Not your regular everyday heretics – they were accommodated in the holding cells adjoining the Temple Guard barracks before being transported off to Gerda. A prisoner could be incarcerated in the dungeon for years and no-one would know they were there. It had become the private jail of the Executive Council, and one of the Great Temple's darkest secrets.

Tobias and Alban were escorted into the labyrinth and interned in neighbouring cells within the dungeon. The heavy wood and metal doors used an old-fashioned key and lock mechanism. The locks were large and tight with age, but still highly effective. The keys hung on a hook at the entrance to the dungeon passage. One could even see them through the small windows on the cell doors, tormentingly close. But only Elite Guard ever came down here, and only when there was a prisoner to watch. There was no escaping the dungeon.

A solitary guard was posted. He sat with his feet up on a small desk just inside the entrance, playing a puzzle game on a portable AV. He was used to this duty and had come prepared. The dungeon bore evidence of other recent use – fresh blood on the stone floor leading from one of the larger cells, and various torture devices could be seen within, glinting in the shadows.

'What do we do now?' Alban asked Tobias softly between the cells.

'We wait.'

'For what?'

'Patience, brother Alban. I suggest you get some rest. We have a long march ahead of us.' With that, Tobias closed his eyes, as he tried once again to connect with his other self – Rene.

— ∞ —

Captain Marius should have been prepping his troops for the opening ceremony, but that was not his responsibility anymore. The festival was the Temple Guards' biggest security challenge of the year, on top of which they were expected to stage a series of exhibition drills to entertain the public throughout Festival week. Lieutenant Makoto had it well in hand though. Despite the dramas of the last few days, festival security was a well-planned and practiced operation. Little was left to chance. Marius had something far less important and more interesting to deal with, and since he technically no longer worked there, he was free to pursue his impulses. It was quite liberating.

Driving a GL cruiser through the main gates and across Festival Square, Marius was astonished how quickly the city had bounced back from the massacre of just a few days before. Food and merch stalls were setting up around the fringes. The figure-8 fountain was receiving a spit and polish by an army of cleaners; the water flowing down its channels a pristine blue, all traces of blood eliminated from the cycle. The patterned limestone tiles of the Square had been washed and buffed, and now sparkled in the bright morning light. The festival always brought a positive, optimistic buzz to the city, and it seemed the unrest of the past week was all but forgotten. Despite his grievances, Marius was feeling pretty good. The mood was infectious.

The tracker led Marius away from the city centre and into the Western Borough, not far from the AQ. According to the readout, Rene St. Claire hadn't moved since last night, he was still at the collapsed house. Though his health had miraculously improved. Perhaps his comkey had been damaged and was glitching. If that was true Marius wasn't at all sure his track was accurate. It might even be a bogus marker from a hacked comkey – quite possible for a rebel heretic. Still, he had nothing better to do and was curious to find out.

Festival preparations continued along the streets with banners and decorations draped or hung between buildings and from the GL train tubes overhead. They were gaudy and hazardous, but did give the city a cheerful atmosphere. By night the decorations would illuminate a myriad of patterns and colours and the normally drab city of Lorna would light up the skies like a beacon visible from space. The mural walls that flanked the inner-city streets, some scaling the full height of their host buildings, presented religious art, carefully curated montages of Tobias healing or speaking, inspirational passages from the modern *Shentama*, and other motivational content. From tomorrow, the image of the Prophet live from the crypt would also regularly appear, his frozen face looking down on the city like a benevolent demi-god – the guiding spirit of the modern world.

The closer Marius came to the Western Borough the less conspicuous the festival became. There were no mural walls in this poorer part of town, no sky-scraping towers, and no GL train tubes. No outward effort was taken by the locals to even acknowledge the festival. Here, it was business as usual. Many of them would travel into the city to take part in the opening ceremony though. As always, a huge crowd was expected.

Arriving at the scene of the collapsed rebel safe-house there was the faint smell of rotting flesh. Decomposing bodies were still buried under the rubble, their gases rising from the heap of crumpled wood, poly-brick and plaster, carried by a light breeze into the street. Marius wasn't concerned with the heretics; they could rot to bone for all he cared. But buried with them were several Temple Guard killed in the line of duty.

He checked the clean-up schedule. Dozens of crews were working their way through the city since the raids; restoring order, removing bodies; making Lorna presentable for the world. This house was on the list, but they were taking their sweet time getting to it. If the media got a whiff it would not look good for the Temple. It had also suffered some of the worst casualties on the day. Out of respect for the Guards who had died their bodies needed to be recovered and given a proper service.

'Get a crew down here now!' Marius barked once he got through to someone responsible. 'The place is starting to stink up the street.'

'Yes, sir. Immediately!'

He was going to miss giving orders. If Kasper were Cardinal Hierophant things would be different. Though Marius wasn't sure that meant better.

Leaving his GL at the curb Marius pulled on a power-glove, and followed the signal locked on to Rene St. Claire's comkey. Climbing through a broken doorway he found himself in a concealed hollow on the far side of the property. He checked the signal – dead ahead. A few more fumbling steps on the uneven ground and Marius stopped short, seeing what appeared to be a large ape of some kind. The creature turned to face him – startled, fearful – but did not run. Instead, it looked back and grunted to someone hidden behind a shard of wall. Marius raised his glove hand, shifting his weight to look around the wall. Rene St. Claire sat in a dusty, busted sofa chair, staring eerily back at him. His clothes were torn and filthy, his face scratched, dried blood clinging to his forehead. Despite appearances, he seemed to be in good health.

Marius moved closer, his power-glove raised defensively, as he took up position a few meters from the strange pair. The ape gathered up some food bars and trundled towards him. Stopping at his feet, it offered the food. Marius wasn't sure how to react to this but wasn't about to take any chances. He knocked the creature's hand away, and violently kicked it to the ground. The ape crawled to pick up the food and calmly offered it again. This time Marius did nothing, instead stepping away from the animal, his limp causing him to stumble slightly.

'Don't be afraid.' Rene told him, that eerie stare still fixed on him. 'She means no harm.'

'Tell it to get back.'

Rene clicked his tongue. The ape left the food at Marius's feet and knuckle-walked to Rene, sitting beside him.

'Rene St. Claire?'

'Have we met?'

'Don't you remember? You tried to kill me.'

Rene thought for a moment. 'Yes. Sorry about that. Though it was not my intention to kill you. How's the leg?'

For someone with a power-glove pointed at his face Rene was irritatingly serene, like his mind was somewhere else. Perhaps he was on drugs or something. 'You're wanted for heresies against the Church, escaping lawful custody, and as an accessory to murder.'

'Murder?'

'There are a dozen good men and women lying in the pile behind you.'

'Yes. That is unfortunate. Do you mean to kill me?'

'… I have some questions first.'

'Of course.'

'The man you prevented me from capturing, the one who looks like the Prophet. Do you know where he is?'

Rene cocked his head thoughtfully. 'Hmm. I'm not sure how I should answer that.'

'It's a simple enough question.'

'To be sure. But it is not so simple an answer. The man you seek is already in custody.'

'Where?'

'Right under your nose. I mean that both literally and metaphorically.'

'What?' Marius figured this Rene was another intellectual fuckhead, giving ambiguous answers just to mess with him.

'The question you should be asking, Captain, is: who is this man really? And why is the Church so determined to see him dead?'

'He's an escaped prisoner and a heretic. Just like you.'

'Are you sure?'

The question was plump with implication, as if he knew of the Marius's doubts – but Marius was not about to confess them to a heretic. 'Give me one good reason why I shouldn't just kill you now.'

'Who would look after Elly?' Rene said as he patted the head of the ape sitting beside him.

Marius looked into the creature's eyes, seriously considering Rene's response. Not that he should give a damn about some ape, but the creature was an innocent. Plus, now the damn thing had a name, and was female to boot.

'How did you survive this?' Marius indicated the debris heaped around them.

'Just lucky I guess.'

'And what's with the monkey?'

'She's a bonobo,' Rene told him, as if that was answer enough.

Marius didn't understand it, but something in the back of his mind told him this Rene was important. This Rene should live. Perhaps it was those eyes gently drilling into him. Perhaps it was the monkey … or whatever the fuck she was. Perhaps it was the fact he was no longer Captain of the Guard and just wanted to stick it to Cairn. Perhaps it was because the day had started out so well and he just didn't want to spoil it. Whatever the reason, he knew what he was about to do was treasonous. But he didn't care.

'Give me your comkey,' Marius demanded.

'My what?'

'The ring. Give it to me.'

Rene removed the ring from his right hand and tossed it over. Marius dropped the ring on the ground, pointed at it with his power-glove and zapped the device into network oblivion. 'Now you're dead.' Marius turned to leave.

'Why?' Rene asked.

'I don't know. I just don't feel like killing anyone today.'

'On such a whim might hinge the fate of the world,' Rene intoned.

Marius stopped and turned on Rene. 'Keep talkin' shit like that and I'll change my mind. Now get out of here. There'll be a clean-up crew along any minute.'

Rene grinned. 'I look forward to our next meeting, Captain.'

'Don't count on it.'

— ∞ —

Althea and Tank were in the catacombs under the Temple. After driving the GL as far as they could, they walked the same route Althea took just ten days before when liberating Tobias from the crypt. This time their mission was to liberate the Prophet and Father Alban from the dungeon; a dungeon Althea didn't know existed until today, and which even Father Alban was unsure of its exact whereabouts. It connected to the same network of tunnels that led to the crypt, so in principle they should be able to find their way to it if they followed Althea's original route. Tank had synced Alban's comkey signal with his own and was able to track him. From their present position the priest was a couple of kilometres away, and thirty-two meters above them. All vital signs showed he was alive and stationary. This gave them a target, but they still had to navigate a path through the labyrinth. Of course, they had no way of knowing for certain Alban was indeed in the dungeon, or that Tobias was with him. Communication was out of the question, lest it be monitored.

At first, they relied on Althea's imperfect memory to get from the old sewer lines into the natural caves and tunnels that spidered under the city. A bewildering web of ancient catacombs that joined eventually to the man-made tunnels beneath the Temple. With nothing but the orange glow of a battery lantern to light their way and no map to follow, Althea tried to remain calm and trust her gut.

They could very easily get lost down here, never to find the surface again. Many a poor soul had. But Tank was no stranger to the threat of death, keeping his cool even as Althea abruptly changed her mind and backtracked several times. The last thing she needed right now was an anxious companion. When confident they were on the right track, she would tear off a piece of paper and leave it as a marker. With all the technology that might have helped them find a safe route through the catacombs, a scrap of paper was still the most reliable.

After several hours of nervous wandering and false trails they stumbled upon the remains of the original map, a tiny square of Temple parchment on the stone floor at a T-junction. Althea fell to her knees, letting out a grateful sigh: 'Oh, thank God'.

From here the path to the crypt passage was easy to trace. It felt surreal to be walking these tunnels again given all that had happened. This was the second time Althea had set out to kidnap Tobias from the church he had inspired. Last time it was for love of the Prophet, this time it was for love of the man.

They reached the junction that led down to the crypt. Alban's comkey marker was in the opposite direction, still above them by several meters, and slightly behind. They were close, but could still get lost trying to find the right path.

'We're directly under the Temple now,' Tank said softly.

'The crypt is down there,' Althea pointed, remembering the treacherous steps that had almost undone them last time.

'I'll give you this, lady. You've got balls.' Althea thought this a curious thing to say, though he clearly meant it as a compliment. 'Coming all this way, stealing Tobias from right under their noses. And then … doing whatever the hell it was you did to bring him back. Big … hairy … balls.'

'Thank you, I think.'

'Did he tell your future?' Tank asked.

'No.'

'Told me mine.'

'Was it … good?' Althea was reluctant to ask, but Tank brought it up.

'Depends how you look at it.'

'What do you mean?'

Tank pondered how to best answer. 'I'm not afraid of death. I just want to be sure it counts for something.'

'Your life does count. Every life counts.'

'But not every death,' Tank responded.

'You want to be remembered.'

'I'm already remembered.' It was true, as one of the all-time champions of the Games Tank would be celebrated long after his death. 'I want to make a difference. I want my death to make a difference when the time comes.'

'You want to be a martyr.' Althea was joking, but Tank wasn't. He smiled those giant pearly whites at her.

'Yeah. That's the word for it. I want to be a martyr.'

'Are your balls as big as your ego?'

Tank might have been insulted, but he took it in good humour and grinned. 'Bigger.'

'I don't want to be a martyr. And I don't care if I'm remembered or not. I'm not doing this for the glory – no offence.'

Tank snorted. 'Maybe those balls aren't so big, after all.'

'I think maybe yours are too big for your own good.'

Tank laughed out loud. His deep basso profondo voice reverberating through the tunnels. He quickly stifled it, realizing they might be heard.

'Come on.' Althea raised the lantern and started up the tunnel. 'And keep those big hairy balls of yours from jangling. They might hear us coming.'

Tank chortled. He liked this one.

— ∞ —

Tobias emerged from his meditation, eyes slowly opening to the darkness of his prison cell. He remembered the meeting with Captain Marius. It was a soft memory, like a dream unbound by time or space, but coherent even so. In the old days it would have been called channelling, though this was a crude word for such a profound experience. But that's what people saw – the mere mechanics of a spirit speaking through another's body. To experience it for oneself was more intense, and more disturbing. Even though Rene was himself in spirit, he was yet another person – another consciousness – suppressed … sleeping … displaced. Tobias felt as if he was stealing Rene's life. These moments were meant to be his. These choices. This path. The longer Tobias lived the more he took from Rene. For all Cairn's failings he was right about one thing. Tobias didn't belong here. As far as he was concerned the future couldn't come fast enough.

Footsteps were heard approaching – two people. One small, one large. Not Guards; their armour would be rattling. It was time to leave.

'Oh, hello. Sorry, but I'm a bit lost.' Althea put on her best little girl voice as she approached the Guard. He was at first startled, then confused, then distracted by her bountiful red hair and ample cleavage. All in the space of two seconds.

It was just enough to throw him off-guard as the shadows behind the red-headed woman sprung forth, taking the form of an enormous (and vaguely familiar) black man who with one clean strike to the side of the helmet cracked the guard's skull against the stone wall, rendering him instantly unconscious. His body bounced off the wall, sprawled across the table knocking his portable AV and the puzzle game he was playing to the ground, finally falling in a heap on the cold floor.

'Really? Just one guard?' Tank was disappointed.

'You haven't killed him, have you?' Althea knelt to examine the man at her feet.

'Nah. He'll be fine. It's only a mild grade-3 concussion. He'll be out for about fifteen minutes.'

'Tank! Althea!' Father Alban was at his cell door, overjoyed to see them.

'Hey Father.' Tank grabbed the keys off their hook and opened the cell.

Released, Alban embraced Tank's giant black frame in a heartfelt hug. 'Thank you. Thank you...'

'My pleasure. Now where's the man?'

'In here.' Alban pointed to the neighbouring cell. Tank opened the door to find Tobias sitting on a low bench in the shadows at the back of the room. Althea stepped past the two men at the door and threw her arms around Tobias so desperately it seemed she intended never to let him go.

Tobias held her gently, savouring the moment. He was surprised how glad he was to see her as well.

'Guys?' Tank interrupted. 'Can we do this later? We should probably get a move on.'

Althea relaxed, wiping tears from her face. 'Sure.'

Tank dragged the unconscious guard into Tobias's cell and locked him in. He thought about destroying the man's comkey so he couldn't communicate when he woke up, but then he would have appeared dead on the system and that would have aroused suspicion even sooner. He did however take the man's portable AV. It was Temple issue and could come in handy. Tank then turned to Alban. 'Give me your comkey, Father.'

'What for?'

'You're officially a fugitive now.'

'Oh … right.' Alban removed his lemnis medallion. This was not just the symbol of his faith, but his literal connection to the Church and society. It then struck him what he was giving up. 'Do I have to?'

Tank gently took the medallion from him. 'This is no longer your Church, Father.' Tank clasped the medallion with both hands and twisted till it split apart with a metallic crack, destroying the processor within. Alban was now effectively dead.

The party headed back through the labyrinth retracing their steps. If all went well, they would return to where they had left the GL within a couple of hours, and a mere thirty minutes later could be back at the station with the others. Just in time for supper.

33

The truly wise man is silent
He has no desire to speak, but should one ask
He teaches not for himself
But for those who would listen and seek understanding
Ask and he will answer
But do not wait for him to speak first
For nothing is more eloquent
Than that which is said in silence

Shentama
– Stanza 12

'What do you mean they're gone?'

'They escaped Your Eminence.'

'How does one escape the Temple dungeon?' Cairn was still trying to process the implications.

'They had help,' the Elite Guard lieutenant replied feebly. 'The guard was attacked by a large black man and a red-headed woman.'

Cairn was incredulous. Was their security so easily thwarted? 'Is the guard dead?'

'No, your Eminence.'

'Then kill him.'

'Yes, Your Eminence.'

'Where did they go?'

'We think they escaped through the catacombs.'

'Check the surveillance cameras. Find them!'

'There are no cameras down there, Your Eminence.'

'Track their comkeys.'

'Either they weren't wearing any, or they've been hacked. There's no signal to track.'

'I don't believe this. What is the point of having a secret dungeon if prisoners can just walk out whenever they feel like it?'

'They did have – '

' – Don't answer that!'

The lieutenant fell silent, awaiting orders from the Cardinal Hierophant.

'Where's Captain Marius?' Cairn couldn't believe he needed the man he had just fired to come sort this out.

'I don't know, Your Eminence. He signed out a cruiser a few hours ago.'

'Why? Where'd he go?'

'He didn't say, Your Eminence. We could track his comkey, though?'

Cairn couldn't help but laugh. This was too absurd. He should have been angry, but providence was against him and there was no point railing against it. For whatever reason, the Prophet Tobias was destined to be among them, and nothing it seemed was going to stop him fulfilling his mission. Serendipity was on his side. A calm acceptance came over Cairn. It was too late to do anything now. He would have to let things play out and see where it took them. He turned to the lieutenant:

'Let me ask you something, lieutenant. Are you a loyal Tobianist?'

'Yes, Your Eminence.'

'Do you believe in the word of the Prophet?'

'Yes, Your Eminence.'

'Would you lay down your life to protect the Church?'

'Yes, Your Eminence.'

'Are you just saying that because you think you have to?'

'… No, Your Eminence.'

'Then answer me this: what would you do if the Prophet Tobias himself told you you were wrong? That the Church is wrong? That your entire life has been misguided and you are a fool for believing in such things. What would you do, lieutenant?'

The Guard hesitated, not sure if this was another hypothetical he wasn't really supposed to answer. But Cairn held his gaze, waiting for a reply.

'Is this a test, Your Eminence?'

'No, just a question. What would you do?'

'I don't know, Your Eminence. I suppose I would ask the Prophet what I must do to change things. How do I make it right?'

Cairn pondered this for a moment. 'You know. That never occurred to me. Thank you, Lieutenant.'

'Will that be all, Your Eminence?'

'One more thing. There is clearly a passage through the catacombs that leads directly under the Temple. Find it and seal it off. And we need surveillance down there. See to it.'

'Yes, Your Eminence.'

— ∞ —

The walk through the catacombs had been free of incident, and aside from one moment of confusion, when the paper trail seemed to have been lost, Tobias, Father Alban, Tank and Althea made it back to the GL in good time.

Tearing through the train tunnels with Tank at the wheel, they were home within twenty minutes. Althea knew what to expect from Tank's driving, but Father Alban remained curled up in his seat the entire trip, afraid to even look out the side. He would have thrown up if he'd had anything to deliver. Tobias on the other hand enjoyed the ride. His long hair whipped furiously in the vortex the GL created, and there was a smile on his face the entire trip, with no fear of potential death or injury.

'That was enormous fun,' the Prophet said as he stepped out of the GL. 'If nothing else, I'm glad to see the future has finally brought us the flying car.'

'I hate the damn things,' mumbled Alban, clutching his stomach. Then on seeing Tobias's apparent look of disapproval: 'Forgive me.'

Tobias touched the priest sympathetically on the shoulder. 'You are not used to such a pace, my friend. I fear that will have to change.' Was this a prediction, or just some well-intentioned advice? As much as Alban loved Tobias, vague utterances like this were very frustrating.

The party climbed the staircase to the main lobby of the station. As they drew closer, they heard the soft but insistent murmur of many voices. It was hard to know where it was coming from, the domed ceilings and curved walkways of the station scattered the sound in all directions. Emerging into the station lobby they saw an overwhelming multitude. Thousands of people crowded the cavernous space, making it small and inadequate. Most sat on the hard floor, gathered in circles and small groups. Tobias and the others paused at the top of the stairs. The murmur stopped. An unsettling silence fell over the assembly as everyone rose to their feet and turned to face them – to face Tobias.

'You'll have to excuse me,' Tobias murmured. 'My public awaits.' Then taking a deep breath to prepare himself, he stepped forward to greet the crowd.

Watching the Prophet at work was a miracle in itself. The way he connected with people, communicated with them … the way he listened. He made it look so simple and effortless.

Tank had an aversion to large crowds and made himself scarce, a vulnerability Althea would not have expected from a former Games athlete. Alban had gone somewhere to recover after the GL ride. Althea sat with Joanna and Kane in the old coffee shop, watching Tobias work the crowd.

'Where did they all come from?' Althea asked.

'Everywhere,' said Kane, as he sipped his luke-warm coffee through a straw. 'Somehow word got 'round about Tobias. I don't know how they found us, but here they are. I ask for an army, and I get …'

'Disciples,' Joanna finished the thought for him.

'How do I fight a war with that lot?'

'But you're not fighting a war,' Althea countered. 'You're fighting a revolution. You don't need an army; you need the people. And thanks to Tobias, you have them.'

'And if we lose Tobias?'

Kane was doing what he always did – preparing contingencies. But Althea was not going to entertain the idea of losing Tobias. Without responding, she got up from the table and left.

'I can see now why you're a single man, Kane,' Joanna told him. Kane looked at her blankly. 'Can't you see she's in love with him?'

It took a moment, then the penny dropped. 'You mean …? But that's not… I mean he's… Shit. Really?' Kane looked out over the crowd to see Tobias speaking with a young mother. 'I wouldn't have thought he'd be interested.'

'Why not? Althea's a beautiful woman.'

'Sure…'

'He's still a man, after all.'

'Is he? I thought he was supposed to be … I don't know … above all that.'

'It proves he's human. I'd rather that than a god any day.'

'If he *were* a god, I still wouldn't believe in him,' Kane admitted. 'This world has had enough of gods, martyrs and messiahs. They're more trouble than they're worth.'

'What about Rene?'

It seemed an odd non-sequitur, but Kane understood Joanna was recalling their earlier conversation. They had both sensed something special in Rene. Whether that extended to him becoming some kind of messiah was something else entirely.

'When I look at Tobias, I see Rene,' Joanna continued. 'I don't know why, they're not at all alike. And I'm not suggesting Rene could become anything like the Prophet Tobias. But there is something.'

'You think he knows where Rene is?'

There was that Kane tact again, but Joanna could tell he was just as concerned as she. 'Yes.'

'How would he know? They've never even met.'

'How did he know I was pregnant? Or that he would escape the Temple in time for supper. He can see the future. He knows the fate of everyone in this room. And yet he stays silent.' As she said this, they observed Tobias move among the crowd, delicately touching people, and with each touch no doubt a wave of impending destinies assailed his mind. 'Imagine how hard that must be. To know so much about a person, about their future, and not interfere. Even when asked.'

'Do you think he sees his own future?'

'That would be hardest of all.'

As she said this Tobias turned and looked directly at Joanna, as if he had heard her from across the room. He excused himself from the people around him and made toward them. The crowd magically parted for him. It was incredible the way he could command everyone in the room without even trying. Already they had devoted their lives to him.

Tobias stopped beside Joanna. 'Being so loved can be exhausting,' Tobias joked, more as a tribute than a lament. He turned to Kane, observing the transparent patch on his cheek. 'That'll be an impressive scar once it's healed.'

'I'm counting on it,' Kane replied. 'How did your meeting with Cairn go?'

'It was educational.'

'Did you get what you went for?'

'Unfortunately. You're right, Kane. I cannot stand by and let this Church continue to rule in my name. I propose tomorrow, at the festival in my honour, we make a peaceful stand and let the world know I am returned.' Tobias paused as he considered what he had to say next. 'There will be violence. The Temple will not allow us to just hijack the occasion. They will try to stop us.'

'They will indeed,' Kane agreed.

'We cannot be armed,' Tobias told him.

'Of course. We'd never get past security.'

'We go together. Everyone.' Tobias indicated the throng crowding the station lobby.

Kane scanned the room. 'There is safety in numbers.'

'There is also strength. One voice, even my voice, can be ignored. The Church cannot ignore the people once they choose to speak. With this small group – with their voice – we can ignite the hearts and minds of everyone else. I will begin this revolution for you, but you must see it through to its end. Be assured I will be with you every step of the way.'

'What the hell does that mean?' Kane asked.

Tobias smiled. He took Joanna's hand. Turning it over he examined her palm, tracing his finger down the lifeline from above the thumb to her wrist. From birth to death. 'We are more than mere flesh. We forget that sometimes.' He looked Joanna in the eye. 'And we are more alike than you know.' With this characteristically cryptic remark, Tobias rose to leave. 'Now if you'll excuse me. The flesh is weak. I'm starving.' Nodding farewell, Tobias headed for the privacy of the stationmaster's office.

'Prophet be damned, I wish he weren't so goddamned enigmatic all the time.' Kane grumbled.

Joanna didn't dare reply. What she was thinking was too preposterous to be spoken aloud. But whenever she looked at Tobias … she saw Rene.

Tobias entered the stationmaster's office to find Alban lying on the couch with a cold compress against his forehead. Althea sat with him, playing nurse. Alban sat up. 'Brother Tobias.'

Tobias smiled wearily. 'Feeling any better?'

'Yes. Thank you.'

Tobias joined them on the couch. It wasn't till his seat hit the cushion he realized how tired he was. His body just crumpled with fatigue. 'Do we have any food?' he asked Althea.

'I'll rummage something up for you.' Althea touched his hand affectionately, then left the room to get him some rations.

'Brother Alban. I have a favour to ask of you.'

'Anything.'

'When the time comes, I need you to make sure my body is cremated.'

Alban was shocked. He understood the implication immediately, but it took him several seconds to come to grips with it. 'Why me?'

'There is no one else I can trust.'

Alban hesitated. 'We can choose a different path. Change this fate. Find a safer way. One where you don't – '

'– There is no other way.'

'But why? We could stay here. Forget the festival. Forget this revolutionary madness. Wait for a better time.'

Tobias knew where this was coming from. 'I am not the prophesy fulfilled, brother.'

'Why else would you be here?' Alban was desperate not to lose him.

Tobias wondered if he should tell Alban the whole truth. Of all their group he was perhaps the one person who might understand. 'Have you forgotten my first tenet? Death is not an end, it is a renewal of life.'

'But you are not dead.'

'And yet, I am renewed.'

Alban chewed on this a moment. 'That's not possible … is it? … How? … Who?'

'I don't believe you've met him. But you've heard of him.'

'Rene?'

'Yes.'

'Rene is … you?'

'Yes. Every minute I live, I am stealing from Rene. This life should be his. This fate … should be his.'

'Rene is the prophesy fulfilled.' Alban understood at last.

Tobias saw Althea returning with food for him. 'Promise me, brother. When the time comes – '

'I promise.'

Althea burst into the room, smiling. 'I bring sustenance, water, and..,' she pulled a bottle from behind her back, '… wine. I suggest we start with the wine.'

Elly led Rene to the one place she knew to go. The one place they might find help. The place she and Althea had escaped from when the noisy men came. They attracted some odd looks for a while – a bonobo and a raggedy man walking the streets of the Western Borough – until they vanished into the gloom of the AQ. By nightfall they arrived at the old hospital and were safely out of sight. The familiar corridors echoed their footfalls as if welcoming them home. They had been missed.

Elly led Rene to the rooms where Althea and the others had slept, hoping to find them there. But the rooms were empty. Then they looked in the large white room with the table and machines; the room where Elly recalled waking from the dreamless death sleep. Everyone had been there at that time. Maybe they were there now.

Some of them were – they lay on the floor, dried blood surrounding their bodies, the smell of decay saturating the room. Asar, Patric and Isaac. All dead.

Elly wept as she looked upon the bloated, pale face of her friend, Jason Asar. She didn't understand these creatures. Why did they kill each other? Why were they so violent? All they did was destroy. Apart from Althea and Rene/Tobias, she had yet to meet a human who thought about anyone other than themselves. There was no sense of kinship, of the shared life. She just couldn't understand how one could live like that.

Rene turned Elly around and led her away from the scene. They left the white room. There was no help for them here. No sanctuary. No Althea. This place now was for the dead.

— ∞ —

It was a long walk from the AQ to the centre of Lorna. This late at night it was also cold and lonely. Weather Control may be holding back the rain in the days leading up to the festival, but they maintained a perverse normality otherwise. The seasons still passed as nature intended, and temperatures fluctuated accordingly. Dan and Maya had not dressed for a chilly winter's evening, so by the time they reached Stonemote Towers, better known as the *Corkscrew*, they were shivering and numb with cold. Dan carried the plasma rifle in its bag across his back. Maya wore a backpack with some basic provisions. They were going to spend the night here.

When Dan suggested his friend Rene's office would be a good vantage point for the snipe, he didn't think he would be the one to carry out the mission. It's not like he had any special knowledge of the place. He just knew about it, having visited Rene a few times at work. To make matters worse, other floors of the building harboured a variety of legal and financial practitioners. The kind of people who tended to work late if there was no curfew forcing them home to their domestic bliss and frustrated partners.

Dan and Maya could have used their newly modified ghost comkey on the train, which would have saved them a walk, but they only had one, and with the two of them travelling it might have alerted security. So they decided not to risk it.

The first barrier and test was the front lobby doors. These would open to pretty much anyone visiting the building. As Dan and Maya approached there was a moment of dread when it seemed the doors were not going to open. *The ghost 'key didn't work.* But then from a meter away it was recognized, and the doors slid open to allow them entry.

Dan smiled at Maya. 'Brilliant.' Maya dropped her head, blushing. For her, that compliment alone made the day's efforts worthwhile.

They walked across the elegant lobby toward the elevators. So far so good. The space was lit with a soft ambient glow, the giant AV walls disabled. The building was asleep. The elevator opened as if it had been expecting them. This was a good sign. If the ghost 'key had flagged any security measures it was unlikely the elevator would have worked for them. As hoped, the system was ignoring them, even with the curfew in force.

The doors closed with a reassuring whisper and they were whisked up the corkscrew shaft to the 29th floor. Stepping out of the elevator Dan quickly scanned the hallway, looking through the glass walls into the empty office. As below, a soft ambient light illuminated the space, as if it was in standby mode just waiting for the new workday. A good sign, no-one was at home. Stepping up to the office entrance, a short *blip* sounded from the ghost 'key. The door remained closed to them. This was to be expected. One needed the proper sync to gain further access. The glass was unbreakable, but Dan had a key he knew would work. He took the bag from his shoulder and lay it on the ground. Unzipping it he removed the plasma rifle, quickly assembled it, and aimed it at the door.

'You might want to step back,' he told Maya, who promptly ducked behind Dan and covered her ears. She remembered how loud the gun was.

Dan released a short burst from the rifle and a nice round hole was burned into the middle of the door about thirty centimetres in diameter. Too small for them to squeeze through.

'Dammit.' Dan adjusted the focus on the gun, giving a broader spread of the plasma toroid. Maya covered her ears and Dan fired again. This time the door was completely obliterated, the circle burning into the adjoining walls with a diameter of around 3 meters. Plenty large enough to walk through.

'I think I'm getting' the hang of this thing,' Dan grinned. 'Come on.' They stepped up to the hole. 'Watch the edge, it's still hot.' While the glass in the centre of the hole had been vaporized, leaving only the faint smell of negative ions, the edges of the circle were cauterized smooth and still glowed red-hot.

'Shouldn't that have triggered the security system?' asked Maya.

'Why? The door's technically still closed. We just put a hole in it.'

'Aren't there cameras?'

'Maybe. But they'll ignore us as long we don't mess with them. One thing I've learned, the first priory of any security system is to protect itself. So unless we do something to threaten it, it'll just ignore us. Besides, it doesn't know we're not meant to be here. It doesn't know there isn't supposed to be a hole in that door. It's got more important things to worry about.'

'Are you sure?' Maya was clearly anxious Temple Guards, or some local night watchman was going to come storming in at any moment.

'Trust me. I've done this before.'

'Have you?'

'No … not really. But I've read up on it.'

It was impossible to go completely unnoticed in Lorna, even with ghost comkeys, avoiding public transport and all the usual safeguards. You couldn't avoid being tracked, but you could remain inconspicuous. An attack on the system was an instant red flag, whereas damage to private property was barely acknowledged. Of course, Dan was guessing, but it was a well-educated guess.

Once inside the office Dan set-up the plasma rifle next to the window that overlooked Festival Square and the Great Temple. It was too dark to see anything clearly yet. He would wait till morning and line up his shot then. Maya unpacked her bag and laid out a picnic on the carpet near the window. There were some instant meals of butter chicken and rice that one heated by pulling a zip-line on the seal to activate the bowl's built-in magnetron. There were also custard deserts, red wine, and some thermo coffees, also with instant microwave heating. A battery lantern lit the cosy scene in a warm orange glow.

'Well, you certainly came prepared,' Dan joked.

'I brought breakfast too.'

Dan smiled warmly, he was liking this girl more and more. Then over her shoulder he saw the empty desk across the room and became pensive. 'That's Rene's desk right there.'

'Your friend?'

'Yeah. I don't even know if he's alive or not.'

'I'm sure he is.'

'And what makes you so sure?' Dan chastised. 'You don't know him. You have no idea.'

'… You're right. I don't.' Maya lowered her head submissively; she didn't want to fight.

Dan sighed. '… Sorry. I guess … I'm feeling a bit guilty. Rene and Joanna wouldn't have got caught up in all this if it weren't for me. He always said I was too impulsive.'

'That's what I love about you,' Maya blurted.

Dan looked at her intently. 'You love me?'

'… No … that's not what I said. I said I love how impulsive you are. That doesn't mean I love you – I don't *love* you. Not like that.'

'Just as well,' Dan teased.

Maya was blushing again. 'Shutup and eat.'

'Yes, ma'am.'

Part 4

Everything begins and ends with you.

Shentama
– The Fourth Tenet

34

The drama of reality is first written
In the pages of the mind
Thought becomes desire
Desire becomes action
Action becomes experience
The writer becomes the actor
And the drama that is called life
Is guided by the All—In—All

Shentama
– Stanza 25

It was not widely known, but there were more Temple Guards mingled inconspicuously among the crowd during the festival than there were uniformed Guards patrolling the perimeters. It allowed them to keep a low profile and be on the spot within seconds if an incident should occur. The Guard had a no-tolerance policy toward any misconduct. One could be transported to Gerda for little more than starting a fistfight. As a result, people tended to behave themselves. The worst the Guard had to deal with frankly was fraudulent souvenir hawkers and illegal drug peddlers, which were either a breach of the

Temple's Intellectual Property or Lorna's controlled substances laws. IP breaches were taken more seriously, so if you wanted to make some illegal money during the festival, you were better off selling drugs. For the Temple Guard, everything else was just crowd control.

The moment curfew lifted at 6am, the crowds began to gather in Festival Square, waiting for the Temple gates to open at 9 o'clock. Despite curfew some early birds camped out overnight to claim the best positions at the gates, so they could then grab prime positions for the Cardinal Hierophant's opening address, and have ready access to the free food that would be on offer at lunchtime. The Temple Guard turned a blind eye to this practice – they had more important things to deal with than a few eager beavers. The festival was a family occasion and many brought their kids along to take part in the biggest spiritual and social event of the year. Stall-holders were already open for business in the Square, offering breakfast, souvenirs, cheap portable AVs and other disposable tech. The address was to be streamcast around the world, which anyone could access via their comkey, along with maps to the Temple grounds and facilities, event schedules, and constant live updates. For 'keys without holo displays (the cheaper kind), a disposable AV made it easy to see what activities were on offer throughout the week.

The figure-8 fountain flowed clean and blue. Children played in the shallows of the pools that days before had run crimson with blood. The sun was shining, not a cloud in the sky – weather control at its finest. The AV billboards screened inspirational images of the Prophet Tobias, along with propaganda of the early days of the Church, the construction of the Great Temple, and the momentous legacy of Tobianism. One could tune in to the soundtrack via comkey. Everything was shaping up for a spectacular opening day to the Festival of Renewal. The excitement was palpable.

Marius had seen it all before. This was his fifteenth festival as Captain of the Guard. At first it was exciting to be part of such a massive celebration. Then it just became hard work, which he quickly learned to delegate to junior officers. These days it was little more than an inconvenience. The one thing about the festival he still enjoyed was the drills. All those virile young men (and women, it must be said), marching in precision rank and file around the Temple forecourt still gave him a hard-on. It was third only to actual sex and driving a GL at speed. Which is precisely what he was doing – speeding through the streets of Lorna, ostensibly on security detail.

No-one questioned it when he signed out a GL vehicle the morning of the opening ceremony. As Captain of the Guard (which everyone still believed he was) he clearly had important business to attend to. And despite the many problems leading up to it, arrangements were going smoothly. He would not be missed. Security was so focused on the thousands of people visiting the Temple, they wouldn't even know he was gone. Omnipresent comkey surveillance had its limitations on a day like this. Marius didn't pretend to understand it, but leniency was built into the system. Something to do with chaos theory and error-correction, which was just a fancy way of saying it made mistakes. As sophisticated as it was, the security AI didn't understand half of what its irrational human subjects did. Marius was counting on this.

When Cairn discharged him he'd been furious, and his first impulse was to take revenge on the Cardinal Hierophant and the Church. He was betrayed. Worse, he was being made the scapegoat for things beyond his control. He had been a loyal soldier of the faith. He deserved better. But after sleeping on it, Marius changed his mind. After fifteen years, he'd had enough of this place. Enough of being a devoted servant to an indifferent Church. Revenge was no longer on his mind. He was ready to move on. Cairn had thought to punish him but had instead freed him to live the life he'd been denied all these years. Just one thing stood in his way.

Outside the city centre the streets were mostly empty and Marius could pick up speed. The closer he came to the AQ the faster he went. Until he found himself tearing through the derelict streets of the old city inhabited only by rats and overgrown weeds. He pulled the GL to an abrupt stop at an intersection. Had there been rubber wheels on the vehicle it would have drifted loudly and left a satisfying skid-mark on the pavement. As it was there came a slight crackle of static discharge, and the gentle purr of the engine tuning down. Very disheartening. It was almost impossible to lose control in one of these things – which took all the fun out of it really.

Obstinate vines pushed through the pavement and scaled the walls of the surrounding buildings. The AQ wasn't completely reclaimed by nature yet, but it was losing fast. He knew there were heretics hiding out in these buildings; lights had been seen in the abandoned towers, and comkeys had a habit of magically dying on the border near here. If comkeys had been embedded like they did at Gerda this wouldn't have been an issue. As a former prisoner Marius's comkey was surgically implanted into his chest. It was called nano-tagging and was incredibly effective in tracking and controlling inmates. It was the reason no-one had ever escaped from Gerda. Each chip contained a toxin that when released into the bloodstream would kill in seconds. To attempt escape, or removing a chip, was suicide. At times like this it would have been very handy to have nano-tagged heretics. Not only could he track them, but he could trigger the toxin remotely and *presto* – no more heretic problem. But that was not why he was here. Today he didn't want to kill heretics, he wanted to talk to them.

Without comkeys to track he resorted to searching the old-fashioned way with heat sensors, audio impetration analysis, and spatial divergence reckoning. He was close. In fact, based on the readout he could tell there were several armed heretics observing him right now. A dozen or so were in one of the towers a few blocks up the street. Four more were at ground level, watching from a discrete distance. He couldn't see them with the naked eye, but he could clearly make them out on his scanners. Marius expected this. Knowing he could not sneak up on them, he made a point of being as conspicuous as possible. He wanted to arouse their curiosity, without arousing hostility. Keep 'em guessing.

He walked towards them, his uneven steps resounding off the overgrown buildings. Stopping a few meters short of where they were hiding, he raised his hands. 'I'm not armed. I'm here to talk. Got a proposition for you.'

Althea marched at the head of the multitude, alongside Tank, Kane and Tobias. Behind them were Alban and Joanna, followed by a legion of allies and devotees that stretched the length of the underground tunnel as far as one could see. Battery lanterns dotted throughout the crowd lit the scene, casting an uneven, kinetic glow on the walls. Faces stood out a bright orange from the lanterns. Pockets of humanity amidst a surge of anonymous figures falling into the deep shadows of the tunnel.

Some were there to fight the revolution with Kane and Tank. Some were there simply because they had nowhere else to go. Most however were there for Tobias. It was astonishing how fast word spread that the Prophet Tobias was alive. Astonishing also how many believed it enough to seek him out. Most astonishing was that they had successfully tracked him down to a supposedly secure hideout in the old underground rail network of the AQ. If regular people could find them so easily, Althea was baffled why the Temple Guard hadn't. Especially as they seemed to have known all about their previous refuge, and so many others scattered across the city.

Trudging through the dank tunnels they sounded like a thunderous army of ants. Few spoke. To have murmuring voices added to the din would have made it too unbearable. Althea feared someone above ground would surely hear them passing below – a low rumbling tremor. But then the trains of old travelled these tunnels and went unnoticed. It would be different once they broke the surface.

Reaching the station at the edge of the AQ they climbed onto the platform and up the stairs to street level, stopping at the caved-in entrance. There was room enough to squeeze through the debris of fallen building bits, but with so many people, young children and infirmed among them it would take forever to get everyone through. As the crowd gathered in the station lobby Tank considered the rubble blocking their path. 'Why don't we just clear it?' he suggested.

'That'll take forever.' Kane leant against one of the larger chunks of concrete.

'Not if we all chip in. We've got a lot of able-bodied men back there. I figure it wouldn't take more than an hour.'

Kane slapped the boulder in front of him. 'How are you going to move a rock like this? It's too big to carry.'

Tank stepped up to the boulder, looking at it from all sides, evaluating its form and position. It was once the corner of a large tower and had a jutting flat angle on one side, exposed concrete and metal reinforcement on the other. It must have weighed several tons. Having assessed its angle and stresses, Tank grabbed a rough edge and braced himself.

Tobias stepped forward, coming in close to Tank, 'Are you sure you want to do this?'

'Why, have you seen something?' This wasn't the moment Tobias told him about, surely.

'No. It just looks very big. I don't want you to hurt yourself.'

Tank grinned. 'You might want to step back.' He got a firm footing, then pulled. His muscles tensed, his face grimaced. Biceps bulged and legs strained. A determined guttural roar rent from his throat, and with one mighty haul the boulder came loose from the pile. It rolled towards them with a crashing thud and everyone scattered for fear of being crushed. The rocks surrounding the now gaping hole left by the boulder cascaded and likewise rolled onto the tiles in an avalanche of stone and glass. A thick dust cloud floated through station lobby, obscuring the scene. When it finally cleared Tank could be seen sitting on the lower step of the exit, covered in chalky white powder. He coughed, waving the particles away from his face.

'Come on then!' he called to the crowd of stunned onlookers. 'Do you expect me to do all the work?!'

Several of the men came forward and began pulling at the debris. A line quickly formed, passing chunks along to be dumped out of the way, while larger pieces were pushed, dragged and rolled away. More people came forward – women and children all keen to help – and pretty soon several dozen devotees were clambering through the rubble, clearing their way up the shattered staircase.

'Maybe you brought me an army after all,' Kane told Althea.

As the faithful worked to clear the staircase Tobias led Althea across the lobby to where Joanna and Father Alban stood. Alban had become very protective of Joanna since he found out she was pregnant. She had been his first refugee and her welfare represented everything this struggle meant to him. He seemed especially protective today.

Tobias looked at her intently. 'Joanna. You cannot come with us to the festival. There is something far more important you need to do.'

'Rene?' It was more a plea that a question.

'Yes. I think I know where he is. He is safe, and he is not alone. But you need to find him before the day is out.'

'Where?'

'An old hospital. I believe Althea knows the place.'

Judging from Althea's stunned reaction, she clearly did. 'How did he end up there?'

'He was taken there. By Elly, who I understand is a bonobo.'

'Elly's alive?' Althea couldn't believe it.

'Yes. They are both safe.' Then turning to Joanna: 'But I would prefer it if you did not go alone.'

'I can take her, I know the way,' Althea offered eagerly, her maternal devotion to Elly surprising even herself.

Tobias paused before answering, as if he had to choose his words carefully. 'Yes. You could take her.'

Althea was skeptical. She grabbed his robes and pulled him towards her. By anyone else this would have been a brazen affront upon the person of the Prophet. By Althea it was belligerent affection. 'What are you not telling us?'

Tobias smiled warmly, but there was sadness behind his eyes. 'I must go to the festival. Joanna must go to Rene. But I will not tell you or Father Alban what you must do. The choice is yours.'

Althea looked at Tobias, the man she loved. Then at Joanna and the chance to be reunited with Elly. Then back at Tobias. Tears welled in her eyes. Something was going to happen at the festival, and he was trying to get rid of her. He wanted her to go with Joanna so she would be safe. She knew then she had to stay with him. No matter what the future held. She was not about to lose him now. By such choices is one's destiny shaped.

A tear tracked down Altheas face. 'You go with her, Father. I'll show you the way.' Looking up at Tobias. 'You're not getting rid of me that easily.' She nestled into Tobias's chest, clutching at his robes. Tobias placed a hand on her head, his fingers lost in her thick red hair. He accepted her choice.

Alban nodded his acceptance to Tobias. He would go with Joanna. By such choices is one's destiny shaped.

— ∞ —

When Dan woke Maya was already preparing breakfast. She was dressed, with her hair tied into a haphazard knot at the back of her head. It was adorable. He watched her in silence. Normally she was either fidgety and nervous, or sullen and shy. But now she seemed full of confidence and purpose. *Is this what she's like when she thinks she isn't being watched?*

Maya stopped and looked at him. 'Good morning.'

Dan sat up, the thermal blanket covering his nakedness. 'Morning.'

Maya pulled the tab on a coffee thermo and handed him the steaming cup. 'Breakfast is served.'

'What time is it?'

'About eight.' Maya joined him on the blanket on the floor and kissed him enthusiastically. This was a different girl to the one he was used to, and already he wondered if it had been a mistake to encourage her. It was an impulse he had with any new relationship. Rene called it his *fear of commitment reflex*. Dan did his best to suppress the feeling. After all, it was just a kiss.

He pulled on his pants and walked to the window. The plasma rifle was set up, pointing roughly in the direction of the Great Temple. Turning on the scope display he zoomed in, scanning the streets and Festival Square. The square was already crowded with pilgrims, while the surrounding streets continued to feed thousands more into the space. The billboards flashed their propaganda, and the fountain sparkled in the morning sun. The gates to the Temple remained closed, the forecourt anticipatingly empty.

Dan zoomed in on the Great Temple. Two giant staircases led up to the main entrance, like the feet of an enormous beast. At the top was a pair of gigantic wooden double-doors. These were closed now, but would open to admit the public once Cairn's sermon was complete. Between the staircases was a platform with a grand pulpit. This was where daily services would be officiated by one of the Cardinals, speeches would be made by various religious leaders or intellectuals, general announcements, or any other business through the course of the week. The exception was the Cardinal Hierophant's opening sermon, which he would deliver from his balcony directly above the pulpit. Dan pitched the gun up slowly and zoomed in on the broad balcony. Tall reflective, glass windows faced onto it. He could not see inside, and guessed they would be bullet-proof and haze-proof; though a plasma shot would probably burn through. But he would wait. Despite the distance, the gun's sight afforded a good, close view. Once Cairn was standing at the railing it would be an easy shot.

Dan caught himself as he thought this. Less than a week ago he was a nobody in a small rebel cell that was unlikely to achieve anything worthwhile. Now, in a few hours, he was going to assassinate the Cardinal Hierophant. He couldn't help feeling proud and slightly terrified at the same time. He did his best to hide this from Maya, sipping his coffee as he returned to their picnic on the floor.

'All good?'

Dan nodded. 'We've got a couple of hours before anything happens. Guess we'll just wait.'

Maya took his coffee from him and set it aside. 'I've got a better idea.' This time it was more than *just a kiss*, but Dan wasn't about to stop her now.

One who does not fear life does not fear death
Wherefore frighten a man with threat of death
When death is of no consequence to him

Shentama
– Stanza 123

'You're either incredibly brave, or incredibly stupid. Which is it?' Rohan sharpened a small white blade against a whetstone in his palm. The sound was unnervingly brittle and sharp. He looked down at the prisoner who was on his knees before him. Unarmed and surrounded by Rohan's men he was pretty much at their mercy.

'I'm Marius. Captain of The Temple Guard. I've come here to talk, not fight.'

'Stupid then.'

'I have a proposition for you.'

'Why should I listen to anything you have to say?' Rohan turned to his men, 'In fact, why is he even still alive?'

'Do you want to defeat the Church or not?' Marius persisted.

'And you're going to help us? Captain of The Temple Guard?'

'Who better?'

Rohan paused. He had a point, but it could also be a trap. He proceeded with caution. 'How?'

'By eliminating one man. I can get you close enough to do the job.'

'You're going to help us kill the Cardinal Hierophant?' Rohan couldn't help but sound condescending.

'No. I'm going to help you kill Cardinal Kasper.'

Rohan was flummoxed. 'Why him?'

'Do you really think Cairn runs the Temple? Kill him and he'll be replaced within a day. Nothing will change. Except you'll provoke a mass slaughter of heretics on a scale not seen since *The Great Purge*. Kill Kasper and you cripple the Temple, without it being seen as an outright act of war. Do it right, and they won't even know it was you.'

Rohan could see his men exchanging worried looks. He knew what they were thinking, he was thinking the same thing. *Is it too late to call off Dan?* But still, he wasn't sure they should trust this turncoat. 'I ask again. Why him?'

'Kasper pulls the strings. He controls what goes on in the Temple. He controls everything. He does it secretly, and quietly. Invisible even to those he manipulates. He's been doing it for years. The fact you don't even think of him as a threat shows how good he is. But I assure you, he's your real enemy. Why take out the puppet, when you can have the puppet-master?'

'You seriously expect me to believe the Cardinal Hierophant is nothing but a puppet to this Kasper?'

'I know these men. I know how things work in there. It's about power. And the best way to get power and keep it, is to be invisible.'

Rohan still wasn't sure he believed him. 'Why are you telling me all this?'

The captain hesitated, sighed, then: 'Because I'm one of those he's manipulated. If Kasper were dead...'

'So this is personal?'

'I'm not the only one in the Temple who would be glad to be rid of him.'

'Why don't you kill him yourself? What do you need us for?'

'I'm Captain of the Temple Guard. Everywhere I go, everything I do, is tracked and monitored. Unlike you lot, I can't simply destroy my comkey and go feral.'

'You're not wearing it now, though.'

'But I am.' Marius placed a finger on his chestplate, near the bottom of his sternum. 'My comkey is here … always.'

Panic flooded through the room. 'I thought you said he was clean?' Rohan demanded.

'He was!'

'Why the hell didn't it show up in the scans!?'

Several of them raced to the window to see if they were being ambushed. But the streets were empty. Rohan picked up his rifle and drilled the barrel into Marius's Temple. 'You've got three seconds to tell me what the fuck this is about.'

Marius remained calm. It wasn't the first time someone had put a gun to his head. 'It's a Gerda 'key. They use a different frequency so don't show up in a normal scan. Don't worry. It's not being monitored right now.'

'Why not? And why the fuck do you have a Gerda comkey?'

'It's a long story.'

'Why didn't you tell us about this?'

'You didn't ask.'

'Why isn't it being monitored?'

'That's another long story,' Marius told him. 'Are my three seconds up yet?'

Rohan turned to his men at the window. They had been scanning the streets as far as they could for any signs of life. 'Anything?'

'All clear.'

Rohan lowered the rifle. 'You were in Gerda?'

'Yes.'

'What for?'

'It doesn't matter.'

'How'd you get to be Captain of the Guard?'

'Kasper.'

Rohan resumed his seat. He was beginning to understand. 'I still don't trust you.'

'I don't expect you to,' Marius replied.

'So what's your plan?'

— ∞ —

Kasper, like every Cardinal, should have been preparing to interview petitioners. Most Cardinals conducted these futile sessions in their offices, with staff on hand to manage any troublemakers. Kasper preferred to do it in a conference room well away from his personal space, surrounded by Temple Guard. This ensured half of those scheduled to meet with him were intimidated away, while the other half could be escorted off within minutes of sitting down. This year Kasper wasn't going to do even this much. All of his plans were coming to a head and he had no intention of wasting time on ceremonial masturbation. Soon Cairn would be dead and he would become Cardinal Hierophant.

The Executive Council was not a concern. He had enough on every one of them that they wouldn't dare oppose his ascension. Likewise, the heretics would dutifully carry out the deed in the name of the revolution or anarchy or whatever the hell they were fighting for. Their sniper was already in position at the Stonemote Towers, and Kasper had a backup in case they missed. Marius was a worry though.

Having been fired by Cairn, Kasper feared he might do something stupid. He wanted to reassure the Captain of his support. Marius and the Temple Guard were Kasper's most important allies. One couldn't stage a coup without an army. But Marius was nowhere to be found.

The one variable he had been unable to control was Tobias. This was a part of his grand scheme that had defied intercession. Helping the heretics steal the body was easy enough, and Cairn's gullible over-reaction only served Kasper's purpose. It was a lot easier to convince the Council where their best interests lay when the Cardinal Hierophant appeared to have lost the plot. But the persistent rumours of the Prophet being alive threatened Kasper's plans. Not because it was true, but because it was not. It was a matter of faith. One thing Kasper had learned working in this place – it was a waste of time dealing with people who believed they knew the truth. They could be broken, but then lost their usefulness; blackmailed, but you could never trust they would not relapse into some noble sacrifice like Trevelle; or directed unawares from the shadows, as he preferred to do, but their behavior was unpredictable. Cairn had become frustratingly capricious once he got it into his head Tobias was alive. Kasper had underestimated Asar. It was a brilliant bit of chicanery.

If only it were true; Kasper could control it easily then. The thing to do with a reborn Tobias was simply to kill him, before he became a focus of yet more religious fervour. Cairn was right about that. A living Tobias was a threat to the Church. But his solution was draconian and heavy-handed. He used a sledgehammer when a well-placed dart was all it required. This Church would be a whole lot easier to run if it weren't for all the religious nutters.

Kasper walked into Cairn's office. He had been summoned. With any luck this would be the last time he would have to respond to such a command.

'Your Eminence.' Kasper bowed low, a semblance of respect.

Cairn sat behind his enormous and largely empty desk. 'Where's Captain Marius?' he demanded.

'I don't know, Your Eminence. Would you like me to find him for you?' Wherever Marius was, Kasper had to get to him first.

'No.' Cairn appeared surprised. Marius it seemed had gone rogue. Cairn was dressed in his festival robes. Black and red, with an elaborate gold embroidered pattern. The collar was high, framing his chiselled features, while the gaping sleeves hung low, without appearing heavy or uncomfortable. A tall conical mitre headdress with similar flourishes capped off the look. It was a masterpiece of design and proportion, perfectly tailored to fit Cairn's tall, lean frame. Quite beautiful in fact, and given his admittedly handsome profile, Cairn looked most impressive in it. Kasper doubted he would look half as regal when it came time for him to wear the festival robes. But then this was a tradition he had no intention of perpetuating. It was gaudy and egotistical. One of the many things he planned to change.

Cairn rose and moved across to the windows, looking out over the Temple forecourt and Festival Square. The main gates were now open and a crowd was gathering below. 'Do you see this?'

Kasper saw nothing unusual. 'What, your Eminence?'

'The people. Do you see the people?'

'Yes, Your Eminence.'

'Those are my people, Kasper. Every one of them. Plus, all of those outside the gates, and throughout the city. And all of those watching on AV. The entire Tobianist world is mine to command. My rabble. My mob. And if necessary, my soldiers. You may have the Temple Guard in your pocket. But I have the people.'

Kasper remained impassive, careful not to reveal anything. Did Cairn actually know something or was he just fishing? Had Marius betrayed him perhaps? Kasper thought a bit of impertinent humour would prod Cairn to reveal more. 'My pockets, Your Eminence, are far too small to carry around a single Guard let alone the entire Temple regiment.'

Cairn scoffed at the ruse. 'Captain Marius was fired because he's become a liability. And no, he didn't tell me about your arrangement. I do have spies of my own. What surprised me though is how brazen you've become. If you're going to stage a coup, at least have the dignity to do it behind my back. I really expected better from you, Kasper.'

Kasper took from this that Cairn anticipated a simple coup, not an assassination attempt. He still had the upper hand. 'Your Eminence, I don't know what you're talking about.'

'Yes, you do. But you could never take my place. You know why?'

Kasper didn't really care but stopped himself from saying as much. The more Cairn pontificated, the more Kasper knew where he stood.

'You have no faith,' Cairn continued. 'Can't run a Church without faith. I tell you the Prophet Tobias is returned. I've met him. I've spoken with him.' Cairn laughed a little. 'I've even imprisoned him. But he has an obstinate destiny that will not be denied. He is our past and our future. All it takes is a little faith.'

'You've spoken with him?' Kasper didn't understand why Cairn was still fixated on this idea of a resurrected Tobias. Perhaps the man truly was mad.

'I know you don't believe me, but it doesn't matter. After today none of it matters anymore.'

'Why? What happens today?'

'The Festival of course; and the return of the Prophet. So you see, I can't have you and your petty little sedition getting in the way.'

Now he was just being patronizing. 'My sedition?' Kasper couldn't help sounding offended.

'Oh, come now, Kasper. Enough with the games.' Cairn was becoming agitated. 'I could have you arrested and put in the dungeon right now if I wanted. I could have you transported to Gerda by nightfall. Are you really going to play dumb with me? Keep it up and I'll just kill you myself and be done with it.'

Regaining his composure, Kasper tried to divert blame to Captain Marius. Cairn was right – soon, none of this would matter. 'Your Eminence. I assure you whatever Marius may be planning, I would have no part in any … coup.'

Cairn sighed, then raised his arms in a gesture of conciliation, palms up. The gold embroidery of Cairn's festival robe began to glow as an electrical charge surged through the cloth. Kasper hadn't noticed it before, but the sleeves of the garment were connected to Cairn's hands by a series of glove-like threads wrapped around the base of his fingers, with opaque conductive tips on each digit. He brought his hands together, as if cupping a large ball. An arc of electricity hazed between the open palms, then spontaneously a lightning ball formed in mid-air a few centimetres above Cairn's hands.

'What's most disappointing,' Cairn explained, 'is that you've been playing me all this time, and I let you. But no more. It's time to change the way things are done around here. The Church will be renewed. And you, dear Kasper, will have no part in it.'

Cairn threw the lightning ball at Kasper with both hands, hitting him square in the chest. Kasper was thrown across the room by the force, slamming into the closed doors behind him. Paralysed, he fell to the floor face first – breaking his nose. Kasper couldn't breathe for several seconds. Eventually his muscles relaxed and he gasped for air.

Kasper struggled to his feet, blood running down his face. His legs and arms shook as his muscles twitched involuntarily.

'Rather ingenious, don't you think?' Cairn boasted. 'It was my idea. But I must say the designer did an excellent job putting it all together. I call it my power robe. Obvious I know, but fitting. It also does this – '

Kasper was struggling to his feet and trying to stem the flow of blood from his nose when Cairn raised both hands once again. This time a pair of smaller lightning balls emerged, one over each hand. Cairn threw them one after the other at Kasper. The first hit him on the left shoulder, throwing him once again into the doors. The second hit him in the head, pinning him momentarily to the wood, until he collapsed in a stiffened heap to the floor.

Cairn walked over to Kasper and knelt beside him. He slapped him on the face with the back of his hand. 'Kasper? Are you dead?'

Kasper blinked. He was conscious but couldn't move. His brain felt like mush. He wasn't sure where he was or what was happening. All he knew was he was in pain. He heard a voice, but his mind was unable to deal with something as complicated as language right now. He felt himself being lifted up and carried away. He was carried like this for a long time, until eventually he was left in a cold, dark place that smelled of mould and shit and blood. Or was that *his* blood? He wasn't sure. One thing he *was* sure of – he was in the dungeon.

36

... let me say to all who read these words
They are given freely
With love and good intentions
But if any part of what you read herein
Does not fit well with you
Do not wear it
Abandon it
Find another teacher
It is a coat tailored, after all, to my reality
And mine alone

Shentama
– Stanza 250

Joanna and Alban parted ways with the others once they emerged from the underground station. Althea's directions to *Saint Olivier's* hospital were sketchy, but the best she could manage under the circumstances. The AQ was a large area, several kilometres across. A maze of indistinguishable towers, their state of decay the most distinctive characteristic. One could easily get lost in the forest of concrete and shattered glass. If they'd had their comkeys they could have used the built-in MaP locator, but that was no longer an option. Coping without modern conveniences was an unexpected drawback to becoming a heretic. Overnight they'd reverted to a primeval state where fire and paper were the most advanced technologies at their command. Anything more was a security risk. But they had a battery lantern to light their way if necessary, and enough supplies to last them several days.

They walked the gloomy old streets in silence, their steps resounding off the steel and concrete bluffs around them, the moist grass and dirt of the pavement crunching under foot. Joanna peered into the glassless windows of the buildings, musing on the people that once lived and worked here. It was a simpler time. When people travelled in wheeled vehicles and carried notes and coins around as currency. When there were nation states and countries with their own laws, their own languages, and their own religions. When freedom and oppression meant two separate things. It was also a time of constant conflict, of economic uncertainties, corruption, fraud, political extremes, and the persistent dread of self-annihilation. This was the time into which Tobias was born. A prophet for the new millennium. And as Joanna now knew, a man abandoned by those he sought to teach. The AQ was symbolic of all the Church had become. The ruin of mankind through self-preservation.

'You are thinking of Rene?' Alban asked, breaking the silence.

'Actually, I was thinking of Tobias, and something he said to me before we left. That he and Rene are more alike than I imagine. They're both loners. Independent thinkers. Natural leaders, even if they don't see it. They both try to avoid conflict whenever possible. And neither of them has a clue how to talk to a woman.'

'You talk of the Prophet as if he were an ordinary man.'

'He is,' Joanna blurted without thinking. 'I mean no disrespect, Father. Meeting him has renewed my faith in a way. I never could abide the notion of a god-man. Knowing he's just like the rest of us, only more-so, kind of makes the whole thing more plausible.'

'Faith doesn't require evidence.'

'No. But it helps. You can't expect a person to believe a thing without some proof or personal experience of it.' Joanna was reminded of the debates Rene and Dan would have. It seemed a lifetime ago.

'I must admit,' Alban conceded, 'meeting Tobias has challenged my faith in the Church, but strengthened my faith in the Prophet.'

'He's the real deal.'

Alban smiled in agreement. 'And Rene?'

Joanna mused on this a moment. It was not such an easy question to answer. 'Rene's just a man.'

'Only more-so,' Alban added.

Joanna wasn't sure if he meant it as a question or a statement of fact. Was he trying to tell her something? 'But you've never met him.'

'…From what I've heard,' Alban clarified, unwilling to volunteer anything more.

Joanna decided not to press the point. She wasn't sure she wanted to hear it anyway. Her thoughts returned to the others marching on the festival. 'They're all going to die, aren't they?'

'We don't know that.'

Joanna placed a protective hand on her tummy. 'I dread the future that will come of this.'

The gesture was not lost on Alban. 'Whatever the future holds, I will stay with you.' It was a commitment Alban took very much to heart. He would give his life for Joanna … and the child of the returned Prophet, Rene St. Claire.

Kane led his group out of the AQ and into the streets of the Western Borough, past *The Light of the Prophet* chapel, bound for Festival Square. Althea and Tobias marched by Kane's right, with Tank on the left. They made an unusually imposing vanguard. Trailing them was a host of new disciples, swelling by the minute as others spontaneously joined their ranks. It was unclear whether they recognized Tobias for who he was, or simply realized the surge of change their procession heralded and were compelled to enlist, but by the time they approached the square they were several thousand strong, moving through the streets as one.

The square and neighbouring streets were crammed with stalls peddling souvenirs – serious, silly, and some downright offensive. There were plates and mugs with the visage of the Prophet emblazoned on them. Pendants and a wide range of comkey ampules sporting the Tobianist lemnis symbol of renewal. Badges, buttons, jewellery, cutlery. Collectible coins illustrated with the face of the Prophet – alll fake, the real ones minted by the Temple were rare and expensive. There were paintings, prints and figurines of all sizes and artistic merit. Action figures of Tobias in his cryo-chamber. Clocks, bottle openers, earrings and hair-brushes. Shirts and hats with a staggering range of Tobianist symbols and images, ranging from tasteful to cheesy to just plain bad. Costume robes in the style Tobias was famous for wearing. Painless tattoos, both temporary and permanent. Rare print editions of the *Shentama* in a range of formats and sizes, including the children's 'easy-read' edition.

Then there was the non-Tobias related merch. Models, images or renderings of The Great Temple, the Figure-8 fountain, and other Lorna landmarks. Stuff relating to the Cardinal Hierophant Cairn or the Executive Council of Cardinals. Collect the whole set! Figurines of the heroic Temple Guard and evil-looking heretics, ideal for staging your own purge re-enactments. Some of the heretic figures wore the traditional garb of the old religions from the era of *The Great Purge,* while others were clearly meant to represent recent events. Other significant figures of the Tobianist era – saints, generals, and previous leaders of the Church – were all represented. Plus a whole raft of bric-a-brac that simply defied description.

This is what Tobias saw as he approached the gates to the Great Temple. It hadn't occurred to any of the faithful this might be a problem. 'I'm reminded of an earlier prophet's reaction to such brazen exploitation,' Tobias told them. Althea didn't know who or what he was referring to. 'Don't worry,' he reassured. 'This kind of thing was common in my time as well. It's pointless getting angry about it.'

'You see now what has become of your religion,' Kane intoned in disgust. 'It's a circus.'

'I do enjoy a good circus,' Tobias joked.

Kane glared at him. He didn't appreciate that the Prophet was taking this so lightly.

'Cheer up, my friend. We may be about to change the course of history. We may even die in the attempt. But this is a festival, after all.' Tobias slapped him on the shoulder. 'Let's enjoy it while we can.'

Tobias stopped at one of the stalls and scanned the wares on offer. There was a rack full of 'Prophet' costume robes of varying styles and sizes.

'What are you doing?' Althea asked.

Tobias pulled a costume robe from the rack and held it against his body to show her. It was a full-length ivory white robe with an ochre waistband and trim around the collar and sleeves. The material was incredibly light yet had a luxuriant feel to it. Like the Egyptian cotton robes he used to wear, but somehow lighter and shinier. *Some new synthetic cloth, perhaps?* he thought. There were several designs to choose from, many of them gaudy and extravagant. He picked out the simplest and most like his original robes he could find.

He didn't have to say anything. Althea just smiled and nodded.

'Is there somewhere I can change?' he asked the stallholder, who directed him to a cubicle off to the side.

Moments later Tobias emerged now wearing the white and ochre robes he was famous for – or at least, a reasonable facsimile of them. Althea grinned. Tank nodded his approval, and even Kane seemed impressed. Now he really looked the part. The others in their entourage were in awe, mouths agape and eyes abugged. Even the stallholder was overcome. The face of the Prophet was on most of his merchandise, and here was a man, wearing the robes of Tobias, looking as if he had just stepped out of one of his framed portraits.

'I'll take it,' Tobias told the staring man. 'How much is it?' He was greeted by a blank look.

'Sorry?'

Althea pulled Tobias aside. 'We don't use money.'

'How do you pay for things?'

'Your comkey records the transaction.'

'I don't have a comkey.'

'None of us do any more.'

'So how do I buy the robe?'

'I'll get it for you!' One of the new disciples jumped forward and waved his comkey at the robe. With the sound of a gentle chime it was purchased.

'Thank you.'

'It's an honour.'

'What's your name?'

'Theo.'

'Thank you, Theo.'

'Anything else I can offer you and your friends?' ventured the stallholder.

Ten minutes later Tobias marched at the head of a thousand-strong entourage dressed almost entirely in white and ochre robes. The investiture of a new Tobianist sect was complete. Kane and Tank conspicuously chose not to wear the robes, but Althea happily complied with the new dress code, wearing a fetching fitted robe that accentuated rather than hid her voluptuous curves. Every stall and shop in the Square were sold out of 'Prophet robes.' Tobias added to his new wardrobe a brimmed ochre cap with a Lemnis symbol embroidered on the front, and a pair of sunglasses. This rather spoiled the populist image of the Prophet, but a little sun protection was not out of place on such a bright day.

The group marched through the ornate gates and approached the Great Temple of Lorna.

Kane turned to Tobias. 'How exactly are we gonna do this?'

Tobias smiled back fearlessly. 'I don't know. Let's find out, shall we?'

Dan watched as the group of white-robed devotees entered the Temple gates. It was not unusual for pilgrims to dress as the Prophet Tobias during the festival, but such a large group was attracting curious looks from those around them. He reactivated the holo display of the plasma rifle's scope, zoomed in a few times, then scanned the faces in the crowd. The man at the head of the march briefly turned to look behind him, revealing his face.

'What's *he* doing there?' he muttered.

'Who?' Maya said from behind him.

Dan zoomed in tighter on the man and tagged him so the scope would follow his movements. 'His name's Kane. I met him in the Temple prison, just before the Festival Square ambush. I think Rene escaped with him, but I can't see Rene anywhere.'

'What was he doing in prison?'

'Arrested as a heretic like the rest of us.'

'Then why is he leading a group of Tobianist pilgrims into the Great Temple?'

'I don't know.'

'Who's the guy next to him?'

Dan tagged the tall fair-haired man walking beside Kane, wearing Prophet robes, an orange cap and sunglasses. From this angle they got a semi-profile of his face as he looked about the square. 'Never seen him before.'

'He looks familiar.'

'Just some tourist by the look of him.'

'Any sign of Cairn yet?'

Dan pulled the muzzle away from the crowd and aimed it at the Cardinal Hierophant's balcony overlooking the Temple forecourt. 'Not yet.'

Cairn watched through the tinted, toughened glass of his office windows as the crowd assembled in the forecourt below. It was almost filled to capacity, with thousands more still streaming in. The problems of the past week were clearly no impediment to people indulging in some free food and spiritual validation. Kasper was safely out of the way. And Tobias would soon be an ally of the Church if Cairn could persuade him. It would take some doing, but his renewed faith in the Prophet gave Cairn hope that a new Tobianist era was at hand; one where the Prophet himself would guide the Church. Just as it always should have been.

Stepping across the room he opened a hidden entrance that led directly to the Temple's Private Library. While he could view the recordings contained in this restricted archive directly from his office or quarters, he sometimes liked to wander through the galleries and smell the old books; browse through the rare photographic prints; or read stanzas from one of the *Shentama* first editions.

He used to come here often, seeking inspiration and solace in the words, but it had been years since he'd done so. As a young priest he studied the *Shentama* endlessly. In fact, he was widely regarded as one of the greatest shentamic scholars of the modern age. His entire career in the Church was built on his deep knowledge and understanding of the holy book. Upon becoming a member of the Executive Council he had been granted access to the private library, and the earliest edition of the book still in existence. He didn't realise it at the time, but that was when his attitude toward the Prophet and his Church gradually changed. The old books differed from the modern *Shentama* in many passages; directly conflicting with one another at times. The inconsistencies disturbed him. He'd struggled to reconcile the old and new editions for half his life, though never quite succeeding. Now, at last, he knew where he had gone wrong.

Cairn didn't understand the paradox that was Tobias, until he met him face to face. He now realized what he meant: ...*your only responsibility is to yourself. All the rest is encumbrance.* As Cardinal Hierophant Cairn felt responsible for the whole world – but this was his encumbrance. It was not him. And it was not why he joined the Church in the first place. He'd been so caught up with the religion, he'd forgotten the spiritual truths at the heart of Tobias's teachings. He'd become a politician and patriarch. A bureaucrat. *What happened to the idealistic young priest who wanted to make the world a better place? What happened to his faith?*

Everything begins and ends with you. It was right there, in the fourth tenet. Once he surrendered to this simple truth, it all became startlingly clear. Just let it go. Let all the encumbrances go. It was a liberating feeling. For the first time in years Cairn was excited by the prospects the future held.

It was not too late to make amends. To renew the Church and all that was good about it. And who better to guide them on a new path than the Prophet himself. As long as he held the office of Cardinal Hierophant, Cairn would ensure that from now on the Tobianist Church truly was the church of the Prophet. This day would go down in history as the day Tobias returned to the world to set things right. And Cairn would be right there beside him. All that stood in his way was Captain Marius. He still controlled the Temple Guard and could still upset things if he went ahead with whatever Kasper had blackmailed him into doing. He had to find Marius before it was too late.

Marius received a missive from Lieutenant Makoto that he was required back at the Temple. Technically he didn't work there anymore, but nothing had been announced yet, so as far as the Guard was concerned, he was still their captain. Marius would like to have made a proper statement to them all at muster, but this was not the day for it. He would already be gone if it weren't for Kasper. But if all went well, by the end of the day that would no longer be an obstacle. He didn't know where he would go yet. Just well away from the Temple. Away from Lorna. He had no family or loved ones to go to, and that was just as well. Once Kasper was dead, he would be free to do whatever he liked.

Getting back to the Temple was not easy. Marius had to navigate slowly through the crowds in his GL until he finally reached the barracks entrance on the east side of the Temple grounds. As he drove the vehicle into a bay Lieutenant Makoto was waiting for him. He saluted as Marius stepped out of the vehicle. 'Captain.'

Marius maintained the pretence he was still in charge. 'Mak. Any dramas?' He started down the long corridor to the barracks, Makoto chasing after him.

'No, sir. Everything's in order. However, the Cardinal Hierophant asked to see you as soon as you returned.'

'What about?'

'I don't know. But Cardinal Kasper has been taken into custody.'

Marius stopped dead. 'What?'

'Cardinal Kasper is under arrest.'

'Why?'

'I don't know. But Cairn had him taken to the dungeon two hours ago.'

This was either very good or very bad. Marius couldn't work out which. 'And now he wants to see me?'

'Yes.'

'Are you arresting me, Mak?'

Makoto seemed genuinely surprised. 'No, sir.'

'Any advice?'

'… Keep your armour on.'

Nodding understanding, Marius made for Cairn's office.

Cairn must know about Kasper's plot to overthrow him. Why else would he have imprisoned him? Part of him wanted to thank Cairn for getting rid of Kasper. It saved him the trouble. But how much did he know about Marius's involvement – such as it was. Was he also destined for the dungeon and a one-way trip back to Gerda? He could explain how Kasper was blackmailing him. Even that he had taken steps to get rid of Kasper for the good of the Temple. … No, maybe not. Conspiring with heretic rebels to kill a Cardinal, even a disgraced one, would not go down well.

He could run. But if Cairn wanted him arrested, he would already have done it. Maybe this was a good thing. Maybe Cairn knew Marius had been loyal all this time and wanted to reinstate him … maybe. Though given what Cairn said at his discharge that seemed unlikely. Or maybe Cairn knew nothing. In which case why did he want to see him? So either he was about to go down with Kasper, be commended for his initiative and asked to stay on … or it was nothing at all. Somehow none of these scenarios seemed plausible. Probably best to say nothing till he knew where Cairn stood. At least Kasper was history. Though dead would be better than imprisoned. Kasper may yet find a way to wriggle out of this.

As he approached the east wing Marius pondered whether he should try contacting the rebels he'd met with. Their plan to dispatch Kasper was still going forward, despite the Cardinal now rotting in a dungeon cell. But Marius couldn't see a way to contact them and change their plans now. Do nothing, he figured, and let fate take its course. Things always have a way of working out. And if not – he could always kill himself.

As he approached Cairn's offices one of the sentries outside the main doors recognized him. 'Go right in, Captain. His Eminence is expecting you.'

Moments later Marius marched into Cairn's office, halted in the middle of the room and announced himself. 'Captain Marius reporting, Your Eminence.' The doors closed behind him and the room was silent. He looked about the room. 'Your Eminence?'

Cairn wasn't there.

He wondered if he should leave. But he was expected. He was likely being watched, so he decided to stand and wait. Scanning the room he noticed a scorch mark on the doors behind him. It looked like something a power-glove might do, but more concentrated. More brutal. If he got hit by whatever had caused that, he doubted his armour would last long.

He waited.

Was Cairn doing this on purpose? Was he trying to rattle him? He remembered the words of the Prophet: *He who understands his fears understands himself. He who overcomes his fears is subject to no one.*

He was not afraid. If anything, he was eager to confront Cairn. One way or another, he would know then where he stood.

Eventually a panel on the side wall opened – a hidden door. Cairn entered the room, glanced at Marius, but then strode to the windows behind the desk. He looked out over the Temple forecourt and crowd below. Without turning he addressed the captain. 'What have you been up to, Marius?'

'Your Eminence?'

'You were in the AQ.'

That was the problem with an embedded comkey, you could be tracked no matter where you went, despite Marius's best efforts to obfuscate his signal. '… Yes, your Eminence.'

'Who did you meet with?' Cairn still did not turn around. His voice was measured and calm. It gave nothing away. Marius couldn't tell if Cairn was guessing he'd met with someone or actually knew. If none of the rebels had worn active comkeys there was nothing for the system to track. But Marius knew there were other ways to surveil a building. If he lied, he might be caught out. If he told the truth, he might be stepping right into a trap.

But he owed nothing to these rebels. And his plan to assassinate Kasper was now scuttled in any case. Ironically, Kasper's protection and wiles would have come in very useful right about now. Marius was not good at these games. When in doubt, speak the truth, Marius figured. If he was about to die anyway, it would be with his honour intact.

Cairn turned to face him. 'Captain. I asked you a question.'

'I met with a group of heretics. I wanted them to assassinate Cardinal Kasper.'

Cairn was surprised by this confession. Rather than become angry however, he seemed genuinely baffled. 'Why?'

'Self-preservation.' Marius was unapologetic.

'Kasper is under arrest.'

'I know, Your Eminence.'

'Whatever arrangement you had with him is annulled.'

Marius wasn't sure what that meant but he could guess Cairn's meaning. 'Yes, Your Eminence.'

'What *was* your arrangement with him?'

Marius looked the Cardinal Hierophant in the eye. He wasn't intimidated by him anymore. Something about Cairn had changed, or something about himself. Either way, he didn't give a damn what Cairn thought or did. He just wanted to be free of this place, one way or another. 'To kill you … if necessary.'

'I thought so.' Cairn paced the room. 'Did you intend to carry this out?'

'Whether I did or not is irrelevant now.'

Cairn's robes began to glow, a web of electrical energy pulsing through them. '… You don't like me, do you, Captain?'

Marius blinked. 'Your Eminence?'

'I don't blame you.' Cairn raised his right arm and a highly charged plasma ball appeared in his cupped hand. 'I haven't exactly made your life easy this past week.' He continued to pace the room, turning his hand over, playing with the glowing ball as it lingered in his palm. 'Loyalty is a rare commodity these days. It must be earned … and it must be nurtured. It may be too late to earn your respect, Marius, but do I have your loyalty?'

Even as Cairn toyed with what was clearly a powerful energy weapon, Marius remained defiant. How dare he talk about loyalty. Where was Cairn's loyalty to him? Fuck him. *I don't owe you anything, you arrogant piece of shit!*

'Your Eminence forgets. I don't work here anymore.'

With that, the former Captain of the Temple Guard about-faced and made for the doors. He heard the sizzle of the plasma ball grow louder and rise in pitch, as if about to be thrown. He kept walking, his armour jangling from his uneven gait. The doors opened. Marius exited the room, the sound of the plasma ball receding behind him.

No turning back.

No stopping.

He was free.

This we call life is but a shadow of greater truths
Obscuring them in a veil of reality
A self-imposed enigma
Expression through constraint

To die therefore is no tragedy
It is, rather, a release
Freeing the spirit to witness
A greater truth than has been known

Shentama
– Stanzas 116-117

C airn had to ask himself: What would the Prophet do? Not the Prophet of legend, oracle of the Tobianist age and demi-god of the Church; but the man he met yesterday. Would he have killed Marius where he stood, or allowed him to walk free? It was a decision that could alter the fate of the world, certainly the fate of Captain Marius. Yet when he asked himself this simple question Cairn knew immediately what Tobias would say.

Sometimes one's fate is determined not by what we do, but by what we don't.

He might also have killed Kasper, but Gerda would be a better fate for him. Perhaps not what the Prophet would choose, but a necessary precaution.

Cairn felt good about his decision to let Marius go. He had granted him a stay of execution. Marius would continue to be tracked and monitored, so if he got up to anything that threatened the Church Cairn could always change his mind. No-one was beyond his reach, and it was foolish of Marius to think otherwise.

Retracting the plasma ball, his robes tuned down and ceased glowing. He looked out across the Temple forecourt from his office windows and watched as a mob of white-robed pilgrims moved steadily through the crowd. They were too distant to make out faces, but he wondered if Tobias was among them.

He waved a hand and his desktop AV sprang to life. He had full access to the festival coverage and could control any of the cameras, including isolating them from the public feed if necessary. Choosing a camera, he brought up a view of the Temple forecourt, and then flew the camera in for a closer look at those leading the white-robed pilgrims. It was Tobias. Cairn smiled at the outfit – white and ochre robes, brimmed cap and sunglasses. He looked like a tourist. How on earth did he gather so many disciples so quickly? Did they even know it was the Prophet Tobias who walked among them?

Whatever happened this day, it would be one for the history books.

'Is that a camera?' Tobias asked, as the droid lens hovered several meters above them.

'Yes,' Althea confirmed. 'There's hundreds of them floating about. The festival is streamcast live around the world. So there's a couple of billion people probably watching us right now.'

'Really? We should wave then.' Tobias grinned and waved at the camera.

Althea laughed. Kane tugged on the brim of his hat in an effort to hide his face. Tank, who was used to celebrity, just nodded nonchalantly – the epitome of cool. 'Smile for the camera,' he told Kane. 'You're about to become famous.'

Dan watched as the white-robed group made their way to the Temple steps. The crowd flowed around them – like waters parting for the brow of a long ship. Maybe there was someone famous at the head. He looked again at those leading the march, and though he could only see the backs of heads, he identified the large man walking beside Kane. It was Tank from the Warrior Games. Even from behind he recognized the bald pate and tattoo. He must be the reason they were attracting so much attention. Though why a thousand white-robed pilgrims were following him didn't make sense. Had the former athlete found religion?

Dan scanned the rest of the crowd. Uniformed Temple Guards patrolled the edges, while others in plain clothes moved among the congregation. They were trying to be inconspicuous, but he could spot them quite literally from a mile away. Instead of looking to the Temple, they were looking at the crowd. Then he spotted Rohan, and two others from their group – Zeke and Andy. They were moving along the southern perimeter towards the rear of the Great Temple – away from the crowd.

'Rohan's down there.' Dan tagged him so the scope would track them through the crowd.

Maya watched them on the holo display. 'Where are they going?'

'Don't know.'

They looked at each other silently for a moment.

'Should we abort?' Maya asked.

'Maybe this is part of the plan and they just didn't tell us.'

'Are you sure you trust these guys?'

Dan thought about it. ' …Yes.'

Maya nodded. 'Okay then.' She was with him no matter what.

It was good to have someone in his corner for once. That alone caused him to have second thoughts about Rohan, it wasn't just his own neck on the line. He watched as Rohan and the others disappeared round the corner. 'I just wish I knew what they were up to.'

Rohan, Zeke and Andy skulked along the southern wall of the Temple forecourt and into the adjoining avenues, towards the Temple Guard barracks – the heart of enemy territory. There were a few people milling about here, tourists getting in some early sight-seeing, but the deeper they ventured the more deserted the broad avenues became. Later there would be a crush of people roaming these streets, but for now, everyone was in the forecourt awaiting the Cardinal Hierophant's address.

The Temple streets were paved with tightly laid angular limestone pieces, polished and buffed to a smooth, though safely textured, surface. Their random pattern provided a kind of chaotic order to the thoroughfares. Like a jigsaw puzzle that would collapse if a single stone were ever removed.

A Temple Guard approached, watching them.

'It's all right,' Rohan murmured to the others quietly. 'We're just looking around.' Then as the guard passed them by, Rohan smiled and nodded, 'Morning.'

The Guard nodded back politely. While serving as security for the Festival, Temple Guards were also acting public relations officers, ordered to maintain a professional courtesy with the public at all times. The Guard passed them by; they didn't dare turn around to see if he was still watching them over his shoulder.

The barracks comprised several buildings facing a central quad for muster and drills. It was securely enclosed by a tall, acrylic fence with inspirational imagery and text floating across it. The facility backed directly onto the rear of the Great Temple, with gates providing ready access to several other major structures in the Temple City as well as direct access to Festival Square and the rest of Lorna. While the barracks were presently empty, Guards were still posted at each of the gates. Captain Marius had assured Rohan that he would disable surveillance at the southern gate, so their lack of comkeys wouldn't raise an alarm. They still had to deal with the guard, though.

Stealth was crucial. They would knock out the guard quietly, without killing him, allowing his comkey to continue transmitting vital signs. Once through the gate they could access the inner Temple. No unauthorized person was permitted back here – even during the Festival. A secure route had been mapped out for them by Captain Marius that would avoid surveillance and hopefully the odd Temple Guard. The good Captain would take no active part during the incursion; instead, he would monitor their progress remotely and help clear the way for them. Their objective was the antechamber to the conference room where Cardinal Kasper was to conduct his public interviews during the festival. The conference room itself would be crawling with Temple Guard, but the antechamber was private and off-limits to everyone but the Cardinal. Their plan was to make it to this antechamber unseen, and wait. Once done, their escape was just as treacherous, but the hope was they could lose themselves in the crowd, and without comkeys to track they would be invisible to any pursuers.

With all that, it was still a highly dangerous operation. Practically a suicide mission. Rohan still feared this might be a trap. Captain Marius's story was bizarre enough to be credible, but he found it hard to trust a Temple Guard, even if he *had* once served time in Gerda. If it wasn't a trap, any number of things could go wrong. But one didn't start a revolution without taking a few risks. That was Kane's problem. He was afraid people might get killed. No guts no glory, Rohan figured. And the chance to take out a key Temple powerbroker was too enticing to pass up. Not because it would shake the Temple hierarchy, or change the world, or even kick-start the revolution, but because it confirmed Rohan as a true revolutionary leader, and would begin the legend of General Zielinski.

Rohan pulled his men up as the gate came into view. As expected, there was a solitary guard stationed at the entrance. The avenue was deserted, but the noise from the Temple forecourt could be heard in the distance. An excitable hub-hub was building.

'Okay, what now?' Zeke asked anxiously, nerves already getting the better of him. They couldn't carry any weapons through the gates, scanners would have picked up anything from a power-glove to a shard of glass. Ideally, they would have used a jet-injected tranq' to neutralize the guard, but even that would have been detected.

But Rohan had a plan, and now was the time to reveal it. 'We take out the guard.'

'How?'

'With this.' Rohan pulled from his sleeve a short white blade. It was sharpened to a keen point and edge.

'What is that?' asked Andy.

'Bone. Human bone.' Rohan flicked it across his own throat,

adding a suitably grisly sound effect to demonstrate his intent.

'We're going to kill him?' Zeke interjected.

'Of course not,' Rohan told them. 'But a nice cut to the jugular should put him to sleep for a while.'

'Won't he bleed to death?'

Rohan glared at Andy, turning the tip of the bone-blade towards him. 'Why do you care?'

Andy swallowed. 'I don't.'

Rohan smiled – they were such sheep. 'I need you two to distract him for me.'

'… How?' Zeke asked.

'Go talk to him. Ask directions or something. Just get him to face the other way.'

'I don't know, Rohan – '

' – General.'

'… General.' Zeke chose his words carefully. 'We're a bit exposed here, don't you think?'

'Just do what I tell you.'

Neither of them much liked the situation, but he was their leader – for better or worse. '… Yes, sir.'

Zeke and Andy marched ahead. Rohan followed a few paces behind, keeping close to the wall and out of sight of the guard, who stood just inside the gate entrance.

'What are we gonna do?' Zeke whispered to his hapless partner.

'You mean about *General* Rohan or the guard?'

'Both.'

'We dance, until the music stops. Then we run.'

Zeke looked askance at Andy. 'You're gonna dance?'

'Just watch me.' Andy picked up pace and stepped up to the guard. 'Excuse me. … Umm, can you tell me where the nearest bathroom is?'

The guard looked at him impenetrably, indicating back in the direction they had come. 'Down there.'

'Isn't there one any closer?'

The guard leaned forward slightly and looked up the avenue, forcing Rohan to hug the wall. 'I can see it from here.'

'No, that one's no good,' Andy lied, moving past the guard to draw his eye. 'Isn't there one down here that's … cleaner?'

The guard pointed a power-gloved finger at him. 'Sir, I suggest you return to the forecourt area. The opening ceremony is about to begin.'

Andy's ruse wasn't working so Zeke moved closer, trying to draw the guard's attention away from the street. 'Damn shame you've gotta be on duty back here. You're gonna miss the Cardinal Hierophant's address and everything.'

'Would you step back please, sir. This is a restricted area.'

'What do you mean restricted? It's the Festival. We can go wherever we like.'

'Not back here you can't.'

Zeke moved intimidatingly closer. He figured an argument was one way to keep the guard distracted. 'Who the hell are you to tell me where I can and can't go! I've got rights, you know. I'm a citizen of this city – ' He tried not to look at Rohan as he crept up behind the guard ' – In fact the Cardinal Hierophant is a personal friend of mine. Me and Cairn are like that! I could have you sacked … or decommissioned or whatever the fuck one does to a Temple Guard. I can see to it personally that you never get to guard anything ever again! What's your name, soldier?! I want to write down your name so I know who to tell Cairn – '

Rohan pounced, lunging for the guard's throat with his bone blade. The guard turned and recoiled as the knife sunk into the side of his neck. Blood spurted. His muscles tensed and the power-glove was triggered. A haze of energy burst from his fingers and found an earth in Zeke. Zeke fell to the ground in uncontrollable spasms. Andy freaked, quickly scanning the avenue to see if anyone was watching.

The guard grabbed Rohan's arm and pulled him away. He was strong. Rohan was thrown to the ground. The guard reached for the knife stuck in his neck, releasing Zeke from the haze. Blood streamed through his power-gloved fingers, causing short circuits and mini-arcs to occur in the still active solenoids on his fingertips. Fumbling, he finally got a grip on the blade.

Rohan leapt into action once more, grabbed the guard's wrist that held the knife still buried in his neck, and pulled sharply so that the blade sliced across his throat. Blood oozed from the long transverse slit, down the Guard's dress armour, dripping on the ground. A final look of disbelief and sorrow, a gentle wheeze as he tried to draw one last breath, then the Guard crumbled to the ground – dead.

Rohan's hands were covered in the man's blood. He turned to see Zeke lying unconscious on the ground, then up at Andy, frozen with fear. Rohan spotted a small floating orb fly into view. A camera. The lens focused on his face. He heard jangling armour as a squad of Temple Guards converged on them from within.

'Come on!' Rohan called to Andy, but Andy ran in the opposite direction – away from the Guards, away from the gate, and away from Rohan.

'Shit!' Rohan dashed through the gate and made for the nearest building, but without a valid comkey the door would not open for him. Leaving a bloody hand mark on the door he darted around the corner just as the pursuing guards reached the gate. Half of them continued after Andy, while five came after him.

Running across the quad Rohan made for the GL terminal. A

haze of energy sizzled behind him. It landed so close he could smell the air around him burn metallic. Another haze. A nearby GL caught the charge and exploded. Their gloves were tuned to lethal force. One hit and he'd be dead. Then a second group of guards emerged from the Temple corridor ahead of him. He was trapped. Weapons trained on him from all sides.

'Hold your fire! Stand Down!'

Rohan turned to see Captain Marius stride through the Guards and approach him. So it *was* a trap all along. And he fell for it. He spat in the Captain's face once he was close enough. 'You fucking parasite.'

Marius wiped the gob off his cheek. 'You should be more grateful. I just saved your life, little man.'

Haze-fire could be heard in the distance. Several Guards ran from their posts in the forecourt to investigate.

'Something's up,' Kane uttered.

'What do you think it is?' Tank asked.

Kane wavered. '… Don't know. But the timing's perfect. Now's your chance, Tobias.'

Tobias turned to Althea. Gently taking her hand, he leaned in and whispered: 'I love you.'

A spontaneous tear tracked down Althea's face. Her throat clenched with emotion; she couldn't breathe. She had loved the Prophet all her life, expecting nothing in return – a transcendent, but reassuringly remote, love. She could never have imagined Tobias would return that love; confrontingly intimate and dangerous, yet more divine than any spiritual passion. This moment was the pinnacle of her life.

He smiled at her. He understood everything. He always had.

The Prophet Tobias stepped over the barrier and climbed the Temple stairs. There were no Guards to stop him, and no citizen saw fit to impede his progress. For all they knew this was part of the show. Kane and Tank took up position at the base of the twin staircases and crowded the area with faithful. They would give Tobias as much time as possible.

Tobias stepped up to the pulpit and surveyed the scene. Before him stood a multitude – over a million people. Just like Central Park. All eyes turned to face him. Several camera drones flew into position to capture his image for the billons watching at home. The crowd fell silent.

Tobias removed his cap and glasses, then combed his fingers through his long hair to pull it away from his face. There were a few gasps of recognition scattered through the assembled, but most still failed to recognize him for who he was. Nonetheless his presence was palpable. The crowd was enthralled, and he hadn't yet spoken a word.

Cairn sensed the change in the crowd. Watching the desktop AV he saw the face of Tobias from several angles. This was it. the Prophet had returned.

'Who's that?' Maya asked.

Dan zoomed the plasma rifle's scope on the man now standing on the stage. He looked like – '… Don't know.'

'Is he meant to be there?'

'Don't think so.'

'You know who he looks like?' Maya wasn't going to say it, but they were both thinking it.

'Bring the AV over,' Dan suggested. 'Let's hear what he says.'

From his cell in the dungeon, Kasper was watching events as they unfolded thanks to a portable AV he had been given. The Guard appeared outside his cell door. 'Are you all right, Cardinal? Anything else I can get you?'

'No thank you, corporal. I'm good.'

'Trying something different this year, I see. Got a Prophet impersonator to kick things off.'

Kasper knew this wasn't the case, but it was interesting it was being perceived that way. 'Yes. A bit of theatre.' So Tobias really was back, and Cairn wasn't mad, after all. No matter. He would do what Cairn couldn't. 'Keep watching,' he told the Guard. 'It gets better.'

Kasper was not worried in the slightest. Everything was unfolding according to plan.

Tobias looked down but could see no microphone on the pulpit. 'Can you all hear me?' he asked at a normal volume, guessing the mic was concealed. There was a general nodding of heads from the crowd all the way back to the gates. 'Oh. Good.' Tobias paused. He knew what he wanted to say. He just had to find the right way to say it. 'Some time ago I gave a talk to a large group, much like this, but didn't get to finish. I thought now might be a good opportunity do that. So, as I was saying:

'Death is not an end. It is a renewal of life.' Tobias hesitated. This was the moment he had been shot last time he gave this speech. 'And while the death of one man may not count for much, it affects us all in ways we cannot begin to fathom. Our fates are bound. Our choices shaped by everyone around us. But they are still our choices. Think of it this way – your fate is the course you have chosen for this life, which you do not remember doing. It cannot be altered. But it can be navigated. There are many ways to achieve the same end, and each way has its own particular lesson to teach. Even now, I am still learning how to best live my life with every choice I make. I'm no different from you. I've just chosen a different path; and who knows where that path will lead. But wherever it is and whatever lessons I learn from it – it was of my own choosing.'

Tobias recognized the delicious irony in what he was saying. He wrote these words just a few weeks ago by his own experience, 246 years ago by history's reckoning, and yet it was as if they were written for this very moment.

A scuffle started at the base of the stairs. A contingent of Temple Guards was trying to force their way past Kane, Tank and the clutch of white-robed devotees who had formed a human barricade. It was getting violent. Tobias had seen this moment. He knew what was coming. He spoke faster. His time was almost up.

'What we do not learn in this life, we will learn in the next. And so the adventure continues. Life after life. Fate after fate. Until all the lessons are learned and there is no more life to be lived. A day that I hope never comes, because I'm enjoying myself way too much.'

Tobias noticed all eyes in the crowd turned up. Cairn had appeared on his balcony directly above the podium. He shouted to the Guards below. 'Stand down! Stand down, I say! Leave them alone!'

Dan whisked the plasma rifle up and got a bead on Cairn as he leaned over the railing. Without hesitation he locked the sites on his target and pulled the trigger. A tightly focused plasma toroid shot from the bell muzzle of the gun, filling the room with a deafening *thrum*. Dan and Maya both turned to watch the result on the AV stream. Two seconds later it hit home.

'Stand Do – !' The plasma shot hit Cairn in the left shoulder, vaporizing it in an explosion of cauterized flesh, blood and bone. The arm, now severed from the torso, dropped at his feet. The festival robes with their embroidered power threads sparkled and glitched as residual plasma energy flowed through them.

Cairn reeled, stumbled and fell headlong over the railing. He plummeted fifteen meters until finally hitting the marbled landing not far from where Tobias stood. There was a bone-crunching *WHAP!* as he hit with the stone, which rattled into the audio pickups for all to hear.

The crowd lurched with horror – the Cardinal Hierophant was assassinated.

Tobias didn't turn to look at Cairn's body, he had already seen it. Instead, he scanned the people below, searching for Althea. He wanted one final look at his beloved. He spotted her desperately clawing past the Guards and faithful to get to him. She looked up and met his gaze. Tobias smiled.

A shot rang out over the crowd and Tobias was hit in the chest by the round. Clean through the heart.

Althea screamed, '*NOOOO!*'

Tobias stood frozen in time as blood from the wound soaked into his ivory white robes. He kept smiling at Althea, until the life vanished from his eyes and he collapsed to the ground – dead.

Dan and Maya watched the stream as a camera honed in on the shooter – a lieutenant of the Guard of Asian descent, wielding an old fashioned ballistic rifle. It zoomed in on his uniform's name patch – Makoto.

Other cameras captured the chaos as the crowd surged with panic. People swarmed away from the Temple, trampling anyone in their path. Temple Guards fired indiscriminately from the perimeter with power weapons set to lethal.

It was a massacre.

Althea broke free of the mob and ran up the stairs to Tobias. With tears streaming down her face she cradled his lifeless body, willing him back to life. When the lethal haze hit her she was grateful for it. Death would take her to him.

All hell had broken loose and Tank did what he did best. Any Temple Guards within reach had their heads crushed or their necks snapped – it was the easiest way to deal with an armoured Guard. He requisitioned a pair of power gloves from two of his victims and returned fire to the Guards on the edges of the court who were shooting indiscriminately into the crowd. Firing double-gloved, hitting his marks, avoiding the innocent, and looking spectacular all at the same time just proved why he was the champion he was. He was magnificent, deadly, and seemingly invincible. It felt good fighting in defence of the people rather than for mere sport and entertainment. He was trained as a warrior, and now he had something worth fighting for.

Tank spotted Kane likewise fending off nearby Guards and

trying to shepherd people away from danger. That's when he saw Kane take a hit from a power rifle and go down hard. Tank fought his way through the fleeing civilians to reach his leader. He picked up Kane's limp body and ran with him into the nearest avenue, finding some temporary cover. Lying Kane on the ground he checked his vitals. 'Kane. Don't you fucking die on me. Kane!'

Kane opened his eyes. 'What happened?'

'You got hit, you idiot.'

'Figures. Is it bad?'

Tank pulled Kane's shirt open. He had a hole in his chest the size of a fist. 'Just a scratch.'

'Right.' Kane knew he was done for. 'Do me a favour? Find Rohan. Look out for him if you can.'

'You know I don't like him.'

'He's my brother. It's my dying wish for fuck's sake.'

'Yeah, okay.'

'And Rene. Find Rene.'

'What makes you think you get two dying wishes?'

Kane laughed. Then coughed so hard he was spitting blood.

'Okay,' Tank finally said. 'And Rene.'

'Now get the fuck out of here. Don't you die on me.' Kane could barely get the words out. His lung must have collapsed.

'Hey. I'm indestructible, remember,' Tank reminded him.

Kane nodded. Then his eyes glazed over, and he was gone.

Kane's spirit rose from his body, joining with the spirits of hundreds of others that were being systematically slain in the Temple forecourt. Tobias watched as their unburdened souls rose high above the killing field, the spirits of loved ones already passed were there to greet them, reassure them, then guide them away. In time they would renew their mortal lives and begin again.

'Why do we do this to each other?' Tobias thought aloud.

'Some people never learn, do they?' Matthew responded with no trace of irony.

The spirit of Althea rose to join them. She embraced Tobias, or what could be considered an embrace in this non-physical form. 'I thought I'd lost you.'

'That could never happen,' Tobias told her. 'But I do need to go back.'

Althea didn't understand. 'So soon?'

'As Rene.'

Althea grappled with this for a moment then understood. '... Oh. Of course. I should have realized....' Then it hit her. 'This is all my fault.'

'No.' Tobias told her. 'This is exactly how it was meant to be.'

'We should go,' Matthew prompted.

'Yes.'

Althea held on to Tobias. 'What about … what about us?'

'I'll need you now more than ever. You'll be my guardian angel. Stay with me. Help me.'

'You'll have Joanna.'

'I need you both for what must be done.'

'What's that?'

Tobias smiled slyly. '… spoilers.'

On the wisp of a thought, they transported instantly to Rene who lay in the dark, comforted by Elly. A thin tendril of light still connected the body of Rene to the spirit of Tobias. An ethereal cord binding them together.

Will was there, watching over Rene and Elly. 'It's about time.'

'Mind your manners, William,' Matthew chastised. 'The Prophet is with us.'

'Tobias will do. This is Althea.'

'Will.'

433

'You're my brother, yes?' Tobias recognized him from his visions. 'That is, Rene's brother.'

'Yeah. If I'd known he was you, I mean you were him, you know … the same … person, I might have been nicer to you when we were kids.'

Tobias smiled. 'You're making up for it now.'

'So everything worked out okay?' Will chirped.

'Everything worked out,' Matthew intoned.

Tobias looked down upon his other self. Unlike most starting a new life, he had some idea where this one would lead. The hard lessons it would teach. Rene's journey was only just beginning. 'Okay then. Let's give this another shot.'

Althea's directions had been accurate enough, and after a couple of hours trek through the AQ, Joanna and Father Alban found the abandoned hospital, *Saint Olivier's*. Wandering the corridors of the ruined building, they searched every ward and room for Rene and Elly. As sunlight didn't make it to some of the internals areas, and there was no power, they relied on their battery lantern for light.

Eventually they came to a wing that was cleaner than the rest and looked as if it had been recently occupied. Despite appearances there was a putrid smell of decay. The stench grew stronger as they approached the surgical theatres. Here they found several blackened, bloated and decomposing corpses lying in a dried bloody mess on the floor of one of the theatres. The orange glow of the battery lantern, and the deep shadows beyond its reach, lent the scene a sickening, surreal aspect.

They quickly left that place to continue their search elsewhere. Joanna was getting worried. 'What if they're not here?'

'Tobias said they would be here,' Alban reassured. 'We'll find them.'

They discovered a large, dark room with several empty cages. There was a smell here also, but this time it was of rotting food, shit … and human body odour.

Alban raised the lantern up, but the farthest corners of the room refused its light. The cages in view were all empty. They heard movement in the shadows at the back of the room.

'Hello?' Joanna called softly.

Something stirred. There was a squeak, a cage door opening, then a figure emerged from the shadows…It was Elly. She let out a cheerful yelp upon recognizing Joanna and leapt into her arms.

'This is Elly, I presume,' Alban observed, gently taking the bonobo's foot that was wrapped around Joanna's waist and shaking it cordially. 'Pleased to meet you.'

'Rene?' Joanna called.

Elly jumped down and took Joanna by the hand, leading her into the gloom. Alban followed, lantern raised to light the way.

In a cage at the back of the room they found Rene curled up in the corner – apparently asleep. His clothes were ripped and dirty. His hair matted and tangled, and a light stubble framed his face.

Joanna climbed into the cage. 'Rene?'

He stirred.

She tried to turn him over. 'Rene?'

Rene opened his eyes and turned to her. His expression was blank, as if he didn't recognize her; but then a veil lifted from his eyes and Rene came to life.

'Jo.'

They embraced.

Alban watched the lovers reunited and sighed with relief. 'Thank the Prophet.'

No one dies who is not prepared to die
Therefore do not mourn their passing too much
It is their fate and their choice
And they are not truly dead after all
For death is not an end
It is a renewal of life

Shentama
– Stanza 125

Lieutenant Makoto marched into the Temple Dungeon, returning the duty Guard's salute as he entered. 'Thank you, corporal. You're relieved from duty.'

The corporal was confused. 'Sir. Are *you* relieving me, sir?'

Makoto looked at him squarely. 'Yes.'

The corporal nodded, 'Sir.' Then about-faced and left.

Makoto grabbed the keychain off the wall, strode to the Kasper's cell, and unlocked the door.

'Your Eminence, sorry for the delay.'

'That's quite all right, Lieutenant. I've been enjoying the solitude. Gives one time to think.'

'The Council is assembled and awaiting your presence.'

'Any problems?'

'None.'

'Good. Captain Marius?'

'He seems to have left the Temple, sir. We're scanning for his comkey but he's done a fair job obfuscating it to the system.'

'No matter. We'll catch up with him eventually. Meanwhile, congratulations. You're promoted Captain of the Guard.'

'Thank you, Your Eminence.'

'Well deserved. You've been a loyal soldier, Makoto. Between the two of us, we're going to change the world.'

Kasper stepped out of the cell, pausing to stretch his legs and straighten his spine. Then marched out of the dungeon and up to the Great Temple. 'Cardinal Hierophant Kasper. Has a nice ring to it, don't you think?'

'Yes, Your Eminence.'

—— ∞ ——

It took Dan and Maya several hours to get back to their base in the AQ. Not for fear of being arrested, all Temple Guards patrolling the city had been recalled to the Temple to deal with the new massacre, but the panic had spread throughout the city and the streets were crowded with frantic citizens and tourists.

Everyone saw it. The whole world saw it. A hundred angles and a thousand deaths. None of it made sense, and already the facts were unclear. Temple Guards had seemingly turned their weapons on innocent pilgrims during the most sacred and public event on the globe – the Festival of Renewal. Within minutes, however, it became clear their intended target was a large group of fanatics who were trying to hijack the ceremony with a Tobias look-a-like. Heretics masquerading as loyal Tobianists. Their intention was to kill as many faithful Tobianists as they could, as publicly as they could. It was an act of pure terrorism.

Unfortunately, and despite the best efforts of the Guard, innocent people were caught in the crossfire. Most of their deaths were attributed to the heretics, and there was clear footage of Kane Zielinski – a known rebel leader – killing many innocent pilgrims. There was also shocking (though thrilling) footage of the famous Warrior Games athlete *Tank* fighting alongside the heretics, killing several Temple Guards with his bare hands – and then with his trademark double-gloved attack. It was as if he had come out of retirement and returned to the arena. People on the street even cheered to see Tank back in action.

More difficult to watch was the footage of a small group of heretic terrorists brutally killing a guard near the barracks, with a very clear image of the murderer – Rohan Zielinski, Kane's brother – committing the deed. Zielinski was now under arrest, his two fellow conspirators killed during the clash.

Footage of the Cardinal Hierophant Cairn shouting from his balcony *'Shoot them down! Shoot them down! Kill them all!'* had shocked the world, even when it became known he was responding to a clear and present terrorist threat. His words sparked a mass panic, and his assassination moments later by an unknown sniper only fuelled the chaos.

Dan seemed to recall Cairn saying something different before he shot him. But the repetition of the *'shoot them down'* clip on the public AV walls they passed was already shaping his recollection of the moment. Dan hadn't paid that much attention after all to what Cairn was saying as he lined up his shot and fired.

It wasn't till later that Dan realized he had actually killed the Cardinal Hierophant, his second murder in a week. He felt they were both justified, but what troubled him most was that he felt nothing about it. Death came easy. And he was discovering he was good at it. Even when he saw on the AV replays Rohan kill the Guard and run away with his hands covered in blood, Dan was not shocked. Only troubled. Not because it was a violent act, but because it meant they had lost their leader.

When Dan and Maya returned to their base camp in the AQ, the mood was bleak. Their arrival lifted spirits temporarily, everyone happy they had survived, but the loss of Rohan, Andy and Zeke hit them hard. They were a ship without a rudder; and while Rohan may not have been the best of leaders, he was going to be hard to replace.

A meeting was called. They had been nineteen in number, now they were sixteen. Dan insisted Maya be present, so all the other women were also permitted to attend. Only one stayed outside as sentry to watch the streets for intruders.

'We need a new leader.' Seth had assumed the role of chair for this meeting. Dan knew him as the one who had met himself and Maya on the street when they first arrived. He was still learning other people's names though.

'Rohan's not dead.'

'He might as well be.'

'We should rescue him.'

'Don't be an idiot,' Seth rebuked.

'We did it once before. Rohan, Kane … lots of people.'

'Things are different now.'

'How are they different?'

'There's a new Cardinal Hierophant for one thing.'

'Kasper,' one of them spat.

'That whole thing was a setup from the start. I knew we shouldn't have trusted that Guard.'

'There's a new Captain of the Guard as well. So whether he set us up or not – he's out of a job.'

'What are you talking about?' Dan interrupted. The conversation had been going round the table so fast he couldn't keep up. Though the women had yet to speak.

'Right. You weren't here,' Seth recalled. 'Captain Marius of the Guard paid us a visit. Convinced Rohan we should kill Cardinal Kasper. That he was the real threat. Suffice to say it didn't go as planned.'

'What about Kane and the others?' Dan asked. 'What were they doing there?'

'Got no idea.'

'Kane was opposed to violence,' another said. 'I find it hard to believe he started it.'

'It doesn't matter who started it. We're gonna finish it.'

'How the fuck are we gonna do that?'

'We start by electing a new leader.'

Maya spoke up. 'I nominate Dan.'

Dan gazed at her in horror. 'No. No, I don't want to be leader.'

'Seconded,' said one of the other women.

'No.'

Seth was indignant. 'Any other nominations?'

'I'm not a nomination,' Dan protested.

There was a pause as the group waited for someone else to speak up.

'Really? No-one else?' He'd moved from indignant to incensed.

'I nominate Seth,' one of the men finally said.

Seth nodded graciously. 'Do we have a second?'

No one spoke.

'Any. Other. Nominations?' Seth was not at all happy.

Silence…

'… Fine. Dan, you're it.'

'What? No. I don't want to be leader.'

'Tough. You've got the job.' Seth rose from the table and left the room in a huff.

Dan scanned the room to be greeted by a gallery of smiles and relieved looks. He sighed, then moved to the head of the table.

By mid-afternoon the bodies from what was already known as the Temple Massacre (to distinguish it from the Festival Square Massacre of the previous week) were laid out in rows on the floor of the Hypogeum Basilica. The hall had been prepared for public petitions to the Cardinal Hierophant, and the run of red carpet still marked the path down the centre and up to the throne. This was now cordoned by row after row of dead pilgrims. They were covered in sheets brought fresh from the Temple laundry, many with an ochre lemnis symbol on them. The rows were neat and ordered, as if part of some giant garden ready for harvest. A field of plumeria plucked before their time.

Brown-robed priests moved dutifully among the fallen. Identifying bodies. Taking photos. Separating out those without comkeys. Some had been ripped from their owners in the panic. Some, in the form of rings and bracelets, were missing because the limb they had been attached to was severed from its host. Others may be heretics who did not carry a comkey. Whatever the reason – man, woman, or child – these victims could not be identified.

Father Alban walked among the fallen. Each unidentified body he passed, he would pull down the sheet and check. After half an hour he found the one he was looking for. He checked to see if anyone was watching. All the other priests were busy with their morbid duties, heads bowed in respect. Alban produced a vial of incendiary reactant and sprinkled the volatile liquid over the sheet from head to toe.

Before he had even finished pouring it began reacting to the cotton. He walked away. Fifteen steps later and he could hear the body explode into flames behind him.

The other priests reacted in horror and ran to douse the flames. But this fire could not be put out. It would burn relentlessly until the body that was its fuel turned to ash.

A tear tracked down Alban's face as he left the Basilica. the Prophet Tobias was finally at rest.

— ∞ —

Rene had no memory of the past five days. The last thing he could recall was clutching Elly the bonobo as the safe-house collapsed around them. There were vague images of other people, other places. Phantoms buried in the back of his brain. Less substantial than a dream, but they nagged him, nonetheless. They seemed important.

'What are you thinking about?' Joanna asked.

'Nothing in particular. Just weighing up what our options are now.'

Joanna and Alban had brought him and Elly to an underground train station in the AQ. This was where they had gone after the safe-house attack. There were several people here, some of whom Rene had met back at the house, but most were strangers to him. All were deeply distressed and grieving. They had lost many friends this day.

Rene and Joanna sought refuge in the stationmaster's office. Elly was with them, sleeping with her head in Rene's lap as he sat on the lumpy couch. He stroked her wiry fur tenderly. She had saved his life. He wasn't quite sure how, but without her Joanna and Father Alban would never have found him. He was lucky. Kane was dead. Althea was dead. Tank was missing. Dan was missing. Rohan was in custody and on his way to Gerda. The revolution, such as it was, had been a disaster. Even the death of Cairn made no difference. Within an hour there was a new Cardinal Hierophant, and it was business as usual.

Nothing had changed.

The death of a thousand people was a mere inconvenience to the Church. The Festival of Renewal is desecrated by Temple Guard and somehow heretic terrorists were to blame. The Prophet Tobias is returned and then assassinated before he could even begin.

Rene didn't want to choose sides. He wanted no part of any revolution. No part of Dan's insurrection against the Church. No blood on his hands. But the choice had been made for him. There was no going back. The phantoms called to him. Demanding action. Demanding justice. Demanding things be set right.

'So, what *are* our options?' Joanna asked.

'I don't know,' Rene told her plainly. 'But it's not over yet. Not by a long shot.'

Then, as Rene combed his fingers through his hair, the choice was made, and the return of the Prophet was assured.

Phil Moore's other books include the *Shentama,*
the companion volume to this novel,
as written by the Prophet Tobias himself.

Also the novel *Terra Utopia,*
available in print, eBook and Audiobook,
and the filmmaking reference book
F*&k Art, Just Tell the Story

Phil is a Filmmaker, Author, Composer and Teacher,
and lives in Sydney, Australia.

He has made three feature films to date –
- *Mortal Fools* (Writer/Producer/Director, etc)
- *Submerged* (Writer/Producer/Co-Director/Editor, etc).
- *A Voyage to Arcturus* – Pro-shoot of the stage musical (Writer/Composer/Lyricist/Producer/Director/Actor, etc)
- As well as dozens of short films, web series and video podcasts series.

- He teaches Screenwriting and Directing, as well as editing, sound and other creative disciplines.

- He also creates music under the name of *GuffNasm,* which you will find on music streaming services.

To find out more, or to drop Phil a line,
visit his website at www.philmoore.net